THE THIEF TAKER

Also by Mick Lee

The Men Who Robbed The Great Train Robbers

Child X

THE THIEF TAKER

Mick Lee

Matador
Unit E2 Airfield Business Park,
Harrison Road, Market Harborough,
Leicestershire. LE16 7UL
Tel: 0116 2792299
Email: books@troubador.co.uk
Web: www.troubador.co.uk/matador
Twitter: @matadorbooks

ISBN 978 1803135 885

British Library Cataloguing in Publication Data.
A catalogue record for this book is available from the British Library.

Printed and bound in Great Britain by 4edge Limited
Typeset in 11pt Adobe Garamond Pro by Troubador Publishing Ltd, Leicester, UK

Matador is an imprint of Troubador Publishing Ltd

PROLOGUE

London, 1725

The cart trundled towards Tyburn and the hanging tree. Mud, rotten food, and human waste were hurled in its direction. Jeers, shouts, the hatred of a city aimed at the condemned inside. The crowd was lined ten deep as the vehicle travelled up Holborn Hill, a procession growing behind it, snaking back through the streets in its wake. On past St Giles in the Fields it went, spectators hanging out of windows and baying from tenement rooftops. Two guards lay on the floor of the cart, shielding themselves from the assault. Beside them, a chaplain crouched and attempted to read scripture to the prisoner, his words drowned out by the noise. Eight mounted turnkeys from Newgate gaol escorted them. The mob surged towards the convoy and fell back in waves when missiles hit them from behind.

One man kept his distance, watching the hangman Jack Ketch lead his horse through the ruts and potholes. The cart turned left onto the Oxford Road for the final section of the journey. Grasping hands rattled the frame and threatened to tip it over as objects continued to rain from the crowd. The guards pulled the prisoner down, his shaven head covered in blood. The chaplain cowered, no longer praying for a lost soul. A stone hit the hangman on the shoulder, and he roared in anger. The mob yelled obscenities in reply, kicks were aimed at the wheels. Ketch cracked his whip at the throng, and they dropped back a step. He drove his horse on.

The observer held back, hoping the laudanum would keep the body on the cart silent. He adjusted his periwig and brushed down the unfamiliar clothes, avoiding eye contact with the crowd. The street stench was as he remembered it: rotting animal corpses, urine, stale alcohol, the foul odour of bodies.

A pamphlet seller yelled above the noise, waving his papers in the air. 'The last confession! Thruppence only.'

A rush knocked the vendor over, his hands grasping at his lost wares. The onlooker picked up a spare from the floor and pulled away to study the Gazette's preview of the hanging. Sharp features stared back at him in sketch form on the front of the pamphlet. The nose was a little longer than its true likeness, the eyes black as coal. It looked like a villain in a play, one you would pay a guinea to attend in Drury Lane and jeer at the lead character. The reader exhaled slowly as he absorbed the words. They told how the condemned had declared his sins before God, a confession to be shared with the thousands who would read or listen to it; then gossip in the coffeehouses on the matter for days afterwards. He screwed up the paper in his fist, silently cursing the newspaper men, the prosecutor, the judge, the politicians who had their own agenda. He cursed the King too, the German inbred.

The onlooker scratched in irritation at his wig, and searched the crowd again for familiar faces, any of the men who had brought discipline to the streets, delivered the guilty to the authorities and reined in those who interfered. He recognised nobody and breathed out slowly, feeling the calmness flow through him. A fresh surge of people swept past. There was another roar up ahead, as the cart approached the gallows, and the hatred in the voices around him rose once more. They were trying to scramble their way onto the cart. Jack Ketch stopped his procession. The turnkeys forced their way through, pushing at the mob. The observer held back. He had attended most Tyburn executions in the previous five years, but none had stirred the emotions like this.

Close to the hanging tree stood a row of benches, erected to provide the better-off folk of London a view of the scene. They would have been in their seats for at least an hour, he imagined, and would not wish to miss this event, paying two guineas each for the privilege. He spotted at least three of the city's Aldermen in the seats, all smiling.

As the cart stopped underneath the scaffold, the horsemen pushed the crowd back. The man on the cart lay still, stretched out. He was dressed in a plain nightgown, the noose tied in preparation around his neck, hands cuffed in front. Escapes had happened before, each subject eventually returned to the hangman. This prisoner was going nowhere but the Triple Tree. So-called because there was a wooden triangle at the top of its frame, to allow for multiple hangings. But this day there would be only one beneficiary of Jack Ketch's skills.

The seated spectators cheered as the hangman tethered his horse. Ketch raised a hand to them in acknowledgement, then climbed back onto the cart, bidding the chaplain and the remaining guards jump off. Two men were left, under the tree. The crowd were at least ten paces back now, quieter, watching the executioner at his work. The observer positioned himself on a shop window ledge to gain a better view. Concentration was etched on the hangman's face as he pulled the noose tight around the prisoner's neck and covered his head with a bag. The rope was attached to the frame above and tied. He tested it and smiled darkly. The head of the figure under the hood lolled to one side, a surrender it seemed. There would be no triumphant speech, no desperate plea for mercy, as arranged. The noise of the crowd started to rise again, and the throwing of missiles resumed. The man on the ledge scanned the faces he could see. The impatience and the hatred were growing, anticipating the fear that was going to be released. A shiver ran through him at the reception. The knowledge of who might have been on the cart instead.

The hangman stepped down and stood beside his horse, soothing its head. Then he untied it and cracked his whip at its behind. The horse bolted forward, taking the cart with it, leaving a man hanging by a noose from the Tyburn tree. The crowd cheered, but then a low groan began to circulate among them, the noise slowly dropping to a hush. The creaking of the rope crept across the square as the body swung in the breeze, twisting its struggle. To the onlooker, time moved slowly, faces around him frozen, the air still. Eventually, he sensed the whispers growing, the chatter return, as the body went limp. There was a lone shout of, 'Justice is served.' The observer on the ledge twitched, struggling to work out where the cry came from. Silence returned. The wind ripped down the Oxford Road.

From his vantage point he saw four men bring a coffin forward and place it underneath the triple tree. Ketch climbed the steps of the scaffold and cut the rope. The body fell. The crowd surged forward, and one of the guards fired a pistol into the air, forcing the throng back. The coffin attendants picked up the deceased, and carefully placed him inside the box, covered it with linen and closed the lid. They lifted it onto their shoulders and carried it to another cart that was waiting at the edge of the square.

Spectators parted to allow the men to take the coffin away. The onlooker was tempted to follow the cart but knew where it was heading. No doctor would carve up the body for experiments, the way they did with most of those who could not afford their own burial. Payments had been made to ensure these remains would be destroyed.

The crowd began to disperse, slipping into the taverns along the Oxford Road, down the alleyways off it to sit in the coffeehouses and the gin shops, to talk about the end of one of their own. To tell stories of murder and betrayal.

The onlooker stood down from his platform and watched the last spectators leave. The reception of the crowd had surprised, then angered him. He had not expected there to be a hero's departure but thought there might be some sense of regret among the people of London. The figure sunk his hands deep into his greatcoat, believing he had made the right choice. And then wondered about whether he truly had any choice at all.

1

Three months earlier

The chink of metal echoed off the stone cellar wall as the captive struggled against his chains. James Neff silently begged the man to stop, watching Hatcher play impatiently with the club in his hand. Neff signalled for his colleague to step aside. This was his project, he did not want Hatcher to overreact.

Their prisoner kicked out wildly, his boots splashing in the puddles in front of him. The head was covered in a small straw sack, tied around the neck, the mouth gagged. He cocked an ear, seemingly to work out where he was. Neff watched him struggle, smiling to himself at the irony of the situation.

A rat scurried across the floor, disappearing into a murky corner. The captive tensed at the sound, frozen. Neff loosened the head covering and lifted it off. Staring into the face of Edward Renshaw, he leaned in carefully, noting the anger in the eyes. Not fear. Not yet. Someone like Renshaw would not take kindly to being tied up. He was usually on the other end of scenes like this. His list of enemies was long.

Renshaw yelled an objection into the gag and choked. He smashed his chained wrists into the wall behind him again. Neff stepped back and contemplated his next move. Eyes flicked around the cellar; Renshaw would be calculating how to escape. Little hope, Neff mused, from this place under the Fleet River. Renshaw's capture had been set up the night before in the Black Dog, one of Emily Jarrett's women lacing his wine. It was a trick Neff knew Renshaw had used before, for blackmail, or extortion. But his situation was more perilous than that.

'You don't recognise me?' Neff asked, teasing.

Renshaw examined him more closely with steady eyes, then grimaced, choking again. Neff kept his distance, both for his safety and because of the stench coming from the cellar floor, where a small pool of liquid was forming underneath the prisoner.

'We have met. James Neff,' he pressed on, looking towards Hatcher, who was lurking in the shadows, then back at Renshaw. 'I'm going to take that off now. Don't bother shouting, nobody can hear you.'

Neff reached forward and cut a slit in the gag with a knife, his hand steady, but taking little care. Blood formed on Renshaw's bottom lip; the prisoner licked at it and growled. His eyes bulged. Neff ripped the restraint off the mouth, pointing his blade in Renshaw's face, a warning to remain still. Renshaw spat a globule onto the floor between them, yanking at his chains again. Neff kicked out, catching Renshaw in the ribs, forcing him to fall to one side.

'There is no point in resisting,' Neff said, standing over the groaning figure. 'You are a dead man, as sure as if you were in Newgate now.' He delivered his well-rehearsed words slowly, designed for Hatcher, rather than the man on the floor. Neff looked across at his fellow Engineer, who seemed to be considering the stones at his feet. The sound of dripping water filled the damp air of the cellar. Neff returned his attention to the prisoner.

'You work for that vermin William Dempsey,' Renshaw muttered. Neff nodded in reply, deciding not to challenge the description. 'He should be here. Is the famous Thief Taker scared of me?'

Neff dismissed the mockery in the voice. Men had different ways of hiding the fear. 'We keep the streets of this city clean. We deliver justice. And you, Renshaw, cannot be trusted.'

Renshaw shook his head and spat again. This time it dribbled down his chin. He roared in anger.

Neff stifled a laugh. 'We are underground, you are wasting your breath.'

'Bring me Dempsey. I do not talk to lackeys.'

Hatcher stepped forward, slapping the club in his palm. The sound echoed around the cellar. Renshaw did not flinch.

'Wait.' Neff held up a hand and Hatcher retreated, his heavy, steady breathing seemingly filling the chamber. 'Dempsey is unhappy,' Neff began. 'You have not been honouring agreements.'

Renshaw said nothing. He tried to stand, lost balance with his hands pinned behind him, and slipped back down to the floor. Neff rolled a blade around in his fingers, savouring the sharpness of the edge.

'Street gambling in London is none of your business. The same with the women. Mister Dempsey suggests you stick to Westminster, and your clubs, the nobility, the politicians.' Neff looked in Hatcher's direction, then back at Renshaw. 'Why muscle in on things that don't concern you? This is a reminder of where the boundaries lie.'

‘What?’ Renshaw shouted. ‘You think I bow down to that prig-napper?’ He showed his rotten teeth, snarling.

Sensing Hatcher move forward, Neff held up a hand once more. ‘Check we are still alone,’ he ordered. ‘Go up and look.’ Hatcher shrugged and slung his club over his shoulder, disappearing through the door, the sound of his heavy footsteps reaching down to the cellar. Hatcher was well known on the streets for his violence, and Renshaw would be pleased to see him leave.

Neff backed away. The light in the room fluttered as he placed his knife in the flame of the lantern for a few seconds. He withdrew the blade, touched it, and winced for effect. The prisoner rose carefully to his feet and shook the metal that bound him behind his back. Neff leaned against the wall; his muscles tensed, readied. Renshaw emitted a guttural scream, and lurched towards him, losing his balance as he neared. Neff took advantage, driving his boot into Renshaw’s side, and followed this with another to the head as he hit the ground.

Neff glanced at the door and reasoned Hatcher would be a while yet. Renshaw’s frantic breathing and low groans reminded Neff he still needed to be cautious. He had seen men overturn advantages like this before through sheer force of will. Dipping his knife into the top of the candle again, Neff studied the prisoner.

‘You might think because you mix with politicians, those honoured gentlemen, you can do what you like. To people, to property. To women.’

Renshaw stared up, eyes flashing, calculating. ‘Women?’ he spluttered.

Neff continued, keeping his voice calm. ‘You think you are better than us. I am here to show you the opposite. All of

London and Westminster wants to see the back of you.' He stepped towards his prisoner and hissed, 'I know what you did to the madam.'

Renshaw aimed a kick from the floor, but Neff saw the move coming, shifting his weight, stamping on an exposed ankle. The crunch of bone reverberated around the cellar; Renshaw cried out again.

Neff leaned over his captive and seized the jaw in his free hand. He tightened his grip as Renshaw tried to twist away and pictured the bruised face of the woman the bastard had lost patience with. 'This is for Emily Jarrett,' Neff snarled, the composure gone.

Renshaw opened his mouth in what looked like horror, a brief flash of recognition at the name. Neff skewered the knife into Renshaw's left eye. There was a faint hiss, the heat from the blade slicing through flesh. It stuck, hitting bone. Neff twisted it, feeling the power and the revenge. Renshaw's arms twitched, his body tensed, and a strangled scream emerged, turning into a bloody gurgle. Neff withdrew the blade, then drove it into the other eye. Renshaw slumped to the floor, lifeless.

Neff extracted the knife, wiping it on Renshaw's shirt, and replaced it in his jacket pocket. The sound of Hatcher's tread echoed down the stone steps. Neff retreated to stand by the lantern at the side of the cellar.

'Well?' Neff asked, as Hatcher entered.

'Nothing,' Hatcher muttered.

'Bit of an accident here,' Neff said.

Hatcher glanced at Renshaw, shrugged, and rested his club against the wall. Neff motioned to his colleague to help him lift the body off the floor. Hatcher moved closer, peering at the blood running down Renshaw's face. A tight-lipped smile emerged, like he was admiring Neff's handiwork. They dragged the body towards the cellar door.

Neff turned to Hatcher. 'This one is for the river. Dempsey doesn't need to know.'

2

William Dempsey paused to take in his reflection in the apothecary's window. He smoothed a hand over his bare scalp and then ran it down a cheek, feeling the history of the scars under his long fingers. Fingers that had once worked this part of London, hustling among the crowds, lifting pocketbooks, purses, watches. Those days were a distant memory now.

He stared at the face in front of him and frowned at the dark lines gathering under his eyes. Enemies still surrounded him, despite the sudden disappearance of one his rivals. Dempsey felt the shape of a package through his coat and breathed out slowly. He scanned the closed off alleyway; no sign of life, as he had demanded for the visit. Dempsey re-traced his steps, picking his way through the mud, the animal remains and the vermin, pinching his nose as he went, towards the opening on to Cheapside.

He peered out of the gap that led into the street and slipped a tricorn onto his head. There was no cause for a wig in this part of town, and his presence did not need to be announced. Dempsey turned out of the alley in the direction of Newgate prison. Business called. The sounds of the street washed over him, familiar and soothing: hawkers selling fish, heather, the rags from the backs of dead men. Ballads were sung on corners, in doorways. Barrowmen yelled for pedestrians to make way. Children squealed as they scampered through the filth.

Dempsey kept close to the shopfronts, his head down as he walked along, looking up only occasionally. He felt a sense of freedom course through him and touched his chest again. Maybe he would not need the potion this time.

As he turned into Fleet Street, a group of three men staggered towards him. They were young and appeared to still be suffering the effects of the night before. One of them raised his eyes briefly in Dempsey's direction, horror flooding across his face. He pointed a finger, muttering breathlessly. His friends took him by the arm and dragged the figure across the street, squelching in the mud, not looking back. Dempsey had no recollection of the man.

He stopped some distance from the Lost and Found office. Six figures were stood in line, all with that sheepish look in their eyes; men who had lost their valuables the night before, who desperately needed their return. And this was the only place it could be guaranteed. Dempsey smiled to himself, at the simplicity of commerce.

One more turn, and then he was standing outside Murray's coffeehouse on Shoe Lane. Newgate, and the prisoners he needed to question, could wait. He paused, waiting for Neff to catch him up, knowing his man would be close behind.

'I need warmth,' Dempsey announced to his companion.

Neff slipped past to open the door, scanning inside. Taking a couple of paces, Neff then turned to indicate it was safe to enter and headed towards a table in the corner. Dempsey followed, pausing to breathe in the aroma; a sharp contrast to that of the street. Freshly brewed coffee, pipe smoke, which billowed to the ceiling; sweat, and yesterday's gin. Every drink was available in a place like this. Dempsey absorbed the constant hum of debate, gossip, and scandal. Typical coffeehouse fare. He plucked a newssheet from a nearby table and checked the front page. More allegations about Catholic officials, reports of financial ruin, something about the heir to the throne returning from Hanover. He flipped the paper over and scanned through the advertisements for the recovery of property. There was no mention of Renshaw and his demise. Dempsey tossed the Gazette to the floor.

Looking up, Dempsey found Neff escorting two men away from his usual table. They scurried to sit at the window, staring straight ahead. One tripped over a chair and spilled some of his drink, but continued to his new seat, eyes fixed in front. Murray himself appeared, greeting Dempsey with a tray and a bowl of coffee.

'One for my colleague as well,' Dempsey said.

'Of course.' Murray left with a slight bow and hurried off in the direction of a large pot over the hearth.

Dempsey caught Neff shaking his head. 'I do not ask for this treatment.'

'But you would be unhappy if it were not there,' Neff smiled.

Murray returned and carefully placed a second bowl of coffee in front of Neff, all the while looking at Dempsey, as if his companion were invisible. 'Anything else?'

'Leave us if you will,' Dempsey directed, with a wave of his hand. This corner of the coffeehouse would be ideal. Nobody would overhear them.

Dempsey leaned across the table and blew at his bowl. The ripples of black sludge shook, and he breathed in deeply. It always smelled better than it tasted.

'James, what have you heard? About who was responsible.'

Neff scanned the coffeehouse, before turning to focus his attention back on Dempsey. 'Everyone is asking,' he said. 'Especially those from Renshaw's territory. There is great confusion. Some say he has just disappeared, gone to France. Others that he was murdered on the road to Bristol.'

'But nobody is naming a culprit?' Dempsey asked.

'No.'

'Have you spoken to Emily? Her girls might have heard something?'

Neff stared down at his coffee bowl. He wrinkled his nose, as if he were displeased. 'I have already asked. Nothing.'

Neff spooned sugar into his coffee. Dempsey did likewise, sometimes it was the only way to make it drinkable. Murray never charged him for it.

'Do you suspect Tindall? He has much to gain,' Dempsey asked. Renshaw's second in command was an obvious suspect. It could be a changing of the guard.

'He has been up north for the past week. Working the highways.' Neff leaned closer. Dempsey could smell his breath, the brandy underneath the coffee. 'He was arrested in Chester. It cannot be Tindall.'

'Then we must arrange a meeting with our friends to the east and the south, get them round the table.' Dempsey stirred the sludge in front of him. Looking at it darkened his mood. 'If one of them raises what happened to Renshaw, he will be the man responsible.'

'You think?' Neff asked, turning away to scan the coffeehouse again. Dempsey took the opportunity to study his closest aide. Over a decade they had worked together, and Neff had not once questioned his instructions. The years had been less kind to Neff, Dempsey thought. His long hair was flecked with silver and tied back in its customary bow. The wide, broken nose was becoming his increasingly dominant feature. But it was the weary expression he always wore that dated James Neff. As if there was a lifetime of regret trapped in there. A man who had escaped one form of service in uniform, and slipped into another, as a key part of his operation.

'Set up the meeting. Let us see what they have to say.'

'Where?'

'Certainly not here,' Dempsey said, scanning the customers around them. Nobody made eye contact in return.

'There is a man who would host such a meeting,' Neff said. 'I will see to it.'

'It will have to be private. Men like Ashford and Kaplan will want to feel safe,' Dempsey prompted, slurping his coffee. 'Especially after what happened to Renshaw.'

Neff nodded, seeming to understand him. 'Do you want them to be safe?'

'For now.'

3

Emily Jarrett spotted the girl leaving the Rose and Crown. She knew her game because it had once been her own. Still was, for the right clients; but these were different days, with different prices, different locations.

Emily switched her attention to the girl's twang, the man whose job it was to step in if she were threatened, or to help her rob the customer. He was sat in a corner of the alehouse, drinking with two men, banging a tankard on a table. The twang did not seem to notice the girl leading a client down an alley. Emily stepped outside to follow her, picking her way through the broken glass at her feet.

The girl took a man by the arm into an alleyway, then raised her skirts, ready for the eager invasion. Emily saw the concentration on her face over the client's shoulder. Slender fingers reached around his back, then subtly lifted a wallet and pocketbook. He carried on with the grunting, oblivious. The jade noticed Emily watching her and looked back at him, one hand now on his nape, the other slipping the items into a purse that was slung over her shoulder. She did not miss a beat.

Emily smiled at her, but the gesture went unreturned. Studying her more closely, Emily noted the prominent cheekbones, the clear skin, the long blond hair. A girl with the potential to be so much more, wasted on the street corners around Maiden Lane.

The man finished his business, and Emily recognised that the girl must have taken the payment first, meaning her mark would not need to fumble for money from a missing wallet. He staggered drunkenly away down the alley towards the river. Emily wondered at what point he would realise he had been fleeced. They were never happy about that. He would probably turn up at Dempsey's Lost and Found office in the next couple of days, asking for the return of his possessions. His indiscretion would be covered up. The thief, the gentleman, and a go-between would all be happy, to varying degrees. It made for a lively economy.

As the girl pulled her skirts down, Emily walked over, checking first if the twang had emerged from the tavern. They were alone in the alley.

'You have deft hands, girl. You make a good buttock-and-file.'

The eyes looked up, defiant, the whites of them stark in the fading light. 'You know my trade.'

'I do. It was mine once.'

'And yet, look at you,' the girl said, a thin smile on her lips. They were a deep red, no smudges from the recent encounter.

Emily recognised the determination and the resistance to help. It was what kept her alive in those first few weeks. She had started out in London with no plan, simply looking to survive, scrape money together to pay for food and lodging. Quickly learned to be suspicious of everybody, male or female.

'How much did you turn?' Emily asked, her hands held up in a friendly gesture.

'A shilling. Plus, what I find in here,' the girl said, holding up the wallet, eyes flicking to her left, checking in case the man returned.

'A shilling for a quick one down an alley? You are better than that. I know places where you could lie down rather than stand up in a doorway. On a soft bed. And make much more.' Emily reached out and stroked the girl's cheek, savouring the softness, surprised the touch had been accepted. 'I would say at least ten shillings for a face like yours. And then there are richer pickings in the wallets of the gentlemen I know.'

'Nobody would pay me that.'

'I know many men who would.'

'I never meet such men.'

'Maybe you should.'

Emily stood back to examine her again. The dress was tatty, the boots worn. Her golden hair was long and loose, could do with tidying up. Emily's gaze came back to the softness of her cheeks. Emily folded her hands together. The girl would require a little investment, but there was potential.

'What do they call you?' Emily asked.

'Alice.'

'Well, Alice, you should come with me.' The girl looked over Emily's shoulder at the tavern. 'Don't worry, you shan't need him again. He has already forgotten you. How old are you, Alice?'

'Sixteen.'

'Really?'

Alice looked at the floor and dragged her foot in the dirt. 'Fourteen.'

The same age Emily started out in the trade. 'That's more like it. We must be honest with each other, even if we are not honest with the men. Come, Alice. I know somewhere safer.' Girls were dying on the streets, and not just from starvation and consumption. Someone was leaving them for dead in filthy alleyways, three murdered in the previous month. No man was going to help them. Emily and her fellow madams were undertaking their own crusade.

'I do alright,' Alice said. 'How do I know you're not like the others?'

Emily looked into those eyes and saw the uncertainty, the fear that came from being repeatedly duped on the streets, in the taverns and the lodging houses. 'You can trust me. I am Madam J.' The girl's eyes widened in recognition. 'Yes, that Madam J.'

Alice smiled for the first time in their encounter, showing rows of rotten teeth. 'Is it true what you say? About better gentlemen?'

'It is.'

Emily held out her hand, and the girl took it. Her skin was rough to the touch. This was a child with sores and scabs on her hands, but long, slender fingers, adept for pickpocketing and a good enough face to make a living.

'Where do you live, Alice?'

Alice pointed at the Rose and Crown. 'I arrived two weeks ago. The woman there, she helped me. But now she says I got to earn my way. I owe her money.'

'You owe nobody,' Emily said. She sighed at memories of the greedy hands that tried to shape her early life. Until she found her own way out. The situation on the streets was getting worse by the day, she thought. Girls trapped by anyone who could offer them a roof over their heads. They were sleeping on tavern floors, in barns, hiding in coffeehouse stores, anywhere for shelter.

'We will make something of you if you are willing to work.'

Another smile. 'I am. London does not appear to be what they said it was.'

Emily led her north, switching in and out of the alleys that snaked their way through Covent Garden. Passers-by whistled at them, and Emily pulled Alice in closer. She could feel the girl shivering in the cool evening bedside her and hear the shallow breathing in response to the stench of rotten flesh, and the vermin that lived off it. Emily knew these streets, but the smell could still catch you out when the wind was blowing up from the river. Alice wiped what looked like tears away from her eyes. The sound of human chatter grew as they approached the piazza, women and their drunken clients falling in and out of taverns, men shouting and arguing about the prices offered to them.

They travelled to the top of Drury Lane, and the safety of Mother Clare's. A place where Emily knew there was room for a girl to stay the night. The next day she would be examined by Doctor Bartlett, to ensure she was fit to work. There would be food on the table, a room with a fire that would not go out at the first gust. Clients who were booked in advance rather than turning up drunk with a few shillings in their pockets and a wild lust in their breeches. This would be another soul saved, as Emily sometimes wished she had been many years before.

4

'A toast before we start.' Dempsey paused to eye the men gathered at the table. 'The King.' Two voices echoed his words.

Each leader had a second stood to attention behind him, hands behind their backs. The landlord of the Fox Tavern flitted about, nervously bringing drinks back and forth, the only other soul in there. Outside, three additional groups of supporters were gathered, suspiciously eyeing their rivals.

'Thank you for meeting today,' Dempsey began. 'There is much to discuss.' He felt Neff's presence, briefed to observe everyone and everything, say nothing. Dempsey leaned forward onto the table, his palms held up, inviting a response.

'It has been some time. There is no harm in talk,' Kaplan said, nodding and glancing at Ashford. Dempsey wondered at the significance of the look. He needed to determine if they were working together. These were the two remaining men of importance. Kaplan, guardian of the east side, was dressed all in black, with a tailored shirt and jacket. Ashford, who ran everything south of the river, fingered his frayed grey collar, and rocked in his seat.

'Indeed,' Ashford agreed. 'No harm.'

'We are all successful in our own ways, in our own territories. I still help to keep the peace,' Dempsey said. 'But despite my best efforts, the authorities feel London is becoming increasingly lawless, with this recent incident.' They would all know he was referring to Renshaw's demise. 'They have accepted us because we provide control. But they see this as a breaking of that unspoken commitment to peace.'

Kaplan picked at something on his sleeve. Ashford sank his chair down to the floor with a thump.

'There is a real danger that they may take a closer interest if we are not careful,' Dempsey continued, eyeing the two men in turn. There were stony stares in reply. 'They are nervous. There are many former soldiers on our streets. An organised force might be introduced, to watch over us, to rein us in.'

'They wouldn't dare,' Ashford said, spittle forming on his fat lips. He swilled his tongue around dubiously and took a long gulp of brandy.

'I am told the King is also interested,' Dempsey added. 'Parliament will soon stick its nose into our affairs. No Renshaw means there is less control over Westminster. I believe we need to discuss how we operate.'

'No politician is going to tell me how to run my business,' Ashford spluttered. He emptied his glass and beckoned to the barman for more. The figure scuttled over and avoided eye contact, pouring from a decanter, which he left on the table.

'None of us want that,' Dempsey said. In his view, London needed change and the end of Renshaw, whatever caused it, was an opportunity. 'We have our areas of strength, but there is no need to fight, or draw attention to ourselves. It is bad for business. Streets are just names. We should open up London to each other.'

Dempsey sat back, and the room fell into silence, as the visitors pondered the concept of sharing. Neither man looked up. Glasses were fingered, supped from. Neff had privately questioned the idea. His closest aide felt man was too beholden to territory to consider surrendering it, but Dempsey thought he understood the other leaders. Their greatest fear was losing control of London to the authorities.

Dempsey focused on Kaplan, who had been listening and stroking his fingers through a beard that was starting to grey. More experienced in these matters than the others in the room, he had run the east since before Queen Anne. Alehouses and illicit alcohol were his strength. On their way to the meeting, Dempsey had voiced his own suspicion to Neff that Kaplan was behind Renshaw's death. Neff had said nothing to contradict his view.

Action was needed. Dempsey opted to fill the silence. 'I offer to concentrate solely on the business of lost and found property, and whorehouses,' he announced. 'To surrender my interests elsewhere.'

'Aye, with your army of pickpockets and footpads, free to roam all of London and Westminster no doubt,' Ashford cut in, rubbing his chin. 'The southern side is not open to you.'

'All of our ventures make money,' Dempsey countered, staring calmly across the table. 'What I suggest is we make them more profitable. We stop competing against each other. Kaplan, you would import the gin, the beer, brandy, anything else you like, at an agreed price to all. Ashford, you set your own prices at the fights, in the skittle alleys, run the gambling, coin at your own rates. You could come to an arrangement over distilleries. I can ensure all the madams do not undercut each other. We maximise our profits this way.'

Kaplan pointed at Dempsey with a bony finger. 'The women need controlling. You seem to think you have them, but they do what they want.'

'I say we let the women run their own businesses, I will merely supervise,' Dempsey said.

Kaplan and Ashford stared at each other, neither blinking. They always seemed to be at war over something. Robberies, assaults, interceptions of drink, breaking up of gambling games; there had been a running battle across their borders for the previous three years. It was a risk asking them to accept peace, and to surrender profitable businesses to the madams. Not even Emily Jarrett and what she called her fellow sisters would expect it.

Ashford smoothed his bald head. 'The whores are parasites. They feed off the taverns, the gamblers, the drink. If we let them do as they wish, we undermine our authority.'

'They must do as they are told,' Kaplan added with a sigh.

'Let me oversee the entire business across London and Westminster,' Dempsey said. 'Renshaw's old haunts as well. Ensure it does not interfere with more profitable enterprises, like gambling and drink.'

Dempsey examined their faces again. Kaplan and Ashford both reddened. Kaplan began fidgeting with his glass. Ashford rocked on his chair once more.

'It was just a suggestion,' Dempsey admitted, hands up in mock surrender. 'Maybe we put that one aside for another day.' There was little point in pushing them too hard. Yet.

'Drop it,' Ashford spat.

'Whores are a devil to control,' Kaplan added. He shuffled in his seat, his gaze flicking between his rivals. 'We all know what the real question is today. Which of you killed Renshaw?'

Dempsey sensed Neff moving behind him but kept his eye on the leaders. The instructions were clear.

Ashford swilled his drink again. 'More importantly, who runs Westminster now?'

Kaplan tapped at his empty glass. 'Tindall is locked up. They say he might hang for being a Jacobite. It is only a few days and already Westminster is lawless. We must agree how we divide the spoils between us before Parliament steps in.'

'Which is why I suggest we forget territory, and specialise instead,' Dempsey said.

'That suits you well, doesn't it?' Kaplan fired back. 'We surround you.'

Ashford belched loudly and laughed. Kaplan wafted a hand in front of his face, his eyes narrowing in distaste, and looked up at James Neff. Dempsey struggled to recognise the expression and hoped his aide would provide his perspective later. The air suddenly reeked of what smelled like rancid pork. Dempsey ran a finger around his collar, feeling his shirt tighten. More convinced than ever that Ashford and Kaplan were plotting his downfall.

'So, neither of you admit to killing Renshaw?' Kaplan asked. 'I thought you would if it were you, Samuel.' He turned to Ashford and grinned. Not for the first time, Kaplan reminded Dempsey of a fox.

'Nothing to do with me,' Ashford spluttered. 'Maybe Parliament had enough of him.'

Dempsey knew the men at the table were the only ones with the means and the will to dispose of someone as powerful as Renshaw. It had to be one of them. Silence returned, as Kaplan sipped at his drink and Ashford continued to swing on his chair.

'Can we agree to stop the warfare?' Dempsey asked, wanting to return to negotiation. 'It is bad for business. Nobody makes money if we fight each other,' he said.

'You would never turn away the rewards for bringing prigs to book,' Ashford smirked. Dempsey knew they both resented his role as a thief taker, and the prominence it afforded him. But he was the first to realise the opportunity, and he had been rewarded for that foresight.

'I would gladly trade those rewards for peace.' Dempsey smiled. 'The alternative is bloodshed, and none of us want that. Renshaw is yesterday's news,' Dempsey continued, examining their reactions. Cold stares had returned. 'We have to look forward.' There were nods from Kaplan and Ashford. The tension appeared to drop, both men replenishing their glasses. Dempsey heard Neff breathe out deeply behind him but kept his own focus in front.

Kaplan leaned forward, resting his elbows on the table. 'We should consider something.' He turned to stare directly at Ashford. 'The bridge and river crossings you control. You should share.'

All eyes turned to the Beast of Southwark, as he liked to be known. Ashford laughed again and took a long drink. 'I share nothing about the river,' he said.

Kaplan shook his head. Dempsey heard a clock ticking somewhere but could not locate the source. He felt his heart pound, and the tightness in his chest return. He gently touched the place where the tincture lay hidden in the lining of his jacket and breathed out slowly.

Dempsey examined Kaplan again. Certain now that this was the rival who had removed Renshaw; he was changing the subject, stirring up trouble with talk of the Thames crossings.

Little either man said could be trusted. Kaplan's whole being, the way he sat, the slow, purposeful movements, his clothes, were designed to project darkness and fear. It seemed a pointless approach, in meetings like these, and contrasted with Ashford's energetic, fidgety demeanour. Light and shade across a dusty tavern table.

The meeting felt like it had lapsed into a stalemate. Dempsey prompted the others with suggestions over sharing the distribution of alcohol, but both men greeted this with more silence, and no commitment to change. Discussion moved to which constables accepted bribes, which was all of them in Dempsey's experience; and then the whorehouses that offered the best rates. Ashford was the more enthused, Kaplan kept gazing into the distance, brooding. Occasionally Dempsey caught movement among the minders standing behind their leaders, confident Neff would be noting anything of interest. The other bosses eventually slipped away, Kaplan last, with little ceremony, no spoken goodbye, leaving only Dempsey and Neff behind.

'Which of them do you think killed Renshaw?' Dempsey asked, pouring Neff a drink, indicating he should sit. 'You were watching their faces.'

Neff slowly lowered himself into a chair and studied the bottle they had been using, imported brandy of the highest quality. 'I don't think they seem to care.'

'But it must be Kaplan, right?'

'He is the one to watch. We know Ashford is violent, but he will not want to venture far from south of the river. He knows he is exposed in London.'

'But we have a plan to draw him out.'

'We do.'

'What do you think of Kaplan?' Dempsey asked, as idly as he could. 'Would you work for him?'

'I cannot believe you ask me that. More than ten years it has been…'

Neff was right. A bond had been formed after such a long time. One of trust between two men with a shared history. Dempsey shook away the small suspicion that had formed at the end of the meeting, that someone closer to home might have removed his Westminster rival. Neff had nothing to gain from it.

Dempsey leaned forward to stare into Neff's eyes. The grey was clear, calm. 'I think Kaplan is the one. He will accuse us, will not want to antagonise Ashford. We need to drive a wedge between them. We will make the move we discussed. James, you and the Engineers have work to do.'

5

Neff watched the bulking shape of Hatcher, bent over the glowing orange line that wound its way to the rear of the alehouse. His colleague's hand trembled as he dropped the match. Then Hatcher turned, as if conscious of being studied, his blotchy face highlighted by the lantern in Neff's grasp. The posture accentuated the slight stoop Hatcher had developed, a physical quirk that identified him as much as the drinking and wild flashes of anger.

This was the third time they had used fire that night, there was no reason to be there when the flames met the alcohol store at the rear of the Watchman. That evening they had selected taverns at random, in Holborn and Newgate, now one in Aldgate, for maximum confusion as to the motive.

As they crossed Fenchurch Street and headed towards London Bridge, a bright red glow began to reach into the sky behind them. The Night of Fire was continuing. They had one more appointment, south of the river.

An unfamiliar figure was waiting at the distillery gates on the corner of Tooley Street and Dock Alley, surrounded by three of the Engineers. Another of their men would be at the foreman's lodgings, a knife to his wife's throat. Insurance against independent action, or the idea of running to Ashford to warn him what was to come.

'Mister Burgess. Good of you to help,' Neff said, as he and Hatcher approached.

'Don't do her no harm,' the foreman spluttered.

'She will be perfectly safe,' Neff replied. A calm voice calculated to prevent panic.

The factory gates were unlocked, and two Engineers dragged a couple of large cloth sacks each inside. Their faces wrinkled in disgust at what they were carrying. One looked at Neff with a questioning eye, but he ignored the voiceless complaint.

'Wait here,' Neff ordered the foreman. The third Engineer dwarfed Burgess as he stood over him. Neff waved a finger in his face and smiled. 'My friend here will look after you. Raise the alarm if anyone comes by.'

Burgess simply nodded, his face a picture of defeat. Neff considered what Ashford would do to him when he discovered his betrayal. There would be no interest in the threats to his family, just the fact that four men had been let into his prime distillery.

Hatcher passed his lantern to Neff, who led the group through the yard, and up the external steps of the factory building to the second floor. Hatcher barged in the door, the other Engineers following behind with their cargo. Neff cast his light along a gantry that ran above a line of tall vats where the fermenting gin was stored. The distillery was much bigger than they had been led to believe. The alcohol below them would be shipped across London, and beyond. A trade that was about to end. The sacks were dropped, one next to each of the four nearest vats. The men who carried them in wiped their hands on their jackets, and stared at Neff again, their distaste barely kept in check.

Neff had contemplated simply setting light to the place but suspected they would all be blown to Hell. Dempsey wanted impact, and there were other ways of delivering it. Putting the Tooley Street gin distillery out of action would not destroy Ashford but would give him something to concentrate on apart from gambling. It would certainly stoke his anger and focus it elsewhere.

Neff directed his colleagues into position along the gantry. Each vat had a door at the top, and the lids clattered as they were opened. The smell of fermenting gin swam up to the top level of the factory, a welcome relief from the artificial flavouring they had brought with them. Neff felt a slight twinge of regret at what they were about to do. Then allowed himself a smile as he thought again of Ashford's reaction. He probably poisoned his gin already. Neff would be sticking to brandy for a while after this.

He gave the signal, and they worked on a vat each. Neff held his breath as he untied the top of his sack, fighting back the need to gag. He tipped it until it was horizontal and shuffled its contents out slowly. Down the delivery dropped, hissing as it met the liquid inside. Steam rose from the vat, throwing off a fearful smell. Neff felt the nausea rise, and unable to fight the sensation, vomited on the gantry. He wiped the tears from his eyes, looked along at his colleagues, and saw the others in similar distress. Hatcher threw up, first on the floor, then into the nearest vat. Neff dropped his empty sack into the liquid and closed the lid, the metallic clang ringing along the gantry. He shut his eyes for a moment, but the smell returned, stronger than before. A mixture of animal innards and horse shit; a new ingredient for Ashford's gin.

The others hurried back along the gantry to the entrance. Hatcher looked green in the light from the lantern. As usual he made no comment on their work. The air inside was thick with a mixture of manure, alcohol, and vomit. The vapour of the devil.

They made their way back down the outer factory steps to the yard. Hatcher led the group towards a pile of tools and picked up a hammer. Another Engineer hefted a plank above his head. The windows to the ground floor of the factory went first, any equipment lying about was smashed. There was a smaller separate one-floor building, the office Neff assumed, and Hatcher lit a torch from the lantern and tossed it through a broken window. The flames rose into the cold night air, and Neff breathed in the smell of burning wood. The fire would soon attract attention and it would be easy to make the link to their earlier activities that evening. Wait until they opened the vats, he thought.

Satisfied with the level of destruction taking place, Neff returned to the gates. The foreman was slumped on the floor outside, the third Engineer standing over him. Neff looked down on Burgess and prodded him with a boot. He murmured. Neff felt no pity for his situation. War was problematic, there were always casualties. And how did you know if you were on the right side? You just followed orders and trusted your instincts to take the correct path.

'Thank you for your time.' Neff pulled out his pocket watch, making a show of consulting it. 'Your wife will be free by now. Go home.' The man stood, shaking, and wiped tears of shame from his cheeks. Or perhaps it was fear of what would happen to him next. Neff pressed on. 'We have a message for Ashford. When he asks you about what happened here, make sure you tell him what we did to you and your wife, how much we enjoyed ourselves. Tell him, greetings from Whitechapel.'

6

The clerk beckoned two visitors from the anteroom into an office. They had been waiting patiently for nearly an hour at the 'Lost and Found' premises on Fleet Street.

'Please be seated. Can I have your names?' He positioned himself behind a table, poised to take down their details.

'Katherine Percival, wife of General Percival.'

'And Emily Jarrett, a friend.'

Emily studied the man she knew was called Croker, although they had never met. His wig wobbled as he carefully scratched away in a ledger, glasses poised precariously on the end of his nose. The odour of pipe smoke filled the room, reminding her of the General in question. An image of his sweaty body fluttered through her mind. She turned to look at Katherine beside her. There was steely determination in her eyes, a woman wronged.

'You need our help?' Croker asked, without looking up. Emily thought she could see a small creature moving in his wig. She watched it wriggling, trapped.

'My house was broken into, and some valuables taken,' Katherine said. 'The General is away, and I would like to retrieve them before he returns.'

'An honourable man.' The voice came from the doorway, from where William Dempsey swept in, his eyes focused on Mrs Percival. Dempsey adjusted a periwig; Emily knew he only wore them in certain company. 'He is away you say?' Dempsey asked.

'Yes, sir.'

'Do tell us everything that is missing.'

Katherine looked across at Emily who offered a smile of encouragement. She seemed to be unaware her husband was an occasional client of Emily's. And this was a chance to satisfy her curiosity over how Dempsey handled these affairs from the other side. He lowered himself into a chair next to Katherine and indicated she should continue with a wave of his hand. Emily looked at the paintings on the wall beside her, to avoid staring directly at him.

'Mostly silverware, including a plate his regiment gave him when he retired, and a valuable necklace of mine.' Katherine smoothed her throat with a shaky hand before continuing. 'Some other jewellery including three of my husband's gold watches.' Her voice quivered as she spoke. Croker scribbled away in a ledger. Dempsey nodded and waved again for her to continue.

'We were robbed yesterday. Will you be able to find it for me?' Katherine asked.

'We will try, Mrs Percival. It is a certain type of robbery, I think,' Dempsey said, finally stealing a quick glance at Emily, one she struggled to decipher, before returning his focus to the other woman. 'We might know some suspects.' Dempsey stroked his neat beard with his fingers. Emily sank back into her chair, engrossed by his performance.

'When will you know?' Katherine asked. The two women played cards regularly, and she had confided to Emily that she did not want her husband to think her incapable of keeping their household secure. Emily knew the General was due back the following week; they also had an appointment.

'Come to us in three days, I can update you then.'

'Three days?'

'Mrs Percival,' Dempsey's tone was soothing. 'We have to find the sort of thieves who might be involved. Then persuade them to part with what they have stolen. It will take some degree of delicacy.'

'And what do I owe you for this task?' Katherine clutched her purse tightly in her lap.

'Nothing, Mrs Percival. There may be a sum that is required to persuade the thief to return your valuables, but that will be a matter between them and you. All we do here,' Dempsey wafted his arm to indicate the office, 'is record what you have lost, and help the return of your possessions as soon as possible. We receive no money for this service.'

A smile crept across his face, and Dempsey raised himself from the chair to kiss Katherine's gloved hand. A true gentleman. Emily examined the paintings once more.

'Do pass your details to Croker here, and we will meet again.'

Dempsey left the room with a short bow and the clerk took a note of Katherine's address in a separate ledger.

When the two women met Dempsey on the next appointed date, in the same room, sat in the same chairs, his attention was once more focused on the General's wife.

'We have tracked down the culprits. They are regular housebreakers, and we found them north of London. They are repentant. For the sum of just thirty guineas, everything that was stolen will be returned. I imagine from your description that the valuables are worth far more than that.'

Katherine and Emily had done the calculations. Over four times that amount, they thought. Emily had arranged for one of her girls to search the pawnbroker shops of Covent Garden and the streets that stretched out to Newgate for the items. Nothing had shown up. Faced with no other means of recovering the stolen goods, thirty guineas would be a small price for the General's wife to pay.

'It can be resolved today,' Dempsey smiled. As if anticipating his customer's questions, he added, 'All we have done is broker a transaction between you and the thief. Remember, I will receive nothing myself in relation to this.'

'I'm not sure…' Katherine had admitted she was not keen to meet the thieves who had broken into her house. 'Could you not pass the money to them for me? You know General Percival is away.'

'Don't worry,' Dempsey smiled back. Emily was amused by his continued act of innocence. 'A courier will bring the valuables to you. So long as you have the payment.'

'I have it with me,' Katherine said, shaking her purse.

'Please, do keep that hidden.' Dempsey turned to Emily this time. Now he looked like William: the sharp eyes, the flashed grin, and underneath it a ruthless edge that drew him to her so many years before. 'You are Emily, I hear?'

'I am, sir,' Emily replied, feeling the glow in her cheeks. They had been business partners in the past, closer than that once. She felt a shiver move through her, excitement at the deceit.

'Enchanted to meet you again,' Dempsey said, lingering, then turning back to Katherine, who had slipped her purse back under her skirts. 'A messenger will come to you and ask for a fee to return your valuables. I can guarantee you will not be robbed again.'

‘I will not be tricked. I have two servants at home for protection,’ Katherine said, her voice rising with determination.

‘A sensible precaution, Mrs Percival, although I do not believe you will need them. It will be an innocent courier who will approach you, not the thieves. Please do not call for a constable. He will only run, and your items will be lost. The men who did this have already left London for good.’ Dempsey rose and swiftly departed through the rear door, bidding them goodbye.

Emily insisted on escorting Katherine to her house on Greville Street. Her companion kept looking round as they headed north through Lincolns Inn Fields, eyes darting, probably seeing thieves at every turn. Emily took her by the arm, to steer the route away from the alleys she knew held the most danger. She felt the woman shake as they stepped in and out of the pedestrians, the vendors, the singers on street corners. A handcart narrowly missed them as its owner swerved to avoid a dog running across the street. Katherine stopped and dropped her eyes to the floor.

‘The General will think me such a fool,’ she said. ‘You must not let him know about this.’

Emily considered what the General might have told his wife about her. ‘You have nothing to fear,’ she replied. ‘I haven’t seen your husband for months now. I believe he gambles in another club these days.’ For Katherine’s benefit, the relationship had always been based around the whist table. ‘Come, let us get you back to Holborn.’

Emily led Katherine along Leather Lane, where the pedestrian traffic began to thin out. Smoke from a nearby factory rose above them, the unmistakable stench of tanning. Katherine, clearly unused to the route, put a handkerchief to her mouth. A beggar held out her hand, ignored by both women. Two streetwalkers paused on the other side, bawdily dressed, accosting passers-by for trade. Elizabeth Manning's girls, Emily thought. She focused on the path ahead, still wary of being recognised. As they entered Hatton Gardens, a man hovered at Katherine's side. Emily wondered how long he had been following them.

'I have something for you.' The figure tipped his hat, removed it, and wiped it on his sleeve. Emily led Katherine into a shop doorway that partially hid them from the street. 'Don't be alarmed,' the man continued. 'I am just the messenger.'

He pulled a sack from over his shoulder. 'This is for you. For the payment of forty guineas, I was told.'

'Forty?' Katherine asked, her voice cracking. Emily held her tightly by the arm.

'Forty. Ten of it is for me, for delivering this. I am an honest man, merely doing the bidding of someone else. I'm sure you realise I do this at great risk to myself.'

'Did Mister Dempsey send you?' Katherine prompted.

The messenger's face did not seem to register the name. 'Sorry, but if I have the wrong lady, I will leave you.' He made as if to back away.

'Please wait, I have the payment,' Katherine said urgently. Both women knew this was the only way to prevent her husband from discovering what had happened.

Katherine withdrew her purse from the safety of her skirts and counted out the money. Emily looked about the street, checking for a lurking constable, or opportunist thieves. She knew that sometimes these could be the same thing. The courier untied a rope at the top of the sack and showed them its contents. They seemed to match what was missing.

'It is all there I am told,' he said.

Emily took the sack from the man, feeling the weight. It was fortunate they did not have far to travel to Greville Street. The figure lifted his hat again and slipped away down an alley.

'I am so relieved,' Katherine said. Her head suddenly flicked up and down the street.

'Do not be alarmed. You are safe now, there is not far to go.' Emily paused, wondering if she had revealed too much. There had been a couple of liaisons with the General at the house when Katherine had been away. Her companion showed no sign of realising why she knew the area well.

As they walked swiftly up Hatton Gardens to the turning for Greville Street, Emily pondered how aware the General's wife was of how her husband behaved. Percival had a violent reputation in the gambling clubs and brothels of London. Perhaps he was adept at hiding his true self. Soldiers often were. Emily felt a sense of relief that she was not so reliant on one man for her livelihood.

The General's servant greeted them on the doorstep and took the sack from Emily with a curious eye, and she snatched a look at Mrs Percival. Katherine seemed to be absorbed with a figure on the first floor, illuminated by lanterns. A maid, Emily assumed. Katherine snapped out of her trance, and hugged Emily at the entrance, thanking her for her help and bidding farewell.

Emily headed for Covent Garden and ducked into the narrow streets that she was more familiar with. She heard a scream in the distance, a common occurrence. Quickening her step in the fading light, she aimed for the certainty of the central piazza. Reminded, as she picked her way through the mud, of the presence that was lurking in the alleyways. A shadowy figure that was putting fear in the hearts of all the working women, leaving them for dead. Two of her girls in the previous fortnight. William Dempsey had done nothing to help so far. All his decisions were business ones. Perhaps she needed to remind him of the value of her network of women.

7

'Kaplan is not happy with you. He thinks you are burning down his taverns.'

Samuel Ashford scoffed at Dempsey's words and wiped his mouth with the back of his hand. 'Where did he get that idea from?' Ashford knew perfectly well that the Thief Taker was involved in what was being called the 'Night of Fires'. This was a natural troublemaker, a man who took money for prosecuting their own kind.

'Search me,' Dempsey said, his eyes glinting in the murky light. They were sat across a table in a coffeehouse near London Bridge, south of the river, Ashford territory. The place was empty apart from the two men and the landlord; a pair of guards were stationed outside to keep things private. Ashford poured them both more brandy and raised his glass.

'He burnt down a couple of my taverns and a whorehouse in Covent Garden the same night he went after your gin distillery,' Dempsey added.

Kaplan was different to this mercenary and had been a thorn in Ashford's side for years, battling over the supply of drink to the city. But this attack on his factory on Tooley Street was an open invitation to war.

'You think Kaplan put shit in my gin?' Ashford asked. 'I thought it was you.'

'Why would I do that? I am not involved in alcohol.'

Historically there had been few issues between Ashford and the Thief Taker. A scattering of his men had been sent to Newgate at Dempsey's hand, although none of them talked about what went on higher up the chain. Marshal Burley, the magistrates, and the Aldermen of London had no clue.

Dempsey sounded insistent and swilled his glass of brandy. 'It must have been Kaplan. Tindall is in gaol and would not know what to do anyway. Kaplan has several stills in Wapping, Cheapside, Whitechapel. He profits from this, not me.'

'I know.' Ashford relied heavily on Tooley Street and his production was severely impacted. 'The foreman and his family have disappeared.'

'Really?' Dempsey raised his eyebrows in surprise.

Ashford folded his arms. The foreman had mentioned something about Whitechapel before he died, but a man dangling upside down like a chicken on a gibbet could say anything to spare his life. The disappearance of Renshaw had made those north of the river jumpy, prompting Dempsey's talk of collaboration. Kaplan and Dempsey seemed to be at odds with each other, probably him as well. Nobody could be trusted.

'We have no word on who did this. Nothing,' Ashford lied. He had contemplated going after everyone, while his anger simmered. And then Dempsey suggested a meeting, claiming he too had been attacked.

'We should move against Kaplan. Between us, we can destroy him,' Dempsey said.

'Kaplan is nothing more than a drink peddler,' Ashford declared. He studied Dempsey, who smoothed fingers over his short beard. The eyes were deep and sunken, dark pits in his face. Like him, Dempsey was bald and did not normally bother with a wig in public.

'Did you burn down his tavern? Mine too?' Dempsey asked. 'Was that why he destroyed your factory?'

Ashford stared across the table, trying to keep his expression blank. 'I have done nothing. Perhaps that is the problem,' he said. 'I did not attack your taverns. My men rarely venture out of Southwark. Kaplan is stirring up trouble.'

'He wants to drive something between us,' Dempsey said.

'Why would he do that?' Ashford asked. He knew the answer and wanted to assess Dempsey's reaction. It had been many years since the last all-out conflict north of the river; a time before Dempsey's emergence, when Renshaw and Kaplan suffered the most from a street war. That battle had consequences: many deaths, a re-shuffle of territory, while Ashford watched on, growing stronger. Staying out of it had served him well.

'To upset you,' Dempsey said. 'He gains massively with your distillery out of action.'

'I have enough capacity for now.' Ashford knew he had to reassert his authority. Nobody had reached that far into Southwark before. Somebody had to pay.

'This could be the end for Kaplan,' Dempsey said, leaning forward across the table. Ashford paused before replying, wondering if Dempsey was reading his thoughts. 'He affects us both,' Dempsey continued. 'Together, we could bring him down.'

'Why would *you* move against him?' Ashford asked. 'They were just taverns.' It was not the same as a factory. 'You make good money from hanging thieves, from brokering stolen goods. Even though they changed the law to stop you, we both know you have found a way round it. Surely what you have is enough?'

Dempsey poured himself a generous helping of drink and raised his glass. 'All of us want more. We both gain with Kaplan gone. You could control alcohol production, take over the importing business. The same with gambling.' Ashford knew there would be conditions for such a deal, nothing he could not overcome.

Ashford nodded. 'I would like to have his distilleries. But that area in the east end is crawling with depravity. Thankfully for me, desperate men looking for sport.'

He studied Dempsey again. Those eyes bore back at him. For the man opposite this meeting had a clear goal, to instigate an attack on Kaplan. Not that he was opposed to it. And Ashford could turn that to his own advantage.

'I assume you want his whorehouses in return?' Ashford asked.

'That is enough for me. My only interest in alcohol is where it helps the women make money. Where the brothels are combined with taverns, I will make sure they stock your alcohol. It could work for both of us.'

Ashford swilled his drink, savouring it on his tongue. This was genuine stuff, not the diluted filth they sold in Covent Garden and Whitechapel.

'It works well for you,' Ashford admitted, sending a cold stare across the table. 'You must stay away from Kaplan's gambling houses. They are mine.'

'I appreciate that,' Dempsey nodded. 'We will avoid gambling in the east end.'

'That should be fine,' Ashford agreed.

Dempsey stroked his bald head. Ashford found himself doing the same. Perhaps they were the two leaders with the most in common; their disinterest in social niceties, and the goal of removing Kaplan, the bastard who put shit in his gin.

'Did you kill Renshaw?' Ashford asked.

Dempsey raised his eyebrows, an attempt at a look of innocence. 'Not me. I thought it was Kaplan. Not you, then?'

Ashford started to shake his head and stopped. Dempsey was clearly responsible for Renshaw and was now looking for his help to remove Kaplan, freeing him from the pressure on both sides. But Kaplan had to go. Expansion north was inevitable for Ashford. To the south there were just fields and villages, and while there was talk of developments towards Deptford and Camberwell, this was not something he wanted to invest in. The east end was easy for him to reach, with his control of London Bridge.

After touching the knife in his pocket, Ashford brought his hands back to the tabletop. This was a whoremonger and peddler of lies in the Old Bailey, there was no physical danger. And every alliance could be manipulated.

'We have a deal. Drink for me, the whores for you. We take him out together.'

Dempsey silently raised his glass in return.

Ashford tipped his drink down his throat, feeling the pleasure of the burn once more. 'You think he is easy to reach?' Ashford asked, his voice lower.

'Kaplan is well protected,' Dempsey said, hushed despite the lack of customers. 'After what happened to Renshaw. If it were easy, you would have done it by now.'

Ashford gave a slight nod of admission. He had briefly contemplated killing both the other leaders at the Fox Tavern meeting, whatever the risks. But was curious to work out who was responsible for Renshaw first. Convinced now it was the man opposite. He signalled for more drink. The landlord scurried away into a back room.

'Let me set things up,' Dempsey said, his eyes shining, his smile betraying excitement. 'We strike together. The east end will be liberated.' Dempsey sounded prepared, as if he had thought about this for some time.

The landlord returned and Ashford uncorked another bottle, topping up the glasses.

When he was out of earshot, Ashford slammed his brandy down. 'To the future.'

Dempsey wiped his brow and pulled a small glass vial out of his jacket, then tipped something from it into his drink. 'A future for both of us,' he said, before throwing back his concoction. Ashford wondered what Dempsey was adding to it, and whether it was something he could provide. People were always looking for distraction, rich and poor, more than just alcohol. Soon, an entire industry would be under his control.

Ashford smiled to himself as he studied the Thief Taker again. Once Kaplan was removed, he could work with Renshaw's former people to squeeze Dempsey out. The man was trapped. He exhaled deeply, pleased to have a territory with natural boundaries, a clear separation between him and London. But soon, with Kaplan's death, the north and the south of the river would be combined as one stronghold against the meddling of criminals and politicians alike.

8

Dempsey stared at the empty chair in the Old Bailey and curled his fists into balls. He relaxed them and took a nip from the glass in front of him. The liquid trickled down his throat, and he breathed out slowly, the calmness returning. He rose to address the court. The issue of Marshal Burley avoiding proceedings could wait.

Dempsey surveyed the open-air Sessions Yard. It was a familiar place, where he had either watched or participated in many trials. He was no lawyer; he did not need to be. Anybody could present a case if they felt they had enough evidence and could earn the reward for a successful prosecution. There were a small number of faces in the public gallery, and he recognised only Neff, who was squinting in the sun. Judge Gregory appeared to be half asleep, resting his head on a gloved hand, the only person afforded any cover in the court, sat beneath a canopy.

Dempsey scratched at his periwig and turned to address the witness. 'Mister Charlton, could you tell us what happened that day on Finchley Common?'

Charlton shuffled on his feet and looked nervously about the court.

'Mister Charlton?' Dempsey prompted. 'What happened?'

'We was doing a robbery. Holding up a coach. We saw it coming over the hill, and they stopped when we drew our pistols.'

Dempsey waited for Charlton to continue. *Stick to the story*, Dempsey screamed in his head. Eventually, he had to wave an arm in Charlton's direction. 'And…?'

'He, Lamont that is, he ordered them to hand over their jewellery and money.'

'And do you see this Lamont, your accomplice in the robbery here today?' Dempsey asked, his eyes pointing towards where the accused stood.

'Over there, that is him.'

Lamont gave a low, demonic chuckle. It had not been difficult to work out which of the two men would turn witness against the other. Charlton was the instigator of all their robberies; Dempsey knew this because they had been working the roads north of London for him for several months. And there was something simple about Lamont and the way he behaved: the glazed looks, the strange outbursts of noise. The world would not miss the hunchbacked figure who had but one skill: to ride a horse like the wind.

'And it was all Lamont's idea, this robbery?'

'It always is.'

Lamont laughed again. 'How…' he began.

'Silence. The accused is permitted to speak later,' Gregory interjected.

Dempsey stared at the judge, wondering when he had regained his interest.

'And who fired the shots?' Dempsey continued, turning to face Charlton.

'Lamont. He did it. My pistol remained in my coat.'

Dempsey paused to allow the jury to take in the fact. They had already heard how the wife of a gentleman had been wounded by pellets to the leg. The case would not have reached this stage if the highwaymen had been more careful. But convictions could be delivered if one witness turned against another, and Charlton was the first of the two to realise how he could save his own neck. One man would be hanged, the other would receive a small reward for his testimony, and Dempsey would secure the thirty pounds for prosecuting. Everyone benefitted. Except for Lamont, but he had been destined for the gallows for some time.

'Tell us what you stole?'

Charlton leaned against the stand in front of him. Dempsey watched the fingers of the witness turn white as he clung to the rail. 'It was some rings, jewellery, and some bills in hand.'

Dempsey returned to his chair and consulted a ledger. The sheets inside it were blank; he wanted the court to see he was not familiar with the missing items, which were safely stored in a warehouse on Bedford Street.

'What was the value of what you stole?'

'I don't know.'

'You don't know?' Dempsey asked, his voice rising to show his surprise. Croker had estimated it to be just over sixty guineas.

'Lamont, he takes things, and he shares it out. I've not seen the takings.'

Dempsey paused for effect again and nodded at the jury. 'Mister Charlton, why are you testifying against this man?'

Charlton paused, as if weighing up the balance of his own guilt. Or so Dempsey hoped the jury would believe. He wondered if it might be because Charlton was still trying to remember the lines he had been given.

'Because he was the instigator of this robbery.' Dempsey held back a sigh, conscious this was one of his own words, and not part of Charlton's normal vocabulary. It did not seem to cause alarm among the jury, who mostly looked bored. Charlton continued. 'I was just there to hold the horses.'

Lamont began to protest again, and Dempsey turned to hold up a hand in his direction. 'You have already been warned by the judge.' Lamont stared at the floor in front of him, shaking his head. Dempsey twirled around and pointed a finger at Charlton. 'So, when Lamont here suggests, as he might well do in his defence, that you have turned evidence merely to save your own neck, he will be lying?'

'Yes.'

There was a nod of the head from the witness towards Dempsey, as if he wanted acknowledgment for the simple task of remembering his story.

Dempsey turned and raised an eyebrow in the direction of the jury. 'You see, Mister Charlton is not vengeful, he is a believable witness. He is merely a gullible dupe in this crime. Lamont is the real villain in this case.' He turned to the judge. 'That is all we wish to present, your Honour.'

Gregory banged his gavel and ordered a short recess, slipping through a rear door into the main chambers of the Old Bailey. The prisoner stared at the floor in what Dempsey took to be disbelief. He was merely the victim of an unfortunate accident. If the lady had not been injured the case might not have brought any attention. Dempsey knew that Charlton and Lamont could not continue as a pair of highwaymen after this mistake, despite their previous success. Their links to his organisation would eventually be exposed. But with any crime there was opportunity. Better to make some profit from them while he could. Charlton would be absorbed into his gang of thieves and Lamont would go to the gallows.

By the time Dempsey returned to his seat, Neff had appeared at the table.

'It looks good from over there,' Neff said in a hushed voice, his eyes in the direction of the jury, who were shuffling out.

'They are with us?' Dempsey whispered back.

'Four of them solidly, and they will shape the rest.'

'They were easy?' Dempsey asked. He knew Neff used a variety of methods to swing juries: sometimes bribery or blackmail, possibly even the threat of violence.

'We made offers they could not refuse,' Neff said flatly.

'We might not need them,' Dempsey said, nodding in the direction of where Lamont had been standing. 'We could have saved ourselves money and effort.'

'There can only be one verdict now,' Neff affirmed.

The pair walked from the court, and paused on the steps outside the Old Bailey, out of earshot of passers-by. Newgate Street was busy with traders and pedestrians jostling for space. Jades of differing ages touted for business, caring nothing for the fact they were so close to the main court of London.

'Ashford is prepared to come in with us. He does not suspect anything.'

Neff's brow furrowed, before he offered a low chuckle. 'Nobody is drinking gin right now.'

'Where did you get that stuff from?'

Neff inclined his head, as if to say do not ask. It was a gesture Dempsey had seen several times before. Like so many things, he did not need to know the details.

'Any more news on Renshaw?' Dempsey asked, changing the subject. Neff surveyed the street, always alert to danger, Dempsey assumed.

'Nothing yet. I will keep digging.'

'I heard a rumour his body was picked up at sea.'

Neff turned back from the direction of the prison, with a thin smile. 'In one tavern I heard he ran off to France, disguised as a woman.' This was a new one to Dempsey. 'Nobody knows for certain, other than he must be dead,' Neff added. 'West London is in chaos.'

'Have you consulted Emily? Or the whores you know?' Dempsey asked. The women heard everything, in his experience. Men struggled to keep their conquests quiet.

Neff appeared to blush and looked across the street. Now that he was so busy with the thief taking, Dempsey wondered how closely Neff and Emily conferred on matters. Perhaps things had moved full circle since Dempsey had allowed her to run the brothels and a network of madams. So long as the whores provided him with valuable information, and the blackmail opportunities that came with it, they were fulfilling their role.

'I will ask her again,' Neff said coldly.

'Do that. The control of crime is a fine balance. We don't want to lose any more prominent criminals, do we?' Dempsey said with a smile.

'Do we?' Neff asked, with the same expression.

'I suppose accidents happen,' Dempsey mused. 'We just need to ensure they don't happen to us.'

9

Neff followed Dempsey into the barn near the river. There was no warning over who would be there, or what might be discussed, just the instruction to attend. Three men stood and scraped their chairs on the wooden floor as they entered. Another remained seated, eyes down. Dempsey indicated Neff should head for the corner, where he positioned himself and looked through a narrow window at the street. Dawn was breaking and traders were shuffling about with their barrows, setting up stalls. His gaze returned to the warehousemen, all familiar to him. He studied the figure of Barwell, who picked at his nose in his seat, wiping what he pulled out on his breeches. The muscular arms were then solidly crossed, as he let out an impatient sigh. Neff attempted to make eye contact, but Barwell raised his head to glare at Dempsey. He hoped the man would do as he was told.

The barn smelled of wet hay. Neff pulled his coat around him, and shivered. A flash of a memory hit, of hiding in stables, in the dead of night, wrapped in blankets, praying the militia men would ride on.

Dempsey dragged a chair across the floor, and Neff was pulled out of his reverie. His boss bid the men sit and poured ale from a large flagon into their tankards. Neff was curious where it had come from: maybe they had brought the drink with them. Warehousemen took ale at any time of day and worked all hours for the Lost and Found business. Neff studied them: these were men of early starts, essential in the storage and distribution of goods, their work hidden in plain sight among the taverns and merchant houses of London. He returned his focus to Barwell, who had not moved from his seat all this time.

'Gentlemen, thank you for coming. I trust all our places are secure with you here?' Dempsey began.

A low chorus of 'aye's came in return. Even Barwell nodded.

'I have a good reason to drag you away from your valuable work.' Dempsey filled himself a tankard and took a gulp. Neff kept an eye on the men, while pretending to observe the street.

'Things are going well?' The question from Dempsey sounded light, unthreatening.

Murmurs in reply, little more.

'I reward you?'

More affirmative nods. Dempsey sat astride a chair in front of them.

'You all know I have eyes everywhere. If people see something unusual, they tell me.'

Barwell spoke up. 'You accusing us of something?' His voice boomed across the space.

Dempsey smiled, as if pleased he had got Barwell to react. 'My clerk keeps a track of everything. And recently when we have come to retrieve some valuable items, they have not been where they should be. It is terrible for business.'

'Mister Dempsey, we are loyal.' Barwell raised himself up in his chair. 'You know we are approached for the goods all the time. We resist strongly, with force if we have to.' Barwell looked round at his colleagues. Their silence begged for him to continue. 'We could make money by betraying you, but we know better. You are the most reliable source in this city. Without you we wouldn't have a trade.'

Barwell supped from his cup. Neff stared at him, wondering at the show of resistance. Barwell still refused to look in his direction. If it weren't for the lost property operation, these men would all be thieving on the streets, as they had been for years before. Or hung. Was he forgetting this?

'I understand that there will be some items which you cannot resist moving on. It is expected,' Dempsey said. From Neff's angle, Dempsey looked calm, his hands in his lap. 'We allow for a certain degree of loss. You are all men of enterprise; you have your own ambitions.' There were shared looks between the warehousemen, eyes trained back on Barwell, their spokesman.

'It is inevitable some goods will disappear,' Dempsey continued. 'But please do not insult me by pretending this does not happen. Or by taking more than you should. We need to keep business running. Too many valuable items are going missing.' The voice was even, measured. Neff had heard the tone before, during negotiation. Usually with people Dempsey had complete control over.

'Maybe we should be informed in advance of what is too precious to lose,' Barwell said, emptying his drink. Nods came from the men beside him.

'That is my business,' Dempsey said, his voice rising slightly. Neff leaned against the wall; his coat felt tight around his shoulders. He hoped the warehousemen were not getting too greedy.

'I am going to increase your payments by a pound a week,' Dempsey continued, the calm restored. 'But if I do this, you are to stop stealing from me, from the organisation. Lost and Found has a reputation. We cannot have this destroyed by valuables disappearing.'

'A pound you say?' Barwell asked, his arms firmly locked in defiance. Neff held back the temptation to cough, to draw attention to himself, and the arrangement. He stared at Barwell, willing him to look over. This was the natural choice to run the largest warehouse on the Strand. Barwell's size, his reputation for brawling, staging dogfights, drinking, all influential.

Neff knew how to work with these men and was surprised at Dempsey's offer of a pay increase. They had certainly not discussed it. It was unlike Dempsey to take an interest in the minor details of this part of the operation. Neff was curious as to what had prompted it. He tried to study his boss's face. The darkness was there, as always, the sunken cheeks and the black eyes that held back many secrets.

'One pound more is a generous offer. That is the deal, and nothing goes missing from now on. Do you all agree?'

'We agree,' Barwell boomed, shuffling in his seat. *Don't overdo it,* Neff worried.

'Fine. Drink up men, go back to your stores, we have work to do. I am told it has been a busy night on the streets, you will have deliveries throughout the day.'

Dempsey stood and carefully placed his tricorn on his head. He clutched at the inside of his coat, before heading for the door. Looking over at Neff, he said, 'give me a few minutes, will you? I have someone to visit. I will see you outside.'

Neff looked out the window once more. The streets continued to come alive; the sound of tradesmen calling, the slopping out of buckets of waste in the gutters, and the chatter of early morning gossip could all be heard clearly from inside the barn. Talk of which prominent man was on the take, who might be hanged next. There was no danger for his boss being alone in this part of London, this early in the day. Dempsey left and Neff turned back to see the warehousemen finish their ale and sidle out the rear. All except Barwell, who remained.

Barwell poured one more from the jug. 'Drink with me. He does not suspect.'

'Just be careful,' Neff said, joining him at the table. 'Croker is meticulous, and clever. Don't let him catch you.'

Barwell shook his head. 'I can look after myself.'

Neff leaned on the table. 'Just don't ruin it for everyone else.'

'Who benefits?' Barwell asked. 'I mean in the end, not the go between. Not you.'

Neff shook his head. 'Best that you don't know.'

'Kaplan, then.' Barwell smiled, seemingly unconcerned.

Neff offered a thin-lipped reply. 'Think what you want. All that matters is we keep turning the trade over.'

Barwell shrugged, carefully placing his chair behind the table. Neff noted the surprisingly deft hands for such a big man. The warehouseman saluted in Neff's direction and headed for the door. 'Times are changing, working men like us are on the march,' Barwell said.

Change was certainly coming, Neff mused. But not every working man like Barwell was going to like the result.

10

Arthur Kaplan held the youth by the scruff of the neck. The light fingers dropped his pocketbook to the floor, and Kaplan's minder swiped it before another scoundrel could grab it. The rest of the group of boys backed away and ran. Kaplan shook the young thief and pushed him against the wall. The lad grinned back, toothlessly. Kaplan could not stand for this type of assault, no matter which part of London they were in. Appearances were important. A swift punch to the ribs, and the lad dropped to the floor.

Kaplan looked around him, suddenly conscious of being in unfamiliar Charing Cross, and the fact the meeting was meant to be in secret. The thief dragged himself to his feet and ran off down an alley, presumably to join his friends. Vermin dodged in and out of abandoned barrows in the darkened lane. A couple of jades turned their backs on Kaplan and his minder, disappearing into a gin shop. This part of London had gone downhill. He almost longed for the old order, the bloody battles with Renshaw and Conway before him.

Kaplan hustled on towards the Black Bear tavern. Inside they were greeted by the innkeeper, who was one of Kaplan's best customers, fiercely independent and the provider of a neutral meeting point. Dempsey was seated a table with his back to the fire, the man he knew as Neff behind him. The smell of smoke filled the room, a fusion of wood and charcoal. The landlord positioned himself at the counter, flanked by two of his own bodyguards, eyeing their four customers.

Kaplan carefully dropped down opposite Dempsey and studied Neff. He had the bearing of a soldier, the piercing eyes and countenance of someone who would not hesitate to act on orders. Sometimes you had to appreciate the strengths of your enemy.

'Mary Grant tells me we have matters to discuss,' Kaplan began. The madam who had passed on the message.

'We have a mutual interest,' Dempsey began. 'We are both under threat.'

'Both of us?'

'Two of my alehouses were attacked as well as one of yours.'

Kaplan feigned surprise. He watched Dempsey run fingers through his neat beard, then stroke his bald head. The last gesture reminded him of Ashford. But they were far from being the same man. You knew where you were with the Beast of Southwark.

'You didn't burn down the Watchman?' Kaplan asked, playing the game.

'Of course not. We were both attacked on the same night,' Dempsey scoffed. 'There is only one culprit.'

'Ashford?'

'The same.'

'Was the Tooley Street distillery you?' Kaplan had benefitted from what happened that night. The demand for his gin had increased.

'I could not let Ashford get away with what he did to the taverns in Covent Garden,' Dempsey said, leering across the table.

'You knew it was him?'

'My people followed the arsonists down to the river, then crossed to the southern side. I did what any man would do. Retaliated. Immediately.' Dempsey reached into a jacket pocket, tapped at something inside, then folded his arms, resting them on the table. Kaplan noticed the hands shake a little as he did this and wondered what troubled the Thief Taker. All weaknesses were worth noting.

'His gin already tasted of shit,' Kaplan said.

Dempsey rocked back in his chair and laughed, showing neglected, dirty teeth.

'We have a common enemy,' Dempsey said. *Everyone is an enemy*, Kaplan mused. 'Although I have let it be known if I discover the men who were responsible for the attack on Tooley Street, I will have them arrested.' Dempsey's lips pursed. The eyes gave little away.

'I'm sure you would,' Kaplan replied.

Dempsey called himself a supporter of the law and frequently claimed the rewards for prosecutions, which always amused Kaplan. He had his own way of balancing the scales with people who wronged him. It never involved proud speeches at the Old Bailey. Guilty men did not need to be hung; they could be punished in more immediate ways.

Kaplan eyed the pretender: A man who had avoided the battles of old. He almost wished for Renshaw to return. Straightforward confrontation was easier to manage.

'We should work together against Ashford,' Dempsey pressed. 'He wants to reach into the east end, across the river.'

They both knew Ashford's continued control of the Thames crossings was a barrier to commerce.

'Yes, as revenge for what you did on Tooley Street.'

'I merely acted to warn Ashford that he cannot strike us in the north. But we can still use the courts to hurt him.'

Kaplan leaned forward on the table and poured himself another drink from the bottle. 'The law can take a long time. I can find out the truth a lot quicker than your constables and marshals. You cannot guarantee justice, Ashford might wriggle off the hook. He never gets his hands dirty.'

'Then we must act against him. Not let it get to the courts.' Dempsey emptied his glass.

Neff moved closer behind his boss and whispered in his ear. Dempsey nodded, scanning the tavern. Kaplan followed his eyes, there were still only four visitors and the owner's men. Kaplan breathed out slowly, savouring his brandy.

Dempsey's voice lowered to a whisper. 'Let me lure Ashford to you. He has set up three new gin stills in the past six months along the South bank. They must be of interest to you, the ones not tasting of horseshit.'

Kaplan pondered the recent arson attacks. Maybe Dempsey's talk of there being no boundaries had emboldened the Beast of Southwark. Dempsey's swift response on Tooley Street made Kaplan look weak. He needed to act.

'If we go after Ashford, I want all of Southwark,' Kaplan said.

'That is acceptable,' Dempsey replied, tapping the side of his glass.

'What do you want in return?'

'I want you to think about the whorehouses to the east. Emily Jarrett and Mary Grant wish to work together. We should let them. Prostitution goes well with drink.'

Kaplan contemplated the idea. His only interest in whores was where they stimulated the consumption of alcohol. This Mary Grant, who oversaw a network of madams from Aldgate to Wapping, was asking for rooms above taverns for trade. The innkeepers resisted. Only one side would get his support: the one that brought in the most money. Drink was King.

'You have no interest in Southwark?' Kaplan asked. Dempsey was trapped in the middle of all the territories with nowhere to expand. That was why he wanted the boundaries to be slackened. But Kaplan had first call on south of the river and the gin factories. If he had an alcohol monopoly across London, he could set his own prices.

'Southwark is yours,' Dempsey said. 'I believe in using our expertise. Whores and thieves are my thing, and alcohol is yours. Put the two together, east of Newgate, we might both do well.' Dempsey leaned forward again, the eyes searching. He wiped his brow and touched the inside of his jacket once more, then returned his hands to the table. Kaplan stiffened, disturbed by the fidgeting. He sensed his own man behind him shift to attention. Dempsey pressed on, black eyes staring. They reminded Kaplan of cold coal. 'We need to stop Ashford expanding. His attack on the taverns was designed to make us suspicious of each other. We should not fall for it,' Dempsey added.

'Why don't you move west?' Kaplan mused. 'Tindall is an easy touch. Renshaw's old territory is ripe for plucking.' They were toying with each other.

Dempsey rocked back in his chair again and sighed. 'I am here to talk about Ashford. There is no sense in ruining each other, we have a common enemy. We can move on him together.'

Images of blood running down the gutters returned to Kaplan. Bad, old days of criminal in-fighting, struggles between him and Renshaw, the vicious Conway before that. But then the sight of Ashford's grinning face presented itself to him, a raging torch in his hand, the Watchman tavern alight.

'Set my men free, then we go after Ashford.'

Dempsey rested his chin on a couple of fingers. The eyes appeared to light up. He stroked his beard again in what looked like quiet contemplation. Kaplan recognised the signals he was trying to give out, had also done this in negotiation before. Making it look like he was considering an offer, when in truth his mind was already made up.

'Your men will be out next week in time to kill Ashford. So long as we have a deal about the women and their trade in your territory,' Dempsey said. Kaplan nodded and finished off his drink. Dempsey continued. 'I shall find a way to lure Ashford across the river. We do not need to hang him. His time is up if we work together.' Dempsey raised his glass. 'To free enterprise, and a free Southwark.'

Kaplan finished his drink and left the tavern. The light was beginning to fade, and he followed the shape of his minder through the streets in the direction of Bishopsgate, checking to see if he was being followed. Nothing. He contemplated how he had managed to maintain his hold over East London for so long. It was by not trusting anyone. Least of all, a Thief Taker whose business thrived on deceit. Once Ashford was gone, deals could always be broken.

11

Emily followed the link lighter across the city, first down familiar streets, then deeper into the east end. As she picked her way through the mud that clung to her boots, Emily tried to focus on the boy and his lantern. She knew this type of journey was used to entrap rich gentlemen, leading them down narrow passageways in places like St Giles, and Moorfields. Dempsey had profited from the trick many times. The message that pushed her on came from her fellow madam, Mary Grant, imploring her to make haste. 'There has been another death', it said.

The boy stopped suddenly in an alley off the furthest end of Lombard Street and beckoned her to walk ahead. Emily could see Mary and Elizabeth Manning crouched in a doorway, over what looked like a pile of clothes. As she approached, the stench of rotten meat hit her, as strong as the gutters of St Giles. She held a handkerchief to her nose to block it out, her own breathing shallow. It became clear the rags covered a lifeless body.

Elizabeth stood and placed an arm around Emily. 'You think this was him again?' Elizabeth whispered. Mary was stroking the hair of a dead girl.

Emily peered down. The victim's stomach had been cut open; the innards bled out onto her dress like the contents of a slaughterhouse slab. Blood spread onto the cobbles from underneath the body. Emily fought the nausea and gagged into the handkerchief. She wondered at what marked this girl out as a target, rather than the hundreds of others.

'Looks like something heavy,' Emily said. 'Like a club or a hammer?'

Mary nodded. 'She was just abandoned, left to die.'

'Have you called a constable?' Emily again.

'Not yet. I wanted you both to see her. To judge for yourselves.'

'It looks the same,' added Elizabeth.

'What are we to do?' Emily asked.

'I'm not sure what can be done.' Mary clutched the dead girl's hand. 'All the men see are whores.'

The wind whipped down the alley, blowing rubbish along it. Silence fell among the three most prominent madams of London. Emily could see the fear in her sisters' faces and wondered if she was showing the same.

Mary Grant knelt; the fingers tightly woven in hers. Emily saw the tears form on the madam's cheeks, the sadness in her eyes despite her experience of the trade since the turn of the century, and the dangers that were always there. Kaplan controlled everything in the east. Emily thought about William Dempsey, and the freedom he granted her to run her business in and around Covent Garden; how things were different for her.

'What was her name?' Emily asked.

'Susan,' Mary replied, swallowing hard. 'She only arrived from the east coast last week.'

Trading on the streets was dangerous, reliable twangs increasingly hard to find. Too many of them had turned to abusing the girls themselves. Gentlemen were always looking for entertainment. Sometimes it was merely company, to travel in a secluded coach, or walk in a park, but at night the thoughts of men turned to sex. And for one it seemed, violence.

'The fourth one,' Emily muttered, 'in the past month.' Her sisters nodded.

First it had been Emily's girls, one in Whitefriars, the next St Giles; followed by Northumberland Avenue under Sister Elizabeth. Now it looked like it was Mary's turn.

'We need to instruct our girls to be careful. To always have their twangs with them,' Emily said.

'There is only so much we can do to protect them.' Elizabeth raised herself up, the taller of the three women. 'The temptation can be too great to make a quick shilling.'

Emily studied the woman who oversaw the western side of London and Westminster. Elizabeth Manning kept a few grand houses, near St James's Park, frequented by politicians, aldermen, nobility. A quality of client Emily was jealous of. Elizabeth crouched down beside Mary Grant and placed a hand around her shoulder. Emily watched the two women, wondering what sort of bond there was between them. The sisters, as they called themselves, did not compete the way the men did. They simply worked different areas of London.

Mary slumped further onto her knees in the dirt. Maybe the presence of a killer on her streets, the stretch from Newgate over to Whitechapel, had hit home. Further west, Emily trained her girls to fight back in their own way, use their deft hands, pick pockets where they could. This kept Dempsey happy, as they provided stolen goods for him to return at a profit. She knew her fellow madams had their own tricks they used on their clients. But what sort of man would attack a defenceless girl? It was hard to imagine.

Mary finally looked up at Emily, her forehead creased, tears down her face. 'Kaplan is only interested in drink. He thinks we interfere with it. You think Dempsey will help us?' she asked.

Emily stared at the dead girl again. 'If it means a loss of money, the men will do something. That is what we must stress to them.'

'Kaplan will not care,' Mary muttered, squeezing the lifeless hand of the girl.

Elizabeth shook her head sadly. 'Without Renshaw we have no protection. To the men, one whore is as good as another. There are so many girls.' Emily had heard about the disappearance of the man who had attacked her a few weeks before. There were no regrets if his end had been painful. It sounded like Elizabeth had been more reliant on Renshaw than she thought.

'I will persuade William,' Emily said. 'He cannot ignore this any longer.' She looked at her sisters; their faces showed only sadness, little belief.

'I shall call for the constable now,' Mary said, rising to her feet, Elizabeth doing the same. Mary's dress was coloured with blood, mud, and tears. 'We will ensure she gets a proper burial,' she added, bending down to stroke the girl's face before placing a jacket over the tiny creature.

'There is a predator out there.' Elizabeth pulled her own coat around her. 'God save us from men,' she spat.

'Leave it to me.' Emily thought there was a beating heart inside Dempsey somewhere. He might recognise the safety of the street girls as well as the loss of trade. And if that failed, there was someone who had known her even longer, that she would turn to. 'Elizabeth, we can walk to Blackfriars. You know where we should go.'

Elizabeth nodded her approval, and they bid Mary farewell. The two women walked arm in arm west through the streets, aided by the link lighter who had waited at the end of the alley. They ignored the shouts of the sellers who continued to ply their trade in the near darkness and pulled up at the rear of a brandy shop close to the river. A place known to the innkeepers and lodging houses of London as the Introduction House.

The door was opened for them by a woman dressed in white linen, a veil drawn across her face. The madams had grown used to her disfigurement. Her smile, when it could be seen, was punctuated by scarring to her cheeks and neck, the result of a customer who tried to brand her with a poker years before. A man who disappeared not long after. Despite this fate, Caroline was the sweetest-hearted woman in the city. She had been rescued from a prostitute's life, and now welcomed all the girls who had been recommended to them.

Emily and Elizabeth moved to a table in the rear of the shop, and Caroline came over to serve them a glass of gin each. 'It is good to see you both,' she said with a slight lisp. 'You can see one of the new ones for yourself this evening.'

A girl sat on the opposite side of the room, picking at a thumbnail with her teeth. Caroline retreated to stand behind a counter and beckoned her over. A low conversation followed, which Emily strained to hear. Caroline offered a patient smile and noted down some details. She had enough of a poorhouse education for basic record keeping.

Elizabeth reached across to Emily over the table. 'This is

more important than ever,' she said. 'The temptation to trade will not go away, even if it is not safe out there.'

'That girl in the doorway. We have to make amends somehow,' Emily replied.

'We do.'

Caroline pointed in their direction, and the visitor turned to look at the madams. After a comforting hand was reached out, the girl made her way over to Emily and Elizabeth's table and curtsied.

'I am looking for Madam Manning,' she said, in a northern accent. Emily cleared her throat, to suppress the jealousy over who had been chosen.

'That is me,' Elizabeth replied, standing, and offering a hand. The girl shook it. Delicate fingers, Emily noted.

'I understand you can find me some employment and lodging.' She gazed at Elizabeth, then her eyes flitted nervously about the room.

'You are new to London?'

'I arrived yesterday. It took me several days by coach from Nottingham.'

'And your story?' Elizabeth prompted.

'Is not a happy one. But I do come from a good home.' There was a timid smile.

'I need to hear the detail.' Elizabeth bid the girl sit with them. The stranger shifted on her feet before dropping into a chair. She sucked at the bleeding nail.

'My mother died.'

'Leaving you with just your father?' Elizabeth asked. The girl nodded. Emily silently congratulated her on the educated guess, although it was not an uncommon tale.

The child blushed and looked at the floor. 'He…' She hesitated, closing her eyes, a single tear falling. 'I had to get away.' Without a mother's protection, some girls became targets in their own home.

'Your name?' Elizabeth asked.

'Anne Cleeves.'

'Your age?'

'Fifteen.'

'Well, if the good lady over there suggests you to me,' said Elizabeth with a nod towards Caroline, 'I am not to disagree. Do you have your paperwork?' she asked.

The girl passed it across the table and then sat on her hands, but not before Emily noticed how filthy they were. The rags she wore looked damp, and smelled of rotten vegetables. Emily offered her a smile, which she returned, showing good teeth. That would be an advantage in the work she would undertake.

'I shall take you somewhere safe,' Elizabeth said, taking the sheet and studying it. 'This is Madam J,' she added. 'You may hear of her name as well as mine. We work together.' Elizabeth folded the paper. 'Did Caroline tell you what we do here? Where we ask girls like you to work?'

Anne sniffed. 'I fear I have no choice. I have nowhere to stay.'

A common situation, Emily mused. Sometimes it felt like they were struggling against an insurmountable tide of girls flocking to the city to escape their troubles. Most seemed unaware that what lay in wait for them could be worse than what they left behind. This was why so many turned to the filthy streets. The aim of the Introduction House was to direct them to safety away from the grasping hands of those eager to make a few shillings at their expense. The tavern owners and the alleyway madams who refused their support.

'You will be a servant to begin with,' Elizabeth said. 'Then we will see what else might suit you.'

The image of the bloodied girl off Lombard Street returned to Emily, and she remembered how she felt when she first arrived in London. Bewildered, lost, hungry, soon imprisoned. She eventually found a way out of the gutter; not exactly holding her morals intact, but it had been an escape all the same. She felt her heart tighten every time she thought about these girls. James Neff had warned her to think of herself as well as saving others. Dempsey saw what she did as purely a business. She had made her choice all those years ago, over which man to follow, and she had benefitted from it. You lived with those choices, there was no point in doubting them.

'Do you have any possessions?' Elizabeth asked.

'Just what I'm wearing,' the girl said, her smile making Emily's heart melt.

'Come, I shall show you where you will be safe in this dark city.'

Emily watched Elizabeth lead the girl outside. She wondered which establishment she would be taken to. There was a place of her own in Covent Garden that was well suited to innocent girls like Anne, run by Mother Gleeson. In the daylight it looked like any other dwelling, but at night it catered for all manner of tastes; shows, dancing, presentations of girls as an ensemble. All designed to tempt the men, and their wallets. A significant step above the filthy life of the girls working on desperate corners.

Emily could not save them all, but God willing, enough could be spared her own early fate, and take control of their lives.

12

1700

The boy dropped his apples to the floor. He scrambled to pick them up and looked around. Nobody seemed to notice. All eyes were on the makeshift stage in the market square. William tried to copy the man again. He used two items this time, managing to keep them both moving. He stopped to look back at the performer, whose fruit seemed to be suspended in mid-air. When William tried to add a third apple, they all tumbled to the ground again. His mother would birch him for the bruising. There was not enough money in his pockets to buy replacements as well as the gin she desperately needed. It was a long walk from Cosby to Narborough market, and she sent her son to fetch and carry now. His mother had not worked since she was thrown out of the village mill but had kept up the rent with the landlord. A man who had his own way of keeping William in check, when her back was turned. There was no father that he recalled. Never a mention of one in eleven years of his life.

The small crowd began to applaud, which changed to a steady rhythm of clapping as a woman walked up and down the stage, singing. Her voice seemed to soar above the square and made him forget his hunger, the pain brought on by shoes that were too small for him, the wheals on his back where his mother reminded him of the penalty for not doing as she bid. The songstress's long, dark hair was tossed each time she made a turn; she added a wink and a smile at certain points for her audience.

The performance then changed again: now there were four people talking in a strange rhyme, waving their arms, and marching about. Then a sword fight, where two men fell to the floor. The victor and the singer kissed. The crowd cheered. William joined in the applause, placing his apples in the bag at his feet. The woman seemed to beam right at him, then looked away into the crowd and called for contributions in the hat that was being walked round. William stood transfixed, wondering at the chills that went through his bones. A strange feeling of wanting to be up there with them, at the same time petrified at the thought of being seen by so many people. He could feel his heart beating faster than he could remember.

As he heard the chink of coins landing in a hat, William stared at his bruised apples, sadness folding over him. He headed for the gin shop where Mrs Brown would know the exact drink his mother needed.

When he emerged into the sunlight, his arms aching from the weight of the bottles along with the fruit, the performers were dismantling the stage. He stayed to watch them, marvelling at how everything was neatly packed away onto their cart. When they finished, the three men and the woman were surrounded by villagers as they made their way into the local tavern. The one with the hat led the procession, shaking the coins.

William sat underneath the cart, remembering the wild eyes of his mother's hate, the swish of the crop as she vented her frustration at him the night before. And then the stinking breath of the man who forbade him to make a sound while his mother was asleep. He called it love, but William knew that it had a different meaning.

Leaning against one of the wheels, the sound of the woman's song echoed around William's head, enchanting, capturing somewhere he would be safe. Tiredness from his early start that morning overtook him, and he closed his eyes.

He woke to his mother's voice screeching across the square. Peeking out, he spotted her standing on a parked barrow, yelling about her missing drink. William wondered how late it was, and how his mother had managed to reach Narborough. Her wide frame was unmistakable, and then he saw the landlord standing beside her, scanning the village. He pulled his arms around himself, feeling the pain, hearing the hushed command to be quiet in the dark, to not shout for help. The pair jumped down and moved away towards the river. William slipped the bottles and the fruit beneath the cart's tarpaulin, and slid under it to hide. His knees trembled. In the dark it smelled of rotten fruit and tobacco, the type that the landlord smoked. He fought back the need to throw up, trying to hold his breath.

There were voices nearby, and he picked out a female one, different from his mother. He guessed it was the woman he had heard singing. She was laughing, and two men joined in the chatter. The words were difficult to understand. William pulled himself into a ball, knowing if he looked out his mother's face would be there, and he would be hauled by the ear home, to a beating like no other he had experienced. And more pleas to stay silent.

The cart dropped under the weight of somebody climbing aboard, then a click resounded, followed by the clatter of hooves. William tightened the grip around his legs, as the cart started to move. Nobody pulled the covering away to expose the shivering figure underneath. He stayed there for what felt like hours, the rise and fall of the cart lulling him back to sleep. Eventually, the cramp in his legs was too much. He wriggled and turned over. There was movement above, then a weight on top of him. A shout, and the cart stopped.

Light rushed at him, and he shielded his eyes. He expected his mother to be standing there with a crop. Instead, there was the face of the singer, and a hand reaching out to him.

'Come, our little stowaway.' Eyes set upon the bottles beside him. 'It seems you have brought us a present. Jake likes a drop of gin. Get out.'

He slipped to the ground and waited, expecting them to leave him there. The earth was dusty, and something itched in his nose, forcing him to sneeze. William wiped his face on a filthy sleeve and looked around him. The road was unfamiliar, a faceless path to nowhere.

The woman crouched down to his height. 'You are lucky. We are due to stop here, the horse needs a rest. Jake is off for a piss.' Her words were difficult to make out, shorter sounds than he was used to. 'Here,' she held out a cup. 'Have a drink.'

William looked over the woman's shoulder, then back at her. Something about her eyes made his breath steady; he felt a tingle run through him. He pulled the cup to his lips, savouring the water, and took it all down.

'Thirsty work, hiding,' she said. 'You should go home.' William shook his head. He could not return to Cosby. 'We could leave you here, at the side of the road. There are robbers in these parts.'

'Where are we?' William asked.

'Lutterworth.'

He had heard the name when people at Narborough market talked of places far away. William had no idea how far, though.

The woman pulled a satchel from across her shoulder and passed him a piece of bread. He realised he had not eaten since lunchtime the day before. William devoured it, his stomach growling. The figure opposite nodded and smiled. He remembered a similar expression from the stage. Suddenly, he knew this was where he wanted to be.

'You can tag along. I will fix it with them,' she said, indicating the men sat at the front of the cart. William looked towards them; they were staring with looks he could not decipher. They raised their hats and turned away. The woman seemed to be in charge.

'You will have to make yourself useful if you are to stay with us. Pay your way somehow. Would you like that?'

William nodded furiously.

'Welcome to the travelling show we call the Largent and Dempsey Players. I'm Lucy Dempsey,' she curtsied dramatically. 'You can call me Luce.'

13

Dempsey swayed to avoid a figure staggering out of the alehouse door. He watched Hatcher swipe at the drunk with his club, the crack against bone echoing in the still night. A pair of dandily dressed culls who were approaching the Goat and Compasses turned and retreated. Wind whipped down the narrow alley, and the sign for the inn creaked, then flapped against the wooden shutters. Something fluttered above, and Dempsey looked up. The rooves of the buildings on both sides seemed to reach out across to each other, blocking out much of the light. He could hear the faint sounds of revelry from inside the tavern. This was Bryan's Passage in Moorfields, also known as Sodomite's Walk, the edge of Hell.

Dempsey led Hatcher inside, his minder slipping his club into his coat. Nobody appeared to notice them as they entered. Most of the attention was focused on two people in dresses parading along a tabletop. Dempsey peered at them, and bundled his fists together, realising they were men. They swivelled and pouted. One raised a hand to the crowd, blowing kisses, prompting cheers. Dempsey closed his eyes to block out the image, trying to focus on their mission, swallowing back the distaste.

The place smelled mostly like any other tavern, a mixture of alcohol, sweat, and pipe smoke which wafted towards the darkly stained ceiling. But Dempsey detected something else, a perfume he recalled from one of Emily Jarrett's houses. It made for a sickening mixture. A pair of uniformed soldiers in heavy make-up raced past them, tickling each other, and began a mock chase across the tavern floor. Dempsey could sense Hatcher twitch next to him, a hand back on his club.

They were approached by a boy, who lifted his skirts, waving an appendage at them. 'Nice to see you,' he screeched.

Hatcher stepped forward and punched the creature in the face. The boy dropped to the floor, groaning. Dempsey turned away to scan the room, feeling the sweat trickle down his back. He leaned against a wall by the door and wiped his hands on his coat, then folded his arms across his chest. This was a job they needed to complete as quickly as possible.

He spotted Mother Petticoat, slumped over a table by the hearth, wig askew. Dempsey side-stepped revellers who were breaking away from the performance in the centre of the tavern and approached the landlord. Petticoat was also in a dress, heavily rouged and made up like a woman. Dempsey sensed the heavy tread of Hatcher at his side; more muscle than he needed for the task, but he wanted to leave no doubt as to the purpose of the visit.

'Where is Burley?' Dempsey demanded, grabbing Petticoat by the collar, raising his voice above the cheers of the boisterous crowd behind him.

Petticoat pulled himself free, jerking back in his seat, startled. He belched, and stumbled his words, as his face fell, studying the spilled drink and broken glass at his feet.

'Upstairs. Last room on the left.'

As a marshal for the City of London, Burley had the right to question, prosecute, even defend criminals if he wished. He also oversaw the prisons for the Aldermen. His was the formal responsibility to keep crime under control. And lately he had been hindering Dempsey's attempts to bring criminals to justice and receive the financial gain that came with it. It was time to remind the marshal of his duty.

As they burst in the door on the upper floor, Burley shrieked. He pushed a figure away and fell into a huddled ball in the corner, whimpering and clutching bedsheets around him.

'Leave,' Dempsey yelled at the moll, who rapidly pulled his clothes on, and scuttled out the door. Dempsey carefully closed it behind him. He bid Hatcher stand aside and eyed the marshal shaking by the bed.

'Mister Burley, this is a surprise. Who would have thought a man as important as you would be cavorting in a place like this?' Dempsey asked, keeping his distance.

Burley snatched at his clothes: a dress and stockings. Most of Moorfields knew what he liked to do with his spare time. The Goat and Compasses was infamous for its male prostitutes and had been protected by Burley for months. Dempsey swallowed hard, thinking about what the customers got up to. He felt his skin prickle.

'The Society for The Reformation of Manners want to stamp out these places. They would hang you for this if they could.'

Burley sat up on the mattress. Dempsey eyed the bawdy pictures on the walls, and scratched at his neck, feeling the urge to cleanse himself. 'You have been taking bribes, I hear,' he continued, finally looking Burley in the eye. The marshal turned away.

'Money is always involved in my position,' Burley muttered.

'It should not be going into your pocket,' Dempsey scowled. 'You are letting places like this do what they like.'

'Where did you hear this?' Burley asked, suddenly straightening his spine, his voice calmer.

'Gillard, your under marshal. He has a conscience, it seems,' Dempsey said. There were rumours that Gillard had his own predilections, but Dempsey was holding on to that information for now. Everything had a value.

'He wants my job,' Burley blurted out.

'Maybe he does,' Dempsey agreed. He stared at the stained bedclothes and cringed, feeling the shivers run through him. 'You are supposed to be above suspicion. The Society influence the Aldermen now. They do not want someone who strolls down Sodomite's Walk in power.'

Burley started to dress himself. Dempsey stepped back, unable to look.

'I am entitled to some leeway,' Burley whispered. 'I have paid for this position. Seven hundred pounds it cost me.'

'You wasted your money,' Dempsey replied, turning to face him again. Hatcher tapped his club against his palm. Dempsey sensed the irritation growing alongside him and put out a hand to stand Hatcher down. He pointed a finger in the marshal's direction. 'You have a responsibility when you prosecute. You must be above suspicion. I expect you to resign in the morning. If you do, we will say no more of this unfortunate incident. But if you are there tomorrow, we shall have to share this information with the world.'

'You can't…'

'We will, Burley. You have lined your pocket for too long. Quit and all will be forgotten.'

'You can't remove me,' Burley protested, his voice barely above a whisper. He pulled his dress about him.

Dempsey addressed Hatcher. 'We should visit that Mister Hobbs. I think the readers of the Gazette would be interested in this story. I can hear the songs in the coffee shops, now, can't you? The ballad of old Burley, how he buggered his way to the top. Something like that.' Then he turned to stare at the marshal. 'Is fame something you crave?'

Burley pulled the bedsheets around him. Dempsey took in the walls and swallowed back the bile.

'I can bring you down with me,' the marshal blurted.

Dempsey stared back at the pathetic shape on the bed. 'I am keeping the streets clean. The leaders of London and Westminster, they need men like me. You are a sodomite. You think they will listen to you when they know that?' he mocked.

Burley started to sob. Dempsey turned his back, reaching for the door. This was a pathetic excuse for a man; dressing as a woman, abusing his public post.

'Resign and all this will be forgotten,' he prompted as they left.

Hatcher and Dempsey thumped down the stairs, and a corridor cleared in front of them as they passed through the ground floor of the tavern. Dempsey paused at the door, and spotted Mother Petticoat, his face flat against the table, wig now at his feet. Moorfields was out of control. Some crimes were simply unacceptable.

The speed of cases coming to the Assizes and the Old Bailey had slowed under Burley. With a new marshal, Dempsey could accelerate the cleansing of the streets. This was, after all, what the authorities wanted. They needed men like him to keep things under control. London's rate of prosecution was about to rise again.

14

On the deck of the Wayfarer, men scrubbed the floor and an overseer bellowed instructions. Gulls swooped and landed, pecking at scraps, drawing annoyed swipes from the crew. Neff followed Dempsey along the Limehouse jetty in the direction of their agent, Joseph Robinson, who gave a small wave, then pulled out a pocket watch. Neff knew how important this man was but wondered at the obvious show of impatience. The ship would not be sailing for a few hours. The captain was drinking in a nearby tavern, accompanied by two of their men.

Neff held back a few steps, and looked along the dockside, searching for the constables who were due to bring the extra passengers. The magistrates were paying them forty pounds for each prisoner, a gang of housebreakers who had worked the better houses to the north and west of London for the previous year. But they had stopped cutting Dempsey in on a share. The Thief Taker ensured they were arrested, found guilty, branded, and sentenced to transportation. As first-time offenders they had escaped the rope but were destined for seven years of servitude on the plantations, preceded by several weeks at sea.

Neff closed his eyes for a moment and imagined the pitching of the ocean. He would rather hang.

The watchmen approached with their retinue. The prisoners were chained together and hobbled their way down to the dock, weaving their way along the cobbles like a comedy troupe. The lead constable pulled ahead of them and greeted Neff with a cursory nod. He seemed eager to pass on his responsibilities and fiddled with a large bunch of keys tied to his belt, removed one and placed it carefully in Neff's pocket.

'They must be bound up until they sail.'

Neff passed over a bag of coins in return. 'We'll take over from here. This is a legal transaction. Don't you worry,' Neff said.

'We've done our bit,' the man replied with a wink, carefully placing the fee in his coat. They were poorly paid men, and Neff knew the tip would more than double his weekly wage.

As he led the shuffling prisoners along the rickety jetty onto the Wayfarer, Neff felt the sense of dread return. Sailing became a part of serving in overseas campaigns, but he threw up every time he took to the water. The nausea grabbed at him from the pit of his stomach at the memory. Neff focused his attention on the captives, and the one they needed to separate. Robinson returned to greet him as they boarded the ship, with a crew member in tow, indicating they should head below, where the men would be held for the passage.

Neff paused on the edge of the deck and pulled one man aside from the rear of the convoy. 'Bennett, you need to stay up here for some work before they sail.' Bennett's face showed his confusion. Neff shifted his attention to the rest of the gang. 'You three,' he said, pointing at the others, 'are starting down there.' Neff unlocked Bennett's chains and the others were led away by Robinson and the other seafarer.

'Wait here,' Neff said. 'The Thief Taker wants to talk to you.' Bennett nodded, then squatted down, his eyes closed. He was half a head taller than Neff, broader than Hatcher. Even in a crouched position, Neff could see the physical benefit of having a man like Bennett alongside them. Neff knew some of the saved man's history. They were from different regiments but had served in the same campaigns, and ex-soldiers looked after their own. Following Neff's advice, Bennett was the only gang member to hand over his share to Dempsey from their last job, which earned him his reprieve.

Dempsey approached them and pointed a finger at Bennett. 'You have been chosen,' he began. 'I already saved you from the noose, and now I spare you a trip across the Atlantic.' Bennett stared below deck, where the rest of the thieves had gone. 'Forget them,' Dempsey said. 'They sail, but you have a new start, working for us. You do as we tell you from now on, you know the alternative. Stay here until we leave.'

Dempsey walked away to talk to one of the crew, and Neff reached down to place a hand on Bennett's shoulder. 'It will be fine. You have made a sound choice.'

'I shall do as he says. Better than being a slave elsewhere.'

'True. Come with me, we have an urgent piece of business to attend to.'

Neff led Bennett back to the jetty, searching for Robinson again. They found their agent pointing at the luggage of a small group of men and women, waving his arms in the direction of the ship. The passengers slowly carried their possessions towards the Wayfarer. These had to be genuine travellers, voluntarily moving to Virginia. The idea baffled Neff. He beckoned Robinson over. This was a safer place to talk.

'You got the message about the other cargo?' Neff asked.

Robinson looked Bennett up and down and indicated to Neff to step closer so they could not be overheard.

'It is fine, Bennett is in this with me,' Neff added.

Robinson frowned and stroked his beard. He looked like a seaman. Their go-between received half the forty-pound fee for arranging the transportation of criminals for Dempsey, and many other items besides. The smuggling of lace from Flanders. The occasional slave back from the Americas. Freshly minted coins from Hull. Robinson watched the docks for early returnees from their forced transportation to the colonies. If they came back within the designated seven years, they could be recaptured and retried. Then Dempsey and Robinson would split the reward again. With an extra pair of eyes along the river, came additional income. Neff knew that Dempsey trusted Robinson implicitly. Nobody in authority seemed to be aware how the pair were manipulating the transportation business.

'I need the payment first. Ten guineas,' Robinson said. Neff handed over a small bag of coins. To an onlooker, it could be any transaction. Bennett busied himself studying the shoreline, stood to attention, arms smartly behind his back.

Robinson smiled at last, revealing a mouth devoid of teeth. Confirmation for Neff that London was better for your health than a life on the seas. 'Show me this extra package,' Robinson said, his voice lowered.

Neff checked that the watchmen had not returned, then led Robinson down to the dockside, Bennett following. The cart had been stationed alongside the ship earlier that morning, the long trunk inside it covered with a tarpaulin.

'Where do you want him?' Neff asked.

'I have a place in the hold. He will be out of sight until after we sail.'

'He should not disturb you for some time yet,' Neff replied.

Neff leaned down to lift his end of the trunk, and Bennett copied him. Between them they carried it onto the Wayfarer, where the crew members had disappeared from the deck. Neff looked about him hopefully, then realised he had to complete the task himself. Robinson directed them down a set of stairs, with Bennett easily bearing the bulk of the weight as they descended. Neff's stomach lurched again as they dropped below the water line, the stench of rotten fish hitting him. Robinson unlocked a cabin, and they placed their cargo carefully on a bench. Bennett stepped back to stand outside the door, as if he automatically understood what was required.

Robinson pursed his lips. 'I am travelling to Virginia this time; I shall personally ensure his transportation.'

Neff lifted the lid a couple of inches. 'He is still alive of course,' he said. Barwell looked like he was sleeping. As he carefully replaced the cover, Neff leaned in towards Robinson, offering hushed advice. 'If he complains when he wakes up, you can remind him it was this or the rope. There are no issues if he does not survive the crossing,' Neff prompted.

Their agent looked at the closed trunk. 'We shall see. I think he will attract a good price, given his build,' he added.

Neff knew Robinson made money from the sale of prisoners to landowners on the other side. Another twenty pounds each time, he heard. 'Up to you,' Neff replied. 'If you can control him.'

One of Emily's girls had applied the dose of laudanum, at Barwell's favourite tavern the night before. It was apparently easy to drug a man when he was thirsty in between sexual encounters.

'You sure you can handle him?' Neff asked. 'When he comes round, he might object.'

Robinson laughed and scratched his beard. 'Where can he go?' Then Robinson gave Neff a more serious look, his face darker. 'You should come one day.'

Neff shook his head. 'I will stick to London. There is much to do here,' he said. 'Like finding a new warehouseman. This one got careless, started taking what was not his. Not wise when we are always watching.'

He bid Robinson a safe journey, and led Bennett back up the stairs to the deck, and fresher air. Neff felt his legs regain their strength. Dempsey was waiting for them on the dockside, leaning against a wall, tapping his foot on the stone cobbles.

'What kept you?' Dempsey asked. 'Not another extra delivery for our friend?'

Neff stared ahead. Dempsey did not need to know all the details. 'Just tidying up a loose end.'

15

Jacob Hobbs poked a fork into his pie and smiled to himself, watching the steam emerge. The Galleon coffeehouse on Haberdasher Square, a short walk from his office on Grub Street, was his favourite eating place. The food was edible and the portions generous, a rarity north of London Wall. They also served large helpings of quality gin, not the stuff that was watered down from the river. This early in the day, there was time to mull over his words in the previous edition of the Gazette.

The first bite tasted good; the gravy ran across his plate. He called the coffeehouse owner over for a refresh of gin and offered a friendly smile, hoping for a discount. Blades shook his head, then scurried away. Hobbs surveyed the establishment, his second home. He was the only customer, save for two scoundrels slumped in a corner, sleeping off the excess of the previous night. Hobbs shuddered, remembering how he had escaped that life, the struggles with drink before the daily newssheet trade took off. He checked his pocket watch. In an hour the place would be full of chattering hacks, would-be poets, and desperate writers begging to be hired.

Two more mouthfuls in, a shadow crept across his plate. He looked up. The visitor smiled briefly, sat opposite, and placed his tricorn on the table in front of him. The bald figure drummed his fingers on the wood loudly.

'Don't mind me, carry on,' he said, quietly. Hobbs had not met the man before but knew by reputation this was William Dempsey.

Hobbs picked up his knife and sliced into the pie but found he could not hold it steady. He had been expecting a loud knock on the door, rather than a polite greeting in a coffeehouse.

'Mister Hobbs, I won't insult your intelligence. You know why I am here.'

'I can guess, sir.'

The publishing industry was in turmoil. The Herald closed, after a fire destroyed their offices. The owner of the Daily Courant, Maxwell Geary, had not been seen for over a week. There were rumours about his forced transportation to the plantations without trial. Worse stories of his body lying at the bottom of the Thames. None of this had appeared in print anywhere, the gossip along Grub Street told its own tales.

The deep-set eyes drew his attention, as if he were under a spell. 'Forget the whispers about me,' Dempsey said calmly, marking lines in the dust on the table with a bony finger. 'The truth can be manipulated, as you well know. All I ask is that you do me a favour. And then I could help you out in return, should you need it.'

'Sir, why would I need a favour from you? You don't work in publishing.' Hobbs could hear the wobble in his own voice and grasped his cutlery firmly. It was now his turn. To be greeted by The Thief Taker in person.

'No, I do not. And nor do I want to. All I hope for is the truth to be shared with the people of London. And you reach so many of them.' Hobbs's publication was essential reading across the city. Penny papers and daily news were the future. With the problems his competitors were experiencing, the Gazette now boasted the highest circulation.

'We are lucky enough to do that,' Hobbs agreed.

'You are reliant on the coffeehouses and the taverns for distribution.' Dempsey swept his arms around, indicating the importance of where they were sat. He clearly knew how many would buy papers in places like it across London.

'Yes.' Hobbs squirmed in his seat. He stared sadly at his cooling pie, then looked up at his visitor.

Dempsey leaned forward, hands stroking his scalp. Hobbs thought he saw a scar down one side but looked away before he could be caught. He swallowed the rest of his gin, to hide the shaking. The Thief Taker's face was passive, eyes dark and steady. Hobbs tried to clear his throat and broke into a spluttering cough. He brought an empty glass to his lips, then placed it silently on the table.

'I can guarantee that they will continue to distribute for you. It would be easy for your dailies to get lost or destroyed,' Dempsey said with a thin smile. 'I want to work with you, Jacob. You are a respected man in this city. People want to read what you publish. All I ask is one small favour. I apologise for surprising you. I was worried you would leave our meeting before I had the chance to deliver my proposition. That is why I disturbed your meal. Do carry on.'

Hobbs stared again at his unfinished pie. Dempsey pulled his chair closer to the table, turning it round to sit astride it. He looked like a Frenchman mounting a horse. Hobbs pushed his plate to one side, and thought about his future, and what it might now hold.

'All I ask is this,' Dempsey continued. 'I know someone who would like to write for your daily newssheets. Nobody would lose their position; he would be an extra person on your staff.'

Hobbs listened, thinking through his visitor's reputation. Bad things happened to people who disagreed with him. They often ended up on the Triple Tree, swinging in the breeze, for stealing anything worth five shillings or more. Hobbs's pamphlets and newspapers had reported the court cases. The Thief Taker took the reward for every successful prosecution. And now he was getting a close-up of how the man operated. Hobbs wiped his sweaty palms on his breeches.

The sound of a gentle cough behind him made Hobbs turn. It came from a man in a shabby brown suit, his lapels worn, the cuffs turned over to hide the poor finish. A hat was removed, and Hobbs received a small, polite bow.

'This is Anthony Fowler,' Dempsey declared. 'I would like you to give him a post. Allow him to write as a crime correspondent.'

'Mister Hobbs, it would be an honour to work for you.' Fowler's accent had a Midland twang to it.

'I would view this as a great favour,' Dempsey continued. 'I would of course cover his wages, so long as you allow him to write what he wishes.'

Hobbs calculated his response. He had been the first to expand into the penny paper trade; it had taken three years of struggle to build up his publication. The recent fate of some of his rivals nagged at the back of his mind. An image of Maxwell

Geary floating face down in the Thames came to him. But if he wanted to stay in business, he would need to negotiate.

'I am the editor. I decide what goes to print. I have the final say.'

Dempsey grinned, reminding Hobbs of a wolf, poised to strike. 'Jacob, this is a humble request. Just a favour. I will guarantee the safety of your presses and your workers.' Dempsey stared directly at Hobbs. 'And you.' Hobbs felt a tightening in his throat. 'You have my word,' Dempsey added.

Hobbs wiped his brow and leaned back a little to study Dempsey. His clothes were unremarkable for a man with such a reputation. You could easily mistake him for an honest merchant. Certainly not the enemy of the unfortunate thief, or even the aristocracy.

'May I think this over?'

'You have until the end of the week.' The eyes narrowed. 'The offer of my help will then be withdrawn. The world is a dangerous place these days, is it not? I shall see you soon.'

Hobbs watched his visitors sweep out of the coffeehouse, tipping their hats at the door. When he looked down at the cold food on the table, Hobbs frowned. Maybe the violent image of William Dempsey was a misconception. This might be a man of reason, and negotiation, the modern way of doing business.

****

Three days later, Hobbs sat in the lobby of the Fleet Street 'Lost and Found' office and tucked his hands under his legs to stop the fidgeting. He had been waiting since dawn. After what felt like an age, a clerk ushered him in, and he was walked through to a drawing room, where Dempsey sat behind a large oak desk. The man did not look up and no attempt was made to shake Hobbs's proffered hand. Instead, Dempsey pointed to a chair. Hobbs sank into the depth of the leather, then raised himself up a little to bring their eyelines level.

'Mister Dempsey, I know now that when a favour is offered, it should be accepted. I have delayed my reply too long. Please accept my sincere apologies.' Hobbs held out his pocketbook. 'Thank you for returning this.'

Dempsey looked up and shrugged. 'I heard a messenger passed it to you.'

'He did, along with most of the money. There was but a trifle missing. It is nothing. Do you not wish to have a reward for its safe return?' Hobbs asked.

'Mister Hobbs, you know it is against the law to accept payment for stolen goods. I had nothing to do with the matter. I merely discovered who might have taken it from you, and ensured they saw the error of their ways. All I did was help a friend.' Dempsey held his palms up and smiled. The teeth were blackened, as dark as the eyes.

'And nothing will be said of where it was lost?'

'Jacob, I care not for where you misplaced your property. If you wish to frequent such disreputable houses, that is your concern.'

Hobbs had done nothing wrong. His wife should count herself lucky he did not want to carry out such acts with her. Busy gentlemen were expected to seek their pleasure where they could.

'Now, this favour that we talked about…' Dempsey paused and sat back in his chair.

Hobbs knew he was beaten. 'Your new writer. Of course, he can work for me.'

'That is good. Mister Fowler will be a great asset to your publication. He has strong opinions on Marshal Burley and his immoral behaviour. He also has a great interest in the past deeds of Edward Renshaw.'

Hobbs considered the names. One jumped out more. He had heard Renshaw mentioned in hushed tones in the alehouses on Grub Street. A dubious figure who had disappeared.

'You knew Renshaw?' Hobbs asked.

'I've heard of him, naturally. The courts would have loved to bring him to justice, but alas…' Dempsey trailed off, staring at a painting to his right. Hobbs examined it. A battle scene, Spain probably. So many lives lost for no gain. Yet none of his readers seemed to be interested in the politics of war anymore. It was crime that sold newssheets.

Hobbs wondered what the connection might be between Dempsey and Renshaw. One had a fearsome reputation for catching criminals, the other for running an organisation of them. There were rumours of the two worlds overlapping, but nothing that could be substantiated. In public, and in the courts, the lines appeared to be clearly drawn.

Whatever the link, Hobbs had a duty to report the truth. 'Send Mister Fowler to me this afternoon,' he said, forcing a smile.

'I think you will find he is already in your office, Jacob. Thank you for the favour. We will work well together, I am sure.' Dempsey pulled a bag of coins out of a drawer and held them out in front of him. 'I believe you dropped this on the way in. Do take it with you.'

Hobbs stared in surprise. He wondered at how easily he had been snared, and how men like Dempsey could shape people to their will. Hobbs stood up straight from his chair and promised himself he would hold out for editorial independence. He ignored the bag and dusted his suit down. 'I came empty-handed, and I leave the same way,' he said.

'I insist.' Dempsey rose and placed the money firmly in his grasp, holding another hand over the top to ensure it was taken. There was a coldness there, in the steely grip, that made Hobbs shudder.

'Remember this day when you have discussions with your new employee over the content he wants printed,' Dempsey added. 'Remember it well.'

16

Ashford smashed a bottle against the nearest table and yelled for the attack to begin. A woman screamed; customers ran for the door. He saw one of Dempsey's men throw the first punch, catching someone flush on the jaw, knocking him backwards over a chair. Ashford's gang moved across the tavern. He spotted Hatcher, grappling with a cull, and heard the roar of pain as the victim was dropped into the fireplace.

A dull thump announced a blow to the back of Ashford's head. He turned groggily, moving a hand to where he was hit, then saw one of his men take the assailant down with a knife. Ashford slumped against a table, his feet slipping in a puddle of alcohol. He gripped his cudgel, ready to defend himself. There was more resistance in the Red Lion than expected. Neff had led them to the right place, but Kaplan's men seemed to be everywhere. Ashford peered through the fighting bodies in the tavern, searching for Kaplan's face. Where was he?

Another pair of hands grabbed at Ashford from behind; a forearm locking around his neck. He smashed a glass as he was lifted, then jabbed it into the face of the attacker behind him. Twisting the broken remains he heard the agonised shout, freeing himself.

There were men spread about the tavern, locked in combat. Flames reached out from the fire, catching hold of a couple of upturned chairs. Amid the noise and the smoke, it was difficult to work out who was on which side. It was meant to be Ashford and Dempsey against Kaplan. Ashford's men had drunk through much of the evening, gathering the courage for an attack on an east end stronghold. He was there to deliver the decisive blow to Kaplan. Four of Dempsey's group had joined them, led by this Neff. More than enough, they thought, to handle Kaplan with the element of surprise in their favour.

Ashford spotted a stairwell behind the counter. His prey would be hiding on the top floor. He vaulted the bar, stumbling as he landed on two fighting men. He recognised neither of them so left them to it. The place seemed to be full of brawlers. Ashford raced up the stairs, his heart pounding as he climbed, adrenalin driving him towards his enemy. This was what he craved, the battle, the smell of a defeated foe. Nobody put shit in his gin and got away with it.

On the landing he found three empty rooms, the fourth was locked. Ashford checked behind him; there was nobody on the stairs. He could still hear glass smashing and the fighting down below. Kaplan would be behind the door, cowering in his bed, ready to beg for mercy, and would not receive it. Ashford kicked at the lock, which splintered easily, and the door swung open. There was a figure huddled under the sheets. Kaplan was a coward.

As he stepped over the threshold, there was a sudden whoosh in his ears, followed by a crack. The floor rushed up to meet him, and darkness descended.

****

Kaplan swung his head from side to side, adjusting to the light. Candles burned above the tavern hearth. The walls were familiar, the Red Lion. But the place he last remembered being was upstairs with a woman.

He was down in the bar, slumped in a chair. He tried to stand and slipped to the floor, cutting his hand on a shard of glass. Kaplan picked the piece out and sucked on the blood, savouring the taste. There were broken bottles scattered around him in pools of drink, upturned chairs, furniture in pieces. Brandy, tobacco and burnt wood filled his nostrils. His spine felt like someone was dancing on it.

Kaplan levered himself up, rested against a table and surveyed the debris across the tavern more closely. Despite the signs of a brawl, he seemed to be alone. He groaned and felt his aching head again. There was a deep hole in his recent memory.

A voice reached him across the room. 'You might need a drink.'

Kaplan swivelled round and blinked at a face he recognised. It was one of the Thief Taker's men, the figure who stood behind him at the last meeting, Neff.

'Dempsey will be with you in a moment. You are safe now. Ashford and his Southwark gang were here. We fought them off.'

'Where are my men?' Kaplan asked. He sank into a chair.

Neff walked over with a bottle, poured two glasses, and placed them on a table, before backing away.

Kaplan sniffed at his drink. It smelled of proper brandy, not the wine of the night before. Memories started to return, of the whore who took him to a room, her red dress and matching stockings, a bottle swinging in her hand as they climbed the stairs. He sipped at it and swallowed hard. It seemed to be the genuine article.

The sound of crunching glass announced the appearance of Dempsey from the rear of the tavern. He stepped forward and offered a handshake. Kaplan accepted, raising himself to his feet.

'Where's Dawson?' he asked. The landlord.

'They arrested him. He was in on it,' Dempsey replied, righting a nearby chair and sitting. Kaplan did the same. They were a few feet apart. Dempsey stroked his scalp and picked at something in his teeth with a long fingernail. The eyes were steady, fixed on Kaplan.

'In on what?'

'The attempt on your life. There was a huge fight in here, they tell me.' Dempsey stared, his dark eyes inscrutable. Even though he was as close to the Thief Taker as he had ever been, it was hard to tell what he was thinking. Not like Ashford, or Renshaw. You knew where you were with bears. Snakes were more devious.

Kaplan's eye was caught by movement as Neff positioned himself in the corner of the tavern, peering through a shutter into the street. Silence filled the room. Kaplan felt strangely calm, despite the carnage around him, and the confusion of the night before.

Dempsey took up the second drink on the table. 'Ashford came after you.'

'Where is he?' Kaplan demanded.

'In Newgate. They have him for attempted murder. Yours.'

'But I was upstairs.'

Dempsey stared into his glass. 'He didn't get that far. We followed his gang here; we thought they were going to burn down more alehouses. A fight started. I'm told several constables were nearby, luckily for you. Everyone involved was taken to Bow Street gaol, my Engineers included. Ashford, they took somewhere more secure. The new marshal is going to be busy tomorrow. Do you not remember?'

The throbbing in Kaplan's head seemed to intensify and he rubbed at his eyes. Nothing about the brawl resonated. There was just a blank where memories should be.

'I thought you were going to lead him to me, into a trap. You did not think to tell me?'

Dempsey shook his head. Kaplan eyed Neff again. If it were just the two of them, he would go for the Thief Taker. Kaplan screwed his fists up and unfurled them, studying the watchful aide in the corner. He seemed to be ignoring them, but Kaplan knew Neff would be on full alert. He took a drink, needing the time to think.

'Ashford decided to kill you first, I imagine.' Dempsey tipped the contents of his glass down his throat. 'We can persuade enough people to say he attacked you with a blade. He is done for.'

Kaplan pondered what the Thief Taker was saying. 'Ashford has persuaded witnesses to change their stories before.'

'He has ventured away from Southwark. We control things here.'

Kaplan stood. The movement was slowly returning to his muscles. The only sound was the gentle crackle of a dying fire in the hearth. He needed to get away from Dempsey and check if what he said about Ashford's attack was true, and to retrieve his men.

'We can work together now,' Dempsey said quietly. 'Ashford will swing for attempted murder, and many other crimes besides.'

'You lured him here. With me as bait.'

Dempsey shook his head. 'Nonsense. I am not Renshaw, or Ashford for that matter. I am respectable.'

Kaplan ignored the lie. 'He can't escape?'

'Nobody leaves Newgate without my permission,' Dempsey replied. 'His case will be heard quickly; the next assizes begin in two weeks, and they hang another batch of the guilty not long after that. The timing is good. Ashford cannot reach inside my gaol.'

'And in return?'

'We talked about it before. Southwark is yours if you want it. Control of the whores for me.'

'I need my men out of prison first,' Kaplan insisted.

'We will all have to make sacrifices. It is worth it to rid ourselves of Ashford. We should work together against him,' Dempsey said. His eyes seemed sunken in their sockets, dark circles underneath. It gave him the impression of a stage actor, made up for a villainous performance.

Kaplan picked up the bottle and glasses and removed them to the bar. This was his tavern, his territory. There was no need to commit to action. He would not be making any concessions until he had more information, and his men. 'You can go now. I have enough people nearby to sort this out,' Kaplan said.

'I will be there when you need me,' Dempsey replied. He rose from his chair and signalled to Neff they were leaving.

Kaplan watched them go and wondered if he might have underestimated Dempsey. There was more to him than the crowing strut of a man who pointed fingers at the Old Bailey. You could never trust a man that made a living from turning thieves against each other.

As Dempsey exited at the rear of the tavern, Kaplan noticed Neff hanging back. They made brief eye contact, before Neff looked away and closed the door behind him. Kaplan paused, his drink in mid-air, pondering his next move. Every opponent had a weakness. It was just a matter of finding it.

17

Neff followed Dempsey down Fleet Street; two paces behind. Most pedestrians steered well clear of them, but outside a gin shop, a stranger blocked their way. Neff stepped forward to intervene, but Dempsey raised a hand. The man wore a plum-coloured jacket and matching breeches, and sported a long dark wig, the sort that was designed to announce importance. It was an unusual outfit for their part of town, making him an obvious target for footpads. The boots betrayed a recent walk through the mud, rather than carriage travel. Neff checked around the street, saw little danger, and focused again on the visitor. A tricorn was removed as he inclined his head slightly.

'Mister Dempsey, I must speak with you,' he began.

'We can walk and talk at the same time,' Dempsey said, indicating the route towards St. Paul's.

The figure stepped into a doorway, then began striding alongside Dempsey. They moved up Ludgate Hill, passing traders hawking food, cloth, trinkets, anything they could lay their hands on. A blind beggar stretched out his filthy hand, ignored. Neff knew this was all part of a wider series of traps, working alongside the pickpockets who stood on corners, watching the rich and the gullible, waiting to pounce. They would have been eyeing up the man who clearly did not belong among them, if he were not walking alongside the Thief Taker. A young lad came up and whispered in Dempsey's ear as he bent down to greet him. Dempsey nodded and the boy ran off. Neff eased closer, to listen to the conversation.

'There is something I need to ask of you,' the stranger implored.

'Join me for a drink and something to eat.'

'My name is Baines. I represent a few merchants who need your help.' He tapped Dempsey gently on the sleeve. Neff placed his hand on his knife, concealed in his coat, poised to act. 'It is a delicate matter; can we talk in private?' The speaker stared at Neff then back at Dempsey, making his point.

Dempsey laughed. 'Nothing is private in this city.'

They stopped at a corner as Dempsey studied his pocket watch. Pedestrians jostled their way past, and Baines flicked his head nervously back and forth as the crowd moved through them. Dempsey started up again, leading them along the raised stone walkway that crossed the street. He stepped carefully over the gulley that ran down the middle of Ludgate Hill, while Baines held his nose, looking uncertainly at the waste. Everything made its way to the filthy Fleet River in the end, Neff mused. Vermin, shit, dead bodies. When they reached the opposite side, Neff moved ahead of Dempsey to open the door to The Gateway tavern and peered inside. Some faces looked up and quickly returned to their business. Neff beckoned his boss to enter, and Baines followed.

There was a steady hum from within: discussion, laughter, and gossip, all typical fare. The landlord, a man called Hamilton, spotted Dempsey, and rushed over to greet him. Neff led them to a table in the corner near the hearth, persuading a group of four men to move. They took one look at Dempsey and scurried away.

'Do sit with us. What would you like?' Dempsey asked Baines. 'The usual for me, and some brandy,' he smiled at Hamilton.

Baines shook his head, scanning the alehouse. 'It is too early.' He fidgeted with his hat, picking at the thread on a corner.

Hamilton wiped their table with a cloth pulled from over his shoulder and motioned to one of the serving girls. She set down the tray of drinks she was carrying and began a new order for Dempsey. Neff positioned himself between his boss and the other customers and poked at the fire. Dempsey busied himself with a napkin, while Baines stared at the table.

Neff surveyed the room and its occupants again. He overheard a conversation nearby, about how Germans could not be trusted. Such discussions were not treason. Taverns and coffeehouses were where men put the world to rights. Slandering the King meant nothing. When Dempsey spoke again, Neff focused back on the Thief Taker.

'What is it you want?' Dempsey asked, sounding genuinely curious.

Baines played with his collar as he spoke. 'I run a linen shop on Panton Street. I represent a few traders in that area. We are under attack,' he said.

'Attack?' Dempsey replied, his dark eyebrows rising.

'The last three nights, a rampaging gang of young men. They drink their fill at an alehouse to the north of us, then work their way along the streets nearby. Some shops have been wrecked and looted; others they set alight. They tear down signs, smash windows.' Baines screwed his eyes shut. Neff believed he had the look of a man with nowhere to turn. Nowhere but the Thief Taker.

'They seem to be having fun at your expense,' Dempsey mused, his eyes fixed on Baines. 'James, have you heard of them?' Dempsey asked, turning to Neff, who held back a smile; they both knew who the miscreants were.

Neff addressed Baines, suppressing the disdain for the men in question from his voice. 'The Mohawks I believe they call themselves. One of them is related to the Duke of Hertford. There is much talk of their antics.'

Dempsey looked up again at his visitor. 'Have you not raised this matter with Marshal Burley, or any of his constables?'

'We have tried. But nothing has been done about it.'

'Interesting,' Dempsey said. 'It is his job to keep the peace. Why come to me?'

'Nobody is listening to us.' Baines screwed up his face, looked around, then lowered his voice further. 'We heard you might be able to help.'

'And where did you hear this?'

'There is talk of how you can solve issues,' Baines said. Neff wondered at the vague term, and what the source might be. 'Of how you can help businessmen in distress.'

Hamilton brought a tray of food over to the table. Baines sat back in his chair, eyes fixed on a steaming bowl of broth and a large chunk of bread. Dempsey began to eat. Neff poked again at the fire, his senses alert.

'You sure you don't want anything? Hamilton makes an excellent soup,' Dempsey asked. Baines shook his head. 'What would you like me to do?'

'We cannot take any more nights of this. Many traders and merchants will go out of business, through no fault of their own.'

'What about Renshaw's former men? Don't they offer you any protection?'

'These attacks started out since he went. We no longer make payments like we used to.'

'For protection.'

'Yes.'

'James?' Dempsey asked, scooping his broth with some bread.

Neff took his cue. 'I hear things have been chaotic in Soho and Mayfair lately, with Tindall in prison and Renshaw gone.' Street women had also been killed in that part of London and in Covent Garden, according to Emily. Neff was unsure how much she had told Dempsey, so did not mention it. He prodded at the ashes; the hiss reminded him of Renshaw's bloody face. Nobody was going to find him, buried that deep.

Dempsey took a long drink of brandy and pointed at Hamilton, who came over and re-filled his glass. When the landlord had moved away, Dempsey spoke. 'We can help you. You work hard for a living; you should not be hampered by these scoundrels. I know of your streets. This was Renshaw's part of London, but we shall do what we can to make your nights quiet again.'

'Thank you, sir. We do not know what to offer you. Renshaw squeezed us hard.' Baines's fingers were white where he was gripping his tricorn.

Dempsey shook his head briefly. 'All I ask for is your loyalty, and that you grant me a favour at some point in the future. That you remember who has helped you.'

Baines's forehead creased. 'No payment?'

'We are not the same as Renshaw. All tithes do is increase your debt. Nobody needs that type of financial obligation, not after what happened with the South Sea business. I ask for loyalty, nothing more.'

Dempsey continued to focus on his broth, and Baines turned his stare to Neff. He offered a brief shrug in return, as if to convey this was how things always worked.

Baines tapped at the table, prompting Dempsey to look up. 'I know all the traders will agree. Thank you. You are sure no payment is required?' The man placed a hand against his breast, Neff guessed to where he had some money secured, ready to pay. He noticed Neff watching him and folded his arms.

'None.' Dempsey sounded dismissive, almost impatient. Then he looked up with his public smile. 'Leave the matter with us,' he said. He scooped the last of his broth from his bowl and shot Neff a quick glance. No words were required.

****

The men who matched the description of the Mohawks were gathered in a tavern on Wardour Street. Neff knew of the young troublemakers, their bold label, and their noble connections. These were bored, frustrated men, with money in their pockets and no sense in their heads. A period in uniform would serve them well, he thought.

Neff and his group of Engineers were gathered across from the alehouse at a discrete distance. They chatted quietly amongst themselves, politely ignoring the attention of the whores who patrolled the lanes.

Five men swaggered into the street from the tavern. They broke into a bawdy ballad, then one led a woman into a nearby alley. Shortly after, he returned to their cheers, and they began to run towards the Oxford Road. They hollered and whooped, swords at the ready, swinging their weapons at passers-by. Stones were thrown through shop windows. Neff and his group followed unnoticed. The Mohawks swept their way up Black Street, then turned right. Two of the gang kicked open the door of a Tobacconists on Frith Street and ran inside. The others followed, screaming their delight.

The Engineers paused outside. The Mohawks did not seem to notice they were being watched, as they knocked over stands and demolished the counter. Neff gave a signal, and Hatcher led them in, smashing his club against the doorframe. One of the young men withdrew his sword and held it out in front of him. He blinked, and Neff saw the doubt in the eyes. His fellows stared, frozen, a costly hesitation. Within seconds, all five of the Mohawks were on the floor, groaning and protesting. Hatcher swung his club around his head, whooping in what sounded like savage celebration. With the door now closed, a set of dim candle lanterns were all that lit the shop. The wreckage of pipes and bottles were scattered about, among the young men.

Neff addressed the figures on the floor. 'This is a warning. You are boys, playing with men, and your games are to stop. No more looting these honest businesses. Go back to your fine houses to the west and stay there.'

'Don't mess with us,' one of them spluttered, rising to his feet. A boot to the chest from Hatcher felled him. Neff's colleague looked down at his victim with a snarl.

'This will be the one,' Neff decreed. He realised it was the Mohawk who took the girl up the alley. Two of the Engineers held him down while his hands were tied. Hatcher pulled a cloth bag from his belt and thrust it over the man's head.

'There has to be one who thinks he can stand up to us,' Neff mocked. 'The most stupid.' He stared into the faces of the young men; they were sobering rapidly; fear had replaced bravery now one of them was in danger.

'Get him up,' Neff commanded. He turned to address the other Mohawks. 'We have a special treat for this one. The rest of you, go. If you misbehave in future, we will come for you, and all your friends. We have eyes everywhere.'

The four accomplices did not move.

'I don't think they believe us,' Neff said, nodding at Hatcher.

Hatcher struck the captive in the belly with his club. The figure doubled over and slumped to the floor. The next blow struck him on the back of the head with a bone-splitting crunch. The sound reminded Neff of a watermelon being opened, something he had seen at the docks. Hatcher bent over the victim and scowled. Neff wondered again at Hatcher's work ethic, and whether they were cut from the same cloth. He shook the thought away and focused back on Dempsey's instructions: how to set a clear example that would be remembered.

'You should leave now, before we start on you,' Neff said, pointing at the four remaining members of the gang. 'But remember this. No more games.' He motioned to Hatcher and Bennett who had moved beside him. 'We will take him with us.' Then back to the remaining Mohawks. 'You might find him one day, you might not.'

The scampering footsteps of the youths echoed down the street as they dissolved into the night. Neff needed them to take their message back to their privileged houses, and the safety of

Mayfair and Westminster. That whatever had gone before with Renshaw meant nothing. That part of London was now under new management.

18

The prisoner was led into the public square where St Catherine's Street met The Strand. In the centre stood a wooden stockade, mounted on a bed of straw. The crowd parted to allow the procession through; two guards from Newgate, dragging Marshal Burley by the arms between them.

As Burley appeared the boos and jeers echoed around. Observers hung from first floor windows, eager to catch sight of the infamous deviant. Rain began to fall, the wind whipping in from the west, bringing the stench of the Fleet River with it. The guards wiped their eyes, focusing on the man they had brought to be publicly humiliated. The downpour began to turn the ground to a sticky mud. The smell of waste seemed to intensify, causing Dempsey to choke. Despite this, from his vantage point in the shelter of a doorway, he was unable to stop a smile forming.

Burley was forced to kneel, and his head placed through a large hole at the top of the stocks, his hands through another two further down. The feet were fastened to metal posts behind the wooden structure. He pleaded for mercy, but the guards had orders to follow. Burley closed his eyes. His hair was matted, and the rain washed the blood from his face. He was shoeless and his clothes looked like they belonged to a larger man. The figure had the appearance of what Dempsey knew him to be: someone who had been imprisoned in one of the filthiest cells in Newgate for a week.

A man in a fine dress coat, black boots and large white wig stepped forward to address the crowd.

'The Society for the Reformation of Manners condemns this man, John Burley. He is guilty of sodomy and bestiality. This pillory session is God's punishment and serves as a warning to others. We will chase these crimes, and the men who perpetrate them, out of London.' He turned to face the prisoner and shook his head slowly. 'May God forgive you.'

The crowd cheered, and the speaker was hit by mud thrown from behind him. He clutched his wig as he disappeared into the throng, slipping as he went. The guards retreated to the edge of the square. Rotten fruit and vegetables were pelted at Burley. The prisoner closed his eyes to the assault and the shouts and curses from around the square.

'Filthy bugger.' 'Sodomite.' 'Burn in hell.'

Two men leaped forward from the crowd and jumped onto the stockade. The guards looked at Dempsey, who held up a hand to advise them to stay in position. Punches started to land on Burley, to his head, into his back. The assailants stamped on his exposed legs. The cries of pain were drowned out by the yells of the crowd as they inched closer. Anger had been fuelled by the work of the Engineers in the nearby taverns that morning. There was a belief that this punishment was deserved. And Dempsey knew it was time for a change of marshal.

Three more men rushed to add their muscle to the beating. They slipped in the mud, falling forward onto the stage. The mob then began to swarm over the prisoner. Dempsey watched impassively as fights broke out, some organised in advance, some not. The rain continued to fall steadily.

Dempsey cast his eye about the square again. He reasoned that the greater the chaos, the easier it would be to control how it was reported. The pillory of John Burley would be discussed in the coffeehouses of London, then recounted in pamphlets and newssheets the following day. The press would repeat the righteous words of the Society spokesman and describe the anger of the crowd. It would also tell of the disgraced marshal's descent into madness, brought on by sodomy. Culminating in the story of a man taking his own life with a desperate leap from London Bridge. A suicide note would be published. It would serve as a lesson to all those in public office.

The rain seemed to intensify, as if a wall of water were descending on the square. Spectators had gone from the windows above. Some of the crowd started to slip away, unable to get close enough to the action. On Dempsey's signal, Bennett and Neff stepped forward and the two Newgate guards joined them. They pulled the remaining mud-soaked assailants off the figure of Burley and urged the last of the gathering to leave.

Dempsey watched as Burley's limp body was freed from his stockade and dragged to a waiting cart and covered in tarpaulin. The Newgate guards were dismissed and paid for both their time and silence. Neff and Bennett led the barrow away to the north, Dempsey trailing a safe distance behind. Nobody seemed to follow them. Neff had already selected the place to lie Burley to rest. Such a beast did not deserve to be buried in consecrated ground.

In a gathering of trees on the other side of Clerkenwell, Neff and Bennett stopped pulling their cart and retrieved their shovels. They dug a deep pit and slung the body into it. Burley was probably clinging on to life but made no sound; he was not going to escape, even if he woke up. The body splashed as it landed, settling in a filthy pool of water. Rats scurried in and out of the grave. The air smelled of burned wood and sulphur, making Dempsey catch his breath in short bursts.

As Neff and Bennett filled the hole with the clingy earth, Dempsey watched them silently at their task. There already seemed to be an unspoken bond between them. Burley's body disappeared under the mud. Dempsey studied Neff closely, wondering at the sacrifice the man had made years before, that he himself benefited from. Still convinced that he was the one that had seized the moment. Neff had enlisted and did not return for two years, on the run from the militia. Still was, as far as Dempsey could tell. Neff was typical of his men, had no hesitation in obeying instructions. Loyalty was crucial to his success.

Dempsey smiled to himself as he followed the cart back towards London. Burley left him no choice but to remove him; his was the weakness of the damned. He sensed change coming. The creation of a new order, one built on the actions of good men, those with a purpose.

19

Neff opened the coffeehouse door for Emily Jarrett and stepped aside. She swept in, purpose to her stride, and headed straight for Dempsey in the corner. Her boots clattered across the stone floor, and many customer eyes turned to watch her. She cut a distinctive figure, with her black breeches and red greatcoat, hair pinned up and hidden beneath a hat. Neff mused that if you passed her at speed in the street, she might be mistaken for a man. He noticed a few avert their eyes when they realised where she was heading. Dempsey was licking his fingers, a half-eaten plate of chicken legs in front of him. He did not look up as she approached. Neff followed and positioned himself between them and the rest of the room. The air was filled with the usual chatter and gossip, and the scent of percolated coffee, making Neff's nose itch. He tuned in to Emily and William.

'It has happened again,' she said, her voice sharp, almost breathless. 'Another of my girls has been murdered.'

Dempsey raised an eyebrow but continued with his meal. Emily shuffled in the seat opposite. Her eyes were fixed on Dempsey.

'This was just off King Street. It was brutal, William.' She reached forward and touched his arm. Neff felt a tingle down his spine. Was he jealous? Dempsey eventually looked up, but said nothing, wiping his fingers on a cloth.

'Her name was Rebecca,' Emily added, pulling Dempsey's hands together. She pressed on. 'This is the fifth one that we know about, there may be more. He stabbed her in the stomach, smashed her head with something heavy, then left her for dead in an alley. William, something must be done.'

'What would you like me to do?' Dempsey asked, pulling his hands free. He signalled to the owner to come over. 'Three coffees,' he announced when Murray arrived.

'Not for me,' Emily said, no smile for Murray. She did not wait for him to be out of earshot. 'You have to catch him. It is what you do.' Her cheeks were flushed, her eyes sparkled. But looking at her hands, Neff felt her skin might crack at the slightest touch.

'James, can you look into it?' Dempsey said, looking down again at his plate.

Murray returned with a tray, and carefully placed another coffee on the table. Neff breathed in the aroma. Several other groups were huddled over their hot drinks, some arguing loudly, others engaged in whispered conversations, all men except Emily. She was the bravest person Neff had ever met.

'This was last night?' Neff asked, his eyes drawn back to her.

'Yes.'

Emily stared at the far wall, and Neff followed her gaze to a painting of a battle scene. It was nothing that he recognised, his mind instantly full of anger at the thought that so few knew what the experience was like. The smell of decaying bodies, the groans of dying men. How could they possibly capture it with oils on canvas? He looked back at her: she seemed lost in thought.

Casting his eye over Dempsey, his boss was still impassive, seemingly captivated by his bowl of coffee. Neff wondered what might move him to act. It was as if the killer had no fear of being caught. The murders seemed to be indiscriminate, and there were many theories on the local streets over who was responsible, ranging from a French nobleman to mad politicians. But no evidence to back up any of the rumours.

'There was a stolen purse I heard?' Neff prompted for Dempsey's benefit.

'One with a gold clasp.' Emily's voice waivered, and she closed her eyes.

Neff started to reach out to touch her, then remembered where he was and who he was with and resisted. Instead, he tapped at his bowl to gain Dempsey's attention. 'I heard such a purse turned up at the pickpocket lair on the back of Whitefriars,' he said, exploring Dempsey's face. It seemed etched in fierce concentration on the drink in front of him. 'The place Hatcher runs.'

'You think it could be one of those boys?' Dempsey asked, looking up, cup in mid-air. A second hand steadied it. Some of the coffee slipped down the side, forming a thin trickle that dripped onto the table.

'Those boys wouldn't have the strength to do what this killer does. They just found the purse,' Neff said.

Dempsey shrugged. Neff took a long drink himself, trying to hide the fact he was closely examining the man alongside him. He could not help thinking about how positions of power brought responsibility. His boss did not sound concerned about the death of a string of women on the streets.

'You may lose business on the back of this,' Neff said, addressing Dempsey. Surely, he understood the financial importance of Emily and her network of women, if not their welfare.

'Look into it, as I asked,' Dempsey cut him off. 'Talk to Hatcher about those boys.'

Emily sat up and seemed to snap back into the room. 'You could publicise this in the Gazette,' she said. 'Or in the Bulletin. Maybe a witness will come forward.' Neff checked Dempsey's expression. His focus was back on his coffee.

'I shall have a word with a newspaper owner, would that be good?' Dempsey said, adding sugar and swirling his spoon around.

'We need your help,' she said, her voice sounding desperate. 'In any way you can.'

Neff turned to Dempsey. 'William, if the girls are being killed, the women may lose money. You will lose money. You must do something.'

'Do as I ask, James,' Dempsey countered, with little emotion. 'But there is one thing you can do for me, Emily?' The smile returned, and she looked across at Dempsey, her face seemingly blank, before she raised her eyebrows slightly. 'I need you to find out something for me. If you do this, we will catch your killer.'

'What?' Her voice sounded flat, resigned.

'Gillard, the new marshal. I want to know about him. His preferences, who he visits, you know what I mean.'

'I have not heard of him.' Emily stared at the wall again.

'Find out. All men have something that entertains them. I want to know what it is with this Gillard. He is short, red haired, and has a strange thing with his lip.' Dempsey stuck a finger in his mouth and pulled it up, gesturing to them both. It reminded Neff of a fish on a hook, a disfigurement he had seen before with a fellow soldier. A man determined to fight, to escape from his deformity. His body buried in the mud of the continent.

Dempsey dropped his spoon into an empty bowl and moved it to one side. 'Emily, James and I have something to discuss,' he said. 'Could you leave us?'

Neff gave her a nod, hoping it provided reassurance, and touched her arm. She did not pull away. He felt the flesh through the material of her coat, remembering a time many years before when he had wanted to touch far more. Emily rose to her feet, freeing herself from his grip, and walked out of the coffeehouse. Many eyes were on her this time. Someone turning their back on the Thief Taker would be remembered. Neff wondered if Dempsey had forgotten the debt that he still owed her. Despite his gentle probing, Emily had not been forthcoming with details over how she secured Dempsey's release from a debtors' prison many years before. But it did not take a genius to guess.

Dempsey leaned forward and lowered his voice. 'We need to distract Kaplan. When Ashford is condemned, he will want his slice south of the river.' Dempsey seemed suddenly energised, his eyes alive, his fingers tapping at the table.

Neff swilled his coffee dregs. 'I have been asking around, and there is much dissatisfaction with Kaplan. He is squeezing the innkeepers. The whores think he is doing nothing to help them. The gambling houses in the east are full of corruption.'

Dempsey nodded. 'I'd love to see Kaplan's face when he hears his people are cheating him. Take this Ingram we know.' Neff recognised the name. A dealer in one of Kaplan's clubs who was on the take. 'He has a thing for very young girls, I hear,' Dempsey added, tapping the side of his head. 'He will do what I ask of him. It is a sick world, James.'

Neff studied the Thief Taker. Beads of sweat had appeared on his brow. Maybe he was drinking his coffee too hot. Dempsey made the familiar gesture of searching his inside pocket for something. Neff needed to visit the apothecary again to find out what his boss was taking. He swept up his hat and stood.

'You be careful with Emily, James. She is sharper than you and me. She will play you better than a hand of whist.'

Neff headed for the door with a nod. What business was it of Dempsey? The Thief Taker had made his lack of interest in her perfectly clear. A lack of interest in all women.

Outside, Neff hurried his way towards the den where Hatcher's gang were housed. A scout stood guard at the rear door. Looking past him, Neff spotted the pickpocket he was searching for. He asked the boy to point out the stolen purse that Emily had mentioned.

'It is gone now,' the lad said.

'You better not be lying to me.' Neff pointed a finger in his face.

The boy merely shrugged. 'Hatcher took it, not ten minutes ago.'

'Where's he going?'

'He don't tell us, just sends us out in the street when he needs us.'

'Does Hatcher look after you all?'

'Yeah.' The boy shrugged. 'In his way. We got nothing else.'

Neff looked down at the wretch, who stared defiantly back. 'Don't tell Hatcher I asked about the purse.'

'Hatcher would kill me if he knew we was talking.'

The boy scuttled away from him into the street. Neff understood. He had seen men take advantage of situations before. His stomach churned at the thought of what Hatcher might be doing with members of his young street gang. Nobody would doubt Hatcher's loyalty, but inside big men Neff suspected demons could lurk. And with these youngsters, it looked like Hatcher was struggling to manage his own.

20

Gillard lit his pipe and puffed smoke above his head. Dempsey watched the shapes form in the stale air of the new marshal's office near Charing Cross and suppressed a cough. Tobacco was a product he had never taken to.

'You have the gaols bursting,' Gillard said. Dempsey stared hard in reply, the southwest accent beginning to grate. 'The constables have been busy, but the Aldermen are asking questions.' Gillard paused to stuff something obnoxious into his pipe and scratched at it. 'They wonder why they are paying so much each session in rewards.'

'They never asked when Burley was in charge,' Dempsey rebutted.

'I'm in charge now.' Did this new marshal dare challenge him?

'I'm not being greedy.' Dempsey shifted in his seat and drew in closer across the desk. 'I deliver a public service. There are many criminals about.'

'Increasingly so.'

Gillard's lip was curled up like a permanent snarl, a defect Dempsey struggled to avoid staring at. The replacement for

Burley was ambitious but did not yet seem to appreciate how the world worked. 'Without me the likes of Kaplan and Ashford would be squeezing the life out of London and Westminster. The economic crash killed off enough of the merchants and the banks. I keep things moving.'

'I don't think the politicians agree.'

Dempsey pulled back into his seat. The leather squeaked. 'They paid for their positions. They are where they are not through ability, but by bribery and corruption.' Dempsey wondered, not for the first time, what would happen if he passed everything he knew to the press. 'I am delivering order. It is our job to keep crime in check.'

'Obviously,' Gillard sneered, tapping at his pipe.

'You are also a servant,' Dempsey pressed on. 'Your job is to prosecute. My role is to find those that can be prosecuted and bring you the evidence. Like we have with Ashford. His fate is sealed.'

'The court will decide,' Gillard countered, blinking slowly.

'It will. And we decide what the court decides.'

Dempsey had been wondering about Gillard for a few days. Maybe Kaplan already had his greedy hands on the man opposite.

'It is the organised criminals we should be stopping,' Gillard said. 'The ones at the top, not just those who do the dirty work.' Gillard looked down to consult something on his desk, shuffling papers about.

'Is this Walpole speaking?' Dempsey asked. Maybe he was wrong about Kaplan. Perhaps the politicians were behind Gillard's sudden emergence from being a minor Westminster official, then under-marshal for London, and now sat in the chair opposite.

Gillard took a slow drink from his brandy glass and nodded to himself. 'Parliament is starting to take an interest. Their view is chop off the head, and the animal dies, as the saying goes.'

'And that is why Ashford is important,' Dempsey countered. 'We remove him, we send a message to the likes of Kaplan and Tindall.' Dempsey detected a slight twitch in Gillard's cheek. Tindall was in prison in Chester, likely to hang. He pressed on. 'Ashford is an enemy of Westminster. He is against another bridge over the river, the one Parliament very much wants to build.' Dempsey leaned forward and jabbed a finger in Gillard's direction. 'I am here to help you carry out your duty, to make your job easier.'

'Maybe I should confer with my Westminster colleagues?' Gillard said without looking up.

Dempsey kept his voice as steady as he could. 'What makes Westminster so special?'

'It is another world,' Gillard sighed.

'Perhaps the marshal over there needs my help rather than yours.'

Gillard looked up and shook his head firmly. 'Walpole controls him. You are best leaving alone.'

Westminster and London were governed by different sets of Aldermen. Perhaps the First Minister had both marshals in his pocket. A dangerous situation, and not good for the business of thief taking. Dempsey brought the conversation back to the elimination of one of his rivals. 'There is no doubt as to Ashford's guilt.'

'Some witnesses have withdrawn their claims,' Gillard said, consulting his notes.

'Withdrawn?'

'Yes.' Gillard picked the paper up. 'Three men have backed out.'

'But there are more?'

'Only two, and one of those is a whore. It will be hard to convict now. The witnesses are melting away. Unless you can find others?' Gillard's face reminded Dempsey of a rabbit evading poachers. The eyes continually flitted about.

'Ashford is dangerous. There is a gang war between the East and Southwark. Gin distilleries poisoned. Taverns burnt down. We cannot have this mayhem on the streets of London. Parliament would not want this.'

'Parliament might not care if the main criminals killed each other.'

Dempsey ran a finger round his collar. His mind returned to Kaplan. Maybe he was manipulating the witnesses, helping Ashford wriggle off the hook, the two working against him. Perhaps they were all paying for Gillard's position, and he was the one who should be concerned about alliances. Dempsey reached inside his jacket pocket and touched the pouch, then breathed out, reassured.

'There is no need for an attempted murder charge,' Dempsey continued, determined to bring Gillard in line. 'Kaplan might back away from that. He will not want the publicity. We will hang Ashford another way. He has been dealing in stolen property, that will be enough.'

Gillard folded his hands in front of him carefully. 'You mean to hang him regardless?'

'He is a dangerous criminal.'

'And what of Kaplan?'

'Kaplan controls the biggest empire in this city. Everything east of Newgate is in his grip. There are women on our streets being killed, the merchants are being sucked dry. You should also be going after Kaplan. As a servant of the law, you must see this?'

Gillard forced out a thin smile. 'I have to act on what is presented to me,' he said, turning to study a painting to his right. He sipped his brandy again and fiddled with his pipe. 'Bring me the evidence, and we shall arrest whoever is guilty. But I need a case that will not crumble in the Old Bailey.'

'Ashford first,' Dempsey confirmed, rubbing at his temples, feeling the blood pulsing in his head. Gillard was focused back on the contents of his desk. Dempsey rose to leave. 'We will have the witnesses you need, for handling stolen goods.' He banged his fist on the desk. Gillard looked up, his eyes suddenly wide with fright. Dempsey pressed his position home. 'Do your job. Convict Ashford. I will hold you personally responsible if he does not hang.'

21

Charles Ingram shuffled the cards with nimble fingers. Emily watched him closely, eager to learn. She sensed Elizabeth Manning alongside her fidget in her seat. They were upstairs at the Excelsior Club, in Whitechapel.

The room contained two long rectangular tables, covered in tatty green cloth, chairs arranged about them. They were sat opposite Ingram at the largest. He stopped manipulating the cards to pull at his elaborate white wig. He sported a smart blue waistcoat and matching breeches, attempting to carry the style of a respectable gentleman, the type she saw regularly in the better parts of Covent Garden. It remained to be seen how much of it was an act.

Emily's knowledge of cards had grown with the help of several clients who were more than willing to entertain her before their encounters. But how to play, and how to cheat, she imagined, were completely different things. Neff told her this man had been cheating Kaplan for months. Dempsey needed leverage.

Ingram held his hands out in front of him. 'Here, watch me deal,' he said. He placed cards on the table. 'Faro first. You know how to play?' he asked.

'A little,' Emily replied. She wanted him to assume she was a beginner, just like the girls they needed to be trained. Elizabeth shook her head.

Ingram dealt some cards onto the table. His fingers moved at great speed, faster than any of the gentlemen Emily had played with before.

'My top card is a King,' Ingram said, then turned it over.

'How did you…?' Emily paused.

Ingram grinned. The few teeth he had were an unsettling mixture of black and yellow. The breath reminded Emily of the fish you could buy in the early mornings on the street. 'I placed it there. Now watch me again. I will do it more slowly. This time see what I do with my right hand,' he added. 'Just focus on that.'

Emily watched closely and thought she saw Ingram slip a card into his sleeve.

'Now,' he said. 'Look at me, then back down again.'

Emily did as he asked. There was now a sixth card on the table, face down. She smiled. It was subtle. 'How did you…?'

Ingram repeated the trick. 'This time, do not look at me, watch the cards.'

And then Emily saw it, a deft passing of a card from his cuff into his collection on the table.

Elizabeth laughed. 'How long have you been doing this?'

'Some time,' he replied, sounding hesitant. Then he coughed and sat up straighter. 'The secret is misdirection. Get them to look at you while you work with your hands. It will be easy for ladies like you to distract them.'

'Let me try,' Emily said. She loosened the sleeve of her shirt and picked up the pack, dealing as Ingram had done, for a game of Faro. She steadily played out the cards and dropped one onto the table. Ingram encouraged her to try again. After a few attempts, she managed to conceal it. The process felt slow and cumbersome, but Ingram smiled.

'Have you done this before?' he asked, sounding impressed.

'Never. I just watch the men play, then join in if they ask. They always win, they do not take kindly to women beating them. Especially for money,' she said.

'Would you like to try, madam?' Ingram asked, turning to Elizabeth.

'I think I will let Emily learn.' She slowly stood and moved to the counter at the side of the room where there was a line of bottles. She poured herself something, knocking it straight back. Emily returned her attention to Ingram.

'Remember, Kaplan does not know what you have been up to. Not yet.'

Ingram looked at Emily, a frown turning into a grin. He did not look like a worried man. 'It is good fun, is it not?' he asked.

'And nobody has caught you?'

Ingram scratched at the scalp under his wig. 'It is a long game, you have to be patient,' he said. 'The house cannot always win, or nobody would return. There needs to be excitement at the table. We play it straight at the beginning of the evening. Most gentlemen will come back when they are worse for drink and lose it all at the end of the night.'

Men must have been cheating her for years, Emily thought. It would only have been the odd shilling here and there, an amount she and her girls would have made up for later in the evening. A harmless bit of sport, but she would study players more closely in future.

'You will teach our girls to do this, it is part of the deal. Otherwise, Mister Dempsey…'

He simply nodded, offering a weak smile. As if he were embarrassed at being discovered, or at having to show them how he had been cheating Kaplan. Ingram had other secrets too, the knowledge coming from Mary Grant and her local girls. Apparently he liked them incredibly young.

'If that is what you wish.'

'It is,' Emily replied, determined to show him her resolve. 'That is the price for our silence, with Kaplan. There is a place near Covent Garden you can use,' Emily said. 'Away from prying eyes. You start there tomorrow. Kaplan will not know you are there.'

'What about here?'

'The Excelsior belongs to us now.' Emily pointed at Elizabeth, who smiled in return. 'Miss Manning and I will be in charge. Unless you wish to discuss this and what you have been up to with Kaplan?'

'I thought...'

Emily shook her head, and the realisation seemed to hit him. 'I understand.' The words were whispered, defeat on his lips.

Out in the street, Emily walked arm in arm with Elizabeth Manning in the direction of more familiar territory, and Newgate.

'You may have to manage this yourself,' Elizabeth said. 'I have too many worries. Not just this killer on the streets.' She tucked a stray hair into her bonnet, pausing, looking as if she were weighing up what to say. 'It is all since Renshaw disappeared. Before, there was order, we knew where we were. Now it is chaos. Customers refusing to pay. More violence in the houses against the girls.' Her voice trailed away.

'Have you not asked Dempsey to help you?' Emily asked.

'There would be no point. The politicians would not allow him to interfere. Not in Westminster, or even Mayfair.'

'You could try.'

Elizabeth reached out to her. 'Emily dear, you are so well protected, and you do not know it. Every time we stand up to the men, they knock us down.'

As they reached Ludgate Hill, Elizabeth nudged Emily in the ribs, her mood seemingly brighter. 'Someone is here to see you,' she teased.

Leaning against a wall was James Neff. He unfolded his arms and made his way across the street towards them, picking a path through the mud.

'Perhaps he is spying on you,' Elizabeth whispered, with a smile. Emily found herself blushing and turned her face away from Neff as he approached.

'James Neff, what brings you here?' Elizabeth said. Emily was tempted to kick her but managed to bring her eyes up to him. He seemed amused by her sister's tone.

'Just taking a walk.' He played with the tie that held his hair in place at the back. Emily noticed him doing this increasingly. Maybe he was nervous.

'Come with us to Maiden Lane,' Emily prompted, taking him by the arm.

'I shall make my own way,' Elizabeth said, winking at Emily. 'I leave you both. Nice to meet you again, James Neff.'

Emily wanted to scream at her sister. Elizabeth disappeared down an alley, leaving the two of them walking side by side. They moved through the alleyways, picking a path between the vendors shouting their wares, mostly fresh fish, and meat, enticing passers-by to part with a shilling here, a few pennies there. One woman was selling cloth, rolled off a wheel, doubtless stolen the night before, looking to unload it before it was discovered. Her face was dirty, her words desperate. Next to her, an old man begged for change, a cup held out in front of him, empty. It might stay that way all day, Emily mused. Then, to her surprise, Neff pulled apart from her and dropped a coin into the man's hand.

Emily pointed at the beggar. 'There is no sense giving them money.' She straightened her spine, addressing Neff directly. 'They need to think about how they can earn it. Like the girls we employ do.'

Neff did not object to her outburst, simply shrugged and thrust his hands into his coat pockets.

Emily leaned in close to him. 'You know if you find this killer that haunts us you would be a hero of the women on the streets. No Mother would ever charge you again.'

Neff said nothing, merely continued to trudge through the mud at her side.

'I am starting a new venture,' Emily said, pulling Neff close to her. 'With my fellow sisters.' For once, he did not seem to resist. 'Do you think William would help me financially? He owns a lot of property.'

She gazed at him. The crow's feet tightened, then relaxed as he smiled. 'You had better ask him.'

'He has no time for me now. Does not bump into me in the street the way you do.'

'I was not…'

Emily placed a finger on his lips. 'I know.'

'William is distracted. By Kaplan and Ashford, others. Maybe when issues with those men are resolved…' Neff looked to his feet, watching where he trod carefully.

'He was never interested in me in that way, you know,' she said, hoping he believed her. He shook his head. Perhaps it was regret. She wondered again about the decision she took long ago, over which man to follow. A choice helped along by the fact that Neff disappeared with no notice, enlisting, never to return she assumed at the time.

Neff pulled himself away from Emily and folded his arms across his chest. Could he sense her concern? Did he think she was living a life of regret over him?

'You need to tread carefully. These are complicated times. And men like Kaplan are dangerous. Be wary if you deal with him.'

Those grey eyes stared into hers. Do not play with my heart. Do not make me choose again.

Emily placed a hand on Neff's arm, feeling she needed to explain further. 'Places like the Excelsior, we will improve them, make them better for the girls. Combine alcohol, gambling, shows, girls of course. But it will be safer. This is the future of our trade, James.' Neff looked across briefly and furrowed his brow. She tightened her grip on his sleeve. 'I need somebody to help me with security for the women. Someone I can trust.'

Neff looked away, then consulted his pocket watch. 'I should be elsewhere,' he said. 'I am already late. It is good to see you again,' he added, 'I will try to help.' He bowed and hurried away in the direction of the Thames.

Emily pondered again what first drew her to Dempsey. Perhaps it was the easy authority he exuded that pulled her away from a more established friendship. It was only recently that she had considered she might have made the wrong decision. She smiled to herself, realising the confidence she had in persuading one man to work alongside her. Casting a glance in the direction of the river, she saw the outline of Neff fade into the distance. He might not know it yet, but he was going to be her future.

22

1703

The crowd hushed, as William took in the faces in front of him. He loved the pause and held it for as long as he dared, then stole a look to his left. Jake and Luce both nodded in reply. William stepped forward towards the audience and held his hands out wide.

'And she never let me play with meat again.'

The laughter seemed to ebb and flow, followed by a small cheer from deep inside the throng that had gathered at the corner of Dunstable town square to watch the show. William bowed.

'It is time for you to be entertained. Please welcome the Largent and Dempsey players to the stage.'

Gentle applause began in front of him, during which he heard a couple of shouts for them to hurry up and begin. William stepped to one side and watched the actors take his place. He had become the precursor to the show, a test of the mood of the crowd: how bawdy to pitch the later jokes. If they laughed at a young lad making lewd comments, there was a piece where Jake wore a large fake appendage that would go down well.

Luce began this time with a song, and William slipped around to the side of the crowd, to observe their reaction. Faces were eagerly turned upwards, smiles of people with little enjoyment in their lives, as far as he could tell, apart from that to be found in a tavern. Their shows always seemed to be welcomed, with one exception. A summer's evening in Alvechurch where the Largent brothers had to fight off a drunken, baying mob, and some of their props were thrown into a river. The bruises had stayed with him for a week. Moving around the stage pieces was developing his physique, and he was hardening up.

William watched Luce captivate the crowd. He still marvelled every time at how she could control a gathering of men and women with a wink, a saucy laugh, and a tune. Three years on from that nervous lad who used to hide in the cart as they travelled, afraid his mother would appear at the shows they pitched up at; slowly his confidence grew so he sat up front with Jake and even handled the reins. He worked hard for his new family, cared for the horse, cleaned the stage, their equipment, the costumes. William guarded their belongings while they got drunk in the taverns. In time, he walked around with the hat, collecting the contributions from crowds at fairs and in market squares. He was robbed a couple of times, before he developed the appropriate scowl to ward off potential thieves, switching back to the smile when it was needed. He even perfected the juggling of fruit.

Most of their performances were learned by heart. But Luce taught him to read, as some pieces they put on were taken from pamphlets or had been scribbled on paper. He stole books from taverns and houses whenever he came across them, to practice. Some of his own ideas for the stage were thrown in, most rejected with a kindly laugh. William had found somewhere that valued him. The image of his mother faded into the dark past. The smell of the landlord's rancid breath disappeared.

The Dunstable show seemed to have gone well, and Tom and Jake were drunk when they returned from the tavern. William sat up front with a pamphlet he had lifted from an alehouse in Brickhill the day before. He found he had fast hands and a gift for making people look the wrong way.

As they left the town heading south, the cart pulled up suddenly and William counted five men on horseback with their pistols raised. One reached over and took the reins from Jake. The players were ordered to line up on the verge behind the vehicle, guarded by the rest of the gang, who dismounted. William was herded alongside them. They had been held up before, but only by a lone highwayman near Warwick, and they overcame him with ease. This number of robbers was more serious.

William had picked up that travellers were proud people. They defended their honour, and their possessions. He stared, transfixed at the guns, vaguely aware of demands and argument. There was movement alongside him, the players charging towards the thieves. Luce let out a shriek as she dived at the one who had ordered them to stop. There was a crack of pistols firing. Luce fell to the floor, blood pouring from her stomach. The sight of her in the road drove William to his knees and he covered his eyes. He could hear the shouts of fighting around him, but he felt invisible, as if he were hiding under the tarpaulin again.

The robbers were in close combat with the other players at the side of the road. More gunshots and shouts rang out. William crept forward to Luce, to stroke her cheek, and grasp her hand. As he held her, blood stuck to his fingers, and he wiped it on his shirt. She whispered one word to him: 'Run.'

Her hand slipped from his, and William sprinted towards bushes to the east. As he drove himself on, he heard a crack, the echo of a pistol firing, a whoosh as a pellet hit a tree to his right. William did not look back, kept running, and stumbled down a steep bank, tasting the mud as he went. It felt like he was falling down a deep well, into blackness, never ending. Eventually his tumbling stopped. His heart pounded in his chest; his eyes were wet with fear. William slowly climbed back up for a view of the road. The cart had gone, but Luce's body was still there, unmoved. He remembered the final look in her eyes, one of love, the first person to show him it. She had pleaded with him to flee. He saw the dust further up the road to the north and realised the highwaymen had gone in that direction. William Dempsey stood, and without a backward glance, headed the other way through the trees, in the direction of London.

23

Dempsey squinted into the darkness of the Haymarket Theatre. The floorboards creaked under his weight, and he closed his eyes, breathing in the smell of the wood and the polish, reminders of makeshift stages, where the tread of men would make the world tremble. A time when he would look up and an audience would be waiting for him to speak.

He called out into the Haymarket auditorium. 'Talbot? Are you there?'

'Mister Dempsey.' The voice came from behind him, and Dempsey turned, trying to make out the human shape in the shadows. He had travelled alone, because if a personal story needed to be told to help put his point across, he did not want his men to know it.

Joseph Talbot emerged from the wings, striding across the stage, and Dempsey could tell from his walk this was a man at home. He owned the theatre and everything in it; managed the shows, occasionally starred in them, certainly took all the profit. This was an area of entertainment Dempsey had been meaning to understand more.

'It is good of you to see me. I'm sure you are a busy man,' Dempsey began, with a pleasant tone.

Talbot stepped a little closer but then stopped, poised, hands on hips. 'We begin rehearsing a new show today. One that should be launched next month. A political tragedy.'

'Your stage and your players have a reputation,' Dempsey said. He stared at the man opposite. 'But you are never full.'

'People do not have the money they once did. But we still have a noble audience from time to time.'

'I hear certain gentlemen get special treatment, after the show,' Dempsey smiled.

Talbot's face dropped as he studied the floor of the stage. 'Nothing unlawful goes on here,' he said.

'Yes, the activities are elsewhere. I heard about the services provided to some of your customers.' Dempsey stared at Talbot intently. 'Quite… brutal, apparently.' Emily said the after-show entertainment she arranged cost ten guineas.

'I am not involved in any of that,' Talbot said. His denial sounded weak.

'There are other matters we need to discuss,' Dempsey prompted.

'Let us sit somewhere comfortable.' Talbot indicated the stalls with an exaggerated movement of his arm, then turned his back to lead Dempsey down a short set of steps. From behind, the figure looked smaller once he was off the stage.

They settled on the wooden benches that looked up at the performers. The odour of sweat and alcohol was strong. Talbot broke out into a coughing fit, pulling a handkerchief from his waistcoat pocket and spitting into it, before replacing it with care. Dempsey inched further away on the bench.

Dempsey pulled a leaflet out of his waistcoat and waved it in Talbot's direction. 'I want to talk about your current offering. The Escape Artist.' He jabbed a finger at the sheet. Below the title was a sketch of a man climbing down a wall. It was clearly meant to represent Jack Drewett, who had absconded from prison twice in the previous year. Each time returned to gaol by Dempsey when the price on his head had increased in value. And now this Talbot had seized on the arrangement for the purpose of entertainment.

'I hear that I am in this.' Dempsey tried to make it sound light-hearted.

'There is a thief catcher character, yes. Jack Drewett spends his time on the run. Somebody has to chase him down.'

'Me?' Dempsey asked.

Talbot rubbed a nervous foot in the straw in front of him.

'Remind me what I am called in this play?' Dempsey prompted.

Talbot coughed again. 'Snatchem.'

'Snatchem, yes.' Dempsey had discretely witnessed the show the night before, seething with anger. The likeness was clearly deliberate. The actor even wore a false bald crown and a close-cropped beard. Dempsey was being made fun of in public, and this Talbot was making it happen.

'It is just a name,' Talbot said, looking up and forcing a smile.

'And not a flattering one.' Dempsey moved closer, wiping at the dust on the bench in front of him. 'Did you not think I would be insulted? Or that it might impede my ability to deliver justice to the people of London? This play of yours is a personal affront.'

Talbot shuffled on the bench and dropped his eyes back to the floor. 'Mister Dempsey, this is just a play, a satire.'

'A satire against me.' Dempsey reached over to jab a finger into Talbot's chest. He felt the theatre owner shudder at the touch. 'And you do not even think to ask me to play the part.'

'I hardly think…' Talbot began, appearing to hesitate over whether this was a serious suggestion.

From what he had seen of the actor involved, Dempsey could easily have done a better job. He pulled a knife from his jacket and pushed it against up against Talbot's heart. There was fear in the wide eyes and Talbot's lips trembled.

'It is time this Escape Artist was consigned to history,' Dempsey continued. 'You should go back to Marlowe, or that Shakespeare. Or maybe bring your new play forward.'

'Our audiences like it. And it has gone down well with Parliament.' Talbot leaned back, away from the knife, and had to stop himself from falling into the next row.

Dempsey pressed forward and whipped a button off Talbot's shirt with a flick. Talbot stared down at the hole, then fixed his eyes on the blade. Anywhere but looking at me, Dempsey thought.

'Have you not read the reviews?' Dempsey asked.

'There have not been any yet,' Talbot stammered. 'It only opened this week.'

'That is about to change.' Dempsey pocketed his knife and pulled a sheet out of his waistcoat. 'I have an advance copy of the review from the Gazette. Shall I read it to you?'

Talbot dabbed at a sweaty brow with a handkerchief.

There was no need to consult the sheet. A memory for words was a skill he had retained, and he kept his eyes on Talbot as he spoke.

'The Escape Artist is one of the worst pieces of theatre it has been this critic's misfortune to see. This was an empty tale of woe.'

Talbot continued to avoid eye contact, and Dempsey pressed on. 'It was neither entertaining nor enlightening, nor amusing or sharp. It would be kind to call it mediocre. Many audience members fell asleep during the performance this correspondent witnessed. One vomited on the seat in front of him, he was so upset. I recommend you avoid this play. A dreadful experience.'

Talbot jerked his head up and stared open mouthed. Dempsey folded the paper and continued. 'You should show something else, Mister Talbot, before your reputation, and that of this great theatre, is tarnished.'

'None of that is true,' Talbot spluttered. 'People were not falling asleep. Nobody has been sick in here. They cannot publish that.'

'They will, Talbot. Worse perhaps, in the Bulletin.'

'You…' Talbot sank back and closed his eyes, the realisation finally hitting home. 'You cannot do this.'

'I will unless this play is withdrawn. I expect to see your doors closed tonight, and after that a new show to delight the public. You remember what happened to the Lyceum earlier this year?'

'The fire?'

Dempsey nodded. 'These theatres are tinderboxes. Accidents happen.'

'That was you?'

'Nothing to do with me, Mister Talbot. I help to keep crime down, not instigate it. If your plays reported that, rather than these false tales of conspiracy and villainy, the critics might look on you more favourably. They are reasonable men; they recognise the truth. I leave you to consider the future of this theatre.'

Dempsey climbed the steps back up to the stage. His head began to throb, and he breathed deeply, taking in the smell once more. He turned to look down on the stalls. Talbot had disappeared. Dempsey recalled the applause and the laughter that once came his way, then contemplated the different path he had eventually taken, once he had reached London. He was thankful he had not continued with that travelling life; fortunate he had chosen another route that made more than just a passing mark on people's lives. One where he could maintain control over the environment around him, and not allow it to be shaken from his grasp by the greed of others.

Steadying himself outside the theatre, Dempsey leaned into a doorway. Two women crossed the street to walk on the other side. A blind beggar shifted along the gutter, pleading to thin air. The early morning stench reached him: vermin, gin, smoke from a furnace closer to the river. He took a sip from the vial in his pocket and shook it; empty. He needed more. Dempsey closed his eyes. When he opened them, the world looked the same: full of threat. He still wondered which of his rivals was responsible for Renshaw. Both Ashford and Kaplan would gain from his demise. They were working together against him, despite his best efforts to turn them on each other. Once there had been a time when you knew who your enemies were, where they lurked in the shadows. Despite there being one less rival, things were increasingly complicated.

He looked up and tried to hide his surprise as the figure of James Neff came into view, carefully picking his way across the mud of Drury Lane. Then Dempsey remembered: they were due to meet. There was so much to keep a track of, and his mind was sometimes lost elsewhere. As Neff approached, Dempsey replaced the empty container in his jacket, and beamed a welcoming smile. At least there were people he could still trust.

24

Neff studied Ashford in the dock. The accused carried the air of a confused innocent bystander and had performed well so far, considering their contacts in Newgate had ensured he had not slept for two nights, forced to share cells with some noisy prisoners.

For once, Dempsey was not playing the role of prosecutor, with the new marshal looking to claim the reward for a guilty verdict. There was always a risk in presenting a case: if someone was found 'Not Guilty', they walked free with a grudge as wide as the Thames. Neff was yet to see Dempsey fail at the Old Bailey. All juries appeared to agree on the story when he presented it, regardless of whether they had been bribed or not. But Neff was sure Dempsey had a reason.

With the eyes of the court on Gillard, Neff watched Ashford glaring at the marshal, then the magistrate. The innocence was turning to rage in those narrow eyes. Standing in the front row of the public gallery, Neff was jostled from behind, and pushed back at two women seemingly keen to get closer to the infamous Beast of Southwark. The attempted murder charge had now been forgotten. Dealing in stolen goods would be enough to hang him, and Ashford knew it.

Gillard stood and addressed the jury, and as he spoke, he turned to ensure the packed crowds heard him. 'Mister Baines, could you tell the court how you know the accused?'

The witness fidgeted with his hat and said nothing.

'Mister Baines?' Gillard pressed.

Baines looked across briefly at Ashford, who stared back. Baines turned his face away, as he spoke. 'I saw him, one day last month. He asked for money for the return of some silver,' he stumbled.

Neff could see Ashford's anger growing, his hands tightening their grip on the rail in front of him. 'Nonsense,' Ashford blurted out. Murmurs rose among the crowd behind Neff. A laugh came from the corner of the gallery. Ashford scowled in the direction of the noise.

The Judge demanded silence, and then Gillard cleared his throat, ready to continue.

'Some silver? What silver was this?' Gillard asked, his voice rising. The Judge shuffled in his seat. An experienced observer would guess something untoward was happening. Baines needed prompting. It was time to return the favour he owed. Neff coughed, hoping the witness would look up, but he merely stared at the floor.

'I had some silver stolen from my shop.'

'And how much was this silver worth?' Gillard persisted.

'Twenty guineas, sir.'

Ashford let out a short laugh, then stifled it. Neff wondered what he would do if he were in the same position. He reasoned he had been fortunate to avoid it until now. Even his old regiment did not seem to care where he was. This did not stop him sleeping every night with a cudgel at his side. Neff glanced at the figure next to him. There were tears forming in the boy's eyes.

'Twenty guineas?' Gillard said, deliberately. 'So, more than five shillings, then.'

'Yes.'

Everyone in the court knew the significance of the value. You could be hung for stealing that much, the same for handling the goods. Property was worth more than life.

Neff returned his focus to Ashford. The cheeks had turned purple with rage, as he scratched at his bald head. The accused's eyes were fixed on the witness, who swayed gently on his feet. Neff knew there would be no friendly faces when Ashford looked at the gallery. All his thugs were locked up, courtesy of a staged brawl and a gathering of constables, two nights before.

'Back to your conversation with the accused,' Gillard continued. 'Where did this take place?' The witness finally looked up.

'Erm…'

Do not forget what you were told, Neff pleaded under his breath. Baines mopped his face with a handkerchief, and glanced around the gallery, eyes dancing, avoiding looking at Ashford. He settled on the person standing next to Neff and froze, then swallowed hard as Neff grasped the boy by the arm. A lad of sixteen, one they had brought to court, to provide Baines with the confidence to speak up. The boy gazed at his father in the witness area. His expression looked like he was imploring him to speak the truth. The truth he had been instructed to tell.

'Mister Baines?' Gillard prompted, the impatience growing in his voice.

Baines returned his focus to the marshal, nodded and the words tumbled out.

'This man, this Ashford, he came to my house on White

Lion Street. He said he could provide me with my stolen silver and ensure its safe return. For a fee, he said.'

Ashford scoffed; the judge ordered him to be silent. Ashford glared at Gregory and shook his head, muttering under his breath.

'A fee of how much?'

'Ten guineas,' Baines said, this time with more resolve. He quickly stared at his son then looked away again. Neff felt the boy tremble next to him.

'So, your silver worth twenty guineas was being sold back to you for ten?'

Baines nodded slowly.

Neff felt Ashford's eyes on him. He appeared to be squinting. The accused ran his measured fingers over his scalp then nodded slowly at Neff, who kept his expression as blank as he could, staring out into the court.

'And then what happened?' Gillard probed.

Baines wiped his face with a sleeve. He looked a shadow of the man who had pleaded for their help. Neff wondered if Dempsey was asking too much of someone not used to the perils of dealing with their kind.

The witness kept his focus on the marshal. 'He brought me the silver in exchange for the money,' Baines said, his voice suddenly louder and more confident.

'And why did you not contact a reputable company for the return of your goods? One that does not charge you for its return?' Gillard asked.

'I was desperate to get the silver back. I didn't realise it was a crime to handle stolen goods.'

'And this was definitely the accused? Stood over there, Samuel Ashford.'

'It was.'

'We would like to proceed to the next witness, Joseph Whittle,' Gillard said, dismissing Baines with a wave of the hand. 'The thief who stole the silver in question.'

Neff escorted the young man at his side from the court. He handed over two guineas to him with the caution to go straight home and not answer the door to anyone. Neff was surprised to find Dempsey waiting for him in the street outside. There was a sly smile on his face.

'How is our friend?' Dempsey asked.

'Ashford is fuming. He will need some persuasion you are on his side. He saw me readily enough.'

'Don't worry, he is running out of options. The gaols are not as secure as they once were.'

'You mean him to escape?' Neff asked. It seemed a strange notion to forge a bond with someone who was so dangerous. And then to spring them from prison. Ashford could not be controlled the way the infamous gaol breaker Jack Drewett had been the year before.

'I have plans for Samuel Ashford.'

Dempsey tugged at Neff's sleeve. His eyes darted around, finally settling on Neff. 'Have you heard from our man Barwell?'

'Barwell?' Neff stared into his boss's eyes. They seemed startled, panicked almost. Neff held the gaze for as long as he could. 'I don't work with him.'

'He is missing, along with some money, so Croker tells me.'

Neff shrugged and turned away to study a woman pushing a barrow of rotten fish across the street. She stumbled, dropping her wares, then picked them up from the floor and replaced them on the cart.

'Must be Kaplan's doing,' Dempsey muttered, before letting go and vanishing into the crowd.

There was something manic about his movements. Neff wondered why Dempsey was outside the Old Bailey at all. Perhaps his boss was checking up on whether Neff was following orders correctly. Loyalty was a strange thing. He pondered his decision to choose a life in uniform rather lead a street army years before. There was too much danger if he had stayed. The move was ultimately forgiven by the Thief Taker when he returned as a fugitive. By then, much of the gang warfare had died down. He was one of the few without those scars of the past. His own were different, deeper.

Neff returned to the court. Four more thefts were still to be described in intimate detail by witnesses Ashford had never met. This meant there was no opportunity to intimidate them in advance. Neff steadily pushed his way to the front row of the crowd, which seemed to be paying little attention to the details now. It was clear Samuel Ashford was destined to hang.

****

Neff scanned behind him again, and relaxed. Nobody seemed to be on his tail. Despite the steady rain that had started up, the streets were still busy with carters, animals, singers, the shouts of merchants. He pulled his greatcoat around him. Mud clung to his boots as he stepped carefully along the gutter. The court proceedings were over for the day. His route took him through the back alleys to a square off Chiswell Street, heading for an upstairs room above the Fighting Cockerel, and a girl by the name of Lucinda.

This was his third visit to her, same time each week. On this occasion, Neff did not go through with the sexual act. Lucinda seemed surprised at his reluctance, had even attempted to encourage him. She gave up and pocketed the payment anyway. He was about to bid her farewell, when the door swung inwards, forcing him back into the room. Kaplan entered and closed the door. Neff made to go for a knife in his coat.

'Don't,' Kaplan ordered. 'I have no weapon,' he said, opening his jacket. 'I am here to talk.'

Neff folded his arms slowly and sat down by the dresser. Kaplan blinked at him.

'What about her?' Neff said, pointing at Lucinda. She shivered, half-dressed on the bed.

'She has done her job.' Kaplan grinned. 'You can go,' he said, with a nod of the head. Lucinda covered her modesty with a dressing gown and did not look back as she slipped out the door. Neff hoped she would be safe.

'I hear things, James Neff,' Kaplan began. 'I hear you are not happy.'

Neff stared across the room. 'What do you mean?'

Kaplan waved an arm. 'The girls hear things. I hear things from the girls.'

Neff smiled inwardly but kept his face as stony as he could. 'I thought you had no interest in whores?'

'Mary Grant's network has its uses,' Kaplan said, stroking his grey beard with care. 'I hear you question Dempsey's methods.'

Neff shook his head and shuffled on the chair. 'I have nothing to say to you. I work for Dempsey.'

'But you have ideas of your own. You want to help the women. Dempsey does not, and it vexes you.'

The proposed betrayal was light on detail, merely that Neff was questioning decisions. Idle discussion with Lucinda, designed to reach the ears of an ambitious man. 'Do you think all your men agree with everything you ask them to do?' Neff asked.

Kaplan did not reply. This was a man who would never admit to any weakness. Neff studied the intruder closely. He was dressed all in black, as always, leaning against the door, blocking his escape. Despite Kaplan's protestation of being alone, Neff wondered how many men were on guard outside the room. Not that he was considering any violence. That was for another day.

Eventually, Kaplan broke his silence. 'We could work together. I can give you what you want, especially now Ashford is locked up. You could run Southwark for me. If that is your ambition?'

'I work for the Thief Taker,' Neff said, his voice as calm as he could make it.

'But Dempsey will not be here forever. You have a better chance of survival with someone like me. I am serious in this; I have heard good things about you, Neff. Do not waste your talents with Dempsey.'

'I have nothing to say to you. This talk of treachery. I am loyal if nothing else.' The initial offer had to be resisted, so that everything that followed would be more believable.

Kaplan nodded, apparently accepting the refusal. He licked his lips and smiled. 'I wonder if your regiment still searches for missing soldiers. And what might happen if someone were to tip them off that a deserter was hiding in London.'

Neff swallowed, staring Kaplan in the eyes. 'They gave up years ago.'

'We shall see. Think on it. If you want to talk, you know where to find me.'

Kaplan saluted Neff with one finger as he closed the door behind him. Neff exhaled and sank back into the chair, thinking about how dangerous his life had always been. From the poorhouse, where children died every day around him, to his spell in a debtors' prison. Then being part of a housebreaking gang with Dempsey in his younger days, his escape from cannon fire and bullets on the battlefield, returning to the streets for the Thief Taker. Violence and intimidation had punctuated everything. He realised it was the thrill of deception, rather than the physical danger, that spurred him on. That, and the face of one woman looking at him many years before, her interest in him foolishly spurned when he took the shilling. Neff was still driven by an unheard promise he had made to her, whispered in the dark, that he would set her free from William Dempsey.

The game they had carefully devised against Kaplan could play out in many directions. Neff considered his options, and the fact that some of them might not necessarily work in the Thief Taker's favour. Faked betrayal could always be turned into reality. If Emily were interested in a life by his side, he would consider anything. He whistled a tune to himself as he strode back in the direction of his lodgings, no longer searching over his shoulder. Perhaps the idea of treachery was not such a bad one after all.

25

The fading tread of Sir Howard Middleton's valet drifted down the corridor, followed by the echo of steps down into the basement. Dempsey pushed the door to the study open gently and signalled to his two men to wait.

Middleton was considering his bookshelves. Dempsey moved silently towards him and was within a couple of strides when the Alderman turned, face frozen in fear.

'Don't make a sound,' Dempsey hissed.

'We have no money here. A few valuables, but...'

Dempsey shook his head. He had been mistaken for a housebreaker. 'Sit down,' he ordered.

'You.' The recognition kicked in; a shaking finger raised in his direction.

'Do not cry out. It would be your last move if you did. Sit.'

Sir Howard slumped into a padded chair and surveyed his oak desk, a place where he would have deliberated as a magistrate. Several were known to be clients in the better brothels, but apparently, Middleton was not one of them. All men could be reached somehow.

Charlton and Bennett emerged from the darkness behind Dempsey and flanked him. Sir Howard shivered in the chair. Bennett stood upright and to attention, hands behind his back. The way he carried himself reminded Dempsey of Neff. Charlton's movements were more languid, and he leaned against a wall, examining a painting, seemingly disinterested.

'We are not here to rob you, Sir Howard.' Dempsey smiled. They needed to begin with persuasion, to place him at ease. Middleton seemed to raise himself up a little in his chair as he looked at the uninvited guests. The hair was grey and thinning, his nightshirt loose and dishevelled.

'Where is the letter I sent to all you Aldermen?' Dempsey asked gently.

'I have it somewhere,' Middleton began, beginning a brief search of a drawer. A selection of papers was removed and placed on the table. Middleton swallowed hard.

Dempsey recognised the petition: his request for the freedom of the City of London. Six pages detailing the miscreants and criminals that the Thief Taker had brought to justice over recent years. A list of over two hundred names, more than eighty of which had been hanged. Without Dempsey the place would be in chaos, violent gangs unchecked on the streets. Deep down, all the Aldermen knew this. They simply refused to publicly recognise it.

'This has been delayed for too long,' Dempsey said, pointing in the man's face. Middleton stared blankly at the letter. 'I need an answer.'

'It is not just down to me. All of us agree, you will not be granted it.' The old man looked away and blinked at Charlton, then turned back to Dempsey.

'How do men like you assume positions of power?' Dempsey strained to keep his voice calm. 'Everything is paid for; nothing you have is through sweat and toil. You must approve this and tell the other Aldermen to do the same.'

'I cannot.'

'I insist.' Dempsey slammed his fist on the desk. An ornament fell to the floor, and rolled towards Bennett, who stopped it with his foot, and crushed it. Shards of glass splintered in front of him. Bennett returned to staring ahead. A soldier at ease.

Beads of sweat ran down one side of Middleton's face. He shook his head vigorously.

'You know how valuable I am to the city,' Dempsey continued. 'It is time that was recognised. Without men like me, crime would be everywhere. Your own home does not look so secure. Approve the request,' Dempsey said, raising his voice slightly, still low enough he hoped not to be heard outside the room.

'We are unanimous. It cannot be done.' The Alderman gazed at Dempsey. There was fear in his eyes, but no surrender. He still had not broken the man.

'All I ask is this little favour. You know I will repay it when the time comes.'

'It is not a matter of money.'

Dempsey sighed. 'Very well. You give me no choice.' He pulled a pamphlet out of his jacket and tossed it onto the desk. 'Read this.'

Middleton leaned forward to examine it, pulling on a pair of spectacles. Scanning down the page, his eyes went wide in horror.

'This will be in the penny papers,' Dempsey went on. 'You know they read these out in the meeting rooms and coffeehouses. Crowds will gather to hear this news. Look at the date.'

'Next week.' Middleton stared across the desk, then back at the pamphlet.

'It tells of your crimes against the King. How you have been revealed as a Jacobite supporter. Information that comes to light following a burglary at this address. Nobody has caught the housebreakers, but your reputation is finished.'

'You cannot do this,' Middleton protested. 'I cannot…'

'This is your last chance.'

Middleton gripped the sheet and closed his eyes, muttering under his breath. It looked like he was praying. 'No,' he blurted out.

Dempsey sighed. Why were they being so obstructive? He pointed at Charlton. 'Start on him.'

His man looked surprised, possibly expecting Bennett to be given the task. Charlton pushed himself away from the wall and pulled a knife out of a jacket pocket, pointing it at Middleton. Dempsey knew this former highwayman preferred to work with pistols, but they were too noisy for this job. Light flashed off the blade from a large candle burning on the corner of the desk, and the Alderman blinked rapidly.

'You would need to do the same with all the others.'

'Oh, we will,' Dempsey cut in. 'Write the letter accepting my application.'

Dempsey watched Middleton's face redden. The magistrate stared at the weapon in Charlton's hand then down at his desk, seemingly examining the pattern in the oak in fine detail. This was a stubborn fool, Dempsey thought, trying to hold his frustration in check.

'Show him we mean business,' Dempsey said.

Charlton gripped Middleton by the hair, brushing the blade against his throat. Dempsey could see the muscles contract in the Adam's apple, the panic in the Alderman's eyes at last. Middleton looked up at Charlton, silently pleading for mercy. Suddenly Charlton released his grip, staring at his own shaking hands, dropping the blade with a clatter on the desk.

'Do as I say,' Dempsey ordered.

Charlton turned away, shuffling into the corner by the bookshelves.

Dempsey felt a tightening in his throat and leaned against the desk, closing his eyes. Tapping at the empty space in his pocket, he sensed the pressure building in his skull, crushing the calm, eating away at the order.

A noise made him look up. Bennett had jumped to the table and grasped the knife. He swept his arm around Sir Howard's neck, lifting him out of the chair. There was a brief struggle, before Middleton settled.

'I will not sign it,' Middleton protested again.

'You people,' Dempsey muttered. What did he have to do to be properly recognised? Action, that was what was needed. 'Do it.'

Dempsey waved a dismissive hand. Bennett brought the blade round and ripped it across the Alderman's throat. There was the beginning of a gurgled protest, Sir Howard flailing an arm in front of him before he slumped forward on the desk. A dark pool of blood spread from under his body. Bennett pocketed the knife and dropped back into the shadows, standing to attention, sneering at Charlton.

Dempsey looked at his new recruits and smiled. At least one of them had passed the test. He snapped his attention back to how the scene needed to look and retrieved a gold snuff box and a few other items from the desk, handing them to Bennett. 'You did well. Take this to The Strand warehouse by morning.'

The three intruders left the way they entered, through a window in the hallway and over the rear wall into the deserted street. Middleton had deserved his fate. They could still get Croker to fake a letter and pass it to the other Aldermen. But somebody was trying to prevent him being recognised for his work. Maybe it was the Westminster politicians, or even Kaplan reaching out across the city. Enemy forces were starting to mass against him. He was hemmed in by people he could not trust.

Having dismissed Bennett, Dempsey pulled Charlton to one side in the street. Distant shouts of drunken men echoed along Grosvenor Mews. He checked there were no molls and their customers in earshot and stared at him under the pale moonlight. The whites of the eyes stood out. He looked petrified.

'I have a different task for you. One I think you are better suited to. There is a gang of highwaymen working the roads between Bath and Bristol, and I have been asked to help by the local authorities. They must have heard what a good job we do of keeping crime in check here.' Charlton nodded slowly. 'They want this gang brought to justice. I thought of you, seeing as Lamont is no longer around. Your job is to capture this gang and take them to Bristol gaol in the name of Lord Malvern. The magistrate wants them to be tried, so they must be taken alive. Go to Croker in the morning, he will give you twenty pounds to cover the cost of hiring any men you need.'

Charlton nodded, then smiled, the first time Dempsey had seen one on his face. 'This is something I can do.'

'It is your chance to prove that I made the right choice in saving you and not Lamont. If you succeed in this, you could run the highways of England for me. It would be a profitable business. You will be famous.' Dempsey gave a low chuckle. 'They might even call you the Highwayman Taker.'

26

Jacob Hobbs watched the smoke billow up from the tavern fire and sipped at his gin. He sighed and savoured the taste; confident it had not come from the infamously tampered distillery in Southwark. A story he had been warned not to publish. He turned to find Dempsey staring at him, papers in hand. His visitor laid the sheets in front of them on the table.

'Here are the Ashford court proceedings. Make sure they are reported accurately.'

Hobbs studied the words in what he recognised as Fowler's careful hand. 'Aren't they still going on?'

'The guilty verdict will come in today as well as the death sentence.'

Hobbs watched Dempsey signal to the innkeeper and take a seat opposite. The landlord scuttled over with a fresh flask of gin and another glass, faster than he had seen him move before. Two drinks were poured before he backed away, eyes fixed on Dempsey.

The Thief Taker sipped his with a look on his face that Hobbs struggled to decipher, the skin of his cheeks gleaming. Maybe it was satisfaction, he thought. Something mirrored in his own life; daily newssheet production was increasing as well as his weeklies.

'You know the result?' Hobbs asked, to fill the silence.

'There can only be one outcome.' Dempsey prodded at the papers. The flash of a gold ring caught Hobbs's eye. 'You have the witness accounts and Ashford's testimony here. Then next week you will be able to publish the Beast of Southwark's confession of all his past crimes. There are many.'

'He has confessed to more?' Hobbs asked.

'They are all here,' Dempsey replied, with an assured nod of the head.

Hobbs struggled to work out what Dempsey was saying. 'What else has he done?'

Dempsey leaned in and lowered his voice as if they were part of a conspiracy. 'Ashford is a dangerous man. You remember the disappearance of a man called Renshaw?'

'No,' Hobbs lied, looking down at his glass.

'You surprise me, Jacob. Renshaw led a criminal organisation that was feared by politicians and paupers alike. Ashford had him killed and has now confessed to it.' Dempsey rocked back in the chair, his eyes peering at Hobbs. 'Ashford's control of the area south of the river is about to end.'

Hobbs studied the sheets in front of him. 'But he is only accused of handling stolen goods.'

'It is enough for him to hang. With this guilty verdict, you can publish details of everything else he has done. You must tell the world what a devil he is.'

Hobbs looked at Dempsey and wondered how it had come to this. Only a month earlier his business was struggling. Accidents with his printing presses had been a common problem, reliable workers hard to find. Now, other publishers were having those issues. He had noticed competitors crossing the street or leaving taverns to avoid him. They no longer sought out his opinion on matters of the day. At first, he had put it down to jealousy over his recent success. Perhaps there was more to it.

'Just make sure Ashford is on the front page of the next Gazette,' Dempsey said. 'People love to read about crime. You can maximise the publicity across the following week with tales of his exploits. You will outsell them all.'

Hobbs thumbed through the bundle of hand-written pages and picked out some gruesome words. He would need to edit judiciously.

Dempsey pulled a discarded copy of the Gazette from the next table. 'I like this headline,' he said, shaking the newssheet. 'Alley Killer on the loose. It catches the eye.'

Hobbs picked up the familiar publication and scanned it, avoiding Dempsey's glare. He breathed out slowly, conscious of being studied. His quiet drink in a different tavern to his usual had been disturbed. He was not surprised the Thief Taker had found him; the man had eyes everywhere, even the murky corners of Grub Street. But despite what he heard was a darker side, there was something intriguing in the way Dempsey conducted himself. It made Hobbs want to know more. He glanced at the bag at his feet, then looked back at Dempsey, hoping his subconscious had not given away his secret. The notes he had made of their previous meeting.

'I'm glad you like it,' Hobbs replied, returning his focus to the whore murders.

'I wondered where you got the story from?' Dempsey asked.

Hobbs pictured a man called James Neff and his hulking figure leaning over him in another tavern a few days before.

There was gentle persuasion to his manner, and the details of murdered prostitutes scribbled barely legibly on a sheet of paper. Enough to form the story in question. The headline had been his own work.

'It wasn't from Fowler, was it?' Dempsey prompted. Hobbs shook his head. 'Was it Kaplan?' Dempsey's eyes darted around the tavern, as if searching for something. 'Or someone who works for Kaplan?'

'A constable,' Hobbs replied. He looked at his glass again. The lie had been agreed with Neff. 'One from the east end.'

Dempsey nodded. 'I heard the deaths were horrific,' he said, leaning across the table. 'Bloody, mutilated corpses left in doorways.' Dempsey tutted. Hobbs felt his mouth go dry. There was a sexual attacker in London, preying on whores and it made for good copy. The coffeehouses and gin shops were buzzing with speculation. Some said it was a crazed Spaniard. Others a former Member of Parliament, escaped from Bedlam. Nobody knew for certain, but James Neff had been insistent on him drawing attention to the crimes in print.

'This is the truth? A constable?' Dempsey asked. He did not seem convinced by the explanation.

Hobbs hesitated. They picked up news from so many places. Fowler had been bringing crimes to his attention he had no idea had even taken place. But Neff had insisted this source remained confidential. He pictured Neff's face again and knew that he could not be betrayed.

'I heard it from many places,' Hobbs said. He looked up from the sheets in front of him. 'But it was a local constable at first.'

Dempsey nodded slowly. 'You should tell me more about what you hear.' Then Dempsey cracked a thin smile. 'You are doing your job, I suppose.'

Hobbs swallowed down the rest of his drink and felt his throat tighten. His shirt stuck to the back of his neck.

'The girls keep working, I am told,' Dempsey continued. It looked as if he was idly gossiping in a coffeehouse.

'Whores don't read newspapers,' Hobbs said.

'But they hear them read out,' Dempsey countered, 'in the meeting rooms and the taverns.'

'You want me to write more about this killer?' Hobbs asked.

Dempsey finished off his gin. 'Too much of this publicity is bad for business. You should concentrate on Ashford, rather than men lurking in alleyways. Ashford is a greater menace to London than this mysterious killer.'

Hobbs considered the contrast between the two men who had discussed the murders with him. Neff seemed to be driven by a desire for justice. Dempsey was more interested in the guilt of someone who was handling stolen goods.

'There is also Burley and his crimes. He should not be forgotten. He was a filthy sodomite; his type should be eradicated. And the death was suicide, I heard. Escaped from the guards and jumped into the river, rather than face the scandal. The body has not been found. Fowler will give you more on that.'

Hobbs played with his glass. A new story had reached him that morning, whispered along Grub Street. A magistrate called Middleton had his throat cut in his home in Holborn, a robbery gone wrong apparently. The death of an Alderman would normally make the newssheets. Perhaps more information was being gathered, ready for Fowler to write.

A man bustled up to their table. Hobbs hunched forward to protect his gin. Thieves and beggars often swiped food and drink in alehouses, after distracting innocent men. Dempsey sat back in his chair.

'I have a proposition for you.' The visitor sat alongside Dempsey and placed his hands on the table. Hobbs studied the filthy fingernails and clung to his glass.

'Do I know you?' Dempsey asked calmly.

'I have some takings,' the man whispered. He scanned the tavern, ignoring Hobbs. 'I hear you can provide me with money for these goods.'

'They are stolen?'

'Don't ask such questions,' the man replied, tapping the side of his nose.

Dempsey stared at him, and Hobbs felt the distaste from across the table. 'I don't take money for stolen goods,' Dempsey said dismissively.

'I heard you do a trade.' The visitor's eyes flitted about the room again.

'You heard wrong; I am no pawnbroker.' Dempsey grabbed the man by the collar. 'Leave. This is an honest establishment,' he snapped, looking across at Hobbs. 'You do not want your story splashed across the newssheets, do you?'

The man shook his head, backed away and scuttled out of the tavern.

'This happens all the time,' Dempsey smiled at Hobbs. 'People mistake me for a criminal. I catch them, I am not one of them,' he laughed.

Dempsey stood to leave, and his face suddenly darkened. He pointed in Hobbs's face, frowning. 'Forget this whore killer. I want Ashford and Burley on the front pages. The public deserve to hear about them,' he commanded. 'They make for good stories.' Dempsey waved to the innkeeper as he left.

Hobbs pondered the disruption of his quiet drink and the man who perpetrated it. Checking there were no eyes on him in the tavern, he pulled out the notes from his satchel. They were written in code in case they were discovered, on sheets mixed in with draft pamphlets. He tried to remember the details of the conversation that had just taken place, so he could record them accurately when he returned to his office. Including the strange visitor whose presence was designed to make him think Dempsey was innocent of handling stolen goods.

Despite Dempsey's insistence about the importance of bringing criminals like Ashford to justice, perhaps the biggest story of all would be that of the Thief Taker himself. Hobbs might have to wait some time before he could use the information, but when he presented it to the world, it would sell more than anything he had printed so far. He carefully replaced the sheets in his bag and finished his gin, checking the door again in case Dempsey snuck up on him. Hobbs rubbed his sweating hands together. The man had left, and still he felt his presence. The truth would have to stay hidden, until Dempsey had been brought down by other forces.

27

The front door to the house on Burlington Street swung open and Emily Jarrett stepped inside. An urgent message had brought her to one of Elizabeth Manning's establishments.

Elizabeth led Emily along the entrance hall to the bottom of a narrow staircase. The sound of laughter came from a room at the end of the corridor. A young girl wearing a shift and little else, led a gentleman dressed in just an unbuttoned shirt past them, and began to climb the stairs. She giggled as he slapped her backside on the way up.

'Anyone famous?' Emily asked.

Elizabeth shrugged. 'Just a politician looking for some light relief from the pressures of his job. Nothing unusual.'

'Should I know him?'

Elizabeth grinned. 'Depends on how familiar you are with Walpole's cabinet.'

Emily pondered the clients she entertained in her own houses. Apart from the occasional member of the minor nobility and the military, her trade was mostly the merchant class. Some of them good enough to still be classed as gentlemen, but not of this standing.

'The man you asked about is up there,' Elizabeth whispered. 'I have a place where you can observe,' she added. Her cheeks were flushed, and Emily noticed a cut under her ear. Emily started to reach out a hand and pulled it away.

'Has he done anything to you?' she asked.

Elizabeth swallowed hard and touched her neck. 'Not him. This is nothing to do with the gentleman in question. He is busy with his new favourite. Come, I will show you.'

Emily followed Elizabeth up a flight of stairs. She took in the polished floorboards and the fine paintings on the walls. Her places were barely decorated and thinly carpeted. The customer she catered for had little time to consider their surroundings, their eyes elsewhere.

A series of doors stretched along one side of the landing. Elizabeth unlocked one of them using a key from a chain around her neck. She picked up a candle lantern and placed a finger to her lips, then led Emily into a narrow room, barely wide enough for both women to pass each other. The tiny space sat in between what Emily assumed were a couple of larger bedrooms.

The only furniture was a tall chair at the far end. Elizabeth indicated Emily should sit and placed the lantern on the floor, before reaching across Emily to slide open a narrow grill in the wall. A thin shaft of light entered the room. 'Look,' she pointed. The smell of brandy from Elizabeth made Emily pause. She wondered whether she was drinking it, or using it to treat bruises, as the girls often did. Possibly both.

Emily flattened her nose against the wall below the grill and blinked, adjusting to the light. She peered into the room next door through the hole.

'You cannot be seen. You are the eyes of a portrait,' Elizabeth whispered. It sounded like this room excited her.

The first thing Emily noticed was a naked man, lying face down on a bed, his hands tied above his head. A girl then moved into view, brushing her long hair. She wore only a pair of silk stockings and sat astride him at his feet. The echo of the smack across his buttocks that followed did not surprise Emily; it was a punishment that many men enjoyed. She knew women were beaten in households every day: servants, daughters, even wives. Why some men liked to have this treatment handed out to them was beyond her. She once had a client who came to her to be tied up and tormented. He would beg her to drip wax over his genitals. Emily had accepted the need to inflict pain: at ten guineas a time, you did. But the reasoning behind it escaped her.

The girl administered more than a dozen strokes with the brush, with increasing ferocity. The man grunted after each one, his face obscured by a pillow. She disappeared from view, then returned with a cat o' nine tails, and walked round the bed to flick it in front of him. Moving alongside him she whipped viciously across his back, the effort showing on her face with every stroke. Emily held her breath as she watched the girl's muscles tense, a smile eventually forming across her face. There were more groans from the prostrate figure, but no struggle.

'This is definitely him,' Elizabeth said quietly, touching Emily on the arm. 'The one you said to look out for. With the red hair and the strange lip.'

Emily had not met the new marshal before. William was frustrated at the ease with which he had gained his office and seemed anxious to discover what his weakness was. So many men in power were deviants, Emily mused. The man on the bed turned his head in her direction, and Emily pulled back.

'Remember, he cannot see you,' Elizabeth reassured.

Emily returned to the grill. Gillard was focused on the whip, and the girl brandishing it. He whimpered as she hit him with increasing ferocity. Emily was drawn back to the girl, admiring again the definition in her arms as she applied the punishment, with force and skill. Gillard gave a mighty groan, and the beating stopped. The hostess reached over and smoothed his cheek, then untied him. He dressed quickly, and counted out a pile of coins, placing them on the table by the door. Gillard muttered something Emily could not hear clearly and checked his jacket for his pocketbook, tapping it with a smile. This was a man who had been robbed in a brothel before, she reasoned.

The girl moved away from him and turned, blocking the view of her customer, and winked at Emily, as if she knew she was being watched. She held her gaze for a moment and then spun around in response to something Gillard said. He was visible again, and Emily shuddered at the sneer on his face as he backed out of the room.

Emily watched the hostess scoop up the payment from the table and place it in a purse. She felt her mouth go dry and her cheeks flush, both impressed by the girl's abilities and intrigued by her own new experience as an observer. The control the girl enjoyed was strangely moving. The figure approached Emily, curtsying low. She was still dressed in just her white stockings.

'I hope you liked it. I can do the same for you. Make it more painful if you wish. Knock on the wall if you want me next.'

'No thank you, Anne,' Elizabeth spoke up through the partition. 'Be prepared for your next gentleman.'

The girl put her hands over her mouth in horror. 'Sorry, Mother Manning. I didn't mean…'

'It is fine. Get ready.'

Then Emily recognised the face. It was the girl who left the Introduction House with her fellow madam a short time ago. Emily looked across at Elizabeth, who shrugged, clearly understanding what she had worked out.

'What can I say? She is a fast learner. She is the only one this gentleman will go to now. He likes them young and innocent.'

'He is never violent back?' Emily asked.

'No. Mind you, if he is tied up like that, there is little he can do. There is no sex, just the beatings.'

Emily felt drawn again to the spyhole and looked through it once more. The girl had dressed herself ahead of her next client. Emily wondered at the invention of the room she was in and how it could be turned to an advantage elsewhere. There was a similar space in The Bull Inn, near Bishopsgate. Despite her years of experience, she was still learning about the trade.

'You use this room often?' Emily asked.

Elizabeth shook her head. 'We discovered it was part of the house, and then put the hole in the wall. We mostly use it for the novices to learn new techniques, to watch how to give pleasure. But occasionally we allow a guest to amuse themselves in here, so long as they are quiet. I have one client who prefers to watch. He doesn't use the room for long,' Elizabeth laughed. 'Come, let us get some more light.'

They crept out onto the landing, and Emily heard the front door slam downstairs. Silence followed, so she assumed that was the new marshal leaving.

'Dempsey will be interested in this news,' Emily announced.

'Will he help us find this killer now?'

'Something will be done, I am sure.' Emily looked down the stairs, wondering how committed Dempsey was. He did say the information on Gillard would lead to action.

Elizabeth smiled. 'And will he help you in the gambling houses?'

'He is reluctant. I work alone on that now.'

'You don't think you need his help?'

Emily ran a finger along the landing banister. It was spotless. 'There are other men,' she said, avoiding looking at her sister. They made their way down, Emily leading.

James Neff was waiting at the bottom of the steps when Elizabeth opened the door to the street. Rain had started to fall, and as Emily looked up at the slate grey sky she felt its permanence, as if it had been coming down for days without end, God unhappy with London. Neff jigged from foot to foot, impatiently. She wondered how come he knew where she was.

'That was Gillard came out just now,' he confirmed, moving up the steps towards them. Emily sensed Elizabeth pulling herself more upright beside her, noticed her brushing down her dress. 'What was he doing?' Neff asked.

'He likes to be beaten,' Emily said, taking him by the arm. She looked into his eyes and held his gaze. He seemed to be waiting for her to speak. 'He likes to be whipped by young girls,' she added. 'Men are strange creatures.'

'Some of us are, Emily,' Neff replied. He seemed to consider his words carefully. 'We have Gillard on a hook. After what happened to Burley, this will be valuable information.'

'You do not wish to go inside?' Emily teased, indicating the house behind her.

Neff stared down the street in front of them. 'It is not for me.'

Elizabeth gave Emily a wink. 'I understand what you mean now.' Elizabeth turned to him. 'Mister Neff, you are welcome here any time,' she said, flashing him a smile.

Neff blushed, and Emily pulled him in tighter. 'James do not be embarrassed by places like these,' she said. 'Come, I need to show you something.' Emily steered him into the street, waving to Elizabeth behind her. The door to the house slammed shut.

'I always remembered you being interested in women,' Emily said, squeezing his arm as they walked. It did not matter where they went, just away from Elizabeth Manning. 'In me at one time,' she added. Neff looked at his feet. The awkwardness was painful to see.

'I still am interested. In women, that is,' he corrected. There was a pause and she wondered what caused it. Years before, he had joined the army rather than pursue her affections.

Emily pulled them to a stop, releasing the hold on his arm. Neff seemed unable to look at her. 'James, I trust you more than anyone,' she said. She wondered how hard she could push him, he worked for the Thief Taker after all. But they went back to before Dempsey took a hold of her life. 'I would like you to do something for me.'

'Anything.'

'Catch the Alley Killer. For me if nothing else.' The words were out before she could stop herself. Perhaps she needed Neff to show her how far he would go to help.

'If William grants me the time.'

And there was his standard answer. The needs of William Dempsey still came first. She wondered what she must do to make him choose her over the Thief Taker.

'James, do you ever think about simply running away from London? To go overseas?'

He looked at her with a puzzled expression. As if he had never considered it before.

Emily leaned forward to place a gentle kiss on his cheek. 'One day, James, you might change your mind.'

He bowed and scurried away in the direction of Covent Garden, and the safety of some tavern, she assumed. As far from her as he could get. There was a barrier there that he did not seem to be able to overcome. Something about her past, or perhaps even her current way of life, that was preventing James from accepting her. From seeing where his future might lie.

28

The Apothecary struggled in Dempsey's grip as he pinned him against the wall. 'You sure nobody knows about this?'

Collins shook his head. Dempsey released the pressure around the neck and breathed out slowly, brushing down his waistcoat and backing away. Collins leaned against the table where he worked his sorcery and took a drink straight from a flask. Dempsey stared in surprise: it appeared to be something he had been using to prepare his tincture.

'Be clear what will happen to you if this gets out,' Dempsey muttered.

'This is strictly between us.'

Dempsey glanced about him. They were in the apothecary's secret room, at the rear of his shop. It was the first time he had been granted access to it. The smell was hard to place; something akin to burned flesh mixed with fresh flowers. There were bottles arranged on shelves along all the walls, no labels. How did the man know what was where? It felt like he was in a wizard's lair. He probably was.

The apothecary turned to the side and dragged a rack of tubes towards him. The table surface was littered with glass vials and dishes containing different coloured substances. There were sheets of paper that looked like instructions scattered among them. Collins wore a pair of gloves the type of which Dempsey had never seen before, that offered thin protection to his hands. He wondered at how men like this came upon their potions, what experiments they undertook with near fatal consequences before they discovered the mixtures that delivered relief. Relief from the distant image that still haunted him, of a dead body on a roadside and a whispered instruction to run.

Collins leaned over the table and poured some powder into a bowl, then mixed a liquid into it, beating it with a pestle. His arm worked quickly: his muscles well defined through a thin white shirt. The face was etched with concentration, as he pounded the concoction. A low hum came from deep inside him. Dempsey wondered at the little man who had the power to create so much. Collins poured his mixture into another bowl and lit a flame under it.

'How long will this last me?' Dempsey asked, moving closer, watching the potion froth and change colour to a dirty brown.

'One batch makes twenty doses. I have already prepared yours; it is safely locked away. It has to cool before it can be taken.'

'That is for someone else?' Dempsey asked, pointing at the bowl.

'You are not my only customer. This is also for someone who wishes to remain anonymous.' Collins looked sheepishly at the table and picked up a sheet of paper, then held it in the flame. Dempsey watched the orange glow burn brightly, as if the air in the room were highly conducive to chemical activity.

'You don't keep records?' Dempsey asked.

‘Of course not. That would be dangerous,’ Collins added, smoothing his hands over his jacket.

‘Dangerous for you.’

Collins cleared his throat and looked up. His eyes were steely and clear. ‘I assume the potions are working. That they help keep you calm?’

‘I need more this time.’

Collins raised an eyebrow. ‘Do not take too much, it is very strong. It could unsettle you.’

Perhaps the apothecary thought he was addicted. Dempsey did not use the drug every day, often the knowledge it was on his person was enough. But there was a growing feeling that sometimes he could not recall which man was working on which project, small details but enough to nag at his mind. He needed the potions to provide some clarity, a path through the fog. They also helped to combat the ghost of a dead woman, a fact that could not be revealed, even to a man as seemingly discrete as Collins.

‘I only use it when necessary.’

Collins carefully put the bowl to one side and studied Dempsey. Could this man read his mind, as well as help him control it? ‘I wondered if you might pay me for it this time?’

Dempsey considered the situation. Collins had not sought money before. Did his other clients pay him?

‘Are you also supplying Kaplan?’

‘I cannot reveal anything about my clients,’ Collins said. ‘I would not dream of mentioning the fact you come here.’ He shook a tube in front of him. The hand seemed steady.

‘You know if I am poisoned, my men will kill you. They will know it is you.’

‘Mister Dempsey, I am no fool.’ Collins looked up with a gap-toothed smile. ‘I value my life more than that.’

Dempsey reached into his jacket and withdrew a bag containing ten guineas. 'Perhaps this might persuade you to tell me more.' He dropped it onto the table and the contents gave a comforting rattle as they landed.

The apothecary wiped his hands on a towel on the bench in front of him, his eyes firmly on Dempsey. 'I am most grateful. All I can tell you is this is for a politician. Certainly not one of the men who would count themselves as a rival of yours. But thank you.'

Collins stepped away and removed a painting from the wall behind him, exposing a wooden cupboard. He took a key from round his neck and unlocked a door. Vials of clear liquid sat on a shelf in front of him. Collins took them out one by one, and carefully placed them inside a velvet bag, slipping the tubes into pockets within the material. He closed the bag and held it out for Dempsey. If anyone came across it by accident, and did not have time to examine it, they would not guess its contents. Collins then placed his money in the cupboard and locked it.

Dempsey took up his medicine, placing it carefully in his inside jacket pocket. He pointed a warning finger at the apothecary. 'Remember,' he said, moving closer. 'Nothing changes despite this payment. Nobody, not even my men are to know about this.'

'I understand,' Collins said, returning to his table and swirling the contents of a tube.

'Make sure you do,' Dempsey replied, his voice calm, as if he had just taken a nip of his tincture. He made his way to the rear door, remembering a similar back-room years before, where his destiny had been shaped. 'Nobody betrays me and lives to tell the tale. I know there are stories whispered on the streets about me. Rest assured, Collins, that the worst of them are true.'

29

1706

William leaned forward, and a rat scurried behind his back. He shivered, not just from the cold which bit into his bones in the gaol cell, but also the stench of rotting animals and human waste. The small, stone prison was filled with humanity. Children, old men and women, thieves like him, and an assortment of brooding presences he instinctively steered away from.

But there was one young man who kept returning over the two days he had been inside Bow Street prison. The figure sat down beside him again, looked around the cell and pulled a chunk of bread from his pocket and ripped it in half. He offered a piece, and William grasped it.

'Where did you get this?' William whispered.

The stranger gave a half smile he struggled to decipher and tapped the side of his head. 'Some of us know what to do in here. I could help you.'

William chewed the bread and swallowed. It tasted as bad as the stuff he ate on the outside, but it was food.

His stomach grumbled. He slipped the rest of it down his throat. 'Thank you.'

The figure nibbled at his own piece. 'There is more if you want. You just need to know who to ask.'

'You?'

'The same,' he said with a nod of the head. William stared into his eyes: grey, exuding calm. So many prisoners seemed to rage at everyone with inexplicable hatred, but this one was different. 'James Neff.' He offered a hand. 'What you in here for?' The tone was casual, as if Neff did not overly care.

William pondered what to reveal. This was the first inmate to ask the question. Only the warder had discussed his crime when he was admitted.

'I owe money, more than I can pay.'

'Don't we all?' Neff replied with a smirk. 'You a proper debtor then? Can't get out 'til you pay it back?'

'Yes.'

'Look at these people.' Neff waved an arm to indicate the others in the cell. 'All of them are thieves, one way or another. Even that one.' He pointed to a man who was talking to himself in the corner. Anybody who had gone near him had been shooed away with a snarl. 'He stole from investors, owes hundreds of pounds. He is one of the biggest crooks of them all. It has sent him mad.'

Neff made a circular sign with a finger at the side if his head William had not seen before. So much of what went on in London had been strange to him. His accent had been mocked when he first ventured into the city. Some of the language he picked up travelling on the roads was met with pained looks, even annoyance. He had been forced to break into houses, stealing what he could to survive. Life in the city was harder than on the roads, but more fruitful.

'Why are you here?' William asked.

Neff gave a shrug and finished off his morsel of bread. 'Why are any of us? We were caught.' Another smile. William decided not to pursue it.

'How did you get the bread?

'It all costs money, garnish,' Neff said. 'I help the turnkeys. They do not like shovelling the shit, disposing of the vermin. They pay a couple of us in here to keep the place tidy. It is not much, but enough to live by and not starve.' Neff looked around them, and William followed his gaze. 'Well, as tidy as we can make it. You should join us. It could help you pay off the debt.'

Neff would probably know that William was bound to rot in that stinking hole until he could muster the thirty pounds that he owed to a draper on Leadenhall Street. He was caught shoplifting the store and had arranged to pay back the debt rather than hang. But there was no money to satisfy the merchant, so he was arrested again. William eased away from the wall once more, as another four-legged creature ran behind him.

'They really pay you for that?' William asked.

'Sure. The guards are paid by the warder, who is paid by the city marshal to run this place. Like all the other gaols. The money eventually makes its way down to us.'

The lock on the cell door rattled, it creaked open, and two women entered. A guard laughed, pocketed what looked like a payment, and shut them inside.

Neff caught William staring at them. 'They work the prisons,' he said. 'If you have enough money saved, you can have a go,' he chuckled. 'Strange to see them here,' he added, eyeing the women as they stepped into the throng of prisoners. 'They tend to make their money on the richer side of the gaol, where there is more room. The master's side. A far cry from here.'

William watched as one of the women approached the crazy man in the corner. She sat on his lap and began to undress. William wondered at the openness of it all. There were children in there. He was barely an adult himself, just seventeen. His eye was drawn to the second woman, who had held back. Her dark hair fell loose, over a black dress. The style reminded him of another female presence, one he had shared a stage with. One of the prisoners tugged at her sleeve, and the girl kicked him in the groin. A laugh came from Neff beside him, triggering her to look across at them. She waved in reply.

'You know her?' William asked.

'Everyone in here knows her. That is Emily. A popular lady, on the master's side anyway.'

William folded his arms across his chest as she walked towards them. 'James, who is this young cull?' Her head was cocked to one side, examining him. Her eyes were a clear blue, the same as Luce. He shook his head, trying to forget.

'Someone I just met,' Neff said.

'What do they call you?'

'William Dempsey.' The use of the last name still filled him with pride. He leaned back against the wall and wondered how easy it was to reinvent yourself.

'Do not ask him why he is here,' Neff said with an amused look on his face.

'I'm sure he does not want to be in this place,' she teased. William guessed she looked about twenty, but he sensed a weariness in her face, as if she had already seen many things.

There was another rattling of the door. A man in a greatcoat entered this time, his black boots echoing on the stone floor, a cutlass swinging at his side. Some prisoners moved towards the sides of the cell and William saw fear in their faces. He felt Neff tense at his side. Emily moved to stand between William and Neff.

The figure strode towards the girl who was sitting on the madman's lap. He pulled her away by the hair and she squealed as she was dragged towards the exit. He knocked impatiently on the cell door and turned to the girl in his grasp.

'Never do that again. He has not paid enough.'

William noticed Emily take Neff by the arm and suddenly feared she would also be dragged out.

The door opened, and the man disappeared, pulling the girl with him. After it closed, the chatter in the cell rose, discussions on what they had seen. On who they had seen, William assumed.

Neff seemed to anticipate his question. 'That is Conway. He is not to be messed with.'

'He is above the warder?' William asked.

Neff laughed. 'He is more than even a marshal.' Neff lowered his voice. 'Conway owns Burley, who runs this gaol.' Neff turned to Emily. 'Will he not come looking for you?'

She shook her head. 'He doesn't know I am here. I came to give Georgina support. And to give you this.' She tucked a cloth parcel into Neff's shirt. 'It is roast chicken from last night. I took it from a gentleman's plate in Drury Lane. Eat it quickly, before the geese in here take it. Share it with your friend,' she said, indicating William. 'He looks like he could do with feeding up.'

Her smile made William pause. These were the first unselfish people he had met since Luce and the players had taken him in. After the incident near Dunstable, he had spent a few years on the move through villages and towns, with occasional visits to London, and nobody could be trusted. Two people had suddenly changed that view.

30

Dempsey slipped the St Giles Roundhouse turnkey a shilling and peered through the bars of the common cell. There were no doors on the filthiest of London's gaols. The place was a teeming mass of humanity: men, women, and children without the money for better accommodation. He searched the faces but there was no sign of the thieves he was looking for.

Dempsey conferred with the guard. 'You've not had any men in lately for a robbery down on the Strand?'

The turnkey looked at him blankly and shrugged. 'No, nobody like that.'

Dempsey shook his head in frustration. Hatcher had not turned up as promised for this visit. He was handy for the tasks where you got your hands dirty. Dirty with the blood of men who had wronged Dempsey. But word was Hatcher was increasingly being found on tavern floors in the early hours. According to Neff, Bennett was already proving to be a more reliable man.

Much of the cell floor was covered by a dank pool of water. Scraps of clothing and vermin floated in it. Dempsey took in shallow breaths and a shiver ran through him. He came to gaols strictly for business now. As he scanned the occupants again for his targets, two boys edged towards him. They held out their hands as they approached. Dempsey made a point of never passing money to anyone but the turnkeys in prisons. The inmates had to learn to generate their own income, as he had done, to work the system through their graft and wits.

One of the boys pulled a small yellow flower from behind his back. It looked like it had been freshly plucked from one of the fine gardens near Hyde Park.

'Where did you get that?' Dempsey asked. The boy shook his head, mute. 'You know who you are talking to?'

The other child, six inches taller, took a step forward. Both had dirty faces, were shoeless and dressed in rags; street urchins, Hatcher called them. Hatcher knew what to do with them and how their minds worked.

'You tell us.'

Dempsey smiled. This one was either brave, or naïve. He pointed at the flower. 'They don't grow those in prison.'

'We found it.'

Dempsey nodded. The truth could be a stranger for miscreants like these. 'How long have you been here?'

'Three days.' The taller boy stared him in the face, something few men dared to do. The one with the flower twirled it so the stalk twisted, and it dropped to the floor. It stuck in the filth at his feet.

'What you in here for?' Dempsey asked.

'Thieving, like everyone,' the vocal one shrugged, as if it were an everyday occurrence.

'I guess you are pickpockets?' The boys simply stared back, blankly. 'How old are you?'

'We are ten.' There was a pause for reflection. 'We think.'

Dempsey cast his mind back to that age. He casually held his side where he would be beaten. The image of a deviant in the dark returned, forcing his face into a filthy mattress. His mother was there too, eventually replaced by that of the leader of a group of travelling players. The freedom of the roads and the opportunity that came with his escape felt like a distant past. But he knew a man who could put two young lads to work on the streets, wherever he currently was.

'You any good at this thieving?'

'We get by.'

'But you are in here, you can't be that good.'

'We was set up. This woman dropped a watch she stole. She saw us pick it up and swore to the constable it was us took it in the first place.'

'And where was this?'

'Drury Lane, a few nights ago.'

Dempsey nodded. Emily would probably know the girl making the accusation.

'You know you might swing for this? If they find you guilty and take you to Newgate.'

Dempsey studied their ill-fitting clothes again, stolen he imagined from someone older. He pictured them, wandering the alleyways, scavenging, robbing, sleeping in doorways, bartering what they stole for food. They would have no fear of being caught, because how could a place like gaol be any worse than life on the streets. The rope might even be a blessed relief if it came to that.

'What are your names?'

'I'm Will. This is Alfie.'

Dempsey returned to the guard who had let him into the prison and pointed at the boys. 'I need these two.'

The turnkey failed to hide his surprise. 'Them? They are going nowhere.'

Dempsey put a gentle hand on his shoulder. 'These two are witnesses to a robbery at a shop in Lincolns Inn Fields. I need them to testify against a particularly nasty thief, one we must put away for the good of this city.'

Dempsey slipped another guinea into the man's hand. This was no fool. The life of a turnkey was an opportunity for profit on many fronts.

'Take them, I don't care,' the guard said, with a shrug, pocketing the money.

Hatcher was leaning against a wall outside, seemingly oblivious to his poor timekeeping. He showed no surprise at the appearance of two boys rather than the expected men who would help them persuade a pawnbroker to change his ways.

'They were not there. We shall talk of it later.' Dempsey pointed at the boys. 'These are for you. Take them and train them.'

Hatcher nodded and cracked into a smile. Dempsey knew he would understand the command: to refine their trade on the crowded streets. There would be regular food on the table, possibly for the first time in their lives. Guidance on where and when to steal. A growing army of thieves put to good use.

Dempsey crouched down to talk to the youths. 'Go with my man here. His name is Hatcher. He will see you right. And do not forget that this is a new life. Better than the fate that awaited you.' Their expressions remained confused. They would see the benefit of it one day.

He watched Hatcher and the additions to his retinue walk away to the south, in the direction of Whitefriars. Dempsey could not afford to get lost in the sentimentality of saving children from Jack Ketch. These were long-term investments. Empires were built from the ground up, Dempsey mused. If you recruited them young, they would remain loyal. And loyalty was an increasingly precious commodity.

31

'Samuel, you escape tonight. Your men will be free tomorrow.' Dempsey winked and showed his rotten teeth. 'It will shock London to its core. Kaplan will be finished; he will run for the countryside.'

Ashford looked up from his chains and rattled them in frustration. Dempsey had been absent from court for his trial, supposedly refusing to prosecute. 'We can't do anything about that Gillard?' Ashford asked. The new marshal, who had come out of nowhere. A fool who would not live long when he was free.

Dempsey sat on a low stool opposite him in the cell. 'He is different from Burley. He has the backing of Parliament and Kaplan. I can do little about him.'

'That will be a first,' Ashford snorted.

'Kaplan controls him. And you did go after Kaplan that night.'

'We both did.'

'Yes, but you were caught. There were constables everywhere, Kaplan must have known we were coming.'

'We? There was no sign of you that night.'

'My men helped you.'

'You warned him off,' Ashford spat. He tried to stand and yanked at his restraints, before falling back to his seat. He scowled at the Thief Taker.

'Why am I here if I set you up? I would just let you hang in two days time. I want to get rid of Kaplan.' Dempsey's forehead creased. The dark shadows under his eyes gave Dempsey the look of a man who never slept. 'Kaplan attacked my taverns,' he continued. 'He reaches into many places. But from tomorrow we could remove him together.'

You said that before, Ashford thought to himself, holding back the rage.

Dempsey stood to pace the cell. 'You prefer this master's side to the common hole?' There was no hint of a smile.

Ashford had been moved away from the rats, the cockroaches, the vagrants, and the stench after the guilty verdict, but he was still chained to the floor most of the time; let off to walk around twice a day. It was only better by a small margin; he was still locked up.

'I could be sprung from the cart on the way to Tyburn,' Ashford said. There had been plenty of time inside to think through the possibilities.

'That won't be allowed.' Dempsey turned to stare at him. 'Two men tried and failed that in the past year. And seeing as it is you, they will be doubly careful. There will be soldiers as well as constables on the route.'

Ashford smiled, flattered. 'We could outnumber them.'

'Kaplan is providing extra security. He means to see you hang.'

'What about something strong around my neck, to protect me from the tightness of the rope? What if I can be cut down quickly and spirited away?'

Dempsey shook his head. 'These are myths that I created. In here, there is nothing to talk of but ways of escaping. Prisoners fill their minds with any story that gives them hope. Nobody has ever survived the noose, not once it is around their neck.'

Ashford's visitor returned to the stool, still out of reach. 'We can get you out another way. You remember Jack Drewett?' Dempsey's eyes seemed to brighten, as if the idea of plotting brought him to life.

Drewett's tale was well known. He had become a hero of the criminal world, celebrated in the ballads and stories from the meeting rooms and taverns. Twice an escapee from prison, once even from the very condemned cell Ashford was in.

'A talented pickpocket, but little more,' Dempsey continued, moving his head from side to side as if to weigh up his merits. 'I managed both of his escapes. He has been hiding in the country until tonight. He will be scaling the walls to rescue you. Him and more of my men.'

'How can you be so sure he will help?'

'Drewett has always done as he is told.'

'You were behind him?' Ashford did not recall hearing anything about the link.

'His story entertained the people and distracted the authorities. Jack Drewett, the romantic hero that could not be chained,' Dempsey chimed. 'He served his purpose, we all benefited from his antics.'

'How am I getting out?' Ashford remembered the stories about Drewett's last escape when he walked past the guards dressed as a woman. He had more dignity than that.

'I don't want you to give anything away.'

'I need to know.' Ashford tried his fetters again. He was not used to having his destiny in other people's hands, particularly those of the Thief Taker.

Dempsey sighed. 'Prisons only look for men breaking out, not breaking in. It will happen tonight.' Dempsey walked about the room, adding nothing to his remark.

Ashford fantasised about what he might do to the other man in the cell once he had escaped, and the pain he would inflict. But he needed to play along with him for now. 'Is there somewhere safe to go?'

Dempsey crouched down on the stool again. 'No hiding. We go straight after Kaplan, because once he hears about your escape, he will run. We both know he has started to move in south of the river, the place is on its knees without you. You need to reclaim it. The people there will support you. With Kaplan dead, the marshal will be isolated and dare not touch you.'

Ashford had heard the rumours about his territory. The organised gambling was on the slide, his damaged distillery quiet, the coining furnaces idle.

'I will be a wanted man everywhere north of the river,' Ashford said.

'Better wanted than strung up at Tyburn.'

Ashford looked over his visitor's shoulder, and thought he heard footsteps outside the cell. Dempsey followed his eyeline. 'Don't worry, they will give us as long as we want.'

'Can't you just pay them to look the other way?' Money solved so many problems.

Dempsey shook his head once more. 'They would come for me as well. The authorities want all of us who run things to hang. Your mistake is just the excuse they wanted.'

Ashford stamped his feet and rattled his chains. 'I made no

mistake. All the stories about stolen goods are lies. I saw your man Neff, in the court. He was involved. You are involved.'

Dempsey narrowed his eyes, the shadows under them deepening, then spat on the floor. 'Do not say that name. He is a traitor. He is with Kaplan, and you can have the pleasure of killing them both if you wish. They are behind your situation.'

Dempsey was like a fish, wriggling out of his grasp. Ashford would discover the truth when he escaped. 'How annoying for you,' he mused, unable to contain a smile.

Dempsey shrugged, as if losing loyal men was an everyday occurrence. Perhaps it was if you spent all your time dealing with thieves and whores.

'Kaplan has orchestrated what happened to you,' Dempsey said. 'We failed to kill him, and he wants our blood. Yours first, at the triple tree, mine next.'

Ashford rocked against his restraints. He would play the game for one more night, then gather his men around him in Southwark, and eliminate them all, run London and Westminster with a new ruthlessness.

****

A scratching sound from above brought Ashford out of a dozing state in the corner of his cell. He looked up to see fragments of stone coming loose from the ceiling, dropping to the floor. A payment from the Thief Taker had ensured his chains had been removed for the night. Ashford pulled his mattress to where the debris was falling, to prevent rousing the guards. He walked over to the cell door. No sound outside. Dempsey had promised he would be undisturbed.

A rectangular block in the ceiling wiggled back and forth, then fell, breaking into pieces on the bedding. A face looked down on him, then disappeared. The scratching resumed. Another stone was worked loose, then fell intact, making him jump out the way. It bounced on the mattress and rolled to the floor. Ashford checked the door again, still no signs of a guard. A third block fell and settled on the bed. The head poked down through the hole, pulled away, and then a string of tied blankets was passed down, reaching the floor. Ashford calculated the height of the cell to be about three times his own.

'Wait,' the voice above whispered.

The makeshift rope tightened. Ashford pulled on it and it stayed firm. He put two hands around a knot, ready to climb. There was a sharp tug from the other end.

'Come on,' the words came from above. 'It will hold you.'

Ashford steadily pulled himself up to the hole in the ceiling. He clambered through the gap, and sat on the floor, poking his head down. The door was still closed. Ashford breathed out slowly, feeling the cramp in his arms and legs from the effort. The blood pulsed in his ears and his chest tightened. This was the thrill of action again. A small candle lantern illuminated the face of the figure alongside him in the roof space. Ashford blinked, exploring the area above his cell. There were steps at the far end, he assumed leading to freedom. It was barely high enough for him to stand.

'Drewett?' Ashford asked. He had seen the sketches in the pamphlets; this man did not look the same.

'He is waiting for you. Up there,' the figure pointed.

Ashford pinned him to the floor. 'No messing about, I want straight out.' He would take a boat across the river to

Southwark, regardless of whatever Dempsey had arranged and deal with Kaplan another day.

'You need to follow me,' his rescuer said, making no attempt to resist. Ashford relaxed his grip a little. 'It is a maze up here. The floor is weak in places, you must tread exactly where I walk. One false step and you will fall through. My job is to get you out of here.'

There was no fear in the eyes underneath Ashford. Instead, what he took for a steely determination to get the job done.

'Where's Drewett?' Ashford insisted, letting him get up.

'Follow me. You need him to get you down the outside walls, that's the trickiest part.'

They moved to the steps, then up to another level, where they worked their way at crouching height through a series of passageways. Ashford followed the trail of the figure in front who moved delicately. Boards creaked under his own weight, and he caught himself holding his breath. They eventually came to another set of wooden steps that led upwards.

'That way to the roof,' his guide whispered.

Ashford glimpsed the moonlight above through a hole. His muscles relaxed. He almost smiled; he was nearly free. Revenge would follow on all of them: Kaplan, Tindall, the Judge, Gillard, Dempsey. Every politician who lined up in opposition would go the same way. He would become more famous than any of them. Bloodshed was coming that would mark Samuel Ashford out as the most feared man London had ever known.

'What's your name? You should be rewarded,' Ashford said.

His helper ignored the question, a look of intense concentration on his face. At the bottom of the steps, he turned to Ashford and spoke. 'Go up here and turn right. Someone is waiting to get you down. I go back now to tidy up, to ensure nobody raises the alarm.' He disappeared, taking the lantern with him.

Ashford climbed the rotten steps to the roof, feeling his way in the dark. Outside, he made out another figure perched on the edge. It beckoned to him. 'Over here,' the voice hissed.

Ashford crouched low as he made his way towards his next accomplice.

'Drewett?' In the pale light it was hard to tell. He was escaping. What did it matter who was helping him?

The man nodded and pointed over the side. 'Use the guttering to get yourself balanced. Then I will drop the ladder for you.' This was promptly unfurled and laid out across the roof. A more reliable one than bedsheets and knots, made of rope.

Ashford could feel his heart pounding. This was the stuff of legend. He placed one foot over the side and found purchase on a ledge. He settled his other foot next to the first. Gripping the iron guttering above, he peered down, and caught his breath. It was too far to jump. He could make out another shape on the ground below, the next man in the chain he assumed, waiting to escort him away. That would be Drewett.

One of his hands slipped on the gutter, but Ashford regained a hold, pulling himself in closer to the wall. The ladder dropped down beside him. It twisted in the breeze, temptingly out of reach. As he stretched to grip it, the rope slipped away into the dark night, like a lost fish on a line, descending into the murky depths. He followed its flight, his heart sinking with it, his mind racing. Ashford lifted his face up again; the whites of the eyes above him stood out, focused on him, just an arm's length away. He gripped the guttering more tightly and tried to relax as he pressed his body against the wall.

He felt something being wrapped under his chin, then wound around his neck, cutting into flesh. A wire, he quickly realised. Choking, Ashford thrust out a hand to grab the attacker and pulled at a sleeve but lost his grip. His other hand slipped away from the gutter and his feet scrambled against the stone ledge, the garotte tensing around his neck as he fought for purchase. Every movement he made jerked the wire tighter. The world spun and all he saw were those eyes above him. His attacker muttered something, unheard. There was a sense of falling, and a rush of wind against his bare scalp. Then blackness.

32

Neff pushed the ferryman against his upturned boat. 'Don't make me ask you again.'

The man shook his head. Sweat dropped off him. He smelled like dead fish; it must have been living on the river. Neff let him drop to the ground in a heap and wiped his hands on the tarpaulin draped over the side of the vessel where they had found him cowering.

'You will make my friend angry. He's not pleasant when he's angry.'

Hatcher laughed. Neff watched him put his match away, crack his knuckles together and delve into his sack of instruments. The threat of burning the boat seemed to mean little to its owner. Violence might be different.

'Ashford is dead,' Neff announced.

'He is escaped, it is a lie.'

Neff shook his head at the pointless defiance. 'I saw his dead body,' he said. 'He will not be collecting any more fees from men like you.'

The ferryman stared along the Thames in the dim light, and Neff followed his gaze. A couple of small fires burned a hundred yards away closer to London Bridge, the results of earlier visits to other boat owners.

'You are the last one,' Neff said. 'All your friends along the shore have come in with us.'

Neff watched the shivering figure curl up into a ball.

'We have instructions, you know,' Neff continued. Hatcher looked at him inquisitively. He thought he would try negotiation before he let his colleague loose. 'This is a better deal than you had before. You pay a lower cut to us than you did with Ashford. But if you disagree, we cannot guarantee the safety of your boat.'

'I will get by on my own.'

'You are mad if you think you can survive without our protection.' Neff eyed Hatcher, who shuffled his feet on the shingle, jiggling his bag of tools. 'This is your last chance,' Neff said, turning to the ferryman again. 'Trade across the Thames is going to flourish. Your custom will increase.'

'Ashford always did right by me.'

'You don't see it, do you?' Neff sighed. Negotiation was a waste of time. Neff kicked the prone figure in the stomach. He choked and writhed on the floor. 'He is dead,' Neff repeated.

'How painful do you want me to make this?' Hatcher asked.

Neff watched Hatcher pull his club from the bag at his side and twist it eagerly in his hands. The image nagged at Neff, a reminder of the methods Hatcher probably used to keep his army of pickpockets in check.

'I will wait for Ashford,' the man said, pulling himself up to his feet and leaning against the boat for support.

Hatcher's eyes burned with impatience. They had been asked by Dempsey to be subtle, which had worked with most of the men on the shoreline; but as they neared the neck of the river, resistance had increased. It did not seem sensible. They were offering the ferrymen better terms. Hatcher seemed to take this growing reluctance to give in as a personal affront. To Neff, it was the pointlessness of the situation that nagged at him. He was better than this.

The roar that came with the swing of Hatcher's club made Neff look along the Thames again, checking for witnesses. All seemed quiet on the water. He turned back to watch Hatcher's assault, as he caught his target square on the jaw, knocking him down. Then followed this up with a heftier blow to the ribs. The man rolled onto his front and retched.

'I've had enough of this,' Hatcher announced, and marched away, his bag of tools over his shoulder, towards the northern bank. His tread echoed along the river as the shingle surrendered under his weight. Neff looked down at the motionless ferryman and felt he should leave him with an apt summary to remember them by.

'You work for Dempsey now,' was the best he could come up with.

****

By the time Neff reached the noisy streets of St Paul's, he had closed in on Hatcher. This area was more alive at night than in the day; drunken men and molls fell out of taverns, hawkers shouted their wares in the murk, whores propositioned passers-by in doorways. Hatcher strode on, no longer burdened by his sack, making Neff wonder where he had dropped it. As he wound his way left and right, Neff felt Hatcher's movements were those of a man with a definite purpose and direction. He turned onto

Cheapside, where the lights from taverns and gin shops helped Neff maintain his distance and keep his target in sight.

Dempsey's instructions to watch Hatcher preyed on Neff's mind; the concept of disloyalty was clearly occupying his boss. That and the fear of Kaplan moving against him. Neff felt looking over your shoulder all the time was no way to live. He paused, checked behind, and chuckled at himself. A tiny idea began to pull at him, one that might help him escape the strangulation of the streets. The image of a life somewhere else. He pushed it to one side as they continued to switch back and forth through the alleys.

Hatcher stopped outside a tavern on the corner of Cheapside and Bread Street and began talking to two street girls. They toyed with him, showing a glimpse of stockinged leg as they lifted their dresses. He pointed at one of them, indicating inside. The moll slipped a blue flower into her long red hair and teased it with her fingers, before beckoning Hatcher into the alehouse. Neff decided to hold back, and stood in a doorway, pulling his overcoat around him against the cold. He contemplated how far he had come. From a workhouse orphan who survived by his wits on the streets, to one fateful act that shaped his and Dempsey's futures, then a fruitless period in uniform, and now keeping London safe. He had been fortunate to run into Emily Jarrett and then William Dempsey early in his life. Luckier still to have got this far and not met the noose.

A couple of streetwalkers pulled up next to Neff. 'A good time, sir? Just a shilling,' one of them said, leaning forward to show off her bosom.

Neff shook his head. They moved on and accosted two men coming out of another tavern up the alley, then disappeared into the night, no twang with them for protection. Emily said she was trying to get the girls working in safer houses, but he doubted she could save them all. Desperation would always drive the women towards danger. What would be the point in helping any of them? They would just be replaced by more.

Neff waited and looked at his pocket watch a couple of times. He reasoned Hatcher was drinking and carousing inside and could be there all night. It was safe to assume he was not meeting anyone to plot Dempsey's downfall, as his boss feared. There would be nothing more to report other than the compliance of the ferrymen. Neff turned back towards Cannon Street. As he reached the corner, he heard the noise of the tavern door being opened, and Hatcher spilled out, the red-haired girl on one arm. They staggered down an alley towards the river. Neff held back, allowing another whore with a customer to pass him by, then followed Hatcher. Something drew him in to it, a feeling he could not quite place.

The couple continued in the direction of the Thames. Hatcher seemed to be dragging her along. The girl's head lolled as they moved, her red tresses shaking. Neff steadily closed in. As he turned into an alley, his prey ahead, a figure bumped into him, knocking Neff sideways.

'Hey,' the man shouted. 'Watch where you go this time of night.'

Neff pressed him into a doorway, locking a forearm across the man's throat. He checked up the street. Hatcher and the girl carried on walking, oblivious to the commotion.

'Let me go. I shall call a constable,' the figure choked. The eyes betrayed fear. The words were empty.

'You won't find one this time of night,' Neff said, dropping his hands. The stranger brushed his coat down and hurried away in the direction he had been heading. Neff looked up the narrow lane; Hatcher had gone.

Neff wandered the streets down towards the river, then up to Cheapside and circled back again. London had grown quiet, the streets murkier with few link lighters working. Despite this he felt he might see Hatcher at every turn. He stopped down by the Thames at Blackfriars Steps. He sat on the shingle and threw a stone in the direction of the water. It failed to reach, and the sound of it landing echoed along the riverfront. His eye was caught by a distant figure running along the shore in the direction of London Bridge. It was too dark to make him out clearly, he seemed to stumble and picked himself up again, before disappearing inland. Neff walked towards the river, and the upturned boat where they had finished their evening's work earlier.

A shape was slumped on the bank next to the boat. As he got closer, he realised it was a body partly covered by a tarpaulin. Possibly the ferryman, or a drunk sleeping it off. Neff looked across the Thames to the southern shore and could make out the occasional lantern in Southwark. He scanned up and down the river again. They were alone. He kicked the legs and muttered a greeting, but there was no movement. Neff knelt closer, making out a pair of boots. There was something vaguely familiar about them he could not place. When he turned the figure over by the shoulders, red hair spilled out onto the shingle. Under that, a dark liquid. Neff ran his hands down the body and pulled them away when he felt the wetness. A woman, with a knife stuck in her stomach. And by the side of the blood-soaked head, resting on the ground like a sad tribute, was a single blue flower.

33

Emily Jarrett closed the tavern door and stepped carefully into the street, looking back at the next project behind her. The Bull Inn, another tavern conversion that she was going to work on with Mary Grant. The top two levels would be decorated for the ladies to work, a gambling room with card tables would be created under these, and the old bar would continue downstairs to lure the men in.

Drizzle splashed in the puddles; she pulled her hat down tightly and hitched up her breeches, examining her boots. They would be covered in mud by the time she reached her lodgings. The vendors and the beggars cried out along Bishopsgate; the pickpockets bustled in and out of the pedestrians. Every step carried the stench of rotten animal carcases and human waste that shortened her breath. She felt uneasy that side of Newgate, despite the scene being like any in Covent Garden.

Emily watched the local collection of girls in action. They shouted at passers-by, thrusting their chests out, yelling prices and suggestions of what men would receive in return. Here they were still competing over every doorstep, every trick. A different world to a mile to the west and her alleyways. Emily wanted this to change, knew she could deliver it, if only the Thief Taker would support her.

A figure swept past, dressed in black, a face she thought she recognised, but struggled to name. He was followed by two men, one as wide as a passageway, the other thin with eyes that danced about him, studying everyone that approached. She looked again at the man in front. Emily shrugged. London was full of strange men.

She turned towards Aldgate and stopped when she saw James Neff coming out of a brandy shop. Emily slipped into a doorway and watched him scan the street with rapid head movements. She felt her chest tighten, as if something were pressing against her. Neff picked his way through the clinging mud in her direction, and stopped a few strides away, unable to hide his surprise when he noticed her. He briefly removed his hat to smooth his hair, as Emily stepped forward and smiled. It was comforting to see a familiar face in that part of town. The rain had ceased.

'Emily?' he croaked, looking about him again. His voice sounded fragile. She ached to reach out and comfort him.

'James, what are you doing here?' she asked, trying to sound playful. Emily turned to her left, following Neff's eyeline. He quickly pulled his gaze back to her, but she knew he had been watching the three figures who passed her moments before.

Neff frowned. Emily wondered if she was interrupting an important piece of work. She knew he did some things that were necessary for Dempsey's business to flourish.

'Sorry, James, I mustn't stop you.'

'No, no,' he said. One quick glimpse along the street again, then a smile broke across his face. 'It is always nice to see you. What brings you this far east?'

'I was due to meet William here,' she said, pointing at the tavern.

'Here?'

'He didn't turn up.' Emily reached out and touched his arm. 'Why don't I show you what I wanted him to see? If you really are not too busy?' She needed to share her excitement at the new opportunity. Wanted him to see how the rooms would be laid out. Then a thought struck her, about whether it was a coincidence meeting James there.

'Did William send you, in his place?' Perhaps Dempsey was going to back her initiative after all.

'He…' Neff hesitated; his eyes flicked away, then back to her.

'Who were those men? One of them was familiar.' Emily still could not place the man in black with the confident stride.

'Just somebody I was following. Nothing to worry about,' Neff came back quickly. He stared at her with an expression she struggled to place, then shifted his eyes to the floor. He bit his lip; she had not seen James so nervous for some time. He finally stared into her eyes and Emily felt her pulse quicken, swallowing hard. Neff reached out a hand towards her. 'Come with me, there is something I must tell you.'

He steered her into a gin shop. Smoke wafted across the room from a large woodburning fire, and Emily picked out the familiar odour of alcohol and sweat. They took a table and while they waited to be served Neff tapped at the floor with his boot. He ran his fingers through his hair again, avoiding looking at her. After two glasses and a bottle arrived and the waitress left, he finally spoke.

'Emily, I have news. You need to hear it from me first, rather than in the penny papers.'

'News?'

Neff reached out to take her hands. His were rough, but she doubted he did anything with them that would help keep them smooth. The whites of his eyes seemed pink in the artificial light of a lantern behind her.

'We have found the Alley Killer.'

Emily felt her heart pause. Was this true? She stared at Neff intently, pulling her hands away and folding them, feeling her temples throb as she reached for her drink. 'You know who it is?'

Neff closed his eyes. 'It was Hatcher,' he whispered.

'Hatcher?' Emily raised her voice, then looked around the shop to check for reactions from the other customers. Heads were turned away from them, the chatter did not seem to stop. Debate of the day between reasoned men, she assumed. Pity none of it ever came to anything. She clutched her hands together, to stop the shaking. The culprit was a man who worked close to Dempsey. Close to Neff. 'You did not know?'

'Of course not.' He looked miserable. 'He is apprehended.'

Emily let out a deep sigh, and a tingling sensation ran down her arms and into her fingers. The man who had been terrorising women on the streets was caught. 'The girls will rest easier,' she said. Emily grasped Neff's hands again. 'You are certain about this?'

'There is no doubt as to Hatcher's guilt.' Neff looked across the gin shop, at a group of men arguing, and she followed his gaze. Voices were raised, something about Catholics, she caught. When she turned back to examine Neff, a blank look had returned to his face. Then it came to her.

'You found him out, didn't you?'

Neff shrugged. 'I wanted you to know. For the girls… There will be publicity,' he added. 'I hear Hatcher has confessed to many more killings. Not just women.'

'He is in gaol?'

'Somewhere safer than that, for the protection of everyone.'

He seemed guarded. Maybe Dempsey was preparing to punish Hatcher in a different way to the assizes. Perhaps that would be appropriate, she thought. 'What did William say, when he heard?'

Neff folded his arms, and suddenly looked like a lost boy. So different to the one she had first met. Emily took a sip from her glass and examined her fingers. Her skin seemed to be turning into that of an old crow.

'He was surprised, like we all are,' Neff said.

Emily thought about the spectre that had roamed the streets unchecked for weeks. She blamed the gang leaders: Dempsey, Kaplan, Renshaw, Ashford. Their quarrels had pulled the city apart, rendered it a place where depravity and danger had become commonplace. Women were disposable, worthless. The Introduction House seemed to be picking up only a small percentage of the girls who came to London to make a new life. Most were struggling in the backstreets, working in doorways, preyed on by drunken clients and madams with no scruples. It felt like a losing battle to keep the women safe.

'Hatcher should be punished in public. The girls will want to see justice done. For their peace of mind.'

Neff shook his head slowly. 'It is complicated. Let us deal with it.'

He sipped at his drink and stared at his glass. Emily wondered where the energy had gone from that young cull she first met. Whether killing sucked the life out of a man.

'I think William is having second thoughts about our venture,' Emily said. 'To improve the locations, places like the tavern I was at just now.' Neff said nothing. 'His mind seems to be elsewhere. Maybe now this killer is caught he will help me.'

'He is often distracted,' Neff muttered. 'Kaplan, Ashford, Gillard, even Walpole.' Neff re-filled his glass. Emily sipped at her own, musing over how difficult it was to tell what Neff was thinking. He was giving no impression he supported her plan to improve conditions in London either. Would any man help?

'He is certainly not distracted by me anymore,' Emily added. She knew how reliant on men even relatively powerful women were, and had long ago realised that little could be gained from attachment. She reached out to grab Neff's sleeve. This time, he made no effort to resist.

'James, why did William take control all those years ago, and not you? Why did you join the army?' That chance of a connection between them had been buried in the past. And there was another question deep inside of her, bound forever to remain unspoken, over what drove her to attach herself to Dempsey, rather than the man opposite. The regret tugged at her, and she closed her eyes with a deep sigh.

When she opened them, Neff was still staring at his drink. He shook his head. 'He was better suited to leading. He thought so much about the details. How to get people to do what he asked.' He looked up at her. 'I did something that set me on a certain path. Joining up was my only option. When I returned, his power had grown, and I had nowhere else to turn. We are different men now.'

As she studied James, and his shy way with her even after so many years, Emily realised she knew who she wanted to share her future ventures with. And it was no longer the Thief Taker. Emily leaned in and pecked Neff on the cheek. He flushed.

‘I need a partner,’ she said, placing a finger under his chin. Neff did not resist her touch and looked up at her. There was a smile there now, the melancholy gone. ‘Someone with his own mind, who would support me and the girls who work on the streets. Someone who knows those streets.’ She stared into his grey eyes and thought she might have seen a flash of recognition. ‘Do you know anybody who would do that for me?’

34

Neff threw a bucket of water over the figure on the floor. Hatcher wiped his face, and tried to pull himself to his feet, but Bennett kicked him in the chest, knocking him back against the wall. It had taken the two of them some time to drag his unconscious form down the steps to the cellar under the Fleet River. Hatcher had been on the other end of punishment there many times, but now his time had run out.

Dempsey walked out of the shadows. 'You are such a disappointment, Daniel.'

Neff moved to one side of the prisoner and kept his expression as neutral as he could. His boss's attention was on Hatcher's slumped form.

'I have done nothing wrong,' Hatcher pleaded.

'That is not what I hear.' Dempsey raised his voice. The sound echoed off the stone walls. 'I know you killed those women.' He walked back and forth; a movement Neff had seen him use before to control the anger. 'James saw you, on Cheapside and by the river. You have been murdering whores. Why?'

'I…' Hatcher held his nose where they had dropped him

less than carefully. It was puffy, oozing blood, looked broken. Bennett took his job seriously, Neff mused.

'You are a traitor as well as a killer. You side with Kaplan. We think he has men on the inside of our organisation,' Dempsey continued. 'Men like you.'

Hatcher looked up, wide-eyed. 'Not me.'

To Neff, the Thief Taker's face looked to be a pale shade of purple in the faint light of a flickering lantern. Perhaps it was just the damp cellar playing tricks with him. He knew the loyalty ran deep. The bond came from an incident five years before, when Hatcher was a humble member of the Engineers. He killed his wife and her lover in a drunken rage, and Dempsey dressed it up as a robbery, placing two other men there at the time, hanging them both for the crime. Hatcher had obeyed every deadly instruction since.

Contemplating his own compliance, Neff wondered what drove it. On balance, he thought Dempsey owed him more when they first met. But he was indebted to the safety offered by the Thief Taker once he returned from the military. He was secure now, hiding in the murky, dangerous streets of London where the Army feared to tread.

It seemed to Neff that it was the working with Kaplan, a thought he had planted, that worried his boss more than killing jades. Neff felt his mouth go dry and looked at Bennett, who was studying him closely. Maybe Bennett was following him, the way he had been instructed to do with Hatcher. Perhaps Dempsey was worried about everyone, the paranoia growing.

'You were seen with a woman who was found dead the same night. A constable will come for you presently. You are to hang.'

'I beg you, forgive me, William. I am often consumed by hate. Those women, they…'

Hatcher broke off and whined. Neff studied the wall, unable to watch. Water trickled down the stones and made him shiver. He could sense Bennett's eyes on him but resisted the temptation to check.

'You have served me well,' Dempsey continued, on the move again. 'But you have undone yourself. I cannot be seen to be the upholder of justice in this city, and not deliver you for killing so many.' He paused in front of Hatcher and a hand went briefly to his jacket, feeling for something, then grimaced. 'Daniel, you cannot be saved from this.'

'Please, William,' Hatcher begged, his hands clasped together. 'What would you have me do?'

Neff's speech was ready. He stepped forward. 'We can transport him. Spare his life.'

Dempsey continued to look at Hatcher, and a thin smile emerged. 'This might be your only choice.'

Neff continued, directing his words at Hatcher, half an eye on Dempsey for his reaction. 'The authorities are given your name as the killer. Then we make it look like you are murdered, by a vengeful whore. We report you dead. We slip you away on the next ship for the plantations under a new name. Robinson will make it happen. It is your only way out of this.'

Hatcher's sobs echoed around the cellar, and Neff clenched his fists, hands behind his back. It was one thing to kill under orders, like a soldier, for a just cause; something he eventually tired of. But to murder defenceless women, and so brutally, was outside of their code. When Neff looked up, Bennett's glare was there again, making him turn away, at the prisoner.

'We will spare your life, Daniel,' Dempsey said, with a sigh. 'It is a good plan,' he continued, placing a hand on Neff's shoulder. 'James here is clever; I trust him to make it work. And removing the Alley Killer would make some whore a heroine. She would be spared the rope, and nothing need be made public.'

'And we dispose of what is thought to be your body,' Neff added. 'The surgeons would have it if we did not stop them. They like to study criminals.'

Neff hoped to God that when his turn came, as one day it surely would, the medical men would not take his bones. Another scan of the room revealed Bennett was busy this time, throwing Hatcher's sack over his shoulder.

'I shall take care of it,' Neff said, looking at Dempsey. The gloom appeared to have lifted a little from his face.

'I would be a free man? Not a prisoner?' Hatcher sounded like he could not believe his luck.

'So long as you go to the colonies,' Dempsey prompted. 'Daniel, I…' A sad-looking shake of the head followed. 'This is the end for us. Bennett, come with me, I have something for you to do. James, I will leave you to make the arrangements.' The Thief Taker swivelled and promptly left with Bennett in his wake; the echo of their tread resounding as they ascended the steps to the street.

'Come with me, just follow my instructions,' Neff said.

Hatcher nodded sadly, and the two men who had shared much action climbed up towards the Fleet River. As the chill night air hit them, Neff offered his flask. 'Drink down, Daniel, I think you need it. I will take you to a safer place.' Hatcher snatched it and sampled the potion with a renewed look of hope in his eyes.

They walked a few paces, before Hatcher collapsed in the gutter. Neff dragged his body along to a waiting handcart, then hoisted it up, covering it with tarpaulin. A quick look up and down the street revealed no witnesses. It was too dark for anyone to identify them even if he was seen. He could easily have been taking a dead animal away to slaughter. According to the apothecary, there would be no waking an ox from the amount Hatcher had taken. Thankfully, Collins never seemed to question their motives.

Neff slowly wheeled Hatcher's body out to Finchley, to a spot in the woods off the High Road, where Renshaw's remains lay. There would be two devils buried side by side in the deep mud. Men like Hatcher, and what they did to women, could not go unpunished. The false story would be spread about a vengeful woman in Newgate gaol, but Neff owed Emily and her girls appropriate justice. Robinson could be persuaded to create a fake travel docket for a passenger to Virginia, to satisfy Dempsey. All it took was money.

Neff covered Hatcher's body with earth, having checked his neck for a pulse. Dead within an hour, Collins had promised. Neff muttered an angry farewell to his former colleague and tossed his shovel onto the cart. He looked up at the night sky; the clouds were thick and promised rain. He did not care if this body was discovered, nobody was going to claim it, let alone recognise the demon. As he wheeled his load back in the direction of London, Neff wondered if his own end would be similar. Perhaps Bennett was lurking in the shadows watching him the whole time. He scanned the length of the lane that led back to the city but saw no signs of anyone hunting him down. Trying to put the thought out of his mind, Neff whistled a tune to himself as he picked his way through the potholes. It was a soldiers' lament to a lost girl who spurned his attentions and ran off with a thief. But he was no longer a man in uniform. His destiny was in his own hands now.

35

The coach bounced its way along the wide sweep of Cheapside. Kaplan settled deeper into his seat, the comfort growing as they moved east, towards his territory.

The Thief Taker shuffled opposite him. 'Shame about Ashford's accident.'

'And you had nothing to do with it?' Kaplan asked, hiding his amusement at the feigned innocence.

Dempsey shrugged as if to decline and stared out the window, lifting a curtain. They both had a man hanging on to the side rail outside, and inside two rivals were locked in a private conversation in the hired carriage. Kaplan had decided there were too many eager ears in taverns for this sort of meeting to be held in public.

'Did you get to the jury?'

Dempsey hesitated, playing with the sleeves of his jacket. Kaplan looked up to examine the decoration on the inside of the roof: images of Hanoverian Germany, soldiers in bold uniforms, mounted on prancing horses. So much for peaceful revolutions, he mused. England had invited foreigners in to rule them again. Did the politicians never learn?

'There was no need to,' Dempsey eventually said, his voice quiet and low. Kaplan had to strain to hear against the sound of hooves and passers-by. 'Although I know Ashford tried.'

'When will my men be released?' Kaplan prompted, bringing the conversation round to his main concern. Six of them were still detained across the city, in various gaols.

'All the charges will be dropped tomorrow.'

'You said they would be free when Ashford was hanged.'

'Well, he wasn't.' Dempsey looked blankly at him. 'Sometimes the process of law moves slowly. We know that.'

'Yes, but you control the court. Or the Old Bailey at least.'

'I did once. But this Gillard…' Dempsey paused and hit his cane against the floor of the coach. They stopped with a jolt and the driver's head appeared at the window. Dempsey looked surprised and turned away, his cheeks reddened.

'Everything all right?' the coachman asked. Kaplan nodded for him to continue, and the face disappeared.

'I suspect Parliament controls him,' Dempsey said when they began moving again. He seemed to be studying Kaplan carefully now.

'Not like you to let a man in that position do what he wants,' Kaplan said. 'Or let politicians dictate matters.' He knew Dempsey was lying. Gillard would be too frightened to disobey orders.

'You gave me your word about my men,' Kaplan insisted.

'I always keep my word, Kaplan. Everyone knows that.'

Kaplan studied the Thief Taker. The light in the carriage did little to improve the features of the man. The hooded lids, the eyes sunken in their sockets, and the grey complexion gave him the look of a spectre, a man who barely set foot outdoors. Even Dempsey's bald head seemed to be a ghostlier hue than Kaplan remembered. For a moment he felt like he was travelling with his own father. Except this man was not standing over him with a whip, making him cower in a corner.

'You promised me everything south of the river, the distilleries, the factories,' Kaplan persisted. The purpose of the meeting was to gain confirmation of control of his new businesses. That and to tease out how genuine the disaffection among Dempsey's men was.

'It is all yours,' Dempsey said, his expression suddenly blank. Kaplan rarely felt ill at ease in the presence of other men. It was just the not knowing what was going on in this one's head that troubled him. Kaplan kept his own expression as neutral as he could. Dempsey's hand appeared to tremble, before he folded his arms and continued. 'The breweries are idle, there are workers not getting paid. It needs someone who knows about drink to take over.'

'Leave that to me,' Kaplan countered. Monopoly was efficiency, as his father used to say. He could set his own prices for alcohol now.

'I shall,' Dempsey acknowledged. Kaplan noticed his hand go to a jacket pocket, making him stiffen. He felt where a knife was hidden in his waistcoat. Dempsey merely wiped the perspiration off his bald head with a handkerchief. Kaplan folded his arms and breathed out slowly. The coach felt strangely warm, as if the air were being compressed from the outside.

'There are opportunities south of the river,' Dempsey continued. 'The merchants have nobody to pay their tributes to.' Protection, he clearly meant. 'You should step in and resume order.'

'I will when you return my men.'

Dempsey nodded, pulling the curtain aside again. They were passing down Bishopsgate, a sea of faces washing past them as pedestrians and peddlers made their way in both directions. The frantic shouts of traders and the chatter on the street invaded the coach. Kaplan relaxed; they were sounds that made him feel at home.

'With Southwark all yours, you need to open up the brothels from Whitechapel to Wapping to me,' Dempsey said, his eyes snapping up to look at Kaplan.

'You think you can manage them?'

'I can take care of the whorehouses and the gambling. They both lead to more drinking. We both win from the deal, with Ashford out the way.'

'You cannot interfere with my taverns,' Kaplan glared at Dempsey, but the man was suddenly distracted again, staring at the ceiling, his train of thought seemingly wandering. Maybe the Thief Taker had no idea a man called Charles Ingram was feeding his organisation false information about where people were cheating at the tables.

'The madams will do what you ask?' Kaplan asked. In his experience that was never easy.

Dempsey seemed to snap out of his thoughts and nodded. 'I can ensure they will stop competing with each other.'

Kaplan mulled over his next move. Perhaps there was more than one way to bring down Dempsey. 'Just make sure the women don't interfere with the alehouses and the landlords. That is where the money is,' he said.

Dempsey offered nothing in reply, but his eyes flicked about the floor, putting Kaplan on alert. Three of his remaining men were following them, but an attack was always possible.

Dempsey had shown his treacherous hand with Ashford already.

'The likes of Miss Jarrett and Miss Manning are important to you.' Kaplan knew the truth. 'Your lost and found business is built on them.' A plan was forming in his mind. He knew his rival relied on more than just those men he called the Engineers. The women were a key source of information on clients. They also robbed them. Everyone knew it, but with Dempsey controlling who was brought to trial, the whores were protected. For now.

'It has long been this way,' Dempsey said, twitching the curtain. He pulled his free hand to his chest and looked absent-mindedly outside.

'Isn't your business threatened by this Alley Killer being on the loose?'

Dempsey suddenly looked across at Kaplan, his eyes sparkling, a thin smile on his face. 'He is caught. The women have nothing to fear now.'

'You know the killer?'

'It does not matter who it was.' Dempsey closed his eyes and slumped in the seat, and Kaplan wondered for a moment whether the Thief Taker had stopped breathing. Then, Dempsey sat up with a start. 'I know you want to supply the alehouses and shops in Covent Garden with your gin and brandy. You have my permission.'

Kaplan tried to hide a scowl. He did not need the say of a man like Dempsey to sell alcohol across all of London.

'With no interference,' he insisted, jabbing a finger, before pulling it back. The bastard had people everywhere, that was why Dempsey was opposed to boundaries. But an empire could not be built on lost property and whores. You needed the hearts and minds of innkeepers, coffeehouse owners, the lifeblood of London. They travelled on in silence for a while before Kaplan decided to raise another matter.

'London Bridge is mine,' he announced. He had taken over the business of charging every vehicle that crossed.

Dempsey held his palms out in front. 'And the ferrymen belong to me,' he said. 'I will not charge your people for using the crossings if you do the same for the bridge.' Both men knew there were no other means of traversing the Thames until Kingston. 'We must stop the move to build a new bridge at Westminster,' Dempsey added.

'Agreed.'

Promises could be broken. There was no honour left in London, Kaplan knew that. He stared at the face opposite. Dempsey closed his eyes and nodded his head as if he were asleep. Kaplan wondered whether some form of madness was coming over his rival. The coach jolted as it hit a pothole and Dempsey jumped upright in his seat. The eyes seemed to lose focus again; a hand moved to his jacket once more, and he removed something from a pocket, tipping the contents of a glass vial into his mouth, shaking his head vigorously. Perhaps the strange behaviour was related to some form of addiction; it was something to ask James Neff about.

'What happens in Westminster is more of a worry for you,' Kaplan said. There was no harm in pointing out the potential weakness of the Thief Taker's position. 'You are stuck between me and whoever takes over from Renshaw. Do you know what is happening there?'

'I could arrange for Tindall to have a similar fate to Samuel Ashford,' Dempsey said. They both knew he was languishing in some northern gaol, unlikely to return.

'Be careful. After Ashford it would look suspicious. At least we knew where we were with Renshaw.' Kaplan still suspected Dempsey's hand behind the disappearance of his oldest rival. 'The politicians would not like it.'

Dempsey offered no reply, merely sighed, and turned his head to pick at the decoration on the edge of the coach window.

They came to a halt, and it was Kaplan's turn to pull the curtain aside. They were about to go left onto King William Street. Leaning out the window for a better view, Kaplan saw that a barrow had spilled its load across the road, and a merchant was busily chasing escaped chickens, picking up vegetables. A crowd had gathered to watch his frantic pursuit; women laughed, others pointed and mocked.

'That man needs help,' Dempsey said. His face beamed with the excitement of a small child.

Dempsey opened the coach door and stepped into the street, beginning to converse with the barrow owner. Neff jumped down to Dempsey's side, and after a brief consultation both began picking up the man's wares from under carts, in the gutter, out of doorways. Why would someone with this reputation stoop to helping a desperate merchant pick up his lost goods? Kaplan shook his head, retreating to inside the carriage. The behaviour was bewildering. Perhaps the rumours about the Thief Taker losing his grip were true. They would certainly aid Kaplan's ambitions.

Kaplan focused on the figure of James Neff as he scooped turnips and carrots to his breast, dropping them onto the barrow. His movements were powerful and precise. The man appeared to be loyal on the surface; but if there was unrest among men like that, it would become increasingly difficult to sustain a position of authority. As he watched Neff catch a cockerel in his significant hands, Kaplan began to form the impression of Dempsey's potential downfall. It would not involve careful negotiation on carriage journeys. Empires built on treachery could be dismantled from within, through the removal of the people that were the most loyal. He slipped out of the coach and into the shadows of the street, followed by his men. Once the others were released the shape of London was going to change, permanently.

36

Hobbs put down his fork and gazed at the slice of mutton on his plate, to avoid the sight in front of him. He thought he had come far enough north to avoid his visitor but was clearly wrong. Dempsey placed a lone brandy on the table, then tossed a copy of the latest Gazette onto the seat next to Hobbs.

'I am sick of hearing about Samuel Ashford. You need to move on to something else.'

William Dempsey? Hobbs mused but resisted the temptation to say. He wondered again how many readers he might attract for that story. Then dismissed it, the thought of financial ruin too strong.

Dempsey lowered himself into the seat opposite and sighed, running a hand over his scalp. 'Is it good?' he asked, pointing at the food.

Hobbs took a mouthful of his regular lunch and nodded.

'I recommend Murray's on Fleet Street. He uses real meat, you know?'

Hobbs paused, then chewed slowly, and swallowed. He took a sip of his drink to wash it down.

Dempsey's eyes narrowed. 'I know Ashford was a devil. He was responsible for many deaths. But London is safer now he is gone. I have ventured to Southwark since his accident; the locals are grateful. Enough of him.'

'We have published the entire catalogue of the crimes you gave me.'

'This Alley Killer story would make a better read,' Dempsey said, tapping at his glass. 'The man was discovered, then killed by a revengeful whore. They are both dead, but the Newgate chaplain captured their stories. It will sell many newssheets.'

'You have the confession of the killer? The woman as well?'

'The killer, yes, in here.'

Dempsey dropped a bundle of papers in front of Hobbs. He kept doing this, bringing news that had already been written up. It made his job easier, Hobbs supposed.

'A man called Hatcher.' Dempsey stared across the table, prodding the sheets with his finger. 'He was a known criminal. It is a gruesome story; one your readers would love.'

Hobbs stared at the bundle and contemplated another mouthful of mutton, before dropping his fork.

Dempsey continued, a frown forming on his face. 'The chaplain persuaded this Hatcher to unburden his soul. There are over a dozen murders to his name. A prostitute killed him; we think defending her life.'

Hobbs sat back, resisting the temptation to pick up the papers. 'Her name?'

'I forget, it is in here,' Dempsey said, tapping at the table. 'Print the story in stages again, draw the readers in. You could say this Hatcher was one of Kaplan's men.'

'Was he?'

'Does that matter?'

Hobbs pondered how it could be difficult to know how serious the Thief Taker was at times. He lowered his voice, looking around the tavern, conscious they were close to the east end.

'You want me to write about Arthur Kaplan?'

'I could arrange for tales of his crimes to fall into your lap,' Dempsey smiled, showing his black and yellow teeth.

Hobbs considered the image of Kaplan, a man he had also heard fearsome stories about. There seemed to be so many dubious characters at large, all of them newsworthy, including the man opposite. Hobbs took a drink to steady himself and decided to switch his attention back to the infamous killer who had been despatched.

'Did you meet this Hatcher?' Hobbs asked.

Dempsey looked up quickly. There was a darkness there that made Hobbs shiver. 'I saw him testify in court once. He worked for Renshaw and then Kaplan.' Dempsey pointed at the confession on the table. 'According to the story the chaplain related he was consumed by evil urges.' Dempsey pushed the sheets towards Hobbs. 'Here, publish it all.'

Hobbs stared at the documents. Speculation as to the murderer's identity had occupied the coffeehouse gossips of London for weeks. If these were the genuine life and times of the Alley Killer, he would be printing more copies than ever.

'I have this exclusively?' There was still some competition, but if he could print this in the Gazette, the others would look on in envy.

'You do. Provided we hear no more about Ashford. He is yesterday's news.'

'The readings in the meeting rooms have proved to be extremely popular,' Hobbs said, changing the subject.

'The news reaches so many more people now. A good idea of yours,' Dempsey smiled. They both knew it was the Thief Taker's suggestion.

Between them, they had created a fresh industry. Each day copies of the Gazette were read to assembled people in meeting halls where audiences paid a farthing to attend and listen to the news. Hobbs recognised the frisson that came with insights into how the underclass lived. The merchants were titillated by it. The nobility needed it to demonstrate how superior they were, even though many of them were even more crooked. He imagined the criminals revelled in stories about their own kind. People wanted entertainment, above all to hear about crime.

'I shall set the whore killings out across a week.' Hobbs could also use the information Neff had passed to him when he pleaded for publicity earlier.

'There is more to Hatcher's confession than prostitutes,' Dempsey said. 'There were many other killings.' He prodded the papers again. 'Organised warfare between criminal gangs. Be sure to mention Kaplan where he crops up,' Dempsey added. 'And put this on the front page.'

'I may need an advance for extra printing.'

Dempsey waved a cursory hand. 'Put the price up. I want your readers to remember this demon Hatcher and the man behind him for years to come.'

Hobbs knew he could increase the cost once the first edition of the gruesome story of the Alley Killer had been printed. It was about time he made a greater profit from this arrangement with Dempsey. Hobbs breathed deeply, congratulating himself on being one of the few people in London that was indispensable to the Thief Taker.

Dempsey pushed the sheets to one side and placed a new pile of papers on the table between them. 'We have another enterprise,' he announced. The eyes were black as hell, the smile fixed.

'Another weekly?'

Dempsey pointed at the documents. 'These are something new. You will simply set and print them for me. We already have an outlet where we can sell them.'

Hobbs turned over the first sheet, read until halfway down and stopped. He ran a finger round the inside of his collar and sipped at his brandy unsteadily. He could scarcely believe the words.

'I cannot print this. This is surely against the law.'

Dempsey flashed a smile. 'We call this a gentleman's pamphlet. There are men who enjoy this sort of thing. Some would read them alone; others like to hear the content spoken. In certain establishments.'

'This is not Paris, Mister Dempsey. I cannot print this depravity.'

Hobbs pushed the sheet back in Dempsey's direction, and pulled a hand to his chest, feeling it thumping. He reached for his now empty drink and looked towards the landlord, who was nowhere to be found.

'You can, Hobbs, and you will.'

'This is immoral.' Hobbs looked down again. His eyes misted over. 'Where did you get it from?'

'Never ask me questions like that, Jacob. You know better than that.'

Hobbs studied the pile of papers once more. He picked out another page, fixing on a lewd drawing. It was horrific.

'I cannot…'

Dempsey slammed his fist on the table. The eyes were locked on Hobbs. 'If I take these pamphlets elsewhere, I shall take the news with it. And if I do that, you can guess what will happen to the Gazette, and the Bulletin, plus all your future enterprises. Maybe accidents might start happening to your presses, and the people who work there.' There was no smile this time, just a cold glare.

Hobbs swallowed hard. He could not imagine returning to the days when he needed a drink simply to get up in the morning, to face the latest issue that would greet him when he arrived at his tiny old office on the corner of Grub Street. He tried to focus on the words in front of him and fingered the sheets with a shaky hand. Why was Dempsey peddling this sin? And what had he become? Looking up, Hobbs felt he was caught in Dempsey's sights, burning through his soul. He wriggled in his seat, trapped, with too much to lose. With a sigh he nodded his acceptance.

Dempsey wrapped up the pamphlets and stood to leave, placing them neatly on the table.

'This is a fine arrangement we have, Mister Hobbs. You are faring well from it. Keep it that way.'

The Thief Taker strode to the door, not a look back. Hobbs pushed his cold mutton about his plate and thought about the notes locked away in the drawer in his office. Those words might exist in print one day. Perhaps it was simply a matter of cataloguing the story and waiting for Dempsey's inevitable fall. All empires crumbled eventually.

Maybe nobody would believe the tale, even if it were laid out. Hobbs was so heavily entangled in it that he would need to tread cautiously. As he looked around the tavern, he wondered at which men danced to Dempsey's tune, regardless of whether they knew it or not. Perhaps it was all of them. Could he stay in business without Dempsey's help? Deep down, he doubted it now.

When the landlord finally emerged from the back room, Hobbs settled his bill. He watched the smoke billow up from the fire and thought about how it reached out to touch everyone in the tavern, and hung above their heads, an unavoidable presence. He wondered what might happen if the Thief Taker vanished overnight and found himself shivering in his seat. Something even darker might fill the void. Hobbs touched the key to the drawer, secure in his pocket. Swallowing back the thought of the disgusting words in his bag, he reasoned that he had little choice but to play along for now.

37

Dempsey slipped a guinea into the turnkey's pocket, before closing the door behind him. Charlton was slumped in the corner of a cell in Bristol gaol, staring through the narrow window at the sky.

'You are in a perilous position,' Dempsey began.

Charlton did not move. Dempsey could hear the prisoner's shallow breath echo in the empty space. He moved into Charlton's line of vision, blocking the light.

Charlton looked up, tired recognition in his eyes. 'I am to be hanged.'

'You are a murderer, as well as a highwayman. I didn't know you could handle a sword.'

Charlton winced, clutching at his side. 'I was doing your bidding, though I've not told anyone that.' What looked like acceptance was in his eyes, rather than defiance. 'The gang fought back; they were armed,' he added.

'The gang escaped,' Dempsey said. Charlton jerked his head up. 'And I heard the man you hired to help got away, but he was killed in a brawl.' Bennett had removed the only other witness to Charlton's mission the day before. 'You had one simple job,' Dempsey continued. Charlton studied the floor. Dempsey shook his head and tutted. This was supposed to be the start of his expansion outside of London, to run the highways of the country. 'And it turned into a bloody battle.'

Dempsey was thankful the mistake was away from curious London eyes. It seemed justice worked quickly out west. Charlton's execution was set for the following week, at the Clifton gallows.

'I have been loyal,' Charlton croaked.

'But little else,' Dempsey countered. 'You failed me and the local authorities. We sent you to detain a gang of highwaymen, and you killed the son of a magistrate at the roadside. That tied my hands.'

'There was confusion,' Charlton said. 'Matthews and me, we drank the night before.'

Dempsey struggled to stop his voice rising. 'They wanted a public court case, not vigilantes riding the roads, killing at random.' The damage to Dempsey's reputation, if word got out, would be difficult to repair. He needed the matter closed, and swiftly.

Checking nobody was listening at the cell door, Dempsey returned to Charlton. The figure was doubled up on a stool, defeated. Dempsey sighed and paced the room to rein in the frustration. How did he make the mistake of hiring this man? Was his judgement slipping? He turned his back on the prisoner and took a swift tote from the vial in his pocket, feeling the liquid ease down his throat, and the tension begin to ease in his muscles.

'I am damned,' Charlton muttered.

'Yet, I come to help you.' Dempsey moved closer.

'Can you save me?' Charlton's head rose slowly to stare at Dempsey.

'I am no conjurer.'

Charlton shrugged his shoulders. 'You have helped others before, persuaded magistrates.'

'That was in London. I cannot reach them here.'

Charlton started to sob. 'I had hoped…'

'Forget hope of a reprieve. I talk of something else.' Dempsey crouched down so he was level with Charlton. The face of a doomed man stared back at him. It was time to explain what could be done. 'What of your family? How will they come out of this?'

'The priest will pay me for my story. I shall be writing it with him today. People like to read about highwaymen and killers. The money will go to my mother.'

'And what will your story say?'

'That I repent for everything I have done. I merely want this agony, the waiting, to stop.' Charlton looked across at Dempsey. 'If it were not for my family, I would want an infamous end. One that will be remembered for many years. But I cannot put them through that.'

'Who do you have?'

'Three younger brothers, all with no trade. A desperate mother. My life on the highways used to support them. Now, they will be reliant on the charity of their parish.'

'A father?'

'None that I remember.'

'Where?'

'Houghton Regis. It is near Dunstable.'

'I know it,' Dempsey nodded, and closed his eyes. He shook a distant memory away. It was time to throw the opportunity at Charlton. 'Would you like to provide for them? For when you are gone?'

'My story is the only way to do this. The priest tells me perhaps ten pounds if it is published in the local newssheets.'

'There is a way to secure much more. You will still hang, but it might aid your family's situation.'

'My case is lost. I only want to help them.'

Dempsey stood and smoothed his scalp, looking down on the prisoner.

'Your pride will not feed them. Nor will ten pounds for long.' Dempsey cleared his throat. 'You remember the death of Lord Malvern's nephew? During the robbery on Hampstead Heath two months ago?'

'It was not me.' An instant denial.

Dempsey pressed on. 'We don't know who it was. The coachman has no description and is not being bribed for his silence. Yet Lord Malvern grieves heavily.'

'It would have been an accident, the shooting.' Charlton sat upright and stared at Dempsey. His skin appeared almost transparent, the eyes empty and white. Time in prison could waste a man away. 'No man of the road would deliberately use a pistol,' Charlton continued, suddenly more animated. 'It is too loud, attracts attention. All we are concerned about is the loot and getting away.'

Dempsey fought back the temptation to tell Charlton otherwise. 'This Hampstead thing, we will probably never know who it was, unless they get drunk one night and loosen their tongue.'

'Unlikely,' Charlton agreed.

'Lord Malvern is willing to provide a significant reward for information on who the killer was.'

The pieces of the puzzle had come together when Dempsey heard that Charlton had been condemned. Charlton shrugged his shoulders again and slouched on the stool. He would need some prompting.

'His Lordship has offered a hundred pounds for the naming of the culprit.' The crumpled figure gave no indication of understanding yet. Dempsey continued. 'We name you as the killer. You have a record as a highwayman; you confess to both the Hampstead robbery and the murder of Malvern's nephew to the chaplain; it will be believed. You can make something good come of your situation.'

Charlton spoke, his eyes suddenly wet with tears. 'I am sorry I failed you again. I did my best.'

Dempsey shook his head. 'Focus on this. Your story would be worth more if this crime were added. And I give you my word, all the hundred pounds would go to your family. Not a penny for myself.'

'I would be admitting to something I did not do,' Charlton mumbled, turning to the window.

'They cannot hang you twice. Why not profit from confessing to a killing? Say the pistol went off by accident. Tell the chaplain and all will go on record. Lord Malvern will make repairs, and the money would go to your family. I will take care of it.'

'Lord Malvern has vouched for this?'

'He has.'

Charlton looked up. 'I know who the attacker was. Would that interest you?'

Dempsey sighed and curled his fists in his coat pockets, before taking a breath. 'You don't come to me with this information before?' He turned away to study the stone walls. 'You said you did not know.'

'What would you have done? Hang another of us?' Charlton chuckled. 'We are a band, us men of the road. We look after each other.'

'You have nobody to help now but your family. Think of them.'

After a period of silence, Charlton with his eyes closed, Dempsey still motionless and standing above him, the prisoner spoke. 'I shall do it. Promise me one thing, Dempsey.'

'Say it.'

'Do not recruit my brothers into your enterprise. They are innocents, they need to find their own honest way in this world.'

'If you confess to this, I swear I shall ensure they will be left alone.'

'Fetch the priest,' Charlton said, with a look of resignation. 'I have more to tell.'

38

Neff dropped his package to the floor. It groaned when it landed. He put a finger to his lips; there was no point in protesting until Dempsey arrived. Bennett was sitting on the other culprit, pinning him to the stone slabs. Neff pulled his coat about him and shivered. Water ran down the walls, and a rat dived in and out of a puddle.

The sound of boots on steps announced Dempsey's approach. Their boss gave them a nod when he appeared, and Neff and Bennett retreated to a corner.

'You two,' Dempsey began, pointing a finger at each prisoner in turn, 'are troubling. There is a warrant for your arrests. We will find witnesses to convict you. You know there are many who can be persuaded to testify to save their own skin.' Dempsey paused to clear his throat. 'I'm told you have lodgings in Barnard Street. And that you have somewhere else a hoard of gold watches, jewellery, valuable cloth.'

The two men looked at each other then back at Dempsey. Sawyer shook his head. His partner, Callard, nodded. Neff suppressed a laugh. They could not even coordinate their lies properly.

Dempsey leaned in closer to the couple on the floor. 'The old corrupt marshal turned a blind eye to your activities. His constables searched your lodgings more than once and found nothing. You see this made me suspicious. Because I did not know where you were hiding the goods either. We do not take kindly to thieves operating independently,' Dempsey said, his tone still patient. 'You know we are supposed to help you?'

The prisoners remained mute.

'Samuel Ashford suspected you of sabotaging his distillery on Tooley Street,' Dempsey added.

'That was not us.' Sawyer made to stand and rested on his haunches.

Dempsey walked slowly back and forth. 'I am more concerned with where you have hidden your goods. I have decided to make you a special case. This cellar is nothing compared to the conditions in Newgate, especially for those who are destined to hang. I have seen many men take their own lives, to spare themselves the pain of the noose.' Dempsey stopped the pacing. 'Tell me where your store is.'

The prisoners shared another look, one that Neff recognised, of two men who had worked together for some time. His attention was drawn to Dempsey feeling for something in a pocket. He pictured the sweating face of Collins, and his nodding acceptance of how to adjust the tinctures Dempsey was taking.

'You would receive payments for collaborating with us. They are small every time, but they oil the wheels of business. We keep many thieves like you out of the gaols.'

'Mister Dempsey.' Sawyer rose slowly to his feet and glanced at Callard. 'We respect you, but we are free men. We rob as and when we like, take opportunities when they come.

There is little planning.' He swallowed before continuing. 'As such, we answer to no one.'

Neff shook his head at their stupidity and shuffled uneasily. He stared at the puddle at his feet, catching his reflection. He looked older than he remembered. Maybe it was the filthy air of the cellar, playing with his senses. But perhaps, like Hatcher, there was a time limit on his usefulness. Neff stared at Bennett who returned the gesture, impassively.

Dempsey coughed, pulling Neff out of his reverie, folding his arms, and staring at the two men. Neff could sense the Thief Taker was fighting back the anger.

'No longer. This city hangs over thirty men a year now. I am paid to clean up the streets and I cannot stand for thieves like you not playing by the rules. What sort of example would that set to others? You must offer up a share every time.'

More silence as the two men stared at each other, then back at Dempsey.

Dempsey sighed. 'If you tell me where the goods are, one of you shall be picked up by a constable and be convicted; the other will be spared. If you refuse, you will both hang. A simple choice.'

Sawyer and Callard conferred in whispers. Callard's head dropped, and Sawyer spoke up.

'There is a store,' he began. 'In Bishopsgate, at the rear of the wainwright at the junction of Old Street.'

Dempsey turned to Neff. 'I shall go, I know where he means.' The Thief Taker pointed at the prisoners. 'I will let you decide which man is saved, and which goes to meet Jack Ketch. One of you will testify against the other and receive a pardon.'

Sawyer placed his hands together in a plea. 'Can't you

spare us both? We have told you where it is hidden. We will pay from now on.'

Dempsey shook his head. 'You are too late for that. Only one of you survives.' He beckoned to Neff and Bennett to follow him to the door, where he pulled out his pocket watch. Dempsey turned to address Sawyer and Callard. 'Make your choice by the time we return. You have an hour to decide who lives and who dies.'

Neff locked the door and joined his colleagues at the top of the steps. 'Wait here,' Dempsey directed. 'Bennett, come with me. We shall retrieve the goods.'

After watching them disappear into the shadows, Neff walked up and down Whitefriars. Avoiding the whores and the late-night hawkers, he kept the cellar entrance in sight. A pair of drunkards stumbled past him, shouting abuse. Neff shrugged off their stupidity, reminded of Hatcher. And of two graves hidden in the woods to the north. Victims of the fluid changes on the streets. He wondered at what it was that dictated who survived, and who got left behind. Or was forced to seek a new life elsewhere.

His patience was starting to wane by the time Dempsey emerged out of the darkness with a purposeful stride, followed by Bennett's unmistakable shape, some distance behind, scanning the street. Dempsey provided new instructions at the top of the steps, leaving Bennett outside. Neff had to hurry after his boss into the cellar, where Sawyer was leaning over the figure of Callard in a corner, blood pouring from his accomplice's nose.

'I wondered if you would settle it this way,' Dempsey said, as he neared them. 'An honest fight, was it?'

'What else were we to do?' Sawyer's face was lined with what Neff assumed was meant to look like regret.

'I thought you would hold out against us. Refuse to play the game.' Dempsey sounded surprised at the outcome.

'There is no point both of us going to the scaffold,' Sawyer said. 'You can provide a pardon for me?'

Dempsey coughed and once more tapped at his coat pocket. 'You have made the future clear.'

Neff walked over to inspect the blood on Callard's face, lifting his chin. There was no resistance or wincing at the touch. Sawyer probably thought he could break Callard out of gaol. Despite the grudging respect he felt for the bravery of their plan, orders were orders.

****

Neff and Bennett tossed the second body overboard into the Thames. They weighed it down to ensure it sank and had been forced to take them one at a time as they rowed out from a landing area by Temple Bar. Bennett had done the hard work with the oars on both trips, as Neff stared down the river into the night. The stench was eye watering. Nothing could live in there, on the surface or in the depths. It was a common dumping ground for waste. In parts, filthier than even the Fleet ditch.

As he felt the boat rise and fall gently, Neff swallowed back the nausea. He wondered whether Dempsey intended to kill both Sawyer and Callard all along. Playing games with the errant thieves seemed to be unnecessary, almost cruel. As he provided his instructions to Neff earlier in the street, Dempsey said it had been an experiment in what it would take for two men to turn on each other. As if betrayal was playing on his mind. Perhaps a form of madness was beginning to possess the Thief Taker. He had seen many officers lose their minds in the heat of battle. Decisions become random; lives lost for no reason.

After they took the boat back to the shore, Bennett and Neff went their separate ways. As he walked towards his lodgings, Neff paid a link lighter to show him the way. He swung his club about him casually, to stave off the attentions of any would-be thief. Image was everything, and his was an extension of Dempsey's. That of a provider of justice, delivering the authorities what they wanted, a belief that the streets were safe. But what if Dempsey was losing his sense of priorities, forgetting what had brought him to power in the first place, the belief of the people on the streets. How could he control them if he was unstable?

As he turned into the noisy piazza in Covent Garden and saw the mayhem of prostitutes and their customers cavorting openly, he was reminded of Emily and the choices she had made when they were young. Including following the man who everyone believed had freed their part of London from tyranny. Neff was certain she was still unaware of his own part in it, his sacrifice. Perhaps it was time to tell her the truth.

39

Dempsey led Emily Jarrett to a card table. The croupier, dressed in a plum-coloured suit and powdered wig that ran down past his shoulders, offered them a seat, eyeing her suspiciously. He glanced over at the club owner. Lord Malvern nodded in reply. Emily ran a hand down her dress, smiling at the men around her. One of them leered, another bared his jagged teeth. All bowed deeply.

'Gentleman, lady. We play Faro here. You know the rules?' the attendant asked.

'Miss Jarrett is playing. I have business to attend to,' Dempsey replied, easing Emily into a chair. The men resumed their seats.

'My father taught me, many years ago. Do explain it again,' Emily said, fanning herself. Dempsey smiled at the performance. She had set up the meeting for him and wanted to sample one of Malvern's better clubs. A rival to her new establishments, she said. Her businesses appeared to be flourishing. Dempsey no longer cared about the details, so long as the girls continued to deliver both stolen goods and information. He left her to join Gillard and Lord Malvern at a separate table, where three brandies were lined up.

'Do you use this place often, Lord Malvern?' Dempsey asked. The Diamond Club was the most exclusive gambling house in Westminster.

Malvern raised a noble eyebrow, and chuckled. 'I do play here when I can. I am a particular fan of the local entertainment.' He indicated three ladies sat in a corner, waiting to be introduced. Emily had already told Dempsey they worked for Elizabeth Manning, and that their charges were at the high end of the scale.

'Lord Malvern,' Dempsey said, flashing a quick glance at Gillard. 'I have something I need to discuss with you in private.' This was a potentially valuable ally. Malvern was rumoured to be about to take up a position in the War Office.

Malvern took a long drink and nodded at the marshal. 'Leave us to it. Go play one of your games.' The dismissal was accompanied by the wave of a heavily ringed hand.

Gillard frowned and dragged himself reluctantly from his chair. He walked over to the collection of ladies and placed an arm around one of them, staring back at Malvern and Dempsey.

'He likes to be involved,' Dempsey mused.

'He likes a lot of things,' Malvern said. 'He doesn't always get what he wants.'

Perhaps the politicians were controlling Gillard after all, rather than Kaplan, Dempsey assumed. 'Does he do as you tell him?'

Malvern looked blankly in reply. 'There is a way of things in Westminster. It does no harm to show men like Gillard where he stands.' Malvern took a drink, swilling it around his mouth. 'And to remind him this is not London.'

Dempsey leaned across the table and pointed at Emily. 'The lady, she will not be cheated?'

Malvern gave an obvious show of being shocked. 'We play honest tables here.'

Dempsey folded his hands together, trying to hide his own surprise. The rich did not stay rich in his experience by playing fair. 'You know in the city of London this pastime is growing,' he said with a hushed voice. 'With a broader class of gentleman.'

Malvern looked down his thin nose. 'One has to be a member to attend this club. You are only here tonight by my invitation. In relation to the matter in hand.'

'But what if this sort of entertainment were opened up to merchants and other respectable men? Even to ladies?' Dempsey asked.

'Not in Westminster,' Malvern smiled, looking at Emily. 'And certainly not to whores like that one.' Malvern gave a wink. 'Oh, I know exactly what she does, Mister Dempsey. Madam J has a reputation, a good one in her … field. She is an exception for this evening. What you do over in London is of no concern of mine.'

Dempsey doubted this were the case. Despite what happened to Middleton, the Aldermen continued to refuse his freedom of the city, and he suspected Parliament was putting pressure on them. He needed more allies to the west, and to test out what influence they had.

He returned to the subject of fair play. 'Surely, the house holds an edge?'

'This is not Spain, Mister Dempsey. We play by the rules.'

'I am thinking of opening a similar establishment in Covent Garden,' Dempsey said, remembering the expansion plans Emily had mentioned. He knew the thought of a woman, let alone one Malvern knew to be a madam running such a place, would appal him.

Malvern gave a low chuckle. 'Are you serious? I doubt these customers would travel that far simply to play.'

'Deadly serious. There is an appetite for more than cockfighting and bare-knuckle bouts to the east,' Dempsey said, studying Malvern, trying to gauge the interest. He seemed preoccupied with the contents of his brandy glass. 'Despite the Bubble, there is still some money about. This form of quality entertainment would be well received in new parts of London.'

'I fear you are asking for the worst kind to attend. You will need a strict membership policy.'

Dempsey knew exactly the sort of customers he would be interested in. Those that could be placed in compromising situations. Those he could cheat out of their money, with Ingram's help. Emily had no idea the man had been working for the Thief Taker for years, fleecing Kaplan under his nose. But he needed a different approach to work on men like Malvern.

'I think I have a way of insuring myself against loss,' Dempsey said. 'Importantly, I need to know how somebody might try to cheat.'

'I repeat, London is different to Westminster,' Lord Malvern scowled.

'People play here purely for fun?' Dempsey asked. The idea of not trying to win money seemed perverse.

'They do. And a gentleman gambler should allow the house the chance to win it back.'

'Do you not have men in debt to you?'

Malvern appeared to consider his reply, savouring his drink. 'Some. They tend to have benefactors, or a friend who can stand for their loss. Do you wish to participate this evening?'

Dempsey sipped at his brandy. It seemed stronger than he was used to. Perhaps Kaplan supplied the real stuff that far west. He considered his rival, and how easy it might be to lure him into a trap. What his weaknesses were. According to Neff and his investigations, expansion into Southwark was stretching his resources.

'Mister Dempsey?' Lord Malvern repeated.

Dempsey snapped back into the present. 'I gather Miss Jarrett is a keen player of cards. I leave it to her,' he said, smiling. They both looked over at the Faro table. Emily raised a hand in silent reply. The aim for her she said was to gather information on how the games were run, and how the dealers cheated. Dempsey smiled to himself. Ingram could tell her everything she needed to know.

Malvern's brandy glass was attended to again by the waiter. Dempsey took another mouthful from his own. A floral odour seemed to surround them in the room, so different from the alehouses of central London. He felt sharper than he had for some time. He tapped the vacant space where the vials normally sat in his breast pocket. The last time he visited the apothecary's store, there was no sign of the man or his wares. He felt strangely better for going without any of his tinctures. Perhaps Collins had been slowly poisoning him. At Kaplan's request.

'About our business,' Malvern said, changing the subject. 'I hear you have news for me.'

Dempsey held up his own drink, which the attendant reluctantly half filled with a scornful look. He waited for him to move out of earshot. 'I have found the man who killed your nephew, Lord Malvern. He has confessed it. He is a known highwayman.'

Malvern held his glass in mid-air and blinked slowly. There was a pause before the question. 'His name?'

'Charlton. He is to hang tomorrow.'

'That was quick,' Malvern said, eyes fixed on Dempsey.

'That is why I wanted to see you so urgently. He has an appointment with the Bristol hangman. The local chaplain heard his confessions of other crimes, and word reached me. This Charlton has described the scene on Hampstead Heath accurately, including what was taken. There is no doubt that this is the killer.'

Dempsey pulled the handwritten sheets out of his jacket pocket and placed them on the table. 'This is his confession.'

Lord Malvern put a shaky hand out to touch the papers. 'Is this for me?'

'I am a servant of justice, Your Lordship.'

Malvern read the first page, stopped, and closed his eyes. A tear ran down his cheek before he could suppress it with a handkerchief. Dempsey looked away to watch Emily at the card table. She appeared to be scrutinising the other players.

'Could we bring the case to court? For my sister, you understand,' Lord Malvern asked.

'The Bristol magistrates have made their decision on another matter, and he hangs in the morning. But we have a genuine confession,' Dempsey said, pointing at the material in front of them. 'We have your killer, my Lord.'

Swallowing hard, Malvern was barely above a whisper. 'I am indebted to you, Mister Dempsey. You are known for finding those responsible for certain crimes. I have discussed you with many people, and not all I heard was complementary. Even the King has an opinion, and not a particularly good one.' Dempsey tried to keep his face impassive. 'You are sure this is the man?' Malvern added. 'The one who killed Nathaniel?'

‘There is no doubt. It is here, in his own words.’ Dempsey pointed at the confession.

Malvern breathed out slowly, and stared across at Dempsey, his gaze fixed. ‘Very well. I shall have the two hundred pounds brought to you once we have confirmation he is dead.’

Raucous laughter broke out at the nearby card table, and both men turned to watch. Emily was pointing at a hand laid out in front of her. One gentleman rocked in his chair and cradled his head. Another scowled as a pile of markers were pushed in her direction.

‘Thank you, Mister Dempsey. I shall not forget this.’ Malvern picked the sheets up and folded them away inside his jacket. ‘I have learned a lesson today. To meet a man and judge him for myself, rather than rely on the gossip of others. Perhaps you are not the son of a devil they say you are.’

40

Neff checked his reflection in the window of a gin shop on Ludgate Hill, then switched his attention to his target. Across the street, the man he overheard asking for "Madam J" in a tavern in Bishop's Court kept his eyes on the path in front of him, dodging passers-by, seemingly focused on a destination. The incident had put Neff on alert. Everybody from the area knew where to find Emily Jarrett.

The man was moving at speed, frantically searching for something, his head bobbing as he examined door fronts. Was this one of Kaplan's men, Neff wondered. He dropped back into an alleyway to stay out of sight. His heart was pounding, even though he was now the hunter rather than the hunted. Memories of nights in hiding flashed into his mind, listening for the thunder of hooves that announced searching militia. He did not fear them anymore; London was a haven of anonymity.

A moll and her customer tripped over him in the alley. 'One at a time, doll,' she laughed, and led her client towards where a box had been propped up. She stepped onto it and raised her skirts to entertain the man in the way she knew best. Neff turned back to the street. His prey was close to the corner of Chalk Hill, and he resumed his pursuit. He could feel his muscles twitching, sensing danger. They switched in and out of a couple of passageways. There seemed to be more focus to the man's movements now. He halted outside an old tavern and checked the sign above the door, before barging his way in. Neff knew this was the Excelsior; the gambling venue Emily was trying to establish.

Neff waited outside, unsure what to do. Was he overreacting? It could be simply a customer, unsure where to find her. Madam J's reputation was widespread. Neff closed his eyes, picturing that young girl he once knew. The one who had helped both he and Dempsey to be released from gaol. She was a different person now, that opportunity had slipped from his grasp.

He looked up at the shutters. There were splinters in the wood, the paint was peeling off. The alehouse was at the end of a narrow alley, and the two sides of it appeared to be reaching out to touch each other above his head, closing off the natural light. This was going to be a significant undertaking and there was nothing he could offer. Dempsey was the one with the money, the financial security she craved virtue of his properties north of London. The Thief Taker was a more suitable supporter.

A woman's scream pierced the air, coming from above the tavern; then another. Neff ran in the front door and charged up the stairs, his breath coming in frantic bursts, following where the sounds seemed to be coming from. Women scattered in panic and slammed their doors. One man, dressed in just a pair of riding boots, emerged from a room, and scuttled back inside, fear etched on his face. As he reached the second floor, Neff saw the cause of the noise. The character who he had been following emerged from behind a door, with Emily's neck under his arm. Her eyes pleaded with Neff to help. No longer teasing, now desperate.

'Stay back. You don't want her to come to any harm,' the attacker panted, as he lunged to his right, dragging Emily with him along the corridor.

'James, do as he says,' Emily squealed.

She groaned as a punch hit her in the stomach. 'Shut it,' the assailant hissed, reaching into a pocket, and holding a knife to her throat. The blade was dark, covered in old blood, Neff imagined.

'Let her go. This is a dispute between men,' Neff shouted.

Emily struggled, and the man slapped her in the face. She went limp.

'You are a soldier, like me,' he said. 'I have orders.'

'To take a woman? What kind of a man are you?' Neff heard his voice rising.

'One who does as he is told.'

'Who are you working for?' There was no reply, only a cold stare. Neff looked at Emily and began to calculate. He continued more softly. 'You know there is no escape.'

The assailant loosened his hold on her a little, to point the knife in Neff's direction. 'Keep out of it.' The hand was shaking violently.

'Who orders this?' A strange feeling came over Neff, as if Emily were whispering in his ear. She appeared to be unconscious, but he could see her chest heaving. The attacker stared back in silence.

Neff was suddenly reminded of Hatcher, and the body he found on the riverbank with a blue flower crushed underneath it. How pointless many of their battles were, and the way commands to kill affected innocent lives.

The man grunted loudly, and Neff looked across to see a knife sticking out of the assailant's leg, just below the knee. With his grip on her loosened, Emily must have stabbed him. They were both now slumped on the floor. She tugged at the weapon, but it would not budge. The man cursed and leaned into a door next to her. Neff was transfixed, his limbs suddenly heavy. He stared at Emily, admiring the bravery, the fight of the woman. She was stronger than anyone he had ever met.

The attacker roared as he gathered himself and lashed out with his own blade into Emily's side. He thrust it in again, yelling with rage, then twisted it, leaving it in her stomach. Emily clutched at the metal embedded in her; it kept slipping in her hands. Blood poured onto her shirt and breeches, both turning from grey to red. The man grabbed at the weapon in his own leg, struggling to remove it, and fell back again.

Emily moaned and Neff jumped across to her, the weight lifted from him. He reached out and cradled her head, repeating her name. The eyes were closed, the face deathly white. He struggled to make out the words she mouthed. The landing of the old tavern, a place that was supposed to be the start of something new for her, was stained with her blood.

A yell from the assailant made Neff turn. His hands clawed hopelessly at the weapon in his leg. Neff rested Emily's head gently on the floor and shuffled towards him. The man's eyes opened, imploring Neff to remove the blade. He knew the agony he would be suffering, had seen it turn brave soldiers into desperate children, asking for their mothers. Neff ripped the knife out of the leg, twisting it as he did, for maximum pain. The assailant shrieked, as loud as any battle cry Neff had ever heard. But this was no soldier he recognised. Anger surged through him, and he reached over to whip the blade across the assailant's throat. A gaping chasm opened where the head joined the body, blood spewing out down his front. The gurgle that came was another reminder of muddy fields and pointless campaigns.

Neff cursed himself. He had been too slow to realise the plan to take Emily, to give chase and run up the stairs, to leap across the landing and save her. He begged Emily to breathe, to speak, to open her eyes. He promised her he would take her far away from London to a safer place. He grasped her body. It shook in his hands.

'I will have them for this,' Neff cried out. Whoever was responsible, Dempsey, Kaplan, the politicians, they would pay.

Emily's eyes opened slowly. There was the faint hint of a smile, then a tiny shake of her head.

'No more killing,' she whispered.

'I cannot…' Neff hesitated, captivated by the shine in her eyes.

'Promise me,' she said. 'It stops.'

Neff nodded, wondering if he could hold himself to it. Her eyes closed and he felt the last breath fall from her with a gentle sigh. She looked so peaceful. So much better than the pained expression she had often worn in life, he realised.

Neff crushed her to his breast, and looked at the blood on the floor, then back at the face that would never tease him again. All his life it seemed that death was routine. He did not know for certain who the attacker worked for, but it was probably Kaplan. Neff had not provided any information about the Excelsior; it must have come from elsewhere. He pulled at his hair tie, considering the recent coach journey, and whether Dempsey had boasted to his rival of the importance of the infamous Madam J to his success. Whether she had become an obvious target.

He sobbed into her shoulder, feeling the body growing cold. Remembering the whispered promise that he had just made, Neff wondered if he could honour it.

41

The fighter pulled himself to his feet as cheers echoed from the crowd. Men shuffled behind the barrels of straw that kept them back, looking for a better view of the raised platform in the warehouse on Chancery Lane. The smell of damp hay filled Dempsey's nostrils, reminding him of days sleeping beside the horses on the country roads, protected by the players. A time when he knew who to trust.

The air was thick with cursing and insults, disguised as encouragement for the two fighters. The champion, Henry Martin, threw a blow that knocked Parnell to the floor again. Martin had barely been touched in the ten minutes of the bout. His manager, Lampard, rubbed at the champion's shoulders, and a smile spread across his face. Dempsey moved around the edge of the arena to stand beside a wooden table, one of two in the warehouse taking bets. He put a hand on Forrest's shoulder and gave his instructions.

Forrest nodded and yelled out, 'evens on Martin.'

A trickle of men pulled away from the contest to attend Forrest's table. Parnell dragged himself to his feet.

'Even money here,' Forrest bellowed louder above the shouting. As the fighters stayed apart, the punters turned into a steady flow. Dempsey pulled away, watching Forrest's long loose hair bob as he wrote slowly and carefully. The ex-soldier's coat across his shoulders added to his bulk, lending him an air of solidity. It was not unknown for gamblers to contest results in places like this. Neff had assured Dempsey that Forrest could handle himself. This was a man who had been shackled by Ashford in the past. One who was glad to have been granted a licence to operate north of the river now, for a share of the revenue.

Dempsey moved around the room and caught the champion's eye when he was certain Lampard could not see him. He nodded deeply at Martin. There was a tiny shake of the head in reply, then a frown of realisation, before the fighter turned away.

Switching his attention to the challenger and his second, Dempsey noted the animated conversation between them, during the lull in the fight. Parnell wiped blood away from his cheek. The Irishman began jigging about, talking to himself, as if taken by a strange malady. They fought in strange ways, these gypsies. But they were entertaining. And entertainment was what the crowd came to see. That, and a fair fight. Parnell took a straight left from Martin and slumped down onto one knee. Martin stood over him, seemingly wavering. The crowd shouted for blood.

Dempsey positioned himself alongside the other bookmaker at the venue. Bennett loomed into view, partially blocking the line of sight to the ring. Lampard's man scratched his head, his forehead creasing. He would be conscious of the business being attracted by his rival. There was an unsuccessful attempt to catch Lampard's eye. The clerk raised himself up and shouted more generous odds on the challenger Parnell, to attract more business.

Giving Bennett his signal, Dempsey walked away into a neutral corner, the irritation starting to grow over the absence of James Neff. It was unlike him to miss a fist fight. An impromptu brawl began in front of Dempsey, three men among the crowd wrestling furiously, arms and legs tumbling in a frenzy, resulting in one sprawled on the floor unconscious. He studied them, shaking his head slightly.

Turning back at the sound of cheers behind him, Dempsey saw the Irishman drag himself up, shouting something in his own tongue. Out of the corner of his eye he also noticed Bennett slip a piece of paper into his pocket. Dempsey moved again, ensuring Martin could see him, adding another nod of confirmation. Martin held his fists out in front and swayed. Parnell charged towards the centre of the ring, then feinted to his left. The champion swung a punch that landed well short. The challenger resumed his attack, catching Martin with an uppercut to the jaw. He wobbled, then fell when he was struck again on the side of the head. The sound of a giant slumping to the floor was lost as groans rang out across the warehouse.

A small section of spectators then started to roar; a wild, ethereal noise. They were yelling for the champion to rise to his feet. Martin lay face down in the straw, his eyes closed. Dempsey studied Lampard; the realisation starting to dawn in his eyes. His position as manager was abandoned, as he ran to his bookmaker and conferred, then stared down at the ledger, and slammed it shut. The clerk looked up at Lampard, his face eatched with fear. Lampard knocked the man off his chair with one swing. The fight was technically still going on, but that book was taking no more bets.

Another shout prompted Dempsey to turn towards the centre of the ring. Parnell was standing over his prone opponent. The thirty seconds a fighter was allowed, to recover from hitting the floor or going down onto his knees, was over. The constable they had bribed to act as neutral referee, raised Parnell's hand aloft.

Dempsey motioned to Forrest to close his saddle bag, knowing almost every bet they had taken was for Henry Martin to win. Some of the crowd began to disperse, filing out into the street. Two women loitered by the door, hoisting up their skirts, looking for trade. Dempsey remembered they had been there throughout the fight, providing their own brand of entertainment. More of Emily's enterprising girls. Bennett nudged Dempsey, pointing to a procession of supporters who lifted Parnell onto their shoulders, and out through the door. Both the whores followed them. Dempsey glanced over at Martin, who was slumped in the centre of the ring, staring at the floor, pushing straw about with his foot. There was a little blood coming from a cut above his left eye, but no more than he would experience in a punch up outside a tavern.

Bennett led Dempsey to Lampard's table and handed over the chit. In a tidy hand, it read ten to one on the challenger. A wager any bookmaker would have to honour. Dempsey had heard tales of bouts years ago, which were regularly fixed. But these were modern times and fist fighting was supposedly more organised. There were clear champions now, and fewer surprises. Unless you had made plans yourself. This was a new venture for Dempsey, and one that thrilled him. Lampard had let down his guard.

'I hope you can pay this?' Dempsey asked, a polite enquiry as he waved the slip in front of him.

Lampard looked up with anger in his eyes, staring at his new creditor. 'I am a man you can trust.'

'You used to work for Ashford.'

'I am an honest man. I know what you did.' Lampard pointed at the former champion. 'Why do you make this your business?'

Dempsey smoothed his scalp with his hands, feeling the bumps and the scars. The calmness and clarity were returning. 'It appeared to be a good fight.'

'That was fixed.' Lampard stood, hands on hips.

Dempsey stifled a smile. 'Fixed? I know nothing of fighting unless you mean cockerels. I am merely a sporting spectator. My man here placed an honest bet.'

Lampard pointed a finger at Henry Martin and shouted across the warehouse. 'You were winning easily. What happened?'

'He got lucky. I think I hurt myself with a punch.' Martin wrung a fist. The timidity in his voice betrayed the stature of such a large man.

Dempsey eyed Lampard again. 'You are going to reward us for our luck, are you not?'

Lampard pulled himself up to his full height, over six foot. Dempsey imagined the ex-fighter wished he were twenty years younger, might have been able to deal with them all back then. He could have resolved the situation now if Martin were on his side. But Dempsey knew who Martin owed money to. Enough to control him.

Making a show of studying the piece of paper in front of him, Dempsey spoke. 'I reckon this means you owe us a hundred pounds, Lampard. I take it we can collect it now?'

Lampard stared once more at his clerk, with scalding eyes. The bookmaker consulted the floor. 'I don't have that amount here,' Lampard said. They knew that in the past, Lampard would have been able to cover any debt with Ashford's help.

'You don't? You see that puts me in a difficult position,' Dempsey glared. 'I have other enterprises to fund. That costs money. Money you owe me.'

'I will pay you back.' Lampard pulled his arms across his chest.

Dempsey looked about him, finally fixing his gaze on Lampard. He ripped up the chit and dropped it to the floor at his feet. 'I will cancel the bet. My man here placed it in error. So long as you do me a service. And remember how generous I have been today.'

Lampard's jaw dropped in initial confusion. Then there was a slight nod of the head, probably a realisation of what the true price might be.

'Cancel it?'

'Just return our stake. Then we can start off business on a better footing. Mister Martin will still work for you, but I will now take a quarter of his purse, the rest is between you and him. And of course, as you have shown that you cannot honour the payment of winning bets, you will turn over the gambling at your events exclusively to Forrest over there.' Dempsey pointed at the man in the opposite corner, hands clasped around a bulging saddle bag.

Lampard looked to be processing the offer. He scanned the warehouse, a place Dempsey knew he had built up through his own sweat and toil, probably his fists as well. But Ashford was no longer around for security. Surely, he would see that one investor was as good as another.

'Do I have a choice?' Lampard asked.

Dempsey ignored the question. 'Remember that you could be reported for running illegal sporting events. You know the courts are clamping down. I can ensure your business flourishes, so long as my man can hold the exclusive book for fights.'

Lampard nodded agreement, lifting his shoulders, and silently stared Dempsey in the eyes.

Dempsey continued. 'I'd like you to expand. You know the Temple Bar cockfighting pit?'

Lampard grunted. 'I know fist fighting better.'

'No matter. You draw good crowds here. You could run events there on Mondays. We can provide you with security. Ashford's old business is mine.'

Lampard grimaced. 'There is no other option, is there?'

'None.'

Bennett stepped forward and stretched out a hand to Lampard. 'Welcome to the company,' he said. Lampard shook it and held the pose. Something seemed to be shared by the two men in the connection, but Dempsey struggled to determine what. Had Bennett been involved in the fighting game somewhere in the past? It might explain his knowledge over which bout to target. Perhaps Lampard was also a former soldier. Dempsey shook the thought away and ran a finger round his collar. The warehouse was becoming hot and suffocating, and he was overcome with a desperate need to get outside. He tapped at his pocket and remembered the empty space, pulling a handkerchief out of his pocket and wiping sweat off his brow.

'Bennett will sort things out with you.' Dempsey turned to leave. As he reached the warehouse entrance, he noticed Bennett and Lampard deep in conversation. They looked across at him and Bennett offered him a salute. A reminder that it was good to have another man he could rely on, in such treacherous times.

42

1715

'We have an appointment,' William said, looking Torres in the eye.

The man chuckled, as if hearing an old joke, and shifted his considerable weight, before stepping aside. 'Careful. He is not in a good mood tonight.' Torres turned to James and nodded, who mirrored the gesture.

'Remember what we agreed,' William whispered.

'Of course.'

The door to the rear room of the pawnbrokers' store opened without a sound. William gestured to James to wait outside. Conway was sat in a leather chair, a cloth tucked into his neck, probably waiting for Torres to bring him his meal.

'Where is that fucking Jew?'

'He said it would be fine for me to have five minutes of your time. He is preparing the coffee.'

William walked slowly towards Conway, careful to

keep his hands in view. Conway pushed himself up out of the chair, sighing heavily.

'You are the bailiff?'

'That is one of my jobs.'

'I remember. There is talk of you. You and your friends have been housebreaking and not paying me your dues.'

William studied the figure in front of him. The hair was greasy, the skin pitted from some old disease, it was said. His clothes were baggy, but they needed to be to house such a large man. Conway lumbered across the room, peering at his visitor.

'We work hard. We plan our robberies well, are successful. So, we think you should re-consider. Perhaps we could keep everything we take.'

'Everything?' Conway roared. 'You know how things run round here. I licence your activities. The marshal does not know you work for him and rob at the same time. Imagine his reaction. No, half is the price for everyone.'

'We are better than that.'

Conway pointed a finger. 'You forget who is in charge. I have to wet my beak.'

William and his gang had been working the houses to the north of Soho and Mayfair for some time, extremely profitably. The rest of them were for giving in to Conway's demands. William had begged them to give him the chance to reason with the man who ran their part of London. The visit was his opportunity to seal the deal.

'We would work more eagerly if we kept more of the loot. Make you more in the long run.'

'Half!' Conway turned and slammed a fist into the wall. The room shook.

Sneaking a look at the door, William wondered if his friend was looking after Torres. Conway began to cough and stepped back in the direction of the chair, leaning on one of the arms. He took a sip of what looked like gin. By the time he turned around, William had pulled his knife out of his jacket, holding it out in front of him.

'Are you a fool?' Conway laughed, advancing. William felt his hand shaking, clutching at the blade. 'How did you get that in here? That Jew is supposed to search everyone.'

There was no point in revealing the truth. That everybody on the streets was suffering at Conway's hands. That something had to be done, either through talk or action. Torres was easily persuaded of the correct course. Emily Jarrett had ensured that.

William pulled the knife down by his side, hesitating. Now he was in the same room with the man, his courage was faltering.

'Sensible,' Conway muttered. Then he charged at William, with a roar that took him by surprise. Conway launched himself at the hand holding the knife, and it slipped from his grasp, bouncing on the stone floor. William's feet went from underneath him, as Conway pushed him into the wall. They wrestled, but Conway was larger, stronger. William felt himself pinned above the fireplace.

Conway grabbed at William's face, forcing a hand into his mouth, fingers in his eyes. Pain seared through him. He tried to bite the hand, but slipped down, towards the hearth. His hair and then the side of his face felt the heat of the embers, the smell of ash and burning flesh filled his nostrils. William tried to push back, easing Conway off him slightly. He could hear Conway panting, the face contorted above him in an ugly shape with the effort. It felt like he was suspended inches above the ashes of the fire. Then, as quickly as Conway had attacked him, the grip slipped and William wrenched himself away, hitting his head on the wall behind. There was blood at his feet, forming an ugly purple pool, but he sensed it was not his own. It came from Conway's neck, his head had been twisted to one side, the throat cut.

William looked up to see James standing above him, a knife in his hand. Blood dripped from its blade. Conway's lifeless body slumped onto the hearth, which sizzled where the skin met the coals. A position William had been so close to being in moments before.

Wiping the sweat out of his eyes, William pulled himself up to his feet. His throat was tight, breathing in short gasps. He touched the side of his face, and the agony returned. The smell of burning and death filled the room. James stepped back and sank into the large chair where Conway made his deliberations, choosing who lived and who died, how much money people handed over.

'James, thank you,' William croaked. He looked down at Conway's body, and suddenly felt the clarity. Of the future, and how it could map out.

His friend looked frozen, as if the exertion had stopped his body from functioning. William moved over to him and prized the knife from his hand. 'Let me.'

A noise from the door made him turn. Torres appeared, scanning the room quickly. His eyes took in the dead figure in the fire, and the two visitors arranged around it. A quick calculation, William assumed. One where the Jew could see a future released from chains.

'Let us tidy this up,' Torres said, his voice a whisper.

Torres and William laid the body out in front of the hearth.

'A terrible accident,' Torres mumbled. 'You agree?'

William nodded. James remained in the chair. He was the one who had been decisive, possibly saved his life, but not without its consequences. Eventually, they managed to steer James into the street, leaving the body behind. They walked him to his lodgings and laid him in his bed. Neither William nor Torres returned to the pawnbrokers' store.

After staying hidden for two days, avoiding his usual taverns and haunts, the next time Dempsey ventured down the Strand in the direction of Newgate, he was stopped by two passers-by who shook his hand. 'Thank you for what you have done,' one of them said. 'We are free now.' They explained they were merchants. They would no longer be paying their dues to Conway. One offered Dempsey five guineas, which he refused.

On crossing the street, three men steered away from him, slipping into the mud of the gutter. They looked at their feet, avoiding his gaze. Dempsey felt the side of his face, where the scars still ran. When he caught sight of his reflection, Dempsey was reminded of stories Luce used to tease him with, of disfigured men that haunted little children. His hair had already been shaved off, with the help of his only visitor, Torres.

The rest of his walk that day included the same mixture of appreciation and deference. By the time he had reached the gaol to resume his duties of moving prisoners from there to the court and back for trial, his presence was noted in some way by most people. He received a simple nod from the gaol warder when he arrived, no mention of the fact he had been absent, or comment about his injuries. Dempsey cast his eye across the prisoners in the gaol as he moved in and out of the cells. Here, everybody steered a path away from him.

Later, Dempsey visited Neff's lodgings only to be met with an angry landlady.

'He has scarpered. I never trusted him. He kept all sorts of hours.'

'No word of where he is?'

'My son said he ran off to enlist, feared for his life. He owes me ten shillings, the shit.'

Dempsey handed over what she was due and returned to the warder's office, where he was asked to sit down. Given a drink, something that had never happened before.

'We are all indebted to you,' the warder said, his eyes averted.

'To me?'

There was a thin smile. 'Everyone knows what you have done. You have spared us all. The people of this part of London will never forget.'

Dempsey sipped at his gin in silence.

'You killed Conway. Everyone whispers it. Do not worry, the authorities are happy. You have done them a favour. No constable will want to take you in for ridding us of that bastard.'

43

Neff checked the message in his pocket and carefully eased open the back door to the brandy shop. This was White Alley, the wrong side of the Tower, deep inside enemy territory to the east. As he entered two figures pushed him against a wall, searching his pockets. The stolen knife was extracted. Neff tried to appear surprised, but the men stared blankly. Letting him go, one of them flicked his head, indicating a door the other side of the stockroom. They then leaned against the rear exit, blocking his escape.

Neff opened the door out into the main shop itself. Kaplan turned to face him as he walked in, standing by a table where two glasses and a bottle were set.

'You came.' Kaplan's voice sounded dry, as if he was about to choke. A fire crackled in the hearth, throwing off welcome warmth. The place reeked of brandy and woodsmoke.

Neff walked around the room, taking a seat on the other side of the table, with his back to the wall. 'We needed to meet.'

'You have something for me?' Kaplan eased himself down opposite Neff and raised his glass, a gesture Neff mirrored. Both men drank down their brandy and Neff felt the liquid burn his throat. This must have been a quality bottle, imported from Flanders or France. Previous enemies on the battlefield. The lines between allies and foes could be murky, he mused.

Neff stroked his long hair and pulled it back in its tie behind his head. Conscious his moves were being watched; he carefully placed his hands on the table to calm his host. Kaplan was dressed all in black, sported no wig, and scratched at his tight dark curls.

'The organisation I work for is rotten,' Neff began.

'William Dempsey not the saviour he thinks he is?' Kaplan refilled the glasses, a rueful smile etched on his face.

'It is complicated.' Neff concentrated on showing how difficult it was to become a traitor.

'It is just you and me here,' Kaplan said, baring his yellow teeth.

Neff looked around the tables. It was unusual to see such a place devoid of customers in the morning. Neff felt the draught reach him from a nearby window and stared out at the quiet street. Sweat trickled slowly down his back, as he shuffled in the chair.

'Obviously, Dempsey must never know I am here,' he said.

'He has eyes in many places, but not here.'

Neff had carefully wound his way through the streets; he did not want any loose tongues to report back on this meeting.

'Dempsey is rotten?' Kaplan probed, toying with his glass.

Neff tried to control his breathing. 'Things have changed since Renshaw and Ashford.'

'They have. Southwark is coming to me.' Kaplan leaned forward, elbows on the surface between them. 'What concerns me is Dempsey moving in this direction, to the east. He has upset some of my people, the pawnbrokers, the innkeepers.

He upsets a lot of people.' Kaplan stared, his eyes seemed cold and clear. 'I just want to protect what I have. I have no desires for his territory. He should respect me and stay his side of Newgate.'

'Dempsey has the whores in his pocket. They are central to his work,' Neff said. 'The madams answer to him.'

'He can keep them.' Kaplan dismissed the concern with a wave of his hand. Neff checked the face opposite. There did not seem to be a flicker of a confession. Of ordering the murder of Emily Jarrett.

'Him controlling the madams does not concern you?'

'No.' Again, no sign of recognition.

'And the crossings?' Neff asked, changing the subject.

'What of them?' Kaplan replied. Now the man was staring at the wall impassively, at paintings of battle scenes. Neff wondered why they were celebrated so much. He pulled himself back into the conversation, fixing on the man opposite.

'Dempsey is anxious about them.'

'London Bridge is mine.' Kaplan paused and Neff sipped at his drink, looking away. 'You know his time is running out.'

'You have a plan?'

Kaplan shook his head, then put a finger to his lips. 'You do not work for me yet. You ask a lot of questions.'

The smell of brandy wafted towards Neff again as Kaplan poured out more.

'I ask because I need to know where I will stand when I help you against him. If I help you. And what I might get from the deal.' Neff checked the face opposite. 'I mean, do I need to work for you? I am my own man. We could work together.'

'I still need to understand why you contemplate treachery,' Kaplan countered. 'You are an ex-soldier, and soldiers are loyal.

That is not what you show me today. I wonder at whether this is some sort of trick.'

Neff shook his head, unsurprised. 'I cannot trust Dempsey now. Hatcher's body lies at the bottom of the Thames. Dempsey discovered he was this Alley Killer and removed him.'

Kaplan whistled. 'Hatcher killed those whores?'

Neff nodded. 'Dempsey dropped him without a second thought. All of us are dispensable, and I will be next.'

'Hatcher was a vicious opponent. I wondered what happened to him.'

'You do not read the newssheets?' Neff asked. Kaplan gave no impression that he did. 'I do not intend to go the same way. If I am anything, it is resourceful. I know my value.'

'What are you proposing?' That sneering smile was there again.

Neff shrugged, no intention of committing too eagerly. 'It would help a lot of people in London, not to mention Westminster, if he were to lose his power.'

'The politicians have had enough of him and his influence,' Kaplan said. 'They say he had an Alderman killed. You know anything about that?'

Neff shook his head. He was not there; he did not know the details. Even Bennett was tight-lipped about it.

'People like Dempsey and me are the wrong sort for them,' Kaplan continued, screwing up his face as if he had tasted something unpleasant. 'They will pass us scraps, but Parliament will never grant us what we deserve. So, we must forge our own way, enough to have a good life.'

Neff took a drink and lowered his voice, despite them being the only people in the shop. 'Dempsey is making strange decisions.' Neff paused to let Kaplan consider his analysis. What he was saying was true. The repeated image of Dempsey reaching into his pocket and taking a nip from his tincture returned. 'He kept order through disciplined crime.' Neff hesitated again to show a conflicted man. 'But discipline is difficult if you are not in control of your own mind. Dempsey serves a purpose for the authorities, but things may change, and I do not want to be stuck in the middle when they do.'

'You are a selfish man, after all, James Neff.'

'We all are at heart.'

Kaplan emptied the bottle into their glasses and took another hearty swig. Neff was not used to drinking this early in the day, nor the fine taste. He played with his brandy, exercising caution. There were stories of men being drugged and never seen again. Kaplan had been duped before by the move. It was time to stop edging around the issue.

'I can help you bring him down,' Neff said. 'Dempsey likes routine, the same coffeehouses and taverns. It is now me or Bennett at his side. It would be easy for us to look the other way.' Neff sat up straight to deliver a vital element to maintain his credibility. 'But I will not raise a hand against him myself, that must be you.'

'Bennett would stand against him too?'

'He will be distracted when it matters.'

Kaplan nodded. 'I understand. You would need to lure Dempsey over to the east side.'

Neff shook his head. 'That would point the finger clearly at your door. This new marshal would come after you.'

Kaplan's eyebrows rose in surprise. 'I thought Dempsey had him in his pocket?' Perhaps Kaplan was not controlling Gillard after all.

'He aimed to,' Neff said, searching the room again. He thought he sensed movement outside the window and stared in that direction but saw nothing, so turned back to Kaplan. 'But Gillard's mind is shaped by the politicians and allies of the King. Gillard is not as supportive of Dempsey as he hoped.'

Kaplan sat back in his chair. Neff wondered how convincing he was coming across. The eyes opposite seemed to be exploring him, burning into his skull.

'Why not simply remove this Gillard if he is the problem?' Kaplan asked.

Neff searched for clues in Kaplan's face. Nothing came back, other than a blank stare. 'Two dead marshals in quick succession would draw unwanted attention,' Neff said. 'It might prompt them to organise the constables themselves or create their own militia. A specialist force to move against criminals. Dempsey mentioned this before. Nobody wants that.'

'No,' Kaplan agreed. 'But with the Thief Taker gone, I presume you wish to take over?' Neff felt the heat in his cheeks rise and took a drink to compose himself. It was a game, and they were jousting, both looking for the truth, selling their own versions of it.

'I have my own ambitions,' was all Neff offered after a short delay.

Kaplan leaned forward and shook an empty glass in Neff's face. 'If you are testing me out, I warn you, I will not forget betrayal.'

'Nobody forgets betrayal,' Neff said promptly.

'You offer me information on when I can strike at him. You are disloyal.'

Neff held Kaplan's gaze. 'My only loyalty is to myself.'

'And if I remove Dempsey, what is the reward for me?'

Neff shrugged. 'We could work together, a better partnership.' The words came out easily. Neff had thought about them much recently. Perhaps he had convinced himself they were true and could be delivered on. 'I am not as greedy as Dempsey. I have no interest in thief taking. One day he will run out of allies doing that. There will be nothing left but wronged enemies and then Parliament will crush him.'

'You would give up the napping?' Kaplan asked. There was no surprise in his voice.

Neff stared back. 'I would. It is increasingly dangerous. Dempsey has lost his sense of morality, trading men like meat. He has little regard for the code that you and I live by, and plays us all against each other, I see it every day.' Neff shook his head, realising he believed the words. 'I cannot take this way of living any more. Remember, I killed for my country. I prefer… certainty.'

Kaplan stood suddenly and offered a handshake. 'I will think on it and make enquiries. Dempsey is not the only one with eyes all over London. Tread carefully if you move against me.'

After walking to the front door of the brandy shop, Kaplan paused, then knocked. Three men entered and escorted him outside, different from those who had searched Neff earlier. Kaplan was well protected, and gave no indication he knew about Emily's death.

Sat at the table finishing his brandy, Neff went back over the conversation and questioned whether Kaplan would act. With Dempsey gone, could he move the organisation in a new direction? Emily had hinted that there was a different way forward, without the need for violence. Although she had not seen what he had seen, things might play out in his favour. From the middle, he might be able to manipulate the pieces where he wanted them. He had learned much from Dempsey over the years. Neff stared at his empty glass and took in his reflection. The image shining back made him blink. The look of treason.

44

The hunched figure of Gillard was impossible to miss, under a tree, far apart from the crowds in St James's Park. He was dressed in an elaborate greatcoat, a large, powdered wig perched on his head. A peacock. Dempsey wondered if he was a secret Jacobite. The Thief Taker stroked his scalp as he approached, emphasising the contrast between them. He had no need for extravagant attire. Men were defined by their actions, not their clothing.

He offered a handshake as he approached the marshal and held the grip for longer than normal, wanting Gillard to be reassured.

'Good of you to see me,' Dempsey began.

'Why here?' Gillard asked. 'Is this about Parliament? Or the King?'

Dempsey wondered what Gillard suspected. 'They don't concern you too?'

Gillard looked out across the park, to where spectators were massing along The Mall and nodded in their direction. He seemed to ignore the question. 'The King is coming,' he muttered.

Dempsey examined the gathering crush of people in front of them. A mixture of the well-dressed and the unwashed surged towards the wide pathway where the King was due to travel. A procession of horses led the way, and he could make out the royal coach in the distance. The crowd was already five or six deep in places.

'Shall we join them?' Dempsey asked.

'Must we?'

'The King is a rare sight these days.'

'He prefers the country. He must have business with Walpole today.'

Dempsey led Gillard in the direction of the throng. As they reached the edge, the jostling began, many eager to get a closer look. Gillard stumbled, then regained his balance, and pulled his wig straight. There were so many questions Dempsey wanted to ask, but he doubted the marshal would answer them directly. The mystery of who had funded his position was one of them. There was a plan in place to discover the truth.

Pulling his hands out of his pockets to maintain his balance among the crowd, Dempsey kept an eye on Gillard. He tried hard to avoid the picture that Emily had painted for him as they walked away from the Diamond Club, of a man tied to a bed being beaten by a young girl. They settled at the rear of the gathering and Dempsey relaxed, comfortable they were not being overheard.

'Ashford's death was unfortunate,' Gillard said. 'I had hoped to watch him hang.'

'You did a fine job in court I heard.' There was no harm in flattery.

'The witnesses stuck to their story. I'm sure you had something to do with it.'

'I have no idea what you mean,' Dempsey smiled, turning away to watch the crowds. All their eyes were on the coach and its entourage. 'He made a mistake, thinking he could escape so easily.'

'The Aldermen were not amused at his premature death. Or that of Sir Howard Middleton. That had nothing to do with you?'

'What an accusation, marshal.'

'And yet you have not apprehended anyone for his murder.'

'There are a number of housebreakers I could bring in, if you want a culprit,' Dempsey said lightly. He had decided to let the matter lie unsolved, for now.

'They suspect you are to blame.'

'Anyone in particular?' Dempsey studied Gillard from the side. There was a strange smirk on his face, and not one caused by his deformity.

'I heard Justice Gregory wanted to issue a warrant for your arrest.'

'On what evidence?'

'Well, obviously there is none. But…' Gillard paused and half-turned to view Dempsey. His breath caused Dempsey to pull out a handkerchief and emit a small cough.

'The King is also concerned,' Gillard added, nodding in the direction of the approaching coach.

'Why would he care?' Were they all after him? Had they forgotten the important service he performed?

'He keeps a closer eye on crime than you might imagine,' Gillard said. 'I have met him a couple of times.'

There was a grin on Gillard's face, one Dempsey would have loved to remove. Patience, he thought to himself.

'And what about Tindall? I had expected to see him here,' Dempsey asked, trying to sound vague and disinterested. Conscious there was deceit and treachery everywhere.

Gillard shook his head quickly. 'He is still detained in Chester gaol.'

He could be dead within the week, Dempsey thought, keeping it to himself. No sense letting Gillard know everything about his reach.

'With Ashford gone, there will be no opposition to the bridge over the Thames at Westminster. Surely Parliament is happy with that. I have done them a service.'

'By killing Ashford?' Gillard asked out of the side of his crooked mouth.

'An accident, as you well know.'

Gillard waved to somebody in the distance. Dempsey squinted but could not see anyone returning the gesture. He fixed his attention on the upstart marshal. A man seemingly reluctant to discuss how things might change in the future with two of his rivals gone. It was time to test Gillard's knowledge in another area.

'You seem well connected in Westminster, despite your new office,' Dempsey said.

Gillard shrugged. His wig wobbled, prompting a hand to shoot up to balance it. 'I understand the nobility and the politicians. You saw what happened with the South Sea Bubble. That was just a fraction of it, what came out. Bribery is commonplace. Westminster is a murky place.'

Dempsey pondered the difference between the two cities, so close together. They were bordered all the way from Soho down to the river near Charing Cross. Things were less complicated his side, with no politicians involved. You knew where you were with whores, thieves, innkeepers, drinkers, and gamblers.

The crowd began to envelop them as it swelled in size. Dempsey lifted himself up onto his toes, straining to his right, and spotted the royal carriage approaching.

Gillard nudged him. 'You would never consider striking out against the King, would you?'

'Of course not. He is German, but…'

'There are some in Parliament who would welcome it.'

'You talk of treason, marshal. Do not include me in it.' Dempsey had many enemies and did not need to become embroiled in any political plot.

The jostling around them intensified, and Gillard's face wrinkled with disgust, pushing at the man in front of him, knocking off a long, dark wig. The figure scrambled for it, then wedged it back on his head, and was pulled away from them in the flow. Cheers rose as the procession neared, and Dempsey sensed a tightness coming in his throat. He tapped at his coat and felt the reassurance of the pouch within it. Collins had disappeared, but Bennett had broken into the apothecary's old backroom and removed the contents of the safe without raising an eyebrow. He was fast giving up on the idea of being able to live without it.

'How can we stop Kaplan taking Southwark?' Dempsey asked, raising his voice a little above the noise of the crowd, pulling Gillard to one side.

'You sound keen to stop him.'

'I want things to stay balanced. Nobody should control too much. Especially Kaplan.'

Gillard shook his head. 'But what would you want in return? They will not give you a foothold in Westminster, Walpole would not allow it. They passed legislation to rein you in, they are not impressed by your antics.'

'I deliver justice,' Dempsey countered. 'Politicians say they worry about crime, but I am more concerned with Londoners, the shopkeepers and the merchants, than Parliament. I help protect the people on the streets.'

'And you believe this, do you?'

'It is how things are.'

Dempsey stared at Gillard. 'What happened to your goal of removing the criminal leaders? You were all for it with Ashford. Why is Kaplan different?'

Gillard shrugged again and his wig tilted to an uncomfortable looking angle. He pushed it back into place. The lip curled into that snarl.

'So, Kaplan is working with Parliament,' Dempsey said quietly. Gillard gave no indication of having heard his words. The bastard Kaplan was trying to squeeze him out.

The King's carriage passed twenty feet in front of them. Dempsey felt himself being jostled and pushed back against pressing spectators. He was pinned from all sides. He pictured the layout of London, and his enemies doing the same to him.

Dempsey raised his voice, scanning the crowd. 'Do not come asking for help when Kaplan encroaches over the water and starts to nibble away at Westminster.'

'I won't...,' Gillard began, before shooting Dempsey a sharp look. A pause followed, then a shout as he pointed to their left. 'Hey, stop that boy. Stop, thief.' The throng surged to follow the coach along The Mall. 'My watch,' he yelled, tapping at his chest, then pointing in the direction of the procession. 'He has it. Thief!'

Dempsey watched Gillard go, and turned against the flow of the crowd, striding in the direction of Whitehall.

****

Dempsey settled at a table close to the coffeehouse hearth. The acrid aroma mixed with the smoke made his throat itch.

Customers were huddled on benches along both walls of the establishment on Northumberland Avenue. He ordered his drink and warmed his hands by the crackling fire.

After the owner brought his cup over, a small figure bustled in and moved towards him. 'You took your time,' Dempsey said. 'Sit down.'

The boy shuffled onto the chair opposite. Dempsey surveyed the room; there were no recognisable faces.

'You weren't followed?'

'Of course not.'

'Hand it over,' Dempsey demanded.

The lad pulled a worn pocketbook out of his jacket and passed it across the table.

'It is definitely his?' Dempsey asked, opening it up. There were bank notes, messages, folded sheets, letters: Gillard's life in his hands.

'Yeah, the one you was talking to.'

'And he didn't come after you?'

'Nah, the misdirection worked. Alfie got away, too.'

'Hatcher taught you well.'

'We was good already,' the boy replied with a smirk.

'Not good enough to stay out of gaol.'

The boy shrugged and laughed.

'Anything else?' Dempsey asked.

'Got his pocket watch.' It was held out across the table.

Dempsey scanned the coffeehouse again. There was little noise other than the low hum of gossip and the crackle of the fire. Nobody seemed to be taking notice of them.

'You keep that. And here's your six shillings. Make sure you share it between the two of you. I will check that you do.'

The boy grabbed at the coins. 'The watch was easy,' he said. 'I'll be off, then.'

Reaching across the table, Dempsey lifted him up by the ear, twisted, then dropped the figure down. The lad cried out, rubbing at where he had been held.

'Hand it over,' Dempsey demanded.

'What do you mean?'

Dempsey grabbed him by the collar. 'Hand it over, or you will be in Newgate.' He let go.

The boy slumped back in the seat, pulling Dempsey's timepiece out of his jacket, and dropped it on the table. Then added the leather pouch.

Dempsey pointed his finger. 'You're good, but don't ever try it on me again. I catch you taking something I don't approve of; you'll be swinging from the rope. Understand?'

'Yes, Mister Dempsey. I get it.'

Dempsey shooed the boy away. Hatcher had put some fight into them. The man would be on his way to Virginia by now. It was impossible for Daniel to continue in his organisation after what they discovered. Bennett was an able and suitably vicious replacement. More reinforcements to supplement the Engineers were coming. He was going to need them.

Emptying the contents of a vial into his coffee, Dempsey stirred it in. This batch did not seem to be helping so well. Dark figures were following him in the street, seeming to disappear when he looked round at them. He needed the potions to get through the times when the blackness would descend, and the image of a dead body rising from a roadside haunted him, casting shadows everywhere he went.

Dempsey leafed through the stolen pocketbook more carefully. There were letters addressed to Gillard, but none seemed to be from Kaplan, or even Walpole. Perhaps the marshal was exaggerating his importance, and his contacts. Croker would find evidence of Gillard's treachery somewhere within them. In time, a faceless messenger would return the pocketbook to Gillard's address, for no reward. The marshal could afford another watch.

45

Neff followed Dempsey across London Bridge, into Southwark; a place of renewed anarchy, according to talk in the taverns. Marshalsea prison jutted out into the street at Borough, a two-floored structure that had stood there since before the domestic war. The walls were a filthy grey, matching the adjoining shop fronts. As with north of the river, gaols sat side by side with everyday life. The grim stench of rotting meat and stale alcohol was familiar, even if the surroundings were not.

They were led into the gaol by a guard who nodded at Dempsey in what Neff took to be recognition. His boss paused to whisper. 'We shall see the result of my test. An examination of human nature, and how we can take advantage of it. The need to survive, above all else.'

Dempsey scratched at his bare scalp, his eyes wide, staring ahead. There was a nervous energy about him, which made Neff hold back from questioning why they were at such an infamous gaol. One that Neff thought was outside of Dempsey's control. Three whores asked for trade at the entrance, and the image of Emily returned. There had been no talk about her death between them, no desire to push for revenge from the Thief Taker. Perhaps it was guilt that was holding him back.

He studied the frantic movements of his boss in front. Collins had been moved to new premises to keep him safe. Judging by Dempsey's agitation, Bennett had found the potions that had been left behind and passed them on. The apothecary had promised the tinctures would make Dempsey easier to control.

They waited for the warder to greet them. 'I have the freedom to come and go as I please,' Dempsey said with hushed tones. 'This man runs the enterprise as he wishes. Ashford used to insist on half his income; I only ask for twenty percent.' Neff recognised the sense in the policy: not to overtax those further down the chain; it was more important to keep them loyal.

Neff scanned the gaol entrance area and noted what looked like a small coffeehouse, within the confines of the Marshalsea. There were tables, even a couple of women serving customers. An inmate dressed in ragged overalls absent-mindedly wiped down the tables. Through a window Neff could see a garden being tended to by what he assumed were other prisoners. This was a different type of prison to Newgate.

Dempsey caught him staring at the workers. 'It is a modern arrangement,' he said. 'Gaols can turn a profit these days. It only takes a little imagination.'

Neff looked up as the warder offered his boss a handshake. 'Good to see you again, Mister Dempsey.'

'You have the winners?' Dempsey asked him immediately. Neff looked away in the direction of the coffeehouse, to hide his surprise. When he turned back, the warder released his grip.

'They are in the holding cell, away from the rest.'

'Show me.'

They were led into a large stone-walled chamber with several entrances off it. It reminded Neff of an army prison he had seen once, where they kept mutineers. He pulled his coat around him against the cold, and had to lean against a wall for support, unseen by the men in front. The warder unlocked a cell door in the corner. Inside, three men were slumped in a heap. One jumped up and raised his fists, looking at his fellow captives, then sat down again. The others remained unmoved.

The warder paused on the threshold. 'Two of them died. Another three probably will any day, we have them elsewhere. These are the ones that made it.'

Neff stared at the bloodied survivors, men he assumed were the outcome of Dempsey's experiment.

Dempsey leaned in to whisper to Neff, a crooked smile on his face. 'We locked eight men in a room and told them to fight it out. Only the three that were left standing at the end would be released.' Dempsey shared a look with the warder and turned back to Neff. 'There were no rules. If any died, they would be buried. Any injured, thrown back into the common hole. This way we get the strongest for the Engineers and the warder reduces his numbers. It can cost much to feed a hungry prisoner, even on the common side.'

Neff studied the lines under his boss's eyes in the weak light of the cell. Despite the animation in his movements, it looked like Dempsey had not slept for days. The face was dark, as if he was made up for a macabre stage show. Testing men out to see if the strongest survived. It was a strange way to do business. Perhaps the Thief Taker really was losing his way.

Neff scrutinised the prisoners. They stayed crouched in

the corner, shoeless, their filthy clothes in tatters, scabbed and bruised, battle-scarred men. They reminded him of broken soldiers. He did not want to see the losers if these were the winners.

'Have them delivered to my warehouse on Bedford Street,' Dempsey said, turning to the warder at the door. 'They can go over the bridge in a cart, at night. I don't want the good folk of London to be scared by the sight of them.'

'As you wish. You have the er…' the warder began. Dempsey pulled a bag out of his waistcoat; what sounded like coins. He handed them over.

'They know what they are going to do?' Dempsey asked.

'They know they will be working for you. And they knew the stakes at the start. It was this or…'

Dempsey looked at Neff and seemed to note his anguish. 'James, we must be prepared. Bennett will not be enough to replace Hatcher, not if we expand our businesses to the east side, and over here in Southwark. We need more manpower. You will have three resilient new recruits for the Engineers.'

Neff wondered at the mental states of the survivors after their ordeal. Where would their loyalty stem from? This solution was short-term. There would be resentment among them, Neff assumed. How could Dempsey think this would work? Neff pulled at the tie that kept his hair in place, feeling something clawing at him. Did he have the right to question? With what he had already been considering? He pictured the distant back room of a pawnbrokers' store, blood on the floor and a body in the fire, a knife in his bloody hand. He earned the right years ago, had not truly realised it until now.

Neff followed his boss out of the Marshalsea and savoured the fresher air. The stench of the street was still there, but at least outside the prison there were occasional pockets that were breathable. Dempsey had a renewed purpose to his stride, as if something was pushing him on and into action. Neff decided he needed to visit Collins. Perhaps someone else had a hold over him.

They reached the ferry where Clink Street dropped down to the river, and Neff wondered at why they were returning to the north side by a different route. Decisions seemed to be becoming increasingly erratic. He watched Dempsey sit upright at the rear of the boat as a familiar figure rowed them across. It was the final ferryman to succumb to their demands who worked the oars, and there was no hint of recognition in Neff's direction.

But there was one issue he needed to press Dempsey on. Something that had to be discussed. Neff did not care if the ferryman heard. 'Do you think Kaplan had Emily killed?'

Dempsey gazed into the distance down the river, seemingly miles away in thought.

'Are we not going to do something about him?'

'We are gathering our forces. He dare not attack us.'

'But what about Emily?' Neff swallowed hard, could hear the pain in his voice.

Dempsey suddenly stared across at him, his eyes wide. 'We have to think about the future.'

'Have you forgotten what she did for you? How she helped you?' Where was the rage, Neff wondered? Did he not want to strike back?

'James, you've got to trust me. There is a bigger picture to all this.'

Dempsey closed his eyes and rocked at the stern of the boat, as if he was falling asleep. Neff saw the Thief Taker's features reflected in the dull water. A spectre on the murky surface. The past was so easily forgotten. Neff clenched his fists, wondering if he had the nerve to push the Thief Taker into the depths. But he himself had abandoned Emily years before. And now he had made her a promise. About the end of the bloodshed.

Perhaps Dempsey had a plan to go to war with Kaplan, one he had not been told about. But if his boss thought he genuinely sided with his enemy, he would be excluded from the plans. Surely, nobody wanted the bloody conflict of the past to return. Pitched battles in the streets, dead bodies left in doorways, disorder, and chaos, raising questions from politicians. They would not stand for it again. Neff's thoughts turned to how he might be able to survive what was coming. Could he rely on someone like Kaplan to act rationally? He needed to meet the man face to face again, to assess which way to jump. Would it really be betrayal if he managed to maintain the peace and prevent unnecessary death? Emily's eyes stared up at him from the river. They implored him to stop. Neff wondered if he had the strength to obey her.

46

'Mister Hobbs, I appreciate you coming.'

'Anything to help Lord Malvern.'

'And the King.'

'The King, of course.'

Hobbs sat at an empty card table and stroked the green baize surface with his fingers. There were small bumps and scratches on it, like it had seen better days. Pipe smoke hung just below the ceiling. They were in Westminster, a location far from home. A waiter silently brought drinks for them both and slipped away.

'The King reads your publication,' Malvern said.

'He does?' Hobbs felt a flush to his cheeks. 'Which one?'

Malvern waved a dismissive hand. 'I know not which. But when he is in London, it is bound to be something of yours. He is a lover of a good tale. His English is much improved.'

'I am always at the service of the King.' Politicians were one thing; the patronage of the monarch would be another step forward for Hobbs.

'And the First Lord of the Treasury, Walpole,' Malvern added. 'He also shows an interest.'

A third man joined them at the table. His large wig sat uneasily on his head, and a puff of dust emerged as he brushed at it. Hobbs pulled his own headpiece down firmly. It was rarely used in public, one of only two he owned. Unless he was stepping up in society, there was no need for a newspaper proprietor to wear one. The men on the presses would simply laugh at him.

Hobbs briefly wondered if this figure was Walpole, but as he sat down it was clear this was no politician. The man had a curled lip and a thin face that did not exhibit authority.

'Hobbs, this is the local marshal, Mister Gillard,' Lord Malvern interjected, as if reading his mind.

'Would you care to play a hand?' Gillard asked, holding up a pack of cards.

Hobbs shook his head.

'You do not mind if we play while we talk?' Malvern asked, his voice smooth and polite.

'Not at all.'

Gillard manipulated the deck of cards with his fingers and dealt seven each to himself and Malvern. Hobbs watched the two men draw and replace cards from the pile in front of them. He had no idea what game they were playing. The dice game of Hazard was more familiar. Hobbs swallowed, remembering the sleepless nights caused by a past debt that took two years to clear. The room suddenly felt uncomfortably hot; he pulled at his wig and stared at the two players.

'I hear you have some information on William Dempsey,' Gillard said nonchalantly, turning over a card. 'We would love to hear it.'

Hobbs pondered his situation. Malvern was a man of influence and a possible gateway to the ear of other politicians.

News about them could gain his publications some status. He thought again about Dempsey's threats, and how his own business had prospered since the Thief Taker had taken an interest in newspapers. Perhaps Parliament wanted to stake its own claim in the press.

'What information do you mean?' Hobbs studied the table intently. Both men traded cards as the game proceeded in silence apart from the occasional grunt from Gillard.

'I hear he has a set of ledgers where he records all his transactions. Of lost and found property.' Gillard sounded well informed.

'I heard this,' Hobbs agreed, trying to remain non-committal.

Lord Malvern laughed as he turned over a card, then revealed his hand. Four of one kind and three of another. Hobbs assumed that meant he had won. Gillard pulled a wallet from his jacket and handed over a sheet of paper. Malvern studied it and nodded.

'That will do for now. Your money is mine anyway,' Malvern said. 'Again?'

Gillard took a pipe out of his pocket and scratched at its contents with a wire. 'Why not?' he replied. It was Malvern's turn to shuffle the pack and deal. 'You still not joining in?' Gillard asked, turning to Hobbs.

Another shake of the head. He could do with a drink. This sort of establishment would have real brandy that did not taste like it had been stored in the sewers. Hobbs looked around for a waiter but found none.

'We would dearly love to get our hands on those records,' Malvern said, eyes focused on his new set of cards. 'Walpole is particularly interested.'

Malvern clicked his fingers and a waiter appeared. Three more brandies were ordered.

'Walpole?' Hobbs asked. The steward glided away.

Malvern continued. 'In Parliament, we are looking at new ways of tackling crime. There is a desire to take the burden of responsibility away from men like William Dempsey.'

'And the best way to do this,' Gillard added, 'is to remove him from the scene.'

'But Dempsey keeps a lid on things. I thought that was the point,' Hobbs said. He had heard this argument from the man himself.

'The process needs to change,' Gillard interrupted, angrily snapping down a card. 'He has been breaking the law for years. Everyone knows it. Only nobody in his circle has been brave enough to stand up against him. We are looking for someone who has that bravery. Someone who might profit themselves from this service.'

Hobbs had suspected for some time that one of the leading criminals of London would lose patience with the Thief Taker. The catalogue of events he was carefully noting would then become newsworthy. Delivering Dempsey directly to the authorities was fraught with danger while he was still at large; his own hands were too bloody. Hobbs understood that the growth of his printing empire was partly built on Dempsey's activities.

'Are you a brave man, Mister Hobbs?' Gillard asked, placing his hand face down, taking a drink. 'I have a wager with Lord Malvern here that you know where those records are kept. You are seen with Dempsey often enough.'

'I have never been to his office. We only meet in taverns and coffeehouses.'

'But you must have some idea?' Gillard stared at him. The lip was turned up at a strange angle, like a permanent sneer. The eyes were cold.

'I wouldn't know where.'

'Try and remember,' Lord Malvern prompted, leaning across the table.

Hobbs felt a tightening in his chest, as if someone were pulling a restraint around him. He tried to focus on the table. 'Croker, his clerk would know. I hear he looks after the records.'

Gillard snorted. 'This Croker cannot be found, the same for the ledgers. There will be enough evidence in those documents to hang him several times. We thought that as his voice in the London press you might have an idea. He passes you all the stories, does he not?'

A nearby clock ticked slowly. Hobbs tried to muster his thoughts. He would be damned whichever path he took.

Gillard turned to look at Malvern. 'It appears that Mister Hobbs knows nothing. Either that or he is implicated in some way with everything Dempsey does and wishes to avoid prosecution himself. Remember this man is responsible for the death of a magistrate. If you are involved,' Gillard leaned in towards Hobbs, lowering his voice, 'then we will hang you with him. Everyone who works in his enterprise will be taken soon. Better to be on our side when this happens than languishing in Newgate with a noose around your neck.'

Malvern gave another hearty chuckle and flipped over more cards. 'I win again. Do you want to settle up, or carry on?'

Gillard stared across the table at his opponent. 'I will deal. My luck has to change.'

Hobbs sat back in his chair and fiddled with his sleeves. The casual way the two men were discussing such serious events played on his nerves. He wondered if Malvern and Gillard truly understood Dempsey and his methods. There were enough dead men to suggest that betraying the Thief Taker was a risky strategy. Another game began, with Gillard's face growing redder as they played.

'Mister Hobbs. Would you like an interview with Walpole?' Malvern asked. 'I could guarantee a series of them with cabinet members if you help us, in exchange for information on Dempsey. So long as it is proof that could stand up in court; the records of the lost and found property or testimony over his activities. If you could find a way to pass the evidence to Gillard here, I would grant you unprecedented access to senior politicians. You will be the envy of your competitors.'

Hobbs struggled to focus on the green baize. He sipped at his drink and suddenly wanted more of it, much more. 'Let me see what I can find out.'

'You do that,' Gillard replied, playing another card.

Malvern laughed again, turning one of his own, appearing to win another hand. 'We had better stop there,' he said.

Gillard stood and passed more paper from his jacket to Malvern. 'That should cover it.' He then pointed a stubby finger at Hobbs. 'Bring us the evidence. Do not find yourself on the wrong side of this when Dempsey falls. Because one day, he will be gone.'

The marshal pulled a coat around his shoulders, bade Lord Malvern a brief farewell, and left. Hobbs toyed with the now empty glass in front of him, attempting to avoid the aristocratic gaze across the table. He had his readership to consider; the people who absorbed his words were more interested in criminals than politicians. They would skip past Walpole's observations on foreign policy to reach the details of a murder or a daring robbery. He needed time to think through his response.

Lord Malvern picked up the papers left for him and waved a hand in the direction of the departed Gillard, finishing his drink. There was a steel in his eyes now, what looked like cold calculation.

'He will not be around for long either,' he said, his eyes on the door. 'But the current marshal is right. You are going to have to choose a side. The Thief Taker, or Parliament. Make sure you choose the winner.'

47

Kaplan indicated Neff should sit across from him, flanked this time by two of his men. They were south of the river, at Neff's request, in the hope he would not be recognised. Four glasses were laid out along with a bottle of gin. No other customers in the Goose Feathers tavern, just the owner leaning on the counter, cleaning glasses with a grubby towel. Kaplan turned Neff's knife in his hands, one that had been removed moments before in a search of his pockets. Kaplan thrust it into the wooden table, where it wobbled. Neff studied the blade and thought about the damage it had done over the years. One leader it had toppled. Kaplan poured them both a drink from the bottle and pocketed the knife.

'Dempsey aims to have your men removed from the streets again next week. You must act quickly. We are set up for Friday at two o'clock,' Neff announced. 'He will be in the Cross Keys on Whitefriars Street. He will not be expecting you.' Kaplan showed little sign of surprise, staring intently at Neff. The men either side of him avoided eye contact, seemingly captivated by the lurid paintings on the walls.

'For your sake, this better not be a trap,' Kaplan snarled, baring his rotten teeth.

'It is the best place. Stay in the gin shop across the street. Watch for me leaving the tavern at two. If I turn left, it is safe to strike. If I cross towards you, he still has men in there to protect him. All I ask is that you do it quickly.'

'An attack of conscience?' Kaplan raised an eyebrow.

'Just one man to another. None of us would like to suffer.'

'You see this as a mercy?'

'We go back many years.'

'And yet you send him to his death. You are a traitor.'

'I know he only works for himself now. It is simply a matter of time before I am hanged.' Neff stared at the man opposite, hoping he could convince him, realising that a part of him believed the words.

'We are saving your skin.'

'You could say that.'

'There will be customers in the tavern?' Kaplan shuffled in his seat and took a sip of gin. 'Bodyguards in wait? I remember what happened when Ashford came after me.'

Neff knew that that experience was a potential obstacle. 'There will be customers, mostly women that time of day. Nobody will raise a hand against you. Bennett will be at the docks.'

'I have heard of this Bennett,' Kaplan said, with a slow nod.

Neff leaned across the table. Kaplan moved closer; the other men seemed now to be focused on the door. 'Dempsey is on edge,' Neff said. 'He suspects everyone and everything. He even thinks Tindall sides with you, from prison.'

Kaplan laughed. 'That Catholic prig? He is nothing.'

Neff nodded in agreement.

'Does Dempsey suspect you?' Kaplan enquired, knocking back more gin.

Neff started to shake his head and paused. 'Possibly.'

Kaplan played with his greying beard. Neff knew this man had been through wars on the streets before. He might be thinking this would be the final one. 'Dempsey fears you,' Neff added.

He reached for his drink, thinking that complacency might be Kaplan's downfall, if he could instil it. Suddenly, he felt pressure tightening around his neck. Kaplan had him by the throat. Neff grabbed at Kaplan's hands to defend himself and twisted in his seat to break free. His attacker's strength surprised him. The minders did not move.

The hold then relaxed slightly. 'You better not deceive me,' Kaplan hissed. 'If you do, I will ensure your death is painful. I will have you cut up, piece by piece, while you are still alive.' Neff could smell the drink, and see the pockmarks on Kaplan's face up close, the pores dirty, and clogged. He felt the eyes burning into his skull. They widened, and he could make out snaking red veins against the whites, recognising the signs of excessive alcohol. 'You will beg me to stop the agony. And then I will find all your loved ones and do the same to them. Understand?'

That will not take you long, Neff thought. Kaplan let go and wiped his hands on his chest. Neff fell back into his seat, felt for his neck, and coughed. He tried to speak but a croak came out, so he took a long pull of gin. The burn in his throat seemed to bring his vocal cords back to life.

'Do what you need to. But I hope you see my position. I am too far gone now. If this goes wrong, I am a dead man. You must remove him.'

'And afterwards? What do you want then?'

'I have been thinking about this.' Neff took another drink to steady himself, to keep his cautious tone. 'I want a one-off payment. Two thousand pounds, in gold.' The demand was deliberately high, to make it appear genuine. 'It is a fair price to guarantee the running of a city. The blame will be directed at me, so I will go to France.' Neff pulled a scrap of paper out of his pocket and slipped it across the table. 'Here are the details of where the payment should be delivered when Dempsey is dead.' It was an address run by Elizabeth Manning, in Mayfair.

Kaplan examined it and looked back up at Neff. 'How do I know this is not a trick? You already show your treachery,' he snarled.

Neff shrugged. 'You can walk away from this opportunity if you wish. Dempsey will come after you soon. This way, you strike first. London can be yours.'

Kaplan nodded. 'You will be paid. Provided Dempsey is there, and he dies. And that I never see you again.'

The quick acceptance told Neff that Kaplan had no intention of paying. He considered how complex betrayal was. Things might even pan out with both Dempsey and Kaplan removing each other. The financial support could come from somewhere else. Croker perhaps, if the thought of avoiding gaol was strong enough.

Neff's attention was drawn to a heated conversation behind the bar, between the landlord and another man who must have emerged from the rear of the tavern. The intruder leaned against the counter and poured himself a drink, then scowled in the direction of the table where the four men were sat. His features were familiar. Neff felt his breath catching and realised why. This was a ghost. The ghost of the man who had killed Emily Jarrett. Someone he had despatched, and with Bennett's help later buried deep in the earth of Finchley Wood.

Kaplan turned his head to examine the visitor. 'Not now.'

'I have business with you,' the man growled.

'Take him away,' Kaplan said, nodding to the minder to his right, who jumped up immediately and shuffled the protestor out the rear of the tavern by the collar.

Neff sipped at his gin, trying to keep his hand steady. Was he drinking too much? The apparition seemed so real. 'Who was that?' he finally asked.

'Just someone. He is aggrieved. His brother has disappeared without trace.'

'He works for you?'

'No longer,' Kaplan sighed, staring at the rear door of the tavern.

Neff looked at his empty glass, trying to think, while avoiding Kaplan's stare. They must have been brothers working for Kaplan. This was confirmation of who was responsible. There was a blood rush in his ears, his brain shouting at him to act. Kaplan was still turned away, the other minder examining the floor. Then Neff heard Emily's voice, pleading with him to stop the killing.

Before he could act, Kaplan stood as if to leave. 'If you ensure Dempsey is where you say, and he dies, you will be free to leave London. With your money.'

'Two o'clock on Friday, at the Cross Keys,' Neff heard himself saying, rising to shake hands with Kaplan. Neff felt the harsh skin against his own.

'Soon you will be a free man,' Kaplan said.

Neff hoped he was not misreading Kaplan's lust for power, that he would not be able to resist the chance to eliminate Dempsey. The three unknown recruits from Marshalsea prison would be ready.

48

Dempsey emerged from the Old Bailey, squinting at the sun. It had been a busy morning; another gang of housebreakers split up, one testifying against the rest to save his own skin. It still intrigued Dempsey, how men would so easily turn on each other, and consider betrayal. But it was the basis on which his business ran. Fear would always set thieves on themselves.

There was a disturbance across the street, a group of men arguing and shouting. Nobody he recognised. Pedestrians sped past them, ignoring the scene. Dempsey noticed Neff watching the incident, intense concentration on his face. A man he could rely on.

Recognising the opportunity to slip away, Dempsey turned into an alleyway that led towards St Paul's. Bennett said he had more of his potions, hidden behind a fireplace at his own lodgings. He swallowed hard, feeling the tightness in his chest again. The visions were growing stronger, of headless women now, lying in the dust.

A few steps into the alley, Dempsey bumped into a figure blocking his way. He was tall, wiry, his hair matted with sweat. It looked like he had been running. A pair of hands went up in mock surrender, and there was a mumbled comment Dempsey struggled to hear.

There was a sudden sharp pain at his neck, then a warm sensation. Losing his balance, Dempsey felt as if he were suddenly drunk. He slipped to the floor and clutched at his throat. His hand was wet with blood. A strangled sound came, as he tried to cry out, sinking in the mud.

****

Neff leaned against a wall on the corner of Newgate and Bishops Court, watching the small gathering outside the Old Bailey. He recognised one of Kaplan's crew among the group, the larger of the two he met in the Goose Feathers in Southwark. The men were arguing. Neff sniffed the air and tensed, sensing trouble. Things were not due to escalate until later that day.

He had left Dempsey inside, in discussion with the magistrate. Neff tended to lose interest when talk turned to the worthiness of Dempsey's work. He watched the men across the street, wondering what the significance of their presence was, and whether Kaplan would still attack in the Cross Keys that afternoon. A man dressed like Dempsey would be in the tavern with his back to the door at two o'clock. The new recruits, as well as some constables they controlled, would be ready for the ambush.

Out of the corner of his eye Neff caught sight of Dempsey emerging from the courthouse entrance, pause, then head down an alley. There was a plan to keep his boss away from the tavern later, maybe he was heading for somewhere quiet. The intensity of the debate among the men across the street increased. The biggest one raised his fists, then grabbed another by the shirt collar. They began wrestling. Neff edged closer, scanning for activity along Newgate Street. He stationed himself between the dispute and the alley where Dempsey loitered, poised to move in either direction. The struggle continued and two men hit the floor, rolling around in the dust. Three more of the group joined in, as another tried to pull them apart. Nobody called for a constable. Street brawls had a habit of sorting themselves out.

A groan behind him made Neff turn. There was a slumped figure in the alley entrance. He moved closer and gasped when he saw the blood seeping between fingers against Dempsey's neck. Then he saw someone running down Newgate Street, towards St Paul's. Neff reached Dempsey and pulled a handkerchief out of his waistcoat pocket; he held it over the wound, pressing down hard. A trick he had witnessed on the battlefield, having seen it save many a life. Or at least prolong a few. As Dempsey lay motionless, his breath coming in short bursts, Neff's eyes flicked in the direction of where the assailant ran.

Torn between giving chase and holding the makeshift bandage against the wound, Neff looked back across the street. The brawl featuring Kaplan's men had dispersed. An old ploy, diverting his attention; he cursed himself for not seeing it. The flow of blood from Dempsey's neck seemed to have stemmed and Neff's hands were a guilty red. The colour filled his thoughts and drove a decision. The attacker turned left towards Smithfield. There was a market there that day. If he hesitated, the man would be lost.

An orderly emerged through the Old Bailey doors and stared open mouthed at Dempsey on the floor. 'Come, hold this fast,' Neff commanded. He pushed the man's hands against the makeshift bandage. Two more clerks he recognised from the court rushed out of the building, reacting to the noise. 'Get him to a surgeon, now,' Neff shouted. 'There is one in Newgate gaol.'

Neff left Dempsey and raced down a side alley, hoping to intercept the assailant. There was no thought process, just an intensive chase. He heard his feet pounding on the cobbles, his heart thumping in his chest. He caught sight of the figure, at another corner in the distance, looking back at him. The face was that of the man who hung on to the opposite side of a coach when their leaders met. Neff drove on, dodging pedestrians and stray animals, making up half the gap after a swift left and right turn. There was fear in the eyes of his prey the next time he checked behind. Neff knew he would catch him. He was surprised the man was not heading east, to the sanctuary of Kaplan's territory. The man changed direction again, heading for the Cloth Market this time.

A couple of women jeered at Neff as he chased through the gutter, splashing in the filth. 'Leave him be,' one of them shouted. They were supporting what they probably thought was a thief, on the run from a constable or watchman. Neff cursed them. They knew nothing of what went on behind the scenes to keep the streets safe. He prayed for someone to tackle or trip up the fleeing figure. But pedestrians simply cleared the way for the assassin to continue. The anger burned inside Neff, driving him on, that they had been duped over the attempt to ensnare Kaplan.

Neff felt his muscles primed, the blood pumping, attuned to the pursuit. He tried to scream for the man to stop, but his throat was dry. After taking another turn, the attacker pulled a cart into Neff's path, causing him to trip over a pile of rotting fruit. It still sold, whatever state it was in. Picking himself up,

Neff saw him dive down another alley. They were heading for Aldersgate, a busy thoroughfare. Once he reached that point, it would be easy to disappear.

Reaching the exit onto the main street, Neff paused. The man could be waiting around the corner, poised with the same knife that slashed at Dempsey's throat. As he crept closer, the image of Emily returned, her stomach bleeding out onto him, her eyes pleading with him to stop the violence. 'I am nearly done,' he whispered.

Carefully peering out at the end of the alley, Neff found nobody lurking with a blade. The sound of neighing horses resounded, followed by an almighty rumble, as if the world were turning upside down. Neff pushed himself back against a wall, trying to take in the scene. A coach had flipped onto its side, and what Neff assumed to be the driver was frantically trying to untangle horses, reins, the remains of a stall, and a half-broken carriage. A whip cracked against one of the animals and it jumped up, whinnying loudly as it pulled itself free, but the wreckage of the coach did not move. One woman moved forward and hurried about picking up wooden objects and thrusting them into a cloth bag. Pilfering was common at scenes of accidents. A crowd started to form, onlookers creeping closer, gossip beginning. Neff scanned the street for the figure he had been chasing but there was no sign. He edged along the wall in the direction of Clerkenwell, wondering where his target had escaped to.

The driver shouted for help to bring his carriage upright. Neff resisted the pleas and walked along the stretch of shops, checking windows for his quarry. All faces seemed to be focused on the scene. Two men in the doorway of a mercers' store pointed behind him, and Neff turned to see half a dozen men dragging parts of the wreckage away. Finally, what was left of the coach was tipped over, juddering to the floor with a thump. It cracked and broke again. The crowd closed in, blocking Neff's line of sight. A woman screamed, her hands to her mouth. He pressed forward for a better view, now strangely drawn in, as if hoping he would find what he was looking for. Pushing a couple of children aside, he saw that where the carriage had been lying, there was a body in the gutter, face down. The figure he had been chasing was lifeless, covered in filth, his bones presumably shattered under the weight of the horses and the carriage. Neff edged closer and examined the faces of the people around him. A mixture of horror and excitement, he judged. They would be telling stories of how they saw a man crushed to death in the coffeehouses and taverns for some time.

Retreating to the rear of the gathering, Neff studied his reflection in a filthy gin shop window. The face of failure and betrayal stared back at him. Why was he so slow to give chase? Was the hesitancy driven by the thought of how he might benefit from Dempsey's death? Perhaps it was his due. The distant image of a blood-soaked tyrant slumped over a hearth returned. It was Neff that had lifted so many out of his cruel clutches. And then Dempsey that gained the most from his actions.

He closed his eyes, reliving the sight near the Old Bailey, of an attendant clutching a handkerchief to the Thief Taker's neck, and wondered if he wanted Dempsey to live. Kaplan must have seen through the plan to lure him and his gang into a trap and turned the tables. Neff had not killed anyone. He had witnessed an accident on the crowded streets of London, no more than that. His promise to Emily was still intact. But if he had caught up with the assailant, he knew he would have been compelled to act. And Kaplan was next.

49

Dempsey pulled himself out of his chair and repeated his routine. He walked to the shuttered window, turned, and retreated to the seat, clenching his fists as he went. The pain in his neck and down his spine was gradually relenting, but after ten days confined to his Holborn lodgings the anger was building. There were enemies everywhere. They all plotted against him: Malvern, Walpole, Gillard, Kaplan, even Tindall from a prison cell. Only James Neff stood by his side.

'Kaplan must have guessed what we planned,' Neff said, moving over to the shutters to open them. The sunlight crept in, and Dempsey shielded his eyes. Neff's voice carried over the bustling noise of the street behind him.

'Unless there is a traitor in the organisation,' Dempsey snapped. He had thought the consequences of moving against him were clear. The Tyburn Tree was testimony to that. 'Kaplan seems to have the jump on us,' he added. 'Ever since we took on new men.'

Neff stared out the window at the street below. From the side, he looked pensive. His silence probably meant he too had come up with the same name. Eventually, Neff turned and walked towards him.

'Do you mean Charlton and Bennett or the men we took from the Marshalsea?'

Dempsey sighed in frustration. Surely, James knew. 'It goes back further than those three. Charlton is dead. He was a failure, but not a traitor. That only leaves one man.'

There had been plenty of time to mull over what led to the attack on his life. Kaplan had killed Emily, realising how important she was to his business. And then tried to do the same to him. Only the steady hands of a surgeon had saved him. As he convalesced, it was the bloodied face of Luce at the side of a road, that still haunted his dreams. Another woman he had failed to protect. He woke every morning now with his bedclothes tangled and soaked, seemingly more tired than when he went to sleep.

Neff inclined his head a little and screwed up his face. 'I would be surprised if it was Bennett. Why would he?'

Neff's loyalty to a fellow former soldier, was understandable. But misplaced.

'I am the Thief Taker; people expect me to act. When did you last see Bennett?'

'He is where he always is. The alehouses of St Giles.' Neff stared intently, eyes unblinking, like a marksman. 'You really think it is him? You have evidence?'

Dempsey had not yet revealed to Neff the source of his information. 'I saw letters from Kaplan, written to Gillard, about him having someone on the inside.' Dempsey watched Neff, studying his reaction. The glass looked steady in his hand. A useful man under fire. 'You saw no indication when you met Kaplan? When you tried to lure him in?'

'None.' The reply was sharp, an eager denial. It could never be Neff. Not after all they had gone through. 'He sent me away with a few bruises.' Neff touched his side to indicate where he said he had been attacked. 'Perhaps they were planning to squeeze us from both sides. Tindall was released yesterday from Chester gaol, is coming back to Westminster to resume Renshaw's business.'

Dempsey sank deeper into his chair, and felt the dryness in his throat, running a finger over the heavy scar tissue where the blade had struck. It was still tender to the touch. He poured himself a brandy with a shaky hand, knocked the drink back, and took another. The burn was a relief.

'What has Kaplan been doing these last few days?' Dempsey asked.

Neff stared intently at a painting on the wall, one of a man on horseback, leading his troops into battle. 'He has been strangely silent. I would have thought he would be crowing about your plight, but no.'

Dempsey pulled himself up to his feet and slammed his glass down on the table beside him. Neff spun round to watch him. There was a fire in those grey eyes, a look Dempsey recognised from the old days. Back when the two of them had started housebreaking together, roaming the streets, learning how the criminal system worked.

'Kaplan, Tindall, Malvern, Gillard. We strike all of them at the same time so there is no warning. I want them all dead.' Neff would understand, London and Westminster were due a clear out; it was inevitable after the demise of Renshaw.

'You would move against a politician like Malvern?' There was caution in Neff's tone.

'He has not paid me…' Dempsey hesitated, remembering that Neff was unaware of the details of Charlton's reward.

'Paid you?'

Dempsey waved a dismissive hand. 'It is nothing.'

Neff shrugged. 'Be careful not to make enemies of Parliament.'

'I want them all gone. See to it.'

Neff stepped forward to fill the space between them. 'William, we have worked together for a long time.'

'Yes.'

'Are you sure this is the right course?'

'Why do you question me?' The reaction was most unlike Neff. They settled opposite each other in chairs.

'But Gillard?' Neff played with his hair tie. A sign he was uncertain, Dempsey had seen it before. 'After Burley, can we make that many enemies?'

Dempsey shook off the objection. 'We used to be respected. Those in power prospered because we took thieves and killers off the streets. The discipline meant they left us alone. Now they conspire against us. We have to make a statement, exert our authority.'

Neff lapsed into silence. Dempsey wiped the sweat from his neck with a handkerchief, careful to avoid touching where he had been attacked. The movement merely reminded him of how close he had come to being toppled. It could not go unpunished.

'See to it, James. Straight away.'

Neff stood and headed for the door. 'It shall be done,' he said in a low voice.

'Bennett. Use him, and then…' Neff stared back, unmoved. 'Betrayal cannot be tolerated,' Dempsey added. His throat stung at the effort, and he groaned as he slumped deeper into his chair. He reached for another drink, to stem the pain. Neff claimed Collins could not be found.

Neff stood to attention at the door. 'I will take care of Kaplan myself.' That look of steel in his eyes made Dempsey relax a little, knowing his orders would be carried out.

'Is that one personal?'

'I do not like being made a fool of. It has nothing to do with Emily.' Neff seemed to sense his disbelief. 'Kaplan is wary of you, I hear,' he added. 'Word in the taverns is he thinks you are protected by something altogether darker, an unnatural force. Perhaps the Devil himself.'

Dempsey raised a smile. 'Be careful,' he cautioned, indicating his scar. 'Do not be taken in by him.'

'There is no chance of that,' Neff said, nodding deeply.

'I want this done immediately,' Dempsey ordered, the resolution stirring him. He felt the blood flowing through his veins, alive again. If only he were strong enough to get out there and be a part of the action.

Neff's face cracked into a dark smile. 'By tomorrow night, London will be a safer place.'

50

The coach came to a stop at the empty toll booth. Everything passing through Hounslow Common had to pay the shilling that funded the militia patrolling the heath. A new development, instigated by Dempsey, to safeguard travellers.

Neff issued the order, and his three men advanced on the carriage, pistols raised. The driver and the footman must have recognised their situation as poorly rewarded men and jumped down from the coach, running for the trees. Bennett secured the reins and tied them to a post. The horses stirred and kicked at the dust beneath their feet. Neff heard the complaining voices from within the carriage. A face framed by a large wig emerged through a window, one he recognised. Tindall. Neff made the signal the Engineers were eagerly waiting for.

The sound of gunshot echoed across the common, before the men reloaded and fired again into the carriage. Neff kept his pistol at his side, checking the road for travellers. Birdsong returned, shriller than before. Bennett stepped forward and carefully opened the coach door. Tindall's body tumbled out headfirst, blood on his waistcoat. Bennett kicked it into the dusty road and peered inside, Neff right behind him, ensuring

Bennett was in his sights. A second figure was slumped on the leather seat, his hands across his face. Bennett prodded him with a boot and between them they dragged another corpse out onto the dirt. Neff rifled through the pockets of the victims and picked out valuables: money bags, watches, notes in hand; and placed them in a cloth bag. They were destined for the Strand warehouse, as any robbery proceeds would be. That was exactly how it was meant to look. Trigger-happy thieves who panicked and made off with the loot. Despite the precautions in place, Hounslow was still a dangerous place to travel.

Neff directed the other Engineers to ride back to London and send word to Dempsey that Tindall had been removed. They seemed eager to leave, and dust swirled as he and Bennett watched them go. Bennett was leaning against the side of the coach, taking a pinch of snuff. Neff approached and drew his pistol. The fellow former soldier crossed his arms and looked at Neff intently, his eyes narrowing.

'You did not guess what Dempsey planned for you?' Neff asked.

Bennett's jaw dropped, and Neff assumed he was only just working it out.

'You were to be caught in the act. A highwayman, and a murderer.'

Bennett cocked his own gun at Neff, his hand steady. Neff felt a strange calmness come over him. He could feel his own heart beating, and Bennett's face appeared crystal sharp. There had not been enough time for his colleague to reload his weapon. Neff could smell the gunpowder in the air, echoes of combat returning. But this time he was in control and knew what the outcome would be.

'I thought…' Bennett began, dropping his pistol to his side.

Neff tossed his own weapon to the floor and grimaced. 'Dempsey is rotten. We are both caught up in this.'

'Yet you know what is to happen next,' Bennett said.

'I was supposed to kill you right here. But I no longer do his bidding. And neither do you.' Neff offered Bennett the bag with the stolen loot. 'This should be worth a good two hundred guineas, maybe more. It is yours. But you must flee, and never return. Remember, if you are discovered they will know you escaped transportation.'

Bennett looked to be calculating his options. Neff wondered what he would do in the same situation if Dempsey had planned to set him up. He would have taken the goods and run. Then the thought came to him. *It was probably Bennett or me. And Dempsey chose me to live.*

'You promise not to shoot? Or send the others after me?'

'On my honour.' Neff saluted. Bennett chuckled and returned the gesture. 'For what that is worth,' Neff added.

Bennett grasped the bag and made for his horse. Neff followed and they shook hands before Bennett mounted. 'What will you tell him?'

'That you are buried in Finchley Woods.'

Neff thought he caught a hint of a smile from Bennett. 'Good luck, James. You will need it.'

Kicking at his horse, Bennett rode across Hounslow Common, heading west. Neff hoped he would stay away. The game was playing out, and as he mounted for his own escape, Neff pictured the next move, feeling the long knife in his pocket.

****

Neff backed against the outside wall of the Aldgate tavern and stretched his arms out in surrender. Passers-by turned their faces away from a man being searched by one of Kaplan's protectors. Lucinda had provided Neff with the information on where to meet Kaplan. The man loomed into view from behind a heavily bearded minder, a thin figure with razor-shaped eyes, someone Neff had not seen before.

'How do I know I am safe here?' Neff asked.

'You can trust me. I am a man of my word.'

Neff looked away to hide his disdain, shrugging off the attentions of the aide searching him. The long knife was removed, and Neff shrugged. Kaplan did not seem surprised. What sane man would walk the London streets unarmed?

'Come inside, we can talk there,' Kaplan said, leading him through a storeroom into the public bar.

They paused at the counter, where Kaplan whispered something to the landlord, who gave a signal to one of his tap men. Neff was patted down for a second time, before the minder joined the owner in walking about the tables, politely asking everyone to leave. Nobody objected. The last ones to depart, a woman and a small boy stumbled into Neff as they passed. He raised his arms, muttering his objection, warning them to be careful. With the tavern cleared, Kaplan's man slipped out the front entrance, preventing them being disturbed. The landlord and his tap man disappeared out the rear.

Neff picked a table in the middle of the room and bid Kaplan sit, as he scanned the alehouse. There were abandoned glasses and meals on the tables. The smell of pipe smoke and dead meat in the air. Neff rolled his shoulders, the sweat sticking to his back.

'Why are you here?' Kaplan asked, taking a seat facing away from the entrance.

Neff slid into the seat opposite, focused on Kaplan. 'You put me in a terrible position. I am still in hiding. Dempsey and Gillard have a warrant for me. I am cornered. I risked my life to come here.'

'Were you followed?' Kaplan's eyes seemed to burn into Neff's skull. Could he tell what was happening? Neff swallowed and concentrated on his reply.

'You think I am a fool?'

Kaplan shrugged as if to say he was unsure and tapped at the tabletop furiously with dirty fingernails.

'We are alone?' Neff asked.

Kaplan waved an arm, indicating the empty tavern. 'Of course.'

'You know you can trust me. I just wonder if that goes both ways,' Neff said. 'I gave you the details of where to strike against Dempsey, but you made your own arrangements.'

Kaplan stood and held out his hands as if he had no idea what Neff was talking about. Then brought over a bottle of gin from the counter and smiled as he poured them a glass each, dropping back into his chair. 'Just being cautious. You never know these days. One of my men was killed by a famous whore, Madam J. Quite the vicious bitch, it seems.'

Neff stared at his drink, trying to concentrate. He gripped his glass tightly, it felt cool to the touch. Calmness returned, despite Kaplan's words. The man opposite knew how important Emily was to Dempsey's organisation. That was why he had gone for her first. To make a statement to the Thief Taker. Then aimed to kill the man himself.

Examining the empty room again, Neff avoided eye

contact. He tried to control his breathing, locking his fingers together, finally bringing his gaze back to the man opposite. 'I tried to help you,' he said, offering a resigned face, 'and you failed me. Dempsey still lives, and my life is over. No money was delivered to me as you promised. I have nowhere to go.'

'You could always work for me.' Kaplan knocked back his drink and poured himself another.

Neff kept his hands where Kaplan could see them on the table. He checked again that the tavern was deserted, saw the shadow of the minder through the front door, nobody at the rear where the landlord had gone. He closed his eyes and pictured Emily's bloody body limp in his arms. Neff took a drink and looked across the table. Kaplan seemed to be reading the label on the bottle. This was the man who had ordered the death of his oldest friends.

Neff gently touched the place where the knife sat in his jacket. The one the pickpocket had put there as they bumped into each other moments before. The outline of the blade against his fingers brought the room into focus. Kaplan put his glass down and stared at a painting on the wall to his left.

With a sudden surge, Neff brought the knife up into Kaplan's neck and ripped into the flesh. He felt the sinew give way and the crunch when the knife hit deeper, then pulled it out, stabbing repeatedly, feeling the power in his hands. He tore at Kaplan, driving it next into the chest. His victim was frozen, arms out to his sides, too slow to protect himself. Gurgling noises came from the bloodied throat. Then, with a silent cry, Neff thrust his knife into Kaplan's left eye. The blade stuck there. The other eye was wide open, staring at nothing.

'For Emily,' Neff whispered, leaning in. Kaplan twisted in the chair and slumped forward. The side of his head hit the table with a thump. He looked like he had been skewered by a butcher.

Neff ran for the back door, his eyes on the front entrance. He sprinted past the tap man, who loitered at the exit, his eyes averted, as if he had no wish to witness a thing. No sign of the landlord. Neff slipped into the street, and hastened towards Covent Garden, dodging in and out of pedestrians, his feet squelching in the mud as he went. It felt like a force was driving him on, taking him to safety. The death of Kaplan was inevitable, he realised, no matter what Dempsey ordered.

Spinning out of a narrow alley, Neff bumped into a man pulling a cart, knocking him over. He offered apologies and helped him pick up the rotten fruit he was attempting to sell. The vendor wore filthy rags and Neff wondered who would buy his wares. But the man was just trying to make a living on the London streets, like so many others. The seller swore at him even as Neff re-loaded the small barrow with damaged oranges and apples. Neff resumed his escape at a fast walk, checking to see if he was being followed. There were no signs of a constable, let alone any of Kaplan's retinue. Pausing on the corner of Lombard Street and Ludgate Hill, Neff placed his hands on his knees, sucking in the foul air, savouring the filth of it all, the freedom. This was his home. He had been fooling himself in thinking about a rich life in France. That was never an option, with the expanse of water to cross. There could be change on his streets, the way things operated, different from this madness. And Neff knew how to make it happen.

He had not forgotten Dempsey's instruction to remove one more man to bring London to order. Neff took a sharp left turn on Cheapside and headed for the marshal's office.

51

A knock at the door dragged Dempsey out of his sleep. The girl called Molly who shared his bed the night before had disappeared. Once again, he had been unable to meet the challenge. The image of Jake Largent, rather than the girl beneath him, came to his mind at the worst possible time. Perhaps it was the prolonged lack of the apothecary's potions, playing tricks with his mind.

Dempsey pushed himself up from the mattress and gathered his clothes about him. His enemies would be gone, but he was still surrounded by people questioning his honour, laughing at his failings. And Luce had featured in his dreams this time, mocking him as he lay with his hands tied behind his back, a noose around his neck, unable to move.

The knocking turned into a pounding. 'William Dempsey. Open up.'

His whereabouts were supposed to be a secret, new lodgings on the northern edge of London, on the road out towards Highgate. Dempsey dressed quickly and checked the street through the shutter. A cart sat outside, unattended. Otherwise, it was deserted. He was due to meet Neff later that morning to confirm the next steps after the bloody revenge of a few days earlier. This was meant to be a new dawn for London. One where the authorities would finally bow down to him.

'What is it?' he shouted. The hammering continued. Dempsey slowly opened the door.

Gillard stood there with a local constable Dempsey recognised at his shoulder. He wondered who they had come to arrest. Through the fog of tiredness, the reality suddenly hit, that Gillard was supposed to be dead.

The marshal thrust a sheet in front of him. 'William Dempsey, I have a warrant to take you to Newgate.' He swept into the room, searching for company.

'It is just me,' Dempsey confirmed, pulling at his breeches.

'How appropriate,' Gillard sneered. 'Take him,' he commanded of the constable.

Dempsey turned to the familiar face standing at the door. 'Hollister, you know me. What are you doing?' The constable was a wheelwright by day and supplemented this income with his work for the magistrates. Dempsey had known him for several years, even nurtured his progress. Hollister examined his own shoes. William willed the man to look up. 'Matthew?'

The cogs turned in Dempsey's head. They must have Neff as well. Did he succeed in removing any of his enemies? He stared at Gillard, who sneered. Dempsey clutched a hand to his chest, feeling the tightness, the need for something to ease the pain. The idea of betrayal crept into his mind, like a ghostly presence.

'Who's behind this?' Dempsey demanded. 'Is this Kaplan? You would not dare stand me up in court.'

The marshal twisted his lip, which peeled back to reveal rotten teeth. 'There are many who wish to see the end of you. Especially now.'

'Why now?'

'There have been too many killings.'

Dempsey breathed out slowly, feeling some relief pass over him. Neff might have been successful after all, even if that did not include the man opposite.

'Your lost and found business has caught up with you,' Gillard continued, waving the paper again. 'We have evidence and witnesses. Your time is up, Dempsey.' There was a note of celebration in the western drawl. Then, to Hollister in a lower voice Gillard added, 'chain him up and take him to Newgate.'

****

Neff thumped the table, rattling gin glasses. Dempsey was right. Gillard had risen too quickly for it to be on the back of merit. Looking around the marshal's office, Neff eyed the expensive paintings and the trappings of his position. None of it earned.

'We had an agreement. I cannot be a witness against him.'

'You need to find those who will stand up in the Old Bailey. Force them if you must.' Gillard straightened his spine in his seat.

'Are you asking me to intimidate witnesses?' Neff struggled to contain the disgust. He was being played by Gillard, just as Kaplan had done to him before.

'If you want to remove him, as we all do, then somebody has to testify. And the more prominent the better.'

'You can use Lord Malvern. He seems keen to rid everyone of Dempsey.'

Gillard stared open mouthed, betraying his knowledge, before waving a hand. 'There is no way His Lordship can appear in court. It needs to be people Dempsey has dealt with directly. Thieves who worked for him, and those who kept the goods.' Gillard raised a bony finger. 'You must speak.'

'Not me,' Neff replied. 'We have a deal,' he added, remembering their meeting a few nights before. When he forced Gillard at knifepoint to make assurances about his own freedom, sparing the marshal's life, Emily's words in his head. He knew Dempsey's time had run out. Neff simply needed to secure a future for himself, as well as people like him on the streets.

'We only have a deal if you help me deliver a guilty verdict against him.' Gillard played with a pipe, prodding its contents with a cleaner. The words came out with a sneer. 'Things have gone too far.'

'Too far?'

'Don't pretend your innocence. Three murders in one day: a politician and two criminal leaders, all of it the work of this Bennett character you say, under Dempsey's orders. Without Bennett we can't prove anything. A man who somehow did not seem to make it to Virginia under his transportation order a few weeks back. I know your hand is in this somewhere.'

Neff poured himself another drink and drained it. He hoped Bennett had the good sense to stay hidden. His own idea of running away with Emily for a new life had ended with the assassin's knife. But no matter what he had promised her, Kaplan could not be spared. Now Neff was determined to honour her memory the best he could; to command a different business in the Thief Taker's place, one with a more human side to it. The way she would have liked things to be done. And much as it pained him, having Dempsey arrested was the only way to stop him destroying everything. The madness had taken hold and clouded the Thief Taker's judgement.

'I have never been involved in killing,' Neff protested. 'You have no proof on that. Dempsey used men like Bennett and Hatcher.' He was confident nobody would come forward to identify him in the East End tavern. Kaplan's gang were already dispersing, so the word went.

Gillard shuffled in his seat and his lip curled again. 'You think that Walpole and the Aldermen would let the death of a politician go unpunished? After Sir Howard Middleton?' Gillard shook his head and lowered his voice. 'We cannot have warfare on the streets, I cannot be seen to allow it. The authorities will not permit William Dempsey to go on after this.'

Neff realised there was little he could do to save him. Parliament wanted Dempsey gone. There had been too many murders, in too short a space of time. Neff had tried to caution his old boss, to no avail. The removal of Kaplan was a different matter; more personal.

'You hang Dempsey, what then?' Neff asked. 'Crime will carry on. You will lose your means of controlling it, without him.'

'Unless someone else steps in. Somebody who knows how his organisation works. Someone who would work with us, with Parliament.'

Neff understood the implication. 'Dempsey will not be forgotten on the streets. If it were known I brought him down I would not live for long.' One knife in a darkened alley was all it would take.

Gillard slammed his pipe down on the table. The contents spilled out, forming an ugly mess of tobacco. 'The only reason you are not languishing in Newgate with him is because you came to me.'

Neff cursed under his breath. Dempsey had placed him in an impossible position. Ordered to remove enemies, knowing how the authorities would react. How were they to know there would be a Member of Parliament escorting Tindall back to London? They had probably meant to replace Dempsey with the Jacobite snake. Neff reasoned saving Gillard might help retain control in London; there was no need to provoke the authorities any further. Dempsey going after the criminal leaders made sense but removing the marshal did not. Who knew what they might replace him with? Westminster was already thinking about developing its own militia. The same might happen in London. But staring at the man opposite, Neff wondered if he had made a mistake.

'Who is behind this?' Neff asked. 'Walpole? The King?'

Gillard stared, his eyes almost translucent in the light from the lanterns at his side. 'I am well backed,' he said.

'Be wary, marshal.' Neff tried to slow his breathing, maintain control. 'I can easily make the witnesses you need disappear or change their minds.' He stared across the table at what he now saw as an opportunist. Neff sat on his hands, to suppress the desire to strike him. Gillard's reckoning would come. 'I can bring it all down around you,' he added.

'But you will not,' Gillard replied with a placid smile. 'You claim to have saved me, but I know you were involved somehow in the rest of it. You know everything Dempsey does.' Gillard paused to blow smoke above his head. The air reminded Neff of the workhouse, and an overseer who made his young life a misery. He closed his eyes and pictured a future where vain men no longer ran things. A dream.

Gillard continued, seemingly oblivious to how he was viewed by the man across the table. 'Dempsey's trial and execution will be the deterrent we need. I am a practical man. I know the whorehouses, the gambling, the taverns will not disappear overnight. So long as the thief taking stops, you would be left alone to run them, unhindered.'

'With your consent?' Neff laughed. He knew he could not live in a world that relied on men like Gillard to uphold order. There was ammunition to use later, about the marshal and his interests, and Neff realised he was already learning lessons from Dempsey. He blinked at the sudden understanding: he was thinking like a leader.

Neff stared at his gin glass, reminding him of a moment when he and Emily had touched hands. He was not exempt from pain; despite the number of men that she had slept with for money, he kept coming back to her smile, the sideways glances when Dempsey was not looking, the occasional touch of his arm. Her absence weighed more heavily in his heart than the removal of the Thief Taker would.

'The death of Kaplan was frustrating,' Gillard said. 'I wanted to prosecute him publicly. Dempsey took that away from me. I heard you were involved in that?'

Neff shook his head emphatically. 'Word is there was a dispute with a gambler. Do not believe everything you hear about me, marshal.' The image of Jacob Hobbs came to him. Someone he would need to work with; a man with much to lose. 'You could make an appeal in the newssheets.'

Gillard stared open mouthed at Neff. How could he not have seen how public opinion was so easily controlled? That in print, and when the words were read in the meeting rooms and coffeehouses, the truth had been bent to Dempsey's will.

'The newspapers are of little concern. They will not affect the courts. Or what will happen at Tyburn.' He stood, scraping his chair, heading for the door with a sudden energy that caught Neff by surprise. The implication that the meeting was over. 'I have an appointment in Westminster.'

Neff followed the marshal to the door. How had this man become so powerful, with so little effort? *You are worse than them,* he concluded. There had been some honour in how men like Renshaw, Kaplan, Ashford, even Dempsey conducted themselves. Gillard was more of an enemy. As he neared, the strange odour that lived in his wake struck Neff. It reminded him of a horse stable.

Gillard opened the door, showing Neff outside. 'Think on it. This is your opportunity. You will be free of Dempsey when he goes to the hanging tree. We need someone we can trust to keep order. The Thief Taker is the last of the major criminals of London and Westminster. Help us cleanse this place of him, and you will prosper.'

52

Dempsey gripped the rail of the dock in front of him tightly, trying to control the anger. How could they prosecute him, after all he had done to deliver justice for London? Gillard paraded up and down, playing to the gathered crowd at the Old Bailey. Had Dempsey behaved the same way before? He doubted it.

Gillard addressed the witness. 'Mrs Hebburn, you met the accused at his office on Fleet Street?'

'I did.' The woman focused her attention on the marshal. Dempsey had never seen her before.

'And he asked for a fee to return your stolen silver?'

'He did.'

'Then what?'

'I paid him ten pounds reward.'

'The man standing over there, William Dempsey?' Gillard prompted.

The witness glanced over briefly, then stared at her feet. 'Yes.'

Dempsey glared in her direction, begging her to lift her head. But Gillard asked the woman to step down, and she walked away without looking back. It was the same as the two supposed thieves before her; men he had also never heard of. If they truly knew how the system worked, Croker would be testifying, and they would produce the ledgers. The case against him was a mockery.

In the lead up to the trial, Neff visited him every day on the master's side of Newgate gaol. An area that he had helped establish, where those with enough money could pay to have better conditions. There was a cell to himself. Food and drink as he needed. But he was still locked up, and knew his position was perilous. His aide's countenance grew increasingly frustrated and angry as the trial approached. The newspapers seemed to be divided, including those Jacob Hobbs controlled. The Bulletin printed details of how the lost property process worked, with examples that highlighted Dempsey's involvement. It was out there, in black and white, and Dempsey knew that when things were published, they were believed. It seemed Parliament had grown tired of his way of working. Dempsey cursed Bennett for his carelessness, the death of a politician stirring them into action. Neff reassured him that that loose end had been tidied up, but the damage to his reputation had been done.

After two hours of Gillard strutting around the court in front of the judge and the jury, pushing his lies, Dempsey finally got to stand and plead his case. He adjusted his best periwig and cleared his throat.

'I have delivered a service to this city for many years,' he began, looking around the packed open-air court. Spectator heads bobbed around to afford a better view. There was near constant chatter from the gallery. Whilst he recovered from the knife attack, the world at the Old Bailey appeared to have changed. The clerks he used to know had moved on; fresh faces stared back at him from the tables in front of the judge. He felt his legs wobble. There were still moments when his body failed him, maybe he would never fully recover. But he had to make his case in public.

'This was a lawless city not long ago; criminal gangs ran wild. Men like Renshaw, and Conway before him did what they liked. It was not safe to walk the streets in the daytime, let alone at night. Going into a crowd meant you would have your pocket picked. Going into a tavern meant you might be robbed. Your shop could be ransacked. There were murders on the streets. It is because of me that you all sleep soundly in your beds. You remember the Alley Killer? I ensured he was caught.' He paused for effect and coughed heartily, his chest suddenly tighter. Neff had found Collins, but the man was apparently refusing to provide any more potions. Dempsey closed his eyes and wiped the sweat from his brow. When he opened them, everybody in the court seemed to be staring at him. He searched in vain for Neff's face in the audience. His mind went back to his own absence when Ashford was prosecuted. That was designed to distance himself from the case. Was Neff doing the same?

Dempsey returned to focusing on the jury. His throat stung. He searched in vain for a glass of water; the comforts of Newgate were missing. 'I stand here,' he continued, 'accused of such a petty crime. I cannot say why this woman and these rogues have spoken against me. They lie.' He then pointed in the direction of the crowd. 'I am no more a criminal than any of you. I have not met any of these witnesses before. I am well known in this city, and they are strangers. It is easy to persuade people to lie.' He paused, knowing the truth of it so well. 'You cannot forget the hundred or more souls I have condemned to hang, in the name of justice. I have always been a servant of the law, and never a breaker of it.'

Dempsey leaned back and waited for the response, scanning the faces in the crowd. Deference had gone, replaced by what looked like mild amusement. From some, scowls, possibly antipathy. Was he becoming a sideshow, one of the entertainers that would perform at fairs? Had his life turned full circle? There were a few murmurs but no applause in his favour. Maybe Neff was right, that the tide of opinion was turning against him, it certainly had among the authorities. Gillard conferred with the judge, sharing a smile.

'If it pleases the court, we have one more item to present,' Gillard said, staring at Dempsey. 'This has just come to light.'

'I will allow it,' Gregory assented.

A clerk walked in with a heavy book under his arm and placed it on a table in front of the judge. Dempsey felt his chest tighten again, the faces in the room turning into a blur. He tried to focus on the rail in front of him, watching his fingers go white as he held on. When he looked up, Gregory was prodding at the ledger, turning pages over. Dust drifted up into the dank air. Dempsey shrunk back. Under his breath he cursed Croker, adding him to the growing list for revenge.

'Do you recognise these?' Gillard asked, turning in Dempsey's direction with that curled lip of a smile.

The details were not written with his hand, but they would be incriminating. He elected to stay silent, unsure how he could explain them.

'This was found at your Lost and Found offices on Fleet Street. Your honour, you will see it contains details of multiple transactions, where the accused has profited from the sale of stolen items. They have been meticulously noted.'

Dempsey closed his eyes. Chatter erupted in the court. The judge had to call for silence. Dempsey tapped his pocket again, still empty.

Gillard raised his voice, addressing Judge Gregory, then the jury. 'You have the evidence you need to convict William Dempsey. I leave it to your sound judgement.'

There were gasps when the guilty verdict was read out in court later that day, but it did not surprise Dempsey. The judge announced the death sentence moments after; he was to hang in two weeks. The room swirled around the Thief Taker, his head a jumble of traitors and liars. He looked about the court once again, and this time caught sight of James Neff in a corner, leaning against a wall to raise himself up into view. Dempsey studied him closely. Neff mouthed something, and then repeated it, the unheard words cutting through the chaotic sound of the uproar in the Old Bailey.

'Trust me,' he seemed to say.

53

Neff held Dempsey close to him as they staggered their way along the corridor. They carried the look of two drunken Newgate visitors, leaving after a final farewell to the Thief Taker. Neff winked at one of Elizabeth Manning's young girls, her hands draped around the waist of a turnkey, an additional distraction.

Back in the condemned cell, Edward Hillier slept. Collins had guaranteed the effectiveness of the laudanum, a sufficient dose to keep him alive but comatose until well into the next day. Hillier was slightly taller than Dempsey, but he bore a close enough resemblance. He matched the artist's image that had been prepared for the hanging pamphlets. Hillier believed he was taking Dempsey's place in the cell for part of the evening, to allow him to slip out for a last night of revelry. Fifty pounds was paid to the man's family, his wife ambivalent about his possible return. Neff had heard about Hillier's penchant for beating the woman. The sacrifice was justified. Word was passed around the gaol that Dempsey had drunk himself unconscious on his final night and was not to be disturbed. The Chaplain was on strict instruction to stay away.

Neff steered Dempsey across the street outside Newgate gaol and hid him under a tarpaulin on a waiting horse drawn cart. Neff took the reins, a lantern at his side. They trundled south through the murky streets, over London Bridge, then turned left across the open fields towards Deptford. Neff regularly checked that Dempsey was out of sight under the cover as he drove on. Whenever he lifted the tarpaulin, his passenger seemed to be lost in contemplation, the darkness in his face unnerving in the pale light of the swinging lantern. A haunted figure, Neff thought. Perhaps he was already reassessing his limited future. This was an escape from the noose, but Neff wondered what else besides. He dared not ask, but the idea struck him the silence might be driven by the fate of Emily Jarrett, and a realisation of Dempsey's role in her death.

Neff pulled the cart to a stop outside a barn in the village of Greenwich and lifted the cover. Dempsey blinked in the pale light and lifted himself out. Joseph Robinson appeared, with a look on his face that Neff struggled to comprehend. Perhaps it was resignation at fulfilling another task with no questions asked.

'You will be safe here,' Neff said. 'Joseph will take care of you until you sail.'

Dempsey had at first argued he could hide in lodging houses in London but had eventually seen the wisdom in Neff's plan. Dempsey was due to stay at the barn until his ship left for the colonies. Neff pointed at the building. 'You have a new identity, and your trunk is already inside.'

After staring at his new hiding place, Dempsey turned to face Neff. He bowed his head, what looked like an admission of defeat. 'Thank you for all you have done, James. I would have been sunk without you. Perhaps I can catch up with Daniel on the other side of the ocean.' Dempsey walked away into the darkness, following Robinson.

Neff shivered and pulled his coat about him, hoping to find the strength to move things forward as Emily had suggested. It would mark a significant shift in how the organisation worked. There would be no more lost and found property business, Gillard had seen to that. Neff considered the shallow pretender that had come from obscurity to dog Dempsey from the marshal's office. The image of the curled lip came to him as he cracked the whip and trundled back towards London. When he crossed the bridge, he turned west away from Newgate. To a new appointment that he hoped would deliver his own freedom.

****

Neff leaned in closer to the spyhole. He could hear Elizabeth Manning breathing alongside him. She touched his arm gently.

'We will miss his money,' she said.

'He is the one responsible for everything,' Neff replied, tearing his attention away from the man on the bed. 'Emily as well, in part.' In the near darkness, it was difficult to tell Elizabeth's expression, but he thought he saw a tear roll down her cheek.

Neff returned to the subject in the room next door. Gillard was naked, face down with his hands tied above his head; his legs manacled to the posts of a bed. A girl sat next to him, playfully slapping his backside with a brush. Gillard grunted and shifted himself forward a little, muttering something inaudible. Neff moved closer to the hole in the wall. The girl jumped up and walked to the dressing table, then returned with a riding crop. Neff wondered at some men, and what it was that made them want this.

'Anne knows what to do. She is ready,' Elizabeth whispered.

Elizabeth led Neff out to the corridor and handed him a key. 'Do what you need to do. Only, no blood, please.'

Neff nodded his agreement. 'I will make him disappear. He was never here tonight.'

He slowly turned the key in the lock and crept into the room. The girl stepped back from the bed and winked at him, covering herself in a long nightgown, and sat in a leather chair, combing her hair. The figure on the bed looked up, straining at the binding on his wrists and shaking his leg constraints. He grunted wordlessly, gagged at the mouth.

'Gillard, what a surprise to see you here.'

The marshal tried to turn himself over, twisting himself in the bedclothes. Neff swallowed down his disgust at the sight. The sound of the girl laughing made him examine her. She rocked in the chair and smiled. What had brought this creature down this path, he wondered. Was her life destined to be the same as Emily's, the same as all the other desperate girls she talked about? Emily was right, there had to be a better, safer way for them to live. But what could one man do?

Gillard's grunts returned his focus to the marshal. Neff moved closer to place his hands around Gillard's neck. The eyes went white, the cheeks puffed out in a silent protest.

'You must have known this would come,' Neff hissed.

Gillard wriggled, kicking at his leg manacles again. Neff squeezed tightly around the throat, his eyes fixed on Gillard's, the look of horror slowly falling away as the life went from the figure on the bed. When Neff let go, Gillard's lip seemed to be exaggerated in death. Neff wiped his hands mindlessly on his breeches and stared at the picture on the wall behind which he guessed he had been sitting earlier. Elizabeth Manning would be there, watching him kill. He wondered how similar her story was to Emily's. Whether they might be able to carry out her plans together. She seemed a highly combative woman.

The girl coughed, and Neff snapped back into the room. He took the bag of coins from his jacket and dropped it on the table.

'For you, Anne. Spend it wisely and say nothing.'

She looked up at him with a knowing smile. 'It was just a game that went wrong, a professional mishap. It could happen to any gentleman,' she said, handing Neff a key and pointing at the leg restraints. Neff noticed that his hands were shaking. Although Emily had warned against the violence, this man was a justifiable exception. A final one.

'There is no need for you to explain this away. I will remove him,' Neff assured her.

Anne shrugged. 'Here, let me help you.' She seemed so vulnerable, yet so strong. There were Emilys everywhere.

Unlocking the manacles, they wrapped the body up in the bedclothes and lowered the corpse to the floor. Gillard's body would be dumped in the Fleet ditch, to avoid suspicion falling on Elizabeth Manning and her house. Another mysterious disappearance on London's murky streets. There were still men he could call on to complete the task, loyal Engineers of old.

Back in the hallway, Elizabeth embraced him. 'Emily said you were different from the others. That you understand what we are trying to do. What we must do.'

Neff dropped his shoulder into her chest and sobbed. Regret clawed at him, over who he truly wanted to be standing there, and at the missed opportunities. But some things were irretrievable now.

'We shall work together,' she said, as if she were reading his thoughts, stroking his hair. 'London will be a better place after tomorrow when the Thief Taker is hanged.'

54

Picking his way through the crowd, Neff tried to stay out of sight of his target. The figure in the greatcoat was holding back from the throng, to avoid being noticed.

He had advised Dempsey against watching his own hanging but suspected the temptation would be too much to resist. Neff had his own disguise and mingled with the spectators as they followed the hangman's cart, studying the dark eyes and the familiar movements that had become slightly more laboured since the attack outside the Old Bailey. He spotted Dempsey when the procession turned to move along Oxford Road for the last section of the journey. Neff silently congratulated him. If you had not been looking for the man who was supposed to have a noose around his neck, the figure leaning in a doorway could be just another anonymous onlooker.

Neff pondered the fact that there were few remaining men with links to Dempsey. Hobbs had printed his pamphlets in celebration of the demise of the Thief Taker, also unaware that the man on the cart was not who they thought he was. The politicians seemed to be pleased Dempsey was being removed. Only Neff and Robinson knew the details of the body swap.

Croker was safely hidden in Essex, away from prying judicial eyes. Collins had moved to Ireland. Everyone else who knew him intimately, was gone. But the strategy was still at risk, with Dempsey this close to the crowd. Neff suppressed the urge to confront him. His primary concern was keeping the Thief Taker hidden, until his transportation.

'Death to Dempsey', shouted the man beside Neff in the crowd. Others joined in the jeers and the throwing of missiles. The people seemed to have already forgotten what the man had done for them. Neff pondered how loyal he himself had truly been, and how much he might benefit from moving Dempsey to another continent. Hearing the crowd's reaction, he reasoned he had been left with little choice; this was the only way to save Dempsey's life. The authorities wanted him gone, preferably at the end of a rope. Neff tried to read the expression on the face from a distance, struggling to make it out as the crowd jostled and rumbled towards the hanging tree, following the hangman's cart.

A cluster of leaflets fluttered past Neff in the breeze. He grasped at one. Something akin to Dempsey's face stared back at him on the front page. The resemblance was close enough. He checked behind him at the figure and quickly looked away as Dempsey seemed to be scanning the crowd.

The cart came to a halt underneath the Triple Tree. Neff issued a short prayer that Hillier would remain silent. Dempsey had moved slightly closer and was now standing on a ledge. Neff circled around to drop behind him, out of sight. The crowd yelled their frustration at the length of time Jack Ketch was taking. The hangman was a showman and knew his worth, saluting the well-connected spectators sat on the benches. Neff spotted the beaming faces of Judge Gregory and a few other Aldermen. They were glad to see the end of the Thief Taker. He noticed Gillard's empty seat in the front row. If only they knew, he mused.

Mud and stones were now being slung at the hangman, who dodged the missiles, and completed his testing of equipment. Neff watched Ketch step down, then switched his attention between the hanging and the man who was supposed to be in the noose. There was not even a flinch from Dempsey as the whip cracked, the horse bolted, and Hillier was left swinging in the wind. The cheers of the crowd seemed to echo, a collective expression of relief from Londoners. The body twisted, and Neff felt a tightening in his stomach. It was too late to pity Hillier. He had arranged the situation, valued the man's life below that of his old friend. A cheer distracted him, then he spotted four men assume their positions with the coffin. It was necessary to take the corpse somewhere secret, to ensure its identity remained unknown. The men would take great care with their task: they assumed they were handling the Thief Taker's dead body.

The crowd began to disperse, and Neff trailed Dempsey on the long walk back through the streets towards London Bridge. The figure walked with his head bowed, Neff assumed to prevent him being recognised. There was no looking back. When Dempsey turned along the south side of the river towards Greenwich, in the direction of the barn where he was supposed to be hiding, Neff felt his pulse slow. He scratched at his wig, feeling the sweat forming where it met his hair; a reminder of the risk involved in their plan. But it was the only way to save the Thief Taker, the nub of his argument with Dempsey when he persuaded him to escape. Better to be in the colonies than on the end of the rope at Tyburn. Neff had promised to continue Dempsey's work, without providing the detail of his new approach. A safer London beckoned.

55

The pull of the London streets was too strong for Dempsey to ignore. He had been hiding in Greenwich for nearly a week since the hanging. There was plenty of food and drink, supplied by Robinson who visited him daily, but no company, no sign of Neff, no potions to get him through the dark nights. His dreams were still haunted by women, pleading for his help. Staring through a small window at the river and the buildings to the north, he knew being a fugitive was not befitting of a man with his standing, even one supposed to be dead.

'Take me to London,' he pleaded with Robinson.

'You know how dangerous it is.' Robinson scratched at his pipe, seemingly distracted, unable to look Dempsey in the eye.

'Joseph, this is me. Just one last visit. London is all I know.'

The journey to the colonies had been delayed, something about poor weather slowing down the incoming ship. Robinson was getting increasingly edgy, the longer they waited.

'They think you are dead. If you appear, many people will be in trouble. Not just me. You must stay hidden,' Robinson pleaded, finally looking at Dempsey. The beard seemed more unkempt than ever. The eyes betraying signs of worry about me, Dempsey thought.

Robinson drove the cart over London Bridge, with Dempsey hidden beneath some sacking. The smell of rotten fish filled Dempsey's nostrils, forcing him into shallow breaths as the vehicle rocked and rolled in the potholes. Then he thought about the alternative journey he was supposed to have taken with a noose around his neck. A man had given his life to save him, Dempsey realised, willingly, according to Neff. Perhaps there would be some support for him if he were to rise from the dead. His re-appearance could be seen as a miracle. They might follow the Thief Taker once more.

Dempsey slipped off the cart after it crossed the Thames. There was no Ashford or Kaplan to demand payment for the crossing. Regret suddenly overcame him, about not removing his rivals sooner. He walked up Cannon Street towards St Paul's, pulling his modest wig down, the rest of the simple clothing designed to make him look respectable enough, but not stand out. He breathed in the rotten stench of decay that hung in the air, a stark contrast with the fresher smell of Greenwich. The filth of home was preferable. Dempsey stopped and closed his eyes from time to time to take in the sounds: the cries of hawkers, beggars, the chatter of passers-by. This part of London did not seem to have changed. He pressed on cautiously, ducking in and out of doorways when groups of men passed. Catching his reflection in a shop window, he pulled himself more upright, stroking his clean-shaven chin. With the sight, the confidence grew that nobody would know it was the Thief Taker staring back at them. He looked like everybody else: shapeless, a tiny dot in the vibrant and dangerous city that was London. The anonymity made Dempsey question whether he needed to cross the ocean. Perhaps he could blend in and reinvent himself the way he had as a young lad.

As he travelled west, he picked his way slowly through the familiar alleyways. Ignoring the pull of Newgate to his right, Dempsey continued down Ludgate Hill, stopping when he met the ancient and filthy Fleet river. He thought about the hidden cellars nearby where many men had been persuaded to fit their story to his words, to send someone less fortunate to the hanging tree. There was no remorse. He had worked diligently to protect the people of the city, convinced his was the right way. Dempsey wondered how committed Neff would be to maintaining his legacy.

Stumbling over a street beggar pleading for food, he showed his upturned palms as if to say he had nothing to give. He touched the key on a piece of string around his neck. It secured the trunk in Greenwich that contained the money and possessions set aside for his future. Thoughts turned to what he would be leaving behind; the property to the north, his share in what was stored in the warehouses. Neff had promised to find a way to forward him money. A hand went instinctively to his jacket pocket, where he used to keep the vials. Empty.

He continued to tread carefully in the direction of Fleet Street, keeping his head down, side stepping pedestrians, avoiding eye contact. He passed several shops and coffeehouses he used to know intimately. They appeared as if coloured by a dusky hue. A sensation gripped him, like he was a ghost moving unseen among them all. Dempsey found himself outside the Lost and Found office. The door was bolted, the window which used to beckon customers inside boarded up.

'You looking for something, my dear?' A female voice called over to him.

He turned towards an old woman selling heather, nobody he recognised. Dempsey hesitated. He was not invisible after all. She sidled up to him.

'What happened to the…' He paused and pointed at the office front.

'That place? They hung the man who ran it. He was a devil, you know. We are glad he is gone.' She spat on the ground in front of her, and leaned in towards him, smelling of the gutter. 'They say they might put a fancy gaming house there now,' she added, with a knowing nod of the head. His London was changing already.

Dempsey pulled away and retreated towards Newgate. With that one short conversation, he recognised his future. The passage to the colonies would be necessary, if that was how the Thief Taker was viewed. He remembered the reception at the hanging the week before, the objects thrown at the condemned man, the jeers and catcalls of the people who once indirectly obeyed his command. He could not live on with a new identity on these streets, echoes of his lost life all around him. Dempsey paused outside the Old Bailey and looked down the alley where the attacker wielded the knife, where he came within an inch of losing his life, the surgeon told him. His chest felt tight, as if he was being crushed, or buried alive.

Across the street the door to a coffeehouse opened, and a figure emerged, turning right, heading towards Cheapside. James Neff. Dempsey followed, dodging pedestrians. A couple of women stopped to curtsy in front of Neff. They were respectable looking, with parasols and long dresses, not streetwalkers. Another passer-by shook Neff's hand and engaged him in a short conversation. Neff nodded and clapped the man on the back before moving on. Dempsey kept his distance, some thirty yards behind. Was this how he had conducted himself among them? He suspected it was. Uneasiness came over him in a sudden wave, as if he was drowning in the ocean. An ocean Neff was asking him to cross to escape from this place.

Neff stepped onto the raised stone walkway, towards the river, and turned to look in Dempsey's direction. He paused, inclined his head, studying the figure watching him. Dempsey took a pace towards him, and Neff seemed to bring himself out of a trance. First there was recognition, followed by a brief smile.

****

Neff had not expected to see Dempsey again. Word had reached him the sailing was delayed, but he hoped the figure before him would stay out of harm's way in Greenwich until then. If the truth were discovered, Neff would be taken to Newgate and then the infamous tree. He was headed for Blake's coffeehouse, his new favourite. It seemed Dempsey had come back from the dead to check up on him.

Signalling with a slight shift of the head the direction he was going, he led Dempsey away from the river, through a network of alleys, checking behind occasionally to see if he was keeping up. Neff knew these streets better now, on the edge of Kaplan's old territory. They passed the hastily arranged monument to soldiers of the Spanish war, and Neff gazed up at the statue. Only the Generals were remembered, sat proudly on horseback, so many men had been forgotten. London's criminal streets felt different now; only the foot soldiers remained. Neff moved deeper into the twisting warren of east end lanes, his temples pounding, the annoyance at the risk Dempsey was taking growing. He stopped at an Aldgate alehouse door, turned, and realised William was only ten paces behind. Neff slipped inside the rear of the tavern, into a storeroom behind the bar and Dempsey followed. When the door closed, Neff pinned him against the wall.

'What are you doing here?' Neff hissed. He saw the momentary look of surprise in the eyes and let the grip fall.

'I go where I choose.' Dempsey pushed him away.

Neff brushed down his waistcoat and stepped further back to study the man opposite. The eyes were even darker, the cheeks sunken; the wig looked precarious on his head. Dempsey's clothes hung off him as if they had been borrowed from a larger man. He reminded Neff of a spectre; one he had been told of in stories as a boy, when the older children in the workhouse tried to scare the little ones. Neff had not truly considered the impact of being in hiding. This seemed to be a different beast in front of him; one devoid of the life that had made Dempsey an irresistible force. A man he followed faithfully for so many years.

'What if someone recognises you? I spotted you straight away,' Neff whispered. He could hear the chatter of gentlemen discussing the news of the day in the public bar.

'I was not seen.'

'You think we should go and sit in there?' Neff pointed at the wall that separated them from the customers. Dempsey shook his head, so he continued. 'A lot of planning went into this, William. To get you away safely, to keep you alive.'

Dempsey's shoulders slumped. Neff imagined a heavy weight dragging him downwards. 'Is this living? Always hiding?'

'Anything is better than Tyburn.'

The man was struggling to grasp the gravity of his situation. Neff felt the pity rise. He took a deep breath. Dempsey looked a beaten man. 'You would not need to hide in Virginia. You could be whoever you choose. When the ship goes from Gravesend, you will have a fortune with you.'

Dempsey fell back into the wall. 'There are some things I still do not understand.'

Neff nodded to signal he should continue.

'What happened to Gillard? He was supposed to be finished that day, with the others.'

'He is dead now. I did it the night we stole you away from Newgate. The authorities do not seem too concerned by his absence.'

Dempsey's eyebrows shot up. Then a frown formed. 'You did not remove him before he could prosecute me though.'

'He went into hiding,' Neff lied, studying the sorry figure in front of him. 'He must have heard what we were doing. But I got to him in the end. He missed your execution, there is something in that.'

Dempsey let out a long breath. The silence hung between them. From the room next door there was a shout, then a breakout of laughter. Life went on.

'Gillard was not the main force against you. They would have had you anyway. Walpole and Malvern are your real enemies.' Neff surveyed Dempsey again and was struck by the emptiness in his eyes. He pointed to the bar area. 'It was here, you know, that I despatched Kaplan.'

Dempsey did not react, merely stared at the floor.

'Kaplan pleaded for mercy, cursed your name just before I slit his throat. Then I stuck a blade into his evil eye.'

Dempsey blinked slowly. 'Sounds a familiar method,' he said.

Neff shrugged. There was no harm in admitting the truth. 'I was angry.'

Dempsey moved forward and pushed a finger into Neff's chest. He made no effort to resist. 'Renshaw was you.'

'Renshaw was a pig. He beat women. Emily. She said he nearly killed her.'

'And she didn't come to me?'

Dempsey's expression appeared to move from confusion to sadness. The shoulders slumped again. Neff recognised the insult Dempsey would feel; that he was closest to her.

'I have had enough of killing,' Neff said. 'Things have to change.'

Dempsey stared at him and raised a fist. 'But you are so good at it. You cannot keep people in line if there is no threat.'

'The city does not need gang leaders,' Neff countered, lowering his voice. 'Or the organisation of crime as it used to be. People will get by.'

'You will see,' Dempsey scoffed. 'The authorities need the chaos to be managed. If you do not do it, they will replace you with something else. The politicians will control you, like they tried with me.'

'I shall take care of things here,' Neff said. He could not voice the thought that had been plaguing him for days. That Parliament had got its wish to remove the one man that had stood up to them, and Neff had helped make it happen. 'But you will have to let me do it my way.' Crime would continue, it was inevitable in a place with so much deprivation. But he had seen the future of London, and it no longer involved the fencing of stolen goods, and a suspicious web of thieves working against each other. He was no idealist. This was simply practical.

Dempsey straightened himself and stared at Neff again, his eyes suddenly sparking into life. He shook his head slowly. 'You will need to be brutal James, more devious and ruthless than the rest. You saw it yourself; you instigated it remember, with Conway? It is how the world works with men like us. It is the one who goes furthest who will come out on top. That is the lesson I learned. You always had that streak in you, James. You may have to push yourself more than before.'

'I want to do things my way,' Neff said.

Dempsey sighed. 'I suppose I have little choice. I am dead, after all.' He fell back into the wall, his face turned to the floor.

'I have work to do here, William.'

Dempsey looked up. 'Follow me to the colonies,' he implored, urgency suddenly in his voice, his hands clasped together. 'We could start again, work as we did before. We could do it together this time, a partnership on equal terms.'

Neff shivered when he thought of the prospect of two months on the Atlantic Ocean. He would not last a day. 'I owe it to Emily to look after everyone who worked for her, as well as the men who used to answer to us. She taught me so much. I will increase the opportunities for women, be they whores, waitresses or card dealers. I promised her as she died.'

Now he said it aloud, and to the Thief Taker of all people, it confirmed to Neff that this was his new driving force. An epiphany, he thought the priests called it.

Dempsey nodded in resignation. 'She would gladly have had you instead of me,' he said. 'I was merely a better financial option at the time. Her heart was always yours if you had asked for it.'

The Thief Taker turned and walked through the tavern exit into the alleyway. Neff watched him go, the former controller of them all: petty criminals, footpads, highwaymen, brothel owners, working girls, innkeepers. That man was no more. The future of London had a different shape. A new way out of the old madness.

56

The coast of Virginia loomed on the horizon. This was a new world, a place where so many had started afresh. Some by choice, most by directive of the courts. Dempsey realised he had never considered the detail of how the colonial economy worked, until Joseph Robinson explained it. There was a rationality to the process. Many of the prisoners on board would be sold at auction the day they landed. Seven years of servitude before they could return.

Dempsey had remained hidden for as much of the two-month journey as he could, but even on a ship this large meeting other passengers, particularly the free ones who were able to roam as they pleased, was inevitable. He had listened to stories of religious persecution, from Dutch and English settlers with all their possessions in heavy trunks like his own. A few other free travellers heading for new lives. Nobody seemed to care about his tale of a failed South Sea investor, searching for new opportunities.

The voyage had been perilous. A violent storm halfway across claimed a handful of prisoners and crew. Robinson brushed deaths away with a shrug, when Dempsey challenged him, as if they were commonplace. There were constant unanswered complaints from the bowels of the ship from those in chains, where a sickness appeared to take hold. The stench of death reached everywhere, a reminder for Dempsey of the Fleet ditch and the world he had left behind. The concerns of the free passengers seemed to be ignored by the captain, who spent most of his time locked in his cabin.

Sleep had become a stranger to Dempsey, the constant tipping and lurching of the vessel playing with his mind. He frequently struggled to tell what time of day it was, let alone how long they had been at sea, and found himself concentrating on keeping watch over his trunk. There was enough inside for him to start again, and documents calling him William Largent, a name that Neff had puzzled over when he chose it.

With the coastline nearing, Joseph Robinson sat alongside him on the deck. The crew were busy preparing for arrival. Neither man spoke as the ship bobbed up and down, Dempsey feeling the now familiar lurch in his stomach. He wondered how Robinson coped with this journey several times a year. Eventually, the man who had helped him make money from the transportation business broke the silence.

'You have made it, William.' Robinson kept to his hushed tones as he had done every time they conferred on the journey.

Dempsey shrugged. 'Made it to what?'

'To your future. Maybe you are lucky to be alive.'

Luck is something that happens to other people, Dempsey thought. The darkness of his later days in London seemed to have been replaced by an uncertain ache deep inside him. He was not used to his fate being an unknown.

'You never really told me what it is like there,' Dempsey said, pointing towards the land ahead.

'We don't know how far it stretches. There is no end to the possibilities.'

'Cultivating land or slaves. Is that it?'

'There is so much more than that.' Robinson screwed up his wind-battered face. 'A man of your talents will find something profitable to do.'

Dempsey thought again of Hillier, his body twitching in the breeze at Tyburn. But the main memory he carried from his vantage point at the back of the crowd remained the jeers and the hatred, and of how a city had turned on him.

'I want to thank you for looking after me,' Dempsey said.

Robinson grimaced again. 'I have merely followed orders, as I have always done for you.'

'For money,' Dempsey smiled. As Robinson returned the gesture, Dempsey realised it was an expression he himself had not worn in a long time.

'I sail back in two days,' Robinson said. 'James paid me well to escort you here. I have one more task to perform, to give you this.' He handed over a sealed envelope. 'I was supposed to do this when we landed, but I guess it makes no difference now. It is from him.' Robinson stood. 'I just do as I am told.' He clapped Dempsey on the back and left.

The wind whipped around the deck as the ship rocked furiously. Dempsey looked about him, he was still alone. He clung to a rope, and when he felt righted, ripped opened the package. There were two pages in Croker's familiar, careful script. Neff's writing was limited and difficult to read so he must have dictated it. Dempsey recognised that this could be his final contact with England.

William, I trust this Letter finds you well.

We have gone through much together. The Prison days, how we scraped and survived. How when you left the Gaol you led the way – something I was fine with – you showed me how an Organisation could thrive based on its Pillars of loyalty and reward. That will always stay with me and make what I must tell you more painful.

There is much for me to explain. Not how you are headed so far away; the authorities grew tired of your methods. You know this. I promise I shall do everything to continue your work where I can. I despatched many men in your name, willingly. I feel I am deserving of your Position. But I need to do things differently. What happened to you is a Lesson for all of us. I am resolved never to kill again, nor threaten, or bully. You might not agree with this Method, but that is what I shall do. Our old Enemies have gone, replaced by new ones. The Politicians. I have discovered they are worse, and they need to be defeated in a different way. With subtlety, rather than force. They think they removed You, and I will let them believe this.

I must confess that it was me that ensured Gillard got his hands on the Ledger, it was not Croker's doing. What happened to Emily showed me that how you ran London, and me as a part of it, had to stop. You seemed possessed by something I struggled to fathom. There did not seem to be a way to make you change your mind. But I could not see you hang, so I moved to take you out of things another way, for your own good. You probably disagree, and it may be best for a while that you are far away. At least you are alive. That is more than the Authorities, and the Politicians wanted.

William, you have another opportunity, please take it. We can rule two different sides of the great Ocean between us. I shall live modestly from my position, try to work alongside others, not against them. You might think me many things: a Fool, even a Traitor, but I reason what I have done is necessary to save both our Souls. It was too late for Emily. I hope it is not too late for you to find a new way.

Your friend,
James

Dempsey folded the letter with shaking hands. He pulled his coat around him as the sea swelled and the ship bounced. His head throbbed; his throat felt as if it was being scrubbed like a lodging house front step. Neff had stood alongside him for years and had forgotten everything they had done together. The man he had trusted more than any in the world had betrayed him. Deliberately led him to the hangman's noose. Forget the rescue and the body switch. Dempsey ripped the letter into pieces and tossed them over the side. He watched the fragments drift in the breeze, some blew back behind him on board, most fell to a watery grave.

He looked up at the new opportunity in front of him. Neff was wrong. You could not maintain control over hearts and minds without the ultimate threat over a man's life. Neff would not last long; the politicians would devour him. Dempsey had learned that power demanded ruthlessness, to control you required force, not collaboration. He screwed his fists together and roared at the Virginia shoreline. Order was coming to the colonies. A new Thief Taker would soon be among them; one who would never fall foul of traitors again.

AUTHOR'S NOTE

The character of William Dempsey is loosely based on a man who was executed in 1725: Jonathan Wild. According to contemporary accounts, including one by Daniel Defoe, Wild ran a gang of thieves in London at this time, while profiting from prosecuting criminals, operating in a vacuum where an organised police force was decades away.

I have extended his likely reach and influence, and invented criminal rivals, as well as characters such as James Neff and Emily Jarrett – both are composites of contemporary characters. Jack Drewett is based on a man named Jack Shepherd, who escaped from prison multiple times, before finally being executed in 1724.

I am hugely indebted again to Gretchen Smith for her input and guidance – without her keen eye, who knows how this may have turned out. A massive thank you each and every day to Jackie and Peggy, who have to live with the demands of having a writer in the house.

This book is printed on paper from sustainable sources managed under the Forest Stewardship Council (FSC) scheme.

It has been printed in the UK to reduce transportation miles and their impact upon the environment.

For every new title that Matador publishes, we plant a tree to offset CO_2, partnering with the More Trees scheme.

For more about how Matador offsets its environmental impact, see www.troubador.co.uk/about/